TIME
TRIALS

BAEN BOOKS by M.A. ROTHMAN & D.J. BUTLER

Time Trials

BAEN BOOKS by D.J. BUTLER

THE WITCHY WAR SERIES
Witchy Eye
Witchy Winter
Witchy Kingdom
Serpent Daughter

TALES OF INDRAJIT AND FIX
In the Palace of Shadow and Joy
Between Princesses and Other Jobs
Among the Gray Lords

THE CUNNING MAN SERIES
(with Aaron Michael Ritchey)
The Cunning Man
The Jupiter Knife

To purchase any of these titles in e-book form, please go to www.baen.com.

TIME TRIALS

M. A. ROTHMAN
D. J. BUTLER

BAEN

A Baen Books Original

Baen Publishing Enterprises
P.O. Box 1403
Riverdale, NY 10471
www.baen.com

ISBN: 978-1-9821-9315-7

Cover art by Alan Morris

First printing, March 2023
First trade paperback printing, January 2024

Distributed by Simon & Schuster
1230 Avenue of the Americas
New York, NY 10020

Library of Congress Control Number: 2022055258

Printed in the United States of America

10 9 8 7 6 5 4 3 2 1

"May your spirit live, may you spend millions of years,
you who love Thebes,
sitting with your face to the north wind,
your eyes beholding happiness."
—Quotation from the Wishing Cup of Tutankhamun

⇒ CHAPTER ⇐
ONE

Our fatigue is often caused not by work, but by worry, frustration, and resentment.

Marty Cohen was tired. He had stumbled across that Dale Carnegie quote as he researched why he'd been suffering from overwhelming fatigue. Caffeine didn't make a dent. He rose tired from sleep.

He shut his eyes, blocking out the sterile white walls, gray Venetian blinds, and alder-yellow wood doorframes of his room in the sleep clinic.

Were his problems worry, frustration, and resentment?

Maybe. He'd left his aborted academic career behind years ago, along with all the worries it had heaped on him, but his sleep hadn't improved. He'd traded them for the cares of a small business owner. He didn't regret the trade, didn't resent it, but some of the struggles of a small business owner were onerous.

In particular, payroll.

He was going to make payroll this month. He had to.

He had employees who he was responsible for.

Carlos's father had lost his job at the big box store outside New Haven, and Pedro's wife was due . . . when? Soon.

This wasn't like the strategy games he'd played obsessively in college, in which the number of pawns or meeples or tokens sacrificed didn't matter, so long as the victory conditions were satisfied.

The victory conditions *were* the pawns and the meeples.

Making payroll. Providing a livelihood for himself and his people were what mattered.

Some sleep would be nice, too.

The whir of the clinic's air-conditioning sounded like the growl of an unseen beast.

The buyer of the dining room set was due to come by in the morning. Marty had offered a discount for full payment in advance, but the buyer had insisted on paying a deposit and the remainder upon collecting the finished product. Tomorrow. Tomorrow, Marty would get paid, and then he could take care of his people.

Tonight, he needed to focus on his fatigue.

His primary care physician had had him tested for anemia, diabetes, high blood pressure, and all sorts of other ailments that might be the cause. But the doctor had come up with nothing, and ultimately he referred Marty to a sleep study clinic. So now here he was, lying on a clinic bed with a nest of wires attached to his scalp, under his nose, the sides of his neck, and his chest.

The doctor walked in with a clipboard. "Dr. Cohen? I'm Dr. Ramaswamy. I'll be monitoring your sleep activity through the night."

"Call me Marty," Marty said.

Ramaswamy smiled. "Your chart has 'doctor' as your honorific. Are you a physician or—"

"No, nothing quite so practical. Your records are probably back from when I was working at the university as a postdoctoral archaeology researcher."

"Mummies and tombs. Very Indiana Jones, I suspect."

"Not quite that adventuresome, I was more a language nerd," Marty said. "When I learned how Egyptian writing worked as a kid, I got so excited I ran home and started making up my own script. I drew it using images of things in my room, then I started keeping my own personal journal with my made-up language."

"Got the bug young, eh?" Ramaswamy chuckled. "Me too, except I pretended all my action figures had serious organ failure and cut them open to figure out what made them tick. With the amount of toys I'd taken apart, I'm pretty sure my parents were praying I was going into medicine, because the alternative I suppose would be becoming a madman."

"Never too late for such things, I suppose." Marty chuckled. "To be honest, I suppose I was destined for the language thing. My mother's Chinese, and her father, who lived with us, spoke only Mandarin. My father was also born in another country, so when I was a kid I didn't even realize I was speaking multiple languages. I just knew that when I talked with my grandfather, I spoke to him in a certain way, and my dad and I always spoke in a different way. It wasn't until I met another person who spoke Mandarin that I realized it wasn't just some weird family thing. And of course, me looking the way I do, nobody would expect me to speak Hebrew."

Ramaswamy's eyebrows went up slightly, and Marty laughed again.

"Yeah, I get that a lot. You don't often meet very many Chinese Jews."

"That is an interesting background." Ramaswamy looked down at the chart and said, "Well, from what I can see here, there's nothing that immediately jumps up as a warning sign regarding a cause for your fatigue. The chart says you're forty-two, one hundred and eighty pounds, which is about normal for someone who is six-foot-two. Blood pressure is fine, and the blood work all came back within normal parameters, though your iron is on the low end of normal." He looked around at the monitors. "Looks like your connections are good. Did you have any questions before I lower the lights and we begin?"

"Do you really think this will help figure out what's causing my fatigue?"

"At a minimum, it'll get us closer to an answer. By gaining a better understanding of your sleep cycle, we'll know if your sleep patterns are contributing to your fatigue. From there, we'll take a crack at solutions."

He tilted his head toward the TV hanging from the ceiling. "If you normally fall asleep with the TV on, go ahead and keep it on. We want you to do what you normally do. And if at any time you need to go to the bathroom, just say so. Someone will remove and reattach the sensors as needed."

The doctor stepped out of the room and turned off the lights, so that the only light in the room was coming from the TV screen.

The TV was on a news channel, and Marty nudged up the volume to hear what the reporter was saying.

"The rash of earthquakes across the globe have seismologists baffled. But if the scientists can't tell us the why, they can tell us the where—and they've directed the world's attention to Israel, at a spot just south of the port city of Haifa. Regional seismograph stations have detected a massive earthquake registering 8.9 on the Richter scale, and a tsunami warning has been posted by the Hellenic National Tsunami Warning Center out of the National Observatory of Athens."

Marty changed the channel. A dark-haired pitchman was fervently singing the praises of his new kitchen gadget. Marty closed his eyes. He didn't want to slice, dice, or cook *sous vide . . .*

He lurched up in the hospital bed to the sound of his ringing cell phone. Had he fallen asleep? He must have; the TV was now showing some hard-boiled cop show.

He answered the phone.

"Marty?"

He recognized the German accent. "Gunther?" Gunther Mueller was an archaeologist he'd worked with on many digs. "I haven't heard from you since . . ."

"Since the greatest linguistic talent since Champollion himself walked away from the game."

"I didn't walk away, Gunther. I was boxed out."

"If that's a basketball metaphor, I think I am following you. Sorry about calling you so early . . . oh jeez, it's like three a.m. Sorry, Marty, but it's urgent. We really, really need your help."

Marty rubbed his eyes with his knuckles. "Unless you need a bespoke sofa, Gunther, I'm not your man."

"Listen before you turn me down. I'm on a privately financed dig in the Sahara, and we discovered . . . something amazing. It's predynastic, there's no doubt about that, and it's not something I'm able to decipher. The guy paying the bills here is paranoid and doesn't trust academics, though; he won't hear about getting another professor involved."

Marty yawned and the bitter resentment he'd buried long ago welled up within him as he recalled many of the reasons he'd left the academic world. "Does your boss not trust the academics because they stick junior faculty with all the work? Because they're in league with fat administrators against the well-being of their own students? Because they never retire, leaving no room for young professors to get tenure? Because they hoard finds, doling them out to their favorites and the politically convenient?"

He'd been through all of those dishonest games and more. That was why he'd left it all behind for more honest work that valued sweat equity. Work where his success or failure didn't hinge on the whims of someone higher up on the food chain, but instead on his customer's willingness to buy the furniture he made.

"My friend, I know you've been burned by the folks who all too often run things, but I'd wager François has different reasons than you to distrust academia. Some of his ideas are . . . eccentric."

"Eccentric? Does that mean you're hunting Bigfoot? Or maybe you're measuring the celestial alignments of the Aswan Dam to corroborate the Illuminati ideology of Gamal Abdel Nasser?"

Gunther chuckled. "Not that eccentric. Listen, Marty, this really is an amazing find. And better yet, the man has agreed to bring you here at whatever rate you ask."

Marty shook his head. "Let me get this straight. You need someone who can read an obscure bit of Egyptian, but your paranoid boss doesn't trust universities . . . and I'm the only person who fits the bill."

"You're also the best," Gunther said. "But I already said that."

Marty paused. The offer *was* tempting. He missed the adventure of being on a dig site, the camaraderie of a dig team. And the ancient texts . . . There was a thrill in deciphering writing that no one else had even looked at for millennia.

"I tell you what, Gunther. I can't leave here—I have people to manage and train, and one of my guys is about to become a father, and I'll need to cover for him—but if you send me pictures of the texts, I'll see what I can do."

Gunther sighed. "Yeah . . . I figured you might say that. But François . . . he refuses to let anyone take pictures, or even draw what we've found. Did I mention he's an eccentric Frenchman? He's worried that with any leak, the information will grow legs and this place will be overrun. And to be honest, I don't exactly blame him. This is big, Marty. He told me to offer you twenty thousand euros as a convenience fee just to come out here. Once you get on the plane, he'll wire the money. You can take it, come here to look at our little problem, and then fly right back if you want."

"Twenty thousand euros? Is he serious?"

Gunther's voice lowered to a whisper. "He's a hard person to work for, but his checks are good. Marty, set aside the money for a moment. I'm telling you, this is the longest continuous text of predynastic Egyptian I've ever seen. As far as I know, the longest that exists. Marty, this is your stuff. If you come, you won't regret this. Maybe you can publish the translations of these, and they'll invite you back to Yale."

"I've already invited Yale to kiss my ass, Gunther."

"Then forget Yale. Listen, this guy puts Don Quixote in the shade. If he doesn't get some answers quickly, he may shut down the dig until he can find someone he trusts who can decipher what we've got here, and will sign an NDA. That'll definitely take a while, and in the meantime, everybody here will likely be looking for a job. And some of the diggers here...I have a feeling they were begging for baksheesh on the streets of Cairo before coming on board."

Marty felt his breath coming quickly and his heartbeat picking up. Was that his mysterious ailment, or was he actually getting excited about going to Egypt again?

"How long would I need to be there?"

"Need to be here? Knowing you, you'll figure out what the primary texts say in twenty minutes. But once you do that, you'll want to stick around. So bring a change of clothes and a toothbrush."

Marty couldn't believe he was actually considering this. But it was good money, and it did sound like an adventure...

"Can I have some time to think about it? I can't leave immediately regardless; I have to meet a customer in the morning."

"Think about it, but don't take too long, Marty, okay?"

"I won't. Thanks, Gunther."

Marty hung up and set the phone aside. Laying his head back on the pillow, he closed his eyes and tried to clear his mind...

Marty was standing in a desert surrounded by weather-beaten stone structures. The wind blew sand across large fallen slabs of chiseled rock, filling his nostrils with the smell of coriander and sage.

He'd been at many ancient sites, but this place was different. There was electricity in the air, making his hair stand on end. He felt the presence of...something, but he couldn't see it or identify it. He also heard shouting, but he couldn't make out where the voices were coming from or what they were saying. They had the singsong quality of prayer, but the words . . . the words were Egyptian.

Not Arabic, the language of the present-day inhabitants, but Egyptian, the tongue of the Nile-dwellers for thousands of years before the Arabs came.

A full moon had just come above the horizon. The wind grew stronger, blowing sheets of sand from the tops of the nearest dunes. And then Marty saw a swirling dust devil forming between two of the dunes.

The tingling grew more intense as Marty walked from the ancient stones toward the swirling dust devil.

Blue sparks flashed within the vortex. It swirled and expanded, growing to almost twenty feet in height, and began to move, slowly, toward Marty.

The ancient words he'd heard hints of on the wind were more distinct and powerful now, and he realized . . . they were emanating from within the dust-filled tornado.

One word kept repeating, and he strained to hear it. But it was slippery; when he focused on it, it faded away.

The air around him shook with the power of the approaching vortex, and when it was within arm's reach, he heard the word clearly.

Come.

Marty lurched up in bed, his breathing ragged, his heart racing, his brow damp with sweat.

Gray daylight leaked around the corners of the Venetian blinds.

The overhead fluorescent tubes snapped on, and Dr. Ramaswamy walked in. "Very good. We've collected lots of interesting data, including your sleep interruption and how you dealt with resuming your night's sleep."

Marty shook his head. "What time is it?"

"Almost six a.m. If you like, you can try to sleep some more."

Marty shook his head. "I think . . . I'm done for today." He felt unsettled.

Ramaswamy nodded. "That's fine; we have enough data. We should get back to you in about two weeks for a follow-up. Middle of April at the latest."

Marty tried to calm his racing heart. "Two weeks, that's good."

He didn't *have* to go to Egypt. He'd get paid for the dining room set today and then have a leisurely think about whether he wanted to go visit Gunther at the site. But if he did decide to take the money, two weeks was plenty of time to get there and back again.

He had time.

Instead of driving home, Marty drove to the shop. That was one of the advantages of no longer having someone waiting at home for him. Cheryl had made very understanding noises about his frustration with the academy, but as soon as he was no longer hanging about the Humanities Quadrangle, she'd found other reasons to leave him.

He'd dated on and off since, but he knew his preferences, and they worked against him. He wanted a woman with white-collar, university-style curiosity, intelligence, and reading habits—but he wanted that without the condescension, class isolation, and self-importance that so often went along with it. In short, he wanted a bartender who read Karl Marx and Adam Smith, and such women were hard to find.

His shop was in a boxy brick building in a run-down semi-industrial neighborhood of New Haven. It was more than just a shop. The front third of the building was a display room for a few pieces Marty and his team had built, just to show what they were capable of doing, along with space for meeting customers. The middle third contained the workshop. The back third was Marty's space.

The sun was up when Marty arrived, squinting through the trees and across the rooftops, splashing egg-yolk yellow light across the carved and painted sign that read MARTY'S CUSTOM FURNITURE. The door was open, and Carlos sat behind the counter, resting his thick chest on his elbows as he read a trashy gossip magazine.

"Practicing your English again?" Marty said with a smile.

"I don't need to practice my English, you dork, I'm from the Bronx."

"Yeah," Marty said, "that's why you need the practice."

"Doc let you out early."

"It was just a sleep test."

"That mean you didn't sleep?"

"It means I slept enough. They measured me and they'll let me know what they figure out once they crunch the numbers."

Carlos jabbed a thumb at the dining room set—fully stained, varnished, and upholstered. "I think that's our best work so far."

Marty nodded, feeling a sense of pride as his gaze pored over the group's most recent project. It was exactly what he'd imagined in his mind's eye. "Agreed. Customer got a good deal, and we're going to get paid."

He headed back through the workshop into what Carlos and Pedro sometimes called "the Marty Cave." His books were here, on a bookcase he'd made with his own hands. Army War College publications. Clausewitz and Sun Tzu, the obvious stuff. Von Neumann on game theory, which had turned out to be more about choice and economics than about strategy, to Marty's disappointment. Thucydides, Herodotus, Polybius, Caesar.

Not exactly the kind of books every furniture maker keeps in his back room.

Marty laughed, tired to the bone.

Beneath the books were shelves full of games. War games, every last one, covering conflicts from every age of Earth's history, but especially its ancient past. His old game table was here, too. He'd built it by hand, with help from both Grandpa Chang and Grandpa Simcha. Its felt-lined gaming surface was sunk beneath a thick wooden armrest with rubber-lined cupholders bored into it. A wooden cover could be laid over the table to close it, preserving a game in progress.

Right now, the lid was off and the table was arrayed with wooden tokens, stained various colors and buffed to a high shine, laid out to depict the battle of Lake Trasimene. Hannibal's great genius had been in picking his battlefields, choosing time and terrain and weather that were always to his advantage. The model territory around the lake was thick with wooden tokens—along with one Smurf holding a hammer and toolbox.

Carlos. Marty chuckled and left the Smurf where it was.

Cheryl had never precisely told him she didn't like the gaming table. When he'd invited her to play a light, two-hour, two-person Gettysburg game, she'd said, "I prefer grown-up activities." Which had sounded very saucy, but had turned out to mean an evening of reality television and wine.

In the very back of the Marty Cave, a punching bag hung from heavy timbers. It was a canvas Everlast, beaten so hard over so many years that the logo was completely gone. As Marty looked at it, he reflexively touched his knuckles, then his fingertips.

Calluses on the back of the hand may be the mark of the warrior, Grandpa Chang had told him. *Calluses on the front mark the worker.*

Marty had both.

He set himself to a light bag workout. It would get his blood flowing and wake him up, if nothing else.

Pedro showed up half an hour later. He was younger than Carlos, and thinner. He had buzz-cut hair like a young marine, and he immediately set himself to work cutting some of the recently purchased stock for their next project.

Marty finished his workout and glanced up at the wall clock. The customer was fifteen minutes late for the agreed-upon pickup time. He knew people could be flaky about time, but he didn't have to like it.

Joining Pedro in the workshop, he put on safety glasses, set a large chunk of wood on a lathe, and began turning what he envisioned would be a leg for the next dining room table. Then he lathed a matching leg. Then a third.

Still no pickup.

At ten, Marty stepped out onto the crumbling sidewalk and called the customer.

The phone line was out of service.

He double-checked the receipt, dialed again, and got the same result. He felt flushed, and sweat trickled down his forehead.

Gritting his teeth, Marty looked at his phone. "Damn it." He needed that money. He needed it *today*.

Impulsively, before he could stop himself, he dialed Gunther.

The German picked up on the first ring. "Can you do it?"

"You said twenty thousand euros wired to me *the moment* I get on the plane?"

"I just need your bank info and I'll make sure it gets done. Is that a yes?"

"It's a yes." Marty gave Gunther his routing and account numbers and kicked at a chunk of loose concrete. A stray dog yapped at him. "When does he want me there?"

"Right away. He's reserved a first-class ticket on an Air Canada flight leaving from La Guardia at 6:45 p.m."

"That's a bit presumptuous."

"What should I tell him?"

Marty shook his head. "Tell him I'll be on the plane."

"Thank you, Marty. You won't regret it. One of the crew will pick you up at the Cairo airport and bring you to the site. It's been too long, my friend. I look forward to seeing you."

Marty hung up and walked back into the shop. Carlos and Pedro both stood behind the counter, trying to look unconcerned.

"Any word?" Pedro asked.

"I just got another source of cash. A different customer, big one, prepaid." That wasn't exactly a lie, and Marty didn't want to tell his guys that he was dipping a toe back into Egyptology. Even if it was just a toe, it might make them worry about their jobs. "I'll get you both paid by the end of the week. We'll keep chasing the customer about the dining room set. And hey, if we have to find another buyer, it'll just mean we get to keep the deposit, so we get paid extra."

The relief on both men's faces made Marty tear up slightly. He cleared his throat.

"That sounds awesome." Carlos said.

Marty nodded. "I'm going to disappear for a few days. I have to meet this new customer. You guys can run the shop. And Pedro, go ahead and start your leave whenever you need to. Don't wait for me to sign off or anything. Take care of the missus."

"Thanks, boss."

"Don't call me boss." Marty grinned. "It's O Great Khan . . . or Marty."

"Thanks, Marty," Pedro said.

⊰ CHAPTER ⊱
TWO

Marty stepped off the plane onto cracked asphalt. A man wearing a dirt-stained shalwar kameez waved at him and shouted in heavily accented English, "Dr. Cohen, Dr. Cohen!"

"I'm Marty Cohen."

"God be praised." The stranger approached Marty with a big smile, his crooked white teeth a sharp contrast to the mahogany of his skin. "Mueller told me you look like Chinese more than Jew. I'm Abdullah." They shook hands, and Abdullah grabbed the carry-on from Marty's hand and motioned to his left. "Also, it is fine if you are Jew, we are all creatures of God. Please, please. Mueller waiting on the plane. Come . . . come . . ."

Marty hustled after the man and asked in Arabic, "What do you mean, Mueller is waiting on the plane? I just got off the plane."

He knew his spoken Egyptian Arabic was a little rusty, but Abdullah looked surprised and pleased. "Oh, you speak so well. Yes, I'm taking you to Monsieur Garnier's plane. It will get us much closer to the site."

As Marty stepped out of the main terminal with Abdullah, the man lifted his hand and snapped his fingers. A driver standing next to a parked car about fifty feet away responded with a wave and hopped into his vehicle. It was a BMW 7 Series with an orange flashing light on its roof: one of the airport's premier Ahlan welcome services, a VIP service that Marty had seen before but never used.

As Marty pondered the expense associated with hiring such a service, he pulled out his phone and launched his banking app. He was relieved to see that the deposit had been wired while he was traveling, and with a few quick swipes, he arranged for this week's payroll to be deposited directly into his employees' accounts.

The car pulled up beside them, and the driver, in a dark suit and cap plus mirrored sunglasses, hopped out to open the rear passenger door. Abdullah handed Marty's bag to the driver, who slammed it into the trunk, and Marty joined Abdullah in the back. Within seconds, they were off.

"Where are we going?" Marty asked in Arabic.

Abdullah shook his head and put his finger to his lips. "Can talk on the plane," he said in English.

Ramaswamy had mentioned "Indiana Jones," but this archaeology dig was starting to take on the attributes of a James Bond film. Marty covered the growing smile on his face as he imagined what this Frenchman might look like . . . Dr. Evil?

Five minutes later, the car rolled into a fenced-off section of the airport that catered to private aircraft. They stopped beside a beautiful midsize jet with no commercial markings, and the plane's cabin door opened, dropping a set of stairs with a handrail.

Marty got out of the car. Despite his growing curiosity about what he'd gotten himself involved in, he felt that ever-present fatigue weighing him down.

While Abdullah paid the driver and retrieved Marty's bag, Marty heard a voice shout from the plane's door.

"Marty!"

He looked up and saw Gunther at the top of the stairs, his wispy hair, still mostly blond, whipping about in the breeze. Marty smiled and waved. If more of the senior academics he had known had been like Gunther, Marty might still be in academia.

"I packed a toothbrush!" Marty yelled over the growling of jet engines. "When do I get to see the good stuff?"

Gunther waved for him to approach. "Get in the plane and we'll talk!"

Marty climbed the stairs and was greeted by an automated voice saying, "*Welcome to the Gulfstream IV business jet. As you get acquainted with the features of this aircraft—*"

"My friend!" Gunther pulled Marty into a bear hug. His smile couldn't have been bigger. "It's so good to see you." He motioned toward a set of plush leather chairs facing each other. "Grab a seat."

Marty sat, resting his elbow on the polished wood-grain table that extended between them.

"François said he already sent the money," Gunther said.

"He did." Marty nodded. "We're squared away."

Abdullah climbed into the plane, Marty's bag in his hand. He held it up. "I bring to back of the plane."

"Thank you!"

The pilot—a thin, pale gentleman with brown hair and a high forehead—emerged from the cockpit, scanned the cabin, and pressed a button next to the entryway. With the whooshing sound of hydraulics, the stairway folded inward, and the front cabin door closed. The pilot pulled out his pocket flashlight and quickly inspected the door's seal, gave Gunther and Marty a thumbs-up, and disappeared back into the cockpit.

Almost immediately, the jet began moving.

"*We have received clearance for takeoff,*" the pilot said over the speakers. His accent was middle European, maybe Czech or Hungarian. "*Please ready yourself and fasten your seatbelts.*"

Marty and Gunther buckled in, and Abdullah settled in the back of the plane with a dog-eared book.

"*We are first in line and will be taking off on runway two-three-right. Our top altitude will be twenty-seven thousand feet, and we should fly over Luxor before landing at Aswan International Airport. Total distance is approximately eight hundred ninety kilometers, and total flying time should be approximately one hour and twenty minutes.*"

The plane turned, rolled onto the runway, and stopped. The engines grew louder and louder. Then the plane burst forward, and Marty, who was facing the rear, was yanked hard into his seatbelt. He had never been on a private jet before, and he realized this was not his favorite direction to face during takeoff.

Soon they lifted off the asphalt and the jet was cutting smoothly through the air at a steep angle.

Marty looked across the table at Gunther. "Aswan, eh? How far from Aswan is the site?"

"It's very close. Only a twenty-minute drive from the airport."

Marty frowned. "Only twenty minutes and the dig is a secret?"

Gunther grabbed a bottle of water from a compartment in the wall. "Thirsty?"

Marty waved the bottle away.

Gunther took a long swig. "We were working just outside of Nabta Playa."

"The ancient stone circle? I would have guessed that's been picked through so many times you wouldn't find anything of note there."

Gunther nodded. "And you'd mostly be right. It's gotten the reputation of being Egypt's answer to Stonehenge. Very trendy nowadays with the tourist dollars flowing. But we had access to some new ground-penetrating radar technology. To make a long story short, we found a small box buried three feet underground just outside the circle. The box held a clay tablet with writing on it. And that's where you come in."

"A clay tablet with writing. Sounds like Babylon, not Egypt."

Gunther traced a line through the condensation forming on his bottle of water. "It's old. As old as Narmer."

Narmer was one of the names given to the pharaoh believed to have unified Egypt into one country. The name was a reading of two hieroglyphs, transliterated *n'r*, meaning "catfish," and *mr*, meaning "chisel," or maybe "angry." The hieroglyphs appeared on a very old stone palette that showed a picture of an Egyptian king—understood to be named Narmer—driving his enemies before him with a mace.

"I can't wait to see it," Marty murmured.

Gunther chuckled. "Oh, none of us can wait for you to see it. But that's just the beginning. While we were trying to read that tablet, François continued the survey with the ground-penetrating radar. We spent almost a month dragging three radar units behind vehicles, looking for God knows what. A university-funded dig would have run out of cash, but François got up every morning and yelled, 'Let's go spend more money!' Which was the signal to start up the trucks."

"That sounds fairly eccentric. Most rich people I know are only that way because they don't want to spend their money."

"Exactly, but just wait. And then the radar picked up the first signs of an underground passage. We followed it in one direction and the radar lost the trail. But in the other direction, we found an opening. For security purposes, we dug only in the dead of night. Good God, Marty, I took my turn standing guard with a rifle, can you imagine it? And when we finally managed to uncover the entrance..." Gunther leaned forward, eyes wide. "Untouched. Sealed. Immaculate. No sign of tomb robbers, no decay. They might have closed up the passage the day before we arrived, for all we could tell. It was a long tunnel. The writings on the wall were painted with brilliant colors, nothing faded... in the same style and syntax as the tablet. And it's a long text. For all we know, it's an epic tale of some sort."

Marty's heart was racing. It didn't really matter what the writing said, it could have been a collection of cooking recipes for all he cared. It was lucky enough to find an intact site, but to find one that old, and full of writing... it was unheard of. If Gunther was right, and Marty could translate the texts, they might push the horizon on written Egyptian back several hundred years.

Marty's ears popped as the plane began descending.

"We are now at seven thousand feet and will be landing at Aswan International Airport in ten minutes."

Marty peered out the window at the vast expanse of yellow rock and sand. From this altitude, he could only barely make out the Nile, a bluish-green thread weaving its way from the south to the north. This dry land, and this river, had given birth to one of the world's great civilizations, and that birth was still shrouded in a veil of mystery.

The idea that he might be about to get a privileged first look behind that veil put a smile on his face.

After disembarking, the three men got into a waiting SUV. Marty sank into the plush leather seats, trying not to laugh out loud at the contrast with his prior experiences at dig sites, when he rode around in the back seats of twenty-year-old jeeps.

There was absolutely nothing posh about archaeology. No first-class tickets, no private jets, and no G-class Mercedes SUVs, much less one waiting for him on the tarmac. And last but certainly not least, he had never had a twenty-thousand-euro signing bonus wired to his account before he even set foot on the dig site.

Abdullah drove and Gunther rode shotgun. As they raced

through trackless desert scrub northwest of the airport, Marty leaned forward between them.

"If this is only twenty minutes into the desert, how is the dig site kept hidden from prying eyes?" he asked. In his experience, foreigners breaking ground on a dig was an invitation for every unemployed man within twenty miles to come offer his services as a digger or guide.

Gunther smiled and grabbed a device from the center console. "We use this."

The device looked like a garage door opener—a plastic box with a single button and a clip to hang it from the car's visor.

"And that is . . . ?" he asked.

"You'll see."

Abdullah set down the device and turned on the car's LCD screen. Instead of a map, it showed a series of numbers, white on a black background, constantly changing as they drove.

"Are those GPS coordinates?"

"Praise be to God," Abdullah replied in Arabic as he slowed the vehicle. "Monsieur Garnier wants this site to not be found, and we are very careful. We are . . ." He glanced at the display and pressed his lips together. "We are half a kilometer away."

Marty studied the terrain ahead of them and saw nothing other than sand, rocks, and the occasional clump of desert grasses.

The white numbers turned yellow, and Abdullah slowed the vehicle to a crawl. When the numbers turned red, Gunther picked up the garage door opener and pressed the button.

A ten-foot-wide crack appeared in the ground ahead of them, running left to right. As it opened wider, it revealed a ramp down into the earth. Seconds later, Abdullah was easing the SUV down the ramp into an underground chamber.

"How . . . ?" Marty began.

Abdullah turned off the engine and smiled. "This place was here before us."

"He means the chamber," Gunther said. "The ramp and door were installed by a Dutch engineering firm. We brought them out here blindfolded and with no cell phones, all the way from Cairo." He pressed the button on the garage door opener again and the ramp rose on hydraulic pistons.

They got out of the car, and Marty scanned the underground lair, which was a good hundred feet from side to side. "Was there a cave-in?" he asked, pointing at a mound of rubble heaped against one of the walls.

"Oh, no, nothing like that," Gunther said. "Abdullah and Kareem have managed to move a lot of rock in the space of the last month or so. This chamber has made it really easy to excavate without anyone noticing anything from up above."

Marty continued to feel uneasy. "Still," he said, "if you believe the news reports, there are earthquakes happening all over the world nowadays. Isn't the epicenter in Israel or something?" He pointed to the hydraulic ramp. "I mean, what if that thing breaks?"

"In that case we're stuck and someone six thousand years from now will find us and have a good laugh at our expense," Gunther said seriously, then laughed. "Don't worry, we have other exits—shafts, ladders, well-hidden ventilation holes. We can get out if necessary. But ignore the news. This area hasn't felt an earthquake in recorded history."

A beefy man appeared at the far end of the chamber, fast-walking in their direction. "Dr. Cohen!" he shouted, revealing a French accent. He shook hands with Marty, who thought he looked like a blond Gérard Depardieu, only more squared off.

"Monsieur Garnier?" Marty said.

Garnier waved dismissively. "Please. François. First names are good enough for me."

Eccentric or not, Marty liked him for that. "Then call me Marty."

"Marty? Not . . . Kung Fu Cohen?"

Marty shook his head. "I see Gunther has completely robbed me of all dignity."

"No, he has sung your praises. Trust me, otherwise you wouldn't be here. Besides, who doesn't admire the discipline of a martial artist?" The Frenchman draped his arm over Marty's shoulder—enveloping him in a cloud of cologne, body musk, and strong cheese—and steered him back the way he'd come. "I am, as you Americans would so charmingly say, the money guy. A banker by profession, at least at one time. Let me introduce you to the crew, and then we can get started. I'm sure you want to see the alien markings."

"Alien markings?" Marty glanced back at Gunther.

Gunther grinned and shrugged.

Aliens? Marty sighed. But Gunther *had* said the Frenchman was both eccentric and paranoid. Was this about to be a giant waste of Marty's time?

He took a deep breath and let it out slowly. He'd made payroll this week, he reminded himself. If nothing else, that was a positive. A big one.

"I keep telling François," Gunther said, "that there's no evidence that these markings are anything but writing from a prehistoric Egyptian civilization."

"Prehistoric they may be," François groused, "but they're no cave paintings from Stone Age man. I've seen the paintings in the Chauvet cave; it's only ten kilometers from where I was born. They're gorgeous, and show a time of human development that most certainly preceded what we know of as human civilization. But they don't communicate much in the way of a message. These markings are quite different. I can't interpret it—that's why you're here, Marty—but I can appreciate what it is *not*. It's not someone enumerating the nearby wildlife. It's not the wild myth of a shaman. It's precise. It has geometric symbology. It's *language*. And I'm convinced that it's beyond the capability of man at that time. I've done my homework. The Egyptians weren't writing in predynastic times."

"They didn't write *much*," Marty said. "That we have yet *found*." He hated to throw water on the fire of the man's enthusiasm, but it was better to set that expectation now. There were no aliens in predynastic Egypt.

"Do we know exactly how old these writings are?" he asked Gunther.

"Not the ones in the tunnels, but luckily the tablet had organic fibers in it. We sent some scrapings to two labs, and got the results back just yesterday. They both agree: the tablet is about six thousand years old."

Marty's eyes widened. "And how much writing is in the tunnels?"

François laughed. "Books!" he cried. "Books' worth!"

They passed into another chamber, thick with shadows. François clapped his hands, and the lights brightened.

This was a smaller chamber, perhaps twenty feet by thirty. At its center stood three long tables, two of which were stacked with books and paper. Several people lay sleeping in cots along the walls.

François clapped his hands again. "Everyone, please meet our newest team member, Dr. Marty Cohen."

He turned to Marty. "I apologize that everyone is sleeping. We got used to working during the nighttime hours."

A dark-skinned woman with straight black hair swung her feet off one of the cots. She wore a ragged Rage Against the Machine T-shirt and a necklace of small seashells. "Hello," she said, without standing. "You're the language expert?" Her accent was Australian.

François leapt in to make introductions. "This is Lowanna Lancaster, our biological anthropologist. And she makes better tea than the rest of these savages."

"I can read some languages," Marty said in response to her question. "Are you an aboriginal Australian, then?"

"Arrernte," she grunted. "Not that it's any of your business."

"It isn't," Marty agreed. "But I find it interesting."

"I've brought Marty here to give Surjan a little competition for 'hunkiest man on the dig,'" François said. "It's for your benefit, my dear. Ah, and here he comes now."

A man with a thick black beard had hopped up from another cot to join them. He wore a blue turban, a white T-shirt, and khaki cargo pants. He was broad of shoulder and narrow of waist, and his arms and thighs both seemed about to burst free of their confining fabric. Altogether he looked to Marty like a rugby player.

"Marty, this is Surjan, our site security chief," François said. "He's been under my employ ever since he retired from Special Group, India's special forces unit—the one that most people don't even know exists. So if you're thinking, 'Is he as scary as he looks?' The answer is no, he's much scarier than that."

Marty didn't know much about the military, but he had heard of SG. He'd helped on a dig near the Kashmiri border as an undergraduate, and the Indian government had assigned several of these men to guard the site. Those soldiers had dealt efficiently with predators, robbers, and terrorist attacks alike.

The large man offered Marty his hand. "It's nice to meet you, mate. I look forward to seeing you in action." The ex-soldier spoke with a mild London accent, like Ray Winstone playing a member of Parliament.

"Surjan . . . Singh?" Marty guessed.

The big man nodded. "I'm Sikh."

Marty smiled. "I'm glad to have you on my side. Though to be honest, I hope I don't have to see you in action."

"If we do see action, I expect you to pull out some wicked kung fu moves."

Marty gave Gunther a severe look. Gunther suddenly became interested in a stray thread coming off his sleeve.

Surjan looked Marty up and down as if taking stock of an opponent. "You stand like a fighter, and your knuckles are well-calloused. You're ready for a fight, I can tell."

"I was in a lot of fights as a kid," Marty told him, "but recently, I've only fought with a punching bag."

Surjan leaned in. "Is it true you knocked your dean arse over tits when he didn't give you tenure?"

Marty sighed. Of course Gunther had to share that story with these people. "I corrected a professor of sociology's bad attitude. And I did it because he was copping a feel on my grad student at a cocktail party."

"I'll remember that!" François said with a laugh. He clapped his arm on Marty's shoulder. "Now where is Kareem?"

"I'm here, Monsieur Garnier."

Marty turned to see a short, dark-skinned young man standing in the doorway. He wore a dirt-stained shalwar kameez like Abdullah's, and held a broken pickaxe over one shoulder.

"Kareem, this is Dr. Marty Cohen," François said, then to Marty: "Kareem is young, and the young ones are too often full of problems. But he's Abdullah's nephew, and so far he seems to be a hard worker and is doing well." He turned back to the young man. "Did you break yet another axe?" he asked, sounding amused.

The little man frowned. "I couldn't sleep, so I tried again to work on the barrier. It's being cursed troublesome, by God."

He pronounced "cursed" as two syllables.

"Barrier?" Marty asked.

Gunther pointed at the tunnel. "Remember when I said there was a section that the ground-penetrating radar couldn't get through?

We think that's where the stone barrier is, at the end of the tunnel with all the writing."

Kareem sighed. "I'll keep trying. A cursed wall shall not defeat me, by God."

François patted Marty on the shoulder and motioned to the tunnel. "I suppose this would be as good time as any to show you the tunnel."

Marty nodded. "I do want to see the tunnel. But maybe I should take a look at the tablet first."

"Good idea," said François. "I need to have a word with Gunther, so I will leave you in Lowanna's capable hands."

CHAPTER THREE

"What do you think?" Lowanna asked as Marty studied the tablet on the table. "Is it really an example of predynastic writing, like Gunther's been saying?"

But despite the wonder of the tablet, Marty found he was distracted by Lowanna. She was stunning, with skin so dark that the light reflecting off of it shone with an almost purple hue. She was probably in her mid-thirties, just a handful of years younger than Marty, but had the same wide-eyed expression he'd seen from undergraduates when he'd led them to the end of an old wisdom text in the original Egyptian.

"I'm sorry, but I'm quite curious about you," he said. "About what growing up Arrernte was like, and how that led to you becoming an anthropologist."

"Sure," she said. "And I'm quite curious about . . . *Are these really examples of predynastic writing?*"

Marty laughed and shifted his gaze back onto the tablet. So it was none of his business.

"To be honest," he said, "it's an enigma. How familiar are you with Egyptian writing systems?"

"Not familiar at all. My focus is on the biological and sociological evolution of societies, including ancient ones."

"Okay. Well, Egyptian writing is composed of many different logographic representations." Marty pointed at some of the illustrations etched in the clay. "But the images don't necessarily mean the thing they show. Sometimes a picture of a star means a star, but usually the pictures represent letters. Some pictures represent a single letter—like here, this picture of a foot. It makes a sound like our letter *b*."

"Is there a whole alphabet?" Lowanna asked.

"The Egyptians don't seem to have recognized one, but every consonant could be written with a single image, so, yes, sort of. But also, lots of pictures represent multiple consonants."

"Syllables."

"No, because they don't tell us the vowels. And no, because they don't even imply that there *are* vowels. They just show consonants. This picture is the letters *m* and *r*, and this one is *p* and *r*. This picture is three letters together: *n*, *f*, and *r*."

"How do you know which picture makes which letters?"

"For an Egyptian, it was easy," Marty said. "Well, once you had the training anyway. The symbol represents the consonants of the thing pictured. For example, in English, let's say I draw a stick of butter."

"Butter comes in bricks," Lowanna muttered.

Marty smiled. "Fine, a brick of butter. What are the consonants?"

"*B, t, t, r.*"

"We ignore doubles, so *b, t, r*. So when I draw a brick of butter, I *might* be referring to butter. But using those same consonants . . . but different vowels . . . what else might I be referring to?"

"Better," said Lowanna.

"Or batter," Marty added. "Or bitter, or biter. Or maybe even bather or bother."

"How do you know which?"

"Sometimes there are extra signs that give us hints," Marty said. "Or a pattern of signs used consistently becomes a recognizable spelling. Sometimes you can only tell from the context."

"Fascinating."

"Isn't it?" Marty grinned. "When I found out about this, I was just a kid, and I thought it was so interesting that I devised a hieroglyphic system for writing the English language, using only objects located in my bedroom. A picture of a desk was *d, s, k*, and the guitar was *g, t, r*, and the letters *p, n* were made with a drawing of a ballpoint pen."

"Nerd," Lowanna said. "Okay, so what's the enigma?"

"The Egyptian writing system lasted some four thousand years, as far as we have evidence," Marty said. "The language kept going, as Coptic, but it was written with a different writing system, mostly borrowed from Greek. Late in its life, the Egyptian writing system became more and more abstract. It was still these little pictures, but instead of a picture of a mouth, you might just have a straight line, or instead of an owl, you'd get a squiggle."

"This tablet is early, then," Lowanna said. "Because these are clearly painted pictures."

"Yes. And that in itself is interesting, because the oldest written Egyptian we have is writing on objects that have other uses—walls, coffins, statues. Not tablets. And also, at first glance, this looks like really simple writing. Simple syntax, simple sentences, a limited vocabulary. Few determinatives. It does look like very early writing."

Lowanna shrugged. "Nothing about that sounds like an enigma."

Marty smiled. "Maybe 'enigma' was the wrong word. Let's say . . . mystery. You see, the carbon dating says this tablet is six thousand years old, but the oldest known complete sentence in written Egyptian is estimated to be less than five thousand years old. If this writing turns out to be as old as the tablet it's painted on . . . then this is not only the oldest Egyptian writing ever found, it's the oldest human writing anyone has ever seen."

Lowanna was quiet for a moment, her eyes unwavering as she looked up at him. "You would have been a great teacher."

Marty shrugged. "As it turns out, I'm a pretty good woodworker. And tolerably decent small businessman."

"Gunther told us about that. What made you get off the university track? Was it because you punched that guy?"

Marty sighed. "The university finally admitted it would never give me tenure. Punching that guy didn't help, obviously. But the truth is I was already at odds with the whole thing."

"Let me guess: there were never any available tenure slots."

"I take it you've experienced that yourself?"

"Oh yeah."

Marty nodded. "Well, add to that the fellow professor who got tenure ahead of me because his dad paid for new seats in the basketball arena. And the one who had a more politically attractive ethnic background than Chinese-Jewish American."

"I don't know, that sounds pretty exotic."

"Not the right kind of exotic. Mostly it just means I make food for myself on Christmas." Marty grinned. "Bad joke. Oh, and don't forget the associate professor who was sleeping with the department chair. They're all tenured professors now."

"All those wrong reasons aside, do you think those others were deserving of tenure?" Lowanna asked.

Marty felt an old bitterness rearing its ugly head. "Not even close," he said.

It was just before dawn the next morning, and Lowanna was watching surreptitiously from just inside a tunnel opening as Marty went through some kind of exercise routine.

Now, stripped naked to the waist, Marty was performing a complex series of steps involving spinning kicks, punches, and deep sweeping lunges. He was in fantastic shape, and moved with the fluidity of a professional dancer. After hearing Gunther talk about how Marty was into martial arts, Lowanna had figured he was one of those poseur types. But it was obvious the man was the real deal. Humble, quiet, and unassuming.

The kind of guy who would punch a handsy sociologist.

He continued for another two minutes before coming to the end of the form.

Gunther had said Marty was unmarried. Not that it mattered, if he really intended to read the inscriptions and then fly right back to Connecticut.

Marty crouched low, and for a moment he seemed to struggle with his balance as he breathed heavily, facing the rocky floor. Then with a deep breath, he hopped up onto his feet, bowed to nobody in particular, then turned to Lowanna with a smile.

"I see you're awake," he said.

Lowanna's cheeks felt warm as she was caught intruding on this half-naked man's . . . well, she wasn't sure what he'd been up to.

"Sorry, yes," she said. "Was that karate?"

Marty grabbed a towel from a rock and wiped the sweat from his face. "Kung fu, actually. Or at least that's what my Grandpa Chang called it. Honestly, I have nothing to compare it to. Everything I learned was because my grandfather wanted to pass on what he knew."

"Interesting. Was he a monk?"

"My grandfather would vehemently say 'no' to that question." Marty smiled. "But my mother once told me that her father had been one of the senior monks at the Shaolin temple before he left the monastery and never looked back. Anyway, those were just some basic forms, mostly to get my pulse pounding a bit. Helps me clear my head."

"Has it helped? Clear your head, I mean."

With an amused grin, Marty shrugged into his shirt. "Some, I suppose. I have a lot on my mind right now."

Marty looked around at the crew gathered around the table. "It's old Egyptian," he said. "My gut says that Gunther's right, it's predynastic, and *maybe* the text dates to the same time as the making of the tablet. So I think this is the longest text in predynastic Egyptian known to man, and the earliest known complete sentence. By far."

Gunther cackled. "You haven't even looked at the tunnel where there's so much more of the same writing. Even so, just having this much translated would make you famous, my friend."

"But it's still Egyptian," Marty continued. "Knowing the language and knowing how words are spelled later, it was relatively easy to work out the spellings here." He opened his notebook and flipped through the fifty or so pages of scribbles he'd made during his effort to decode the meaning of certain characters.

"Relatively easy for you, maybe," Gunther said. "I couldn't make heads or tails of them."

François, as always, was less reserved. "*Incroyable!* How you unraveled this in the span of twelve hours, I'll never understand."

Gunther patted Marty on the shoulder. "I told you, François. The man's a genius. It's a crime he's not teaching at Chicago right now."

Marty shook his head. "Anyway, I was able to make out about ninety percent of the text. Keep in mind, much of that is guesswork, based on words I know in other Afroasiatic languages. It'll take a lot more study for me to get a translation I have full confidence in."

"Leave some for your eventual grad students," Gunther said, "and for the lesser scholars in your wake."

Lowanna snorted.

François made a rolling motion with his hand, urging Marty to keep going. "Well, what did it say?"

Marty flipped through his notebook and landed on the last page. He cleared his throat, feeling the crew's silent focus, then began.

"As instructed by our fathers, we built a wharf for the great sun to dock. For many generations, men said in their hearts it was a waste. But one night, the sun arrived."

"Son?" François asked. "As in the male child of a father, or the big yellow thing in the sky?"

"The thing in the sky."

"Ra?" asked Lowanna.

Gunther shook his head. "Ra becomes important to the Egyptians by about the Fifth Dynasty. If Marty's right, this text is older than Ra."

Surjan shook his head. "Older than the gods."

François motioned for Marty to go on.

"The stars assembled into the sun and then walked on the land. They breathed like crocodiles, they spoke with the voices of beasts."

"I knew it!" François said, positively giddy with excitement. "That must be an alien visitation! Breathing like a crocodile would be just like the sound of someone breathing through a respirator. Don't you see? Oh, you can mock UFOs all you like, but technology and aliens make a much better hypothesis than gods!"

Marty bit his tongue. He had feared the Frenchman would come to precisely this interpretation.

Lowanna laughed. "I don't know, François. Maybe the tablet is describing someone with a crocodile head. Don't the Egyptians have a crocodile-headed god? I can't read hieroglyphs, but I've seen enough of their art to know that much."

"You're thinking of Sobek," said Gunther.

François turned to Marty. "Please. Continue."

Marty nodded and went on with his reading. *"They spoke of the battle. One that warriors must prepare for. And when the lands unite is when the work begins. Let the son be ready, because he will be the chosen."*

He looked around at the crew. "In this case, 'son' means male descendant. I don't know what the significance is of these battles or being the chosen, but the lands being united immediately set me to thinking of Narmer, who united upper and lower Egypt. Roughly six thousand years ago, much of that area was ruled by the Badari civilization. It's a prehistoric people who populated upper Egypt. And from what little we know, they were a distinct group, separate from other neighboring peoples."

Marty returned to his translation. *"He*—that's referring to the son again—*will guide and set those on a path. A path of death or a path of life. Defeat your foes and continue. Lose and die. Complete the final battle and the sun will come again.* And that 'sun' once again means the thing in the sky."

"The aliens," François murmured.

Marty frowned. *"There will be a final battle at . . ."* Marty shook his head. "I'm not sure how to read the location. It could be Meged." He continued: *"And for all, it will be life or death. We must prepare."*

"Well, that's ominous," said Surjan, breaking the sudden silence.

Marty felt a shiver down his spine. He would normally have laughed off François's aliens and Surjan's foreboding alike.

But what if they were right?

Marty ignored the sound of machinery as he held up the LED lantern to study the precisely painted text on the walls of the tunnel. It was without a doubt the same style and age as the writing on the tablet, with the same naïve grouping patterns and the same idiosyncratic glyphs. But there was simply so much *more* of it here. To really understand this phase of written Egyptian would take much, *much* more time.

François approached. "Anything yet?"

Marty shook his head. "I've only been looking at this section of the tunnel for half an hour. It's . . . a lot."

"Gunther told you to bring a toothbrush," François said with a chuckle. "Are you understanding anything at all?"

"Well . . . I can tell that there's something about a contest or maybe a battle." Marty's gloved finger hovered over a section of the wall. "And here's more about the docking sun. I haven't walked down the rest of the tunnel yet, but is the entire length of the tunnel filled with this writing?"

"The entire thing." François grinned like a child on Christmas morning. "Come," he said, motioning for Marty to follow farther into the tunnel. "Maybe it would be better if you started at the beginning of the text instead of the end. And besides, I want to see how the boys are doing with the new grinders I got them."

"How do you know which end is the beginning?" Marty asked.

"I don't. But isn't that how the Pyramid Texts are supposed to be read? From the inside out?"

A guess, but not as crazy a guess as aliens.

As they continued along, the sound of something grinding echoed from up ahead. Suddenly the noise halted, replaced by a stream of Arabic cursing.

"Sounds as if Kareem and Abdullah are having a rough time," Marty said.

They came around a corner, and saw the workers crouched in a shower of sparks.

François suddenly ran toward them and yelled, "*Khalas!* Stop it, you two!"

The men stopped, but only because one of the cutting discs on Abdullah's angle grinder cracked, sending shards of the broken cutting wheel in all directions.

"What is wrong with you two?" François snapped. "Why didn't you tell me the wall had metal in it?"

"It does?" both workers responded.

François rolled his eyes and began chiding the diggers in a mixture of French, Arabic, and English. Marty took the opportunity to study the wall that sealed the end of the tunnel.

It was simple blank stone. No writing. Smooth. It had the same texture as the sandstone on either side, but when he rapped his knuckles on it, he heard a faint echo, as though there was empty space on the other side. Just as Gunther had said.

Marty then crouched and looked closer at the section of the wall the men had been working on. "This doesn't make sense," he said. "You guys haven't even scratched the surface. Even if this were made of metal, shouldn't we see some marks on the wall?"

At that moment, Gunther came down the tunnel and stepped into the circle of portable LED lanterns. "Hey, guys," he said. "Any progress?"

François ignored him and continued to huddle with Kareem and Abdullah, muttering something about equipment. But Marty picked up one of the broken cutting wheels, showed it to Gunther, and then pointed at the unmarked stone.

"There's your progress," Marty said with a lopsided grin.

Gunther shook his head. "Somehow I figured as much. So what are you doing all the way down here? Come to look at the weird hieroglyphs?"

"Actually I started with the writing at the entrance. But then François said maybe I should start at this end. I'm not sure that it matters, though, it's all the same mystery."

"Not over there it isn't." Gunther pointed to Marty's left, to a section of wall near the floor that had a completely different writing style from the rest of the tunnel. The symbols were carved into the stone but left unpainted, as if the author had been interrupted before they could put the final touches on their work. "I mean, I can't read the rest of the tunnel either, but at least I recognized the style everywhere else. This section—it's utterly foreign to me. I don't recognize a single glyph. Do you?"

Marty got on his hands to look, and his breath caught in his throat. He hadn't seen this writing style in over twenty years. In fact, nobody else had either. They couldn't have.

This is impossible.

He traced the hieroglyphs with his fingers. A teddy bear, a lamp, a curtain, a doorknob. A guitar. And, unmistakably, a ballpoint pen.

François stepped away from his men and walked toward Marty. "Well, magic language guru?" he said. "You see something interesting?"

Marty was at a loss for words. His skin tingled and his hands began shaking. "I . . . I recognize it."

His heart was racing so quickly he was afraid he was going to suffer a panic attack. He swallowed hard and closed his eyes. Using a meditation trick his Grandpa Chang had taught him, he focused on his breathing.

How? How is this . . . here?

The symbols weren't written recently; they had the same patina of age as the rest of the writing on the tunnel walls.

But they were in English.

Written in a script that only Marty knew.

Because he was the one who had made it up in the first place.

This was the silly writing system of his youth. The one he'd invented as a kid. And yet it was carved into the wall at an ancient dig site that Marty was certain was thousands of years old.

Could Gunther be pranking him? He'd told Gunther of his personal writing system, as he'd told Lowanna. It wasn't a secret.

But he hadn't taught them the symbols. Whoever had chiseled these images into the wall didn't just know *of* Marty's juvenile writing system. They knew the *system*.

Because this writing . . . it made sense.

"Well? What does it say?" François pressed.

Marty opened his eyes and stared at the symbols once more. He took a deep breath. His heart had slowed to a manageable rate, but he'd broken out in a cold sweat.

"It's talking about the wall," he said. "The end of the tunnel. It says there are six panels."

Gunther stepped closer to the blank wall, then backed away a few steps, squinting and holding out his lantern. "Interesting . . ." he said. "I never noticed it before, but now that you say it, parts of the wall do have slight color differences. Almost like a checkerboard. A very faded checkerboard."

He turned back to Marty. "What else does it say?"

Marty stood, and now he too could see the faded checkerboard. The wall had been put together with six different slabs of rock.

"It's instructions," he said. "For touching the wall in certain spots. I think I know how to . . . open it."

François's eyes widened. "*Imshi!*" he shouted, snapping his fingers at the diggers. "Hurry, move away from the wall."

Kareem and Abdullah scrambled away, and François and Gunther backed off as well, leaving Marty standing alone before the wall.

Feeling a tingling racing through him, Marty reached up and touched the top left corner of the top left panel. He then touched the center of the top right panel, then continued through the other panels, following the instructions written below. He felt foolish; he had absolutely no idea what this was accomplishing, if anything.

Then, as the glyphs instructed him, he repeated the process a second time. And this time, when he touched the top left panel, the wall trembled.

He looked back at the others, who were staring wide-eyed back at him.

Marty tried to shrug away the tension building up in his

shoulders. He took a deep breath, then continued through the other panels, trying to ignore the vibrations he felt under his finger. When he was done, he stepped back.

Nothing happened.

And then a tremor ripped through the entire tunnel and the lanterns went out, cloaking them all in darkness.

"Kareem! Abdullah!" François said. "Check the lanterns!"

Marty heard the sound of a switch being flipped repeatedly, then Abdullah said, "The lantern. It's not working, by God."

But another light appeared in the tunnel behind them, bouncing along, accompanied by the sound of footsteps.

"Are you gents all right?" Surjan called. "Did you feel an earthquake?"

"We're fine," called François. "Just bring that light over here."

The light came closer, revealing not only Surjan but Lowanna, who was the one holding the lantern.

"What in the world?" she gasped, looking past them.

They all turned to look at the wall. The blank sandstone now glowed with a pale, bluish-white light. And as they watched, the six stone panels vanished with a sound like the crack of a whip, followed immediately by a strong gust of dust-laden wind that nearly knocked everyone off their feet.

"*Mon Dieu!*" François cried.

Marty blinked the dust out of his eyes and passed his hand through the space that had previously held an impervious barrier.

And then a voice spoke in his head.

"*Seer, it is time.*"

Marty felt a surge of energy, like a shot of adrenaline coursing through his veins. The voice in his head was speaking in ancient Egyptian.

"*Bring your crew into the chamber of reckoning. As seer, you are the first. You will know. You will lead. You will tell others. You will seek what is needed. It is time.*"

Marty looked at the others. "Did any of you guys hear a voice?"

They all shook their heads.

Marty did, too. He had no explanation for what was happening here. He'd spent many years in the field—a scholarly man of science and truth for all of those years. And he was at a complete loss.

Then again, there was *one* rational explanation for everything he had seen this day: He was insane.

But deep in his heart, he didn't think that was it.

He motioned for the others to follow him, then stepped through the opening into the space beyond. It was a perfectly round, domed chamber, about twenty feet in diameter. The walls glowed with the same bluish-white light that the panels had.

The others stepped through behind him.

And the world flashed white.

The Administrator felt the ripple in the fabric of space itself, well before the hive reached out to alert him.

"We have a primary test triggering malfunction."

The Administrator frowned. "Give me its local description."

For the Administrator, the time it took for the hive to process the request and return an answer seemed like an eternity. But for those living within the brane, a thin membrane-like universe in which the test had been triggered, the processing time would have seemed like an instant.

"The local name for the event occurred on a planet named Earth, orbiting a G2V star called Sol, in the Orion arm of the Milky Way galaxy, a member of the Virgo supercluster, which is a part of the Laniakea supercluster."

The Administrator's presence appeared instantly above the planet and zoomed down over the test sites. He scanned the entire time from the moment the Builders had established the test sites up through the moment of the triggering, in a place now known as Egypt.

There were seven humans in the transport chamber.

But there had been an anomaly in the triggering. He sensed a wrongness on this planet. It had become unstable.

"The nature of the anomaly is?"

"The time allotted for the planet's dominant species to complete its test is about to expire."

The Administrator checked on the test site that had caused the anomaly. A seer had been assigned. However, the tests had not been run in many Earth years. So many years that the tests themselves should no longer be working. The earthquakes had already begun. This was the beginning of the end for the planet's sentient hominids.

The Administrator made a decision.

One last chance for this species.

"I have stitched the tests to compensate for the delays. I will allow this one last set of champions to contest for their species' fate."

"*Understood. The malfunction is cleared. Testing is underway.*"

Marty tried to speak to the others, but found he couldn't. He had no control over his body. In fact, he wasn't in his body. He was just a mind.

He saw himself, though. He and the others were still standing in the chamber. They were frozen, like statues, and each person was bathed in a beam of shimmering white light.

Then the chamber faded, and he was surrounded by nothing but white. He knew he wasn't alone only because he heard the *thud* of seven individual heartbeats.

The whiteness wavered ever so slightly, and something began to take shape. A shimmering gold image of an ankh appeared, hanging before him.

Marty reached out to it. And though he couldn't see his arm moving or his fingers grasping the object, he felt a white-hot burning in his hand. The golden hue drained from the ankh as the searing heat crawled up his arm and traveled through his body.

And then with a *crack*, a swirling vortex of color appeared before him, and he found himself looking down at a horseshoe-shaped rocky massif. He descended, still bodiless, and swooped along the surface, the land speeding past him at an impossible rate. The sun rose and fell dozens of times as he headed eastward, past villages, farmlands, the outskirts of the desert.

In the distance, a dust cloud arose, as if kicked up by a large number of people traveling on foot, heading into the rising sun. An instant later he was upon them, an army, hundreds of people equipped with weapons of ancient war: spears, slings, bows, an occasional sword or staff. At the center of the army was a covered wagon, and he flew toward it. Toward it, and into it.

Inside, a man with bronze skin sat on a throne.

He looked up as if he could see Marty, and smiled.

"*Welcome, Seer. It is time.*"

The world of white exploded around Marty once more, and his

ears popped. He fell forward onto all fours, overcome by an intense bout of dizziness. He clenched fistfuls of grass and held on. The world spun.

He heard the sound of someone nearby retching and Marty opened his eyes.

Gone was the chamber.

Gone were the rock walls that had surrounded him.

Somehow...someway...they'd been transported to a new place.

He looked up and found himself and the six others standing on a high rocky escarpment. Each of them held a metal ankh, about the length of a forearm.

The images of the flyover replayed in his mind.

As he climbed up onto his feet and scanned his surroundings, he knew that they were atop that horseshoe-shaped formation he'd seen in the portal.

This couldn't be real.

Maybe he'd breathed in some ancient contaminant that was giving him hallucinations?

"It is time." the voice in his head prompted him again.

"Shut up," he told the disembodied voice.

He turned to the others, who were all getting up onto their feet, and Marty's jaw dropped.

⇥ CHAPTER ⇤
FOUR

Marty stood facing an ochre-colored stone wall. His eyes stung and watered. Bricks? Had he turned himself around so that he was now facing into a corner of the tunnel, seeing exposed brick?

But his eyes watered because the light cascading all around him was brilliant daylight, and overhead stretched a piercingly blue sky.

What had happened?

His hand hurt, and he dropped the ankh, which only now did he realize was actually in his possession. It landed on soft stone beneath his feet with a dull *thud*.

"What happened?" François's voice sounded remote.

"Look at that!" Gunther snapped. Then, in a more worried tone, "Step back. Be careful. Marty, watch where you put your feet."

Marty turned slowly. He saw the others all standing on a shelf of yellowish stone. They all wore the same clothing they had been wearing in the tunnel, and each held an ankh. Most of them stared past him, though Lowanna had her head cocked to one side as if listening to something, and Surjan stared at the ankh in his hands. It was the size of a large knife, or a short sword.

Marty left the ankh on the ground for the moment. He felt a tingling sensation from head to toe, as if he'd been shocked. He breathed heavily. Heeding Gunther's advice to tread carefully, he turned around.

The stone at his feet fell away in a hundred-foot drop. At the bottom, the descent ended abruptly on a steep sandy slope, covered with tall green grass that rolled down another fifty feet onto a green prairie. Miles away, he saw ranks of low hills cutting across the savannah, the whole landscape fading into blue in the distance.

Marty controlled his reaction, stepped away from the cliff's edge, and picked up the ankh carefully. The skin of his palms was tender.

"Everyone else get burned hands from this thing?" he asked.

A hesitant, muttered yes rolled around the group.

"I dropped acid once," François said. "Okay, a few times. But the trips were always more interesting than this. That sky, for instance, is just blue. Also, I don't remember taking anything today. Maybe that chamber contained some type of hallucinogenic."

"This is a dream," Lowanna said. "I'm clearly dreaming."

Marty had to concur. Obviously, he had fallen and hit his head, and was suffering oxygen deprivation down in the tunnel, or he'd accidentally been drugged from the ancient dust.

François edged forward toward the cliff. "Since it's a dream, maybe I should try to fly."

Surjan knelt and pressed the long stem of his ankh to a large stone at his feet. "I'm not so frivolous with my life. Even a dream-life."

"We should get away from this cliff." Marty smiled. "Since I'm the dreamer and you're all dream-figments, you don't really get a vote."

François frowned. "I get a vote. I always get a vote."

"Because of your money?" Lowanna asked.

"That's not what I was saying," François said. "But it's not crazy to remember that I'm paying for all the vehicles, and the tents, and the tools, and the food."

"Yes," Lowanna said. "And where is that stuff?"

"That's a really good point," Gunther said. "Where is that stuff? In particular, where is the water?"

Marty realized that he was sweating in the heat. The sweeping vista before him didn't show any sign of a river.

"This . . . this is a dream, or a hallucination." François cleared his throat.

"Right. So, you were saying about your vote?" Lowanna scanned the rock formation they were on and started walking away. "I think I see a path down."

François grumbled wordlessly but followed. The others filed in a line after the anthropologist and Marty came last, following the two Egyptian men. Abdullah had his arm around Kareem, and was murmuring reassuring sounds to the younger man. Kareem trembled, and twice Abdullah had to pull him away from the edge. The boy seemed to be in danger of shaking himself right over the cliff.

Marty, on the other hand, had never felt more sure-footed. Maybe this was the effect of being in his own dream, but his steps were smooth and perfect. Walking down the stone felt something like performing a fighting form, taking the fluid, smooth steps he had practiced thousands of times, in empty airport terminals, standing backstage to give presentations on new text translations, and waiting for the bus.

The rock formation on which they stood was familiar to him. Had he been here before? Was it a famous mountain?

But that was silly. The mountain was familiar because this was Marty's dream.

Though, for a dream, the experience felt awfully crisp.

"This hill has been occupied," Surjan said.

Lowanna stopped and turned, and François took the opportunity to keep going, getting slightly out ahead of her. Surjan looked at a low, time-gnawed line of stones, obviously the remains of an old wall. The ruin of a stone building lay at their feet, clinging to the side of the yellow cliff, overlooking a ravine. Marty looked down; the ravine led from the prairie below up onto the rock massif.

"You're thinking what I'm thinking," Gunther said to him. "This could have been a guard hut. Good control over the access up the arroyo."

"Or a shepherd's hut," Marty said. "In a strong position to control the flock coming up and going down the sole approach."

"We'll publish rival papers," Gunther said.

Marty shook his head.

"What will you say about that in your papers?" Surjan pointed at a vertical slab of stone a few paces from the ruin. Red images covered the yellow space. There were humans, some ten of them, and they seemed to be prostrate. Dead? Bowed to the ground on their faces, as so many ancient cultures bowed? And they faced toward three larger humanoids, with something like a hound at their side. The larger humanoids had heads like dogs', and one of them was raising a mace in his hand.

"Anubis?" he murmured. "But holding a mace of kingship?"

"The ears are square," Gunther said. "That's Seth. And that pseudocanine thing, also with square ears and the forked tail, is the Seth beast. The sha."

"Of course." Marty nodded.

"Although I don't know why there are three Seths," Gunther said. "That seems wrong."

"Oh jammy, even in my dreams, I get to hear this stuff." Surjan shook his head. "I need a new job."

The Egyptians pushed forward to the front of the line and Abdullah addressed François. "Let us go first. We can't read the hieroglyphs, but we can pick a good trail. We're used to the desert."

"They're not hieroglyphs," Gunther objected. "They're just pictures."

"It's the Jebel Mudawwar," Marty said.

Gunther squinted at the rock pictures. "What?"

Everyone else turned to stare at Marty.

"No," Marty said, swinging his arm to capture the vista behind him. "This massif we're standing on. I recognize it. I've been here before. This is the Jebel Mudawwar. It's a rock formation . . ." His voice trailed off. "In Morocco."

"Why not?" François shrugged. "It's my dream, we might as well be in Morocco. I've had some good times in Marrakesh. Lead on, Abdullah."

Abdullah reached the end of the rock shelf and started to pick his way down a boulder-strewn slope into the ravine that descended toward the prairie.

"Only it's way too green." Marty found himself talking to Gunther, Lowanna, and Surjan, all of whom had thoughtful expressions.

"This is definitely spring," Lowanna said. "Look at the vegetation. We're in a savannah, and look how green the grass is. We're in the time of the spring rains, or maybe just at the end of them."

"Morocco is not a savannah," Marty said. "Not in the twenty-first century."

"We're not in Morocco, anyway," Lowanna said. "We're in Egypt. So this is my dream."

"*My* dream," Gunther said.

Surjan shook his head and followed the Egyptians and François down into the ravine.

"We're going to need water, though," Gunther said. "Or we'll be dead by tomorrow. Dream-dead, if you must."

"I'm thirsty," Marty admitted, "dream or not. Other than the greenness of the grass, though, I haven't seen any sign of water."

The ravine took them down into a wider canyon, within the embrace of the U-shaped rock massif. The grass here grew thick and tall. As they hiked, Marty felt an irrepressible urge to let loose his inner teacher. He resisted for a brief time, but then decided that, since this was his dream, it didn't matter.

"The rock formation is very difficult to climb on three sides," he said, pointing. The others all stopped to listen. Lowanna plucked a long stem of grass and sucked at its pith as she examined the other plants around her. "It's open to the west, so at some point in the past, I forget when, it was fortified. We'll cross the ruined remains of the wall that blocks off the open end of the canyon in a few minutes, turning the whole thing into a natural castle."

Lowanna yanked a plant from the ground. It wasn't grass, but some sort of vegetable, with wide green leaves and a long, thick, white root.

"What is that, a wild potato?" Gunther asked.

"You said you were thirsty," Lowanna reminded him. "And no, I think it's more like a radish."

"We're all thirsty," Surjan growled.

"First of all," Lowanna said, "pluck a grass stem. Don't pull it out of the ground, just pluck the top segment. See how it's almost like it's in a little sleeve? Pull it out of its sleeve and you expose the white pith." She showed them. "That's where the grass stores its water."

"Not very much, though," François grumbled.

"Not very much." She nodded. "But also, it stores sugars there. The pith is sweet. Suck on it and you'll start your own salivary glands. It will give you some relief."

Marty plucked a stem and sucked on it. Gunther plucked one for himself and a second for Kareem.

"This won't save us from dehydration," François pointed out, gently tugging a stem from its sleeve.

"I have a theory about this wild radish." Lowanna shook the dirt off the radish. With her knife, she carefully peeled away the outer skin of the radish. The inside of the root was moist and pulpy.

"Good idea," François said. "We can smash that in a pot or something, and pour off the water."

Surjan stepped a few feet away from the others to where a heavy boulder sat at the bottom of a slope of scree. He pressed the stem of his ankh against the stone and pushed it forward in long, firm strokes.

"We don't have a pot," Lowanna pointed out. "But we have thumbs."

She had scraped the radish into a heap of pulp in her palms. Now she held the pulp over her head and wrapped her four fingers around it, pointing her thumb toward her open mouth. She squeezed, and the milky liquid extracted from the root ran down along her thumb and into her mouth. She squeezed out a couple of mouthfuls of water and then cast the remains of the radish aside.

"Do you have a radish for me?" François asked.

"Get your own," she harrumphed.

François immediately began searching through the grass.

"Wait a few minutes," Lowanna said. "Let's make sure I don't have an adverse reaction first. Mmm, tastes peppery."

"Why did you test it on yourself first?" Marty asked. He didn't know what the right answer to his question was. Who was she supposed to have tested the liquid on? Kareem, because he was a low-skilled laborer? Surjan, because he was responsible for physical security?

"I was going to invite François to try it first," Lowanna said, "in case it was poisoned. But then I decided, hey, it's my dream, and I'm thirsty."

"That's it, I'm done waiting." François dug up a radish, his motions more awkward than Lowanna's, so he left a bigger hole behind and had more dirt to shake off. He fumbled with the skin, too, nearly cutting himself, but with two minutes of sustained fiddling, he got the skin off, scraped off some pulp, and drank.

Marty was willing to wait. In case, somehow, this was not a dream and he was in fact in Morocco with a real life to lose. He turned to Surjan. "Are you *sharpening* that ankh?"

Surjan nodded and showed it to him. "I seem to have my belt

knife, but the guns are all still in camp." He seemed vaguely embarrassed about something.

"And your sword?" Marty guessed.

Surjan nodded. "So if any of these Moroccan castle people decide to try to rob us, I'd like to be a little better armed. And I think this can be made to serve as a kind of short sword."

"It's heavy enough to be a club just as it is," Gunther pointed out.

"I want a sword," Surjan said.

"There are lots of these radishes," François said. "We'll make our camp here. It's probably worth exploring, but we'll come back here for the night."

Gunther eyed François and Lowanna. "Neither one of you feels dehydrated? Nauseated? Cramped?"

"I feel revitalized." François thumped his chest.

Lowanna snorted. With her knife, she began cutting blades of grass, close to the earth. She gathered them up in the crook of her left arm as she went, quickly collected a thick sheaf.

"Camping here is problematic," Marty said. "We're under the direct sun, with no shade. We probably only have a few hours of light left today, but if we're going to make a camp, it should be somewhere where we can shelter from the sun."

Lowanna sat cross-legged, with her sheaf of grass beside her. Improbably, she began weaving the grass together.

"Are you making a canopy?" Gunther asked her. "For shade?"

"That might also be a good idea." She seemed distracted, and shook her head as if clearing her thoughts. "But right now, I'm weaving a basket."

"There's no one here to give you merit badges," François said.

"I will use these baskets," Lowanna said, still speaking to Gunther, as if François hadn't spoken, "to carry radishes. There are lots of radishes here, but there's no guarantee once we leave here that we'll find more of them, or even that we'll be able to come back. I don't have a waterskin, which would be a much more efficient way to carry the water, but at least I can carry radishes." She pointed at her long-sleeved T-shirt, which read TOOL. "It separates us from the beasts."

"I'll join you." Gunther smiled. "If you can teach me how to weave."

"You'll get the hang of it quickly. Go cut yourself some grass."

Abdullah and Kareem joined Gunther in gathering grass to weave baskets. Marty didn't have a pocket knife, but found he could snap the grass off close to the ground with his thumb and forefinger, and began plucking strands.

"I don't feel like I'm cut out for weaving." François looked westward, out past the yellowish rock arms of the Jebel Mudawwar. "I'm going to go find that ruined wall. Maybe it will be able to give us some shade."

"Good idea," Marty said. "My memory is that it should be easy to find. It's pretty big. But you shouldn't go alone."

"What are you worried about?" François asked. "Robbers? Snakes? Lions?"

"Any of those, I think," Marty said.

"The only way to stop me from going alone is to come with me." François strode away westward.

Marty handed Lowanna his strands of grass. "How do you feel about keeping watch here?" he asked Surjan.

"It's a good idea," Surjan said. "There could be robbers. Snakes. Lions."

He kept a straight face, but was he making fun of Marty's caution? Marty didn't know whether Morocco had wild lions. This rock formation was clearly Jebel Mudawwar, but the fact that it was surrounded by a sea of grass threw Marty into a pool of deep uncertainty. Was Morocco less of a desert than Marty remembered? Maybe it had wild lions. And robbers.

It certainly had snakes.

The tingling in his limbs had subsided and thankfully, his fatigue wasn't bothering him nearly as much as it normally did. He followed François, setting a fast pace because François had a head start.

"Listen," he said as he caught up to the Frenchman. "Did you, uh, see anything? I mean, between the moment when you were in the tunnel and grabbed your ankh, and the moment when you arrived here, did you see anything else?"

François stopped. "You mean, did I have another dream before this one?"

"Maybe, I suppose that's what I mean."

"No, I went straight from Egypt to, apparently, Morocco." François was staring at the ground. "Why? Did you have a vision?"

"Yes." Marty shrugged. "But, you're right, probably just another dream. Before this dream."

François was staring at the ground. "Where are the ruins of that wall you were talking about? All I see are animal tracks. What makes tracks like this, a herd of antelope?"

Marty looked up at the massif. "Should be nearby, I think. It should definitely be visible. It's twenty-five feet tall in some sections."

Together they walked out farther onto the prairie, looking for the wall. They moved close to one cliff and then the other, looking for the tumbling stone ruins of the ancient fortifications that Marty remembered.

"Looks like you're wrong," François said. "We're not in Morocco."

"Maybe I'm wrong." Marty looked up at the distinctive rock formation above them. "I'm pretty sure we're not in Egypt, though."

⫷ CHAPTER ⫸
FIVE

They reached the rest of the party while the evening sun was still yellow and shadows were long. Under Lowanna's direction, Gunther, Abdullah, and Kareem had woven together seven grass baskets, each with a short, thick, grass rope attached at two points to the rim, like a handle.

"The more I see this place," Marty said, "the more convinced I am that it's Jebel Mudawwar. But . . ."

Should he really betray his doubts to the group? But they couldn't reach anything like a good decision unless they had good data. Which meant *all* the data.

"But there's way too much grass," Lowanna said. "This should be desert. Like the dry, sandy desert of the northern edge of the Sahara. We should see sagebrush and saltbush and succulent euphorbia, barely dotted across the landscape. Not this sea of grass. This looks like, I don't know, some wild corner of Kansas."

"Also, you said there would be ruins in the mouth of the canyon," François said. "Big stone walls. Twenty-five feet tall."

"So we're not in Morocco," Surjan said. "And not in Egypt."

"A dream," Abdullah said. "By God, it *is* a dream."

Marty frowned, not sure what to believe anymore. This had already gone on too long, and the dry sweat now prickling his back between his shoulder blades felt much too real.

"We have water," François said. "The next orders of business are shelter and food."

"We can test your hypothesis," Gunther said, "can't we? We can look at the stars in a few hours, and tell our location from the stars."

"We'll be able to tell latitude," Lowanna said, "but not longitude. I'm a little surprised you'd even think that."

Gunther grimaced and shrugged. "I was just hoping, I guess. I'm a city boy, but I know some of you know your way around the backcountry. I thought maybe you'd know something I didn't."

Marty searched his memory. "Jebel Mudawwar is about thirty degrees north latitude. If we're at some other latitude, I'm wrong, but if we're at thirty, then we have a working hypothesis as to where we are."

"In this cursed dream," Kareem muttered. Abdullah elbowed him into silence.

"But in your hypothesis," Gunther said, thinking out loud, "Morocco has had several really wet years and we just didn't know about it, so the vegetation is different from what we expect. And also, your memory is wrong about the ruins."

"And if this is Morocco," Surjan said, "we should go north. Or maybe west. We get to the sea, and to a more forgiving, Mediterranean climate."

"This climate looks plenty forgiving," Lowanna muttered.

Surjan frowned.

"If this is the place I think it is, we should go east," Marty said.

Gunther snorted. "It's true, Cairo is also about thirty degrees north, so if this is Morocco, we can walk straight east to Cairo. But that would be some two thousand miles, wouldn't it?"

Marty thought about his vision, then pushed it from his mind.

"Well, I don't know," he said. "Yes, we could walk to Egypt, but that wasn't what I meant. If this is the Jebel Mudawwar, then there's a town about ten miles east of here. On a river. The river's intermittent, it's sometimes just a dry watercourse, but right now I imagine, given the grass we're seeing, that the flow is pretty good."

"You know a lot about the geography of Morocco," Surjan said.

Marty chuckled. "I guess so. I was here years ago for a dig at Sijilmassa. That's a medieval ruin, near Rissani—they're both near an oasis on the River Ziz. We came out here on motorbikes a few times, to hike." He looked around. "We had to bring our own water. This place was bone dry."

"How about pot?" François asked. "Did you bring your own marijuana?"

Marty smiled. "I was young and foolish. I can neither confirm nor deny."

"Ten miles is not a long hike, once the sun goes down," François said. "We go east."

"Let's get a look at the stars first," Gunther said, looking to Lowanna and nodding. "If we discover we're not at thirty north, we'll have to figure out another plan."

"So in the meantime," François said, "food."

"There are the radishes," Lowanna pointed out.

"I am grateful for the radish water," François said, "however much it tastes like peppered chalk. But I saw antelope tracks back there, and I think we should kill an antelope."

"With what?" Lowanna frowned. "Are you going to beat it to death with a basket full of radishes?"

Surjan stood, tucking his ankh into his belt. "Agreed, we need food. I'll go get an antelope."

Marty raised his eyebrows at the Sikh's casual confidence. "With your ankh?"

"I'd prefer a gun or a bow," Surjan said. "Or a spear. Since I don't have any of those, I'll use my knife."

"And if that fails, his bare hands." Gunther smiled. Surjan frowned at him, and the German looked away.

"The sharpened ankh should make an effective weapon," Surjan added to Marty. "You might consider sharpening your own."

"I should come," Marty suggested.

"You'll want to stay back some distance," Surjan said, "so you don't frighten the game."

"I can be quiet," Marty said.

Surjan shrugged. "Stay near me, so you're downwind of our quarry."

Marty followed Surjan west out of the mouth of the canyon, trailing slowly behind. As they went, Surjan paid more and more attention to the ground at his feet, stooping to brush aside the grass so he could see the soil, or to pluck and examine the grass itself, and then he froze. Marty froze, too, and followed where the Sikh was looking; a herd of white ungulates with long and twisted horns grazed in the distance.

Addax. White antelope. Native to the Sahara, Marty thought he recalled. Although if this was the Sahara, it wasn't the Sahara as he remembered it.

Surjan motioned with his hands for Marty to get down, and Marty crouched. He looked around, still astonished and frustrated not to see the fortifications he remembered so well. He didn't want to admit it to François, but he had smoked a joint, leaning against a twenty-five-foot-tall stone wall and watching the sunset with three other grad students.

Watching the sunset out over these plains, he was sure of it.

He returned his attention to the addax herd, and could no longer see Surjan. Was he creeping forward on hands and knees, or lying on his belly with his knife in his teeth? The wind rippling the grass was blowing toward Marty, so the antelope shouldn't be able to smell him. If Surjan was moving more or less in a straight line toward the animals, they shouldn't be able to smell him, either.

The sky was a deep purple, sunset was upon them.

If this was a dream, it was unlike any dream Marty had ever had. But what else could it be? A hallucination? A simulation of some other kind? And was the rest of the group really here and experiencing it with him, or was he merely imagining them?

Were they all sitting somewhere in a room, eyes closed, while a hypnotist told them they were seeing tall green grass covering the Sahara Desert?

Something, the image of the Sikh sneaking up on the game animals through the tall grass or the memory of the pot or the ridiculousness of not knowing for certain where he was, struck Marty as improbable and incongruous, and he laughed out loud.

One of the antelope raised its head to look in Marty's direction. At that moment, Surjan sprang up from the grass, knife in his hand, and seized the beast around the neck. The addax leaped forward, but Surjan kept his grip. As the antelope tried to buck and throw him off, Surjan wrapped his other arm around the animal and slit its throat in one smooth motion. A bloody crease opened, vivid even in the dim light against the white hide.

The herd burst into motion, bounding away across the prairie.

Surjan fell to the grass. The antelope slashed at him once with its twisted horns, and then Surjan's prey ran with the other antelope.

But Surjan stood, and as Marty rushed forward to join him, he watched the wounded antelope slow to a canter, and then a walk, and finally collapse to the earth, bleeding out. Surjan jogged to the animal, and then froze.

He stood, staring down at the antelope's body and at his own hands.

Marty stopped jogging. What was Surjan seeing? The sun had hit the horizon and long rays bounded over the prairie, making silhouettes of the Sikh and his dead prey both. Marty moved forward slowly.

Surjan was murmuring something as Marty caught up to him over the antelope's body.

"I'm chuffed you're here, Marty. Now I know I'm safe from snakes." His arm was bleeding.

"I didn't save you from the antelope," Marty acknowledged. "But at least I can tend the wound."

Surjan nodded. Marty tore half his white cotton undershirt into strips and wrapped the long gash in Surjan's forearm. The cotton wasn't sterile, but at least it would be absorbent.

"Did you see . . . something?" Marty asked as he worked. "After killing the addax?"

Surjan hesitated. "Like what?"

"Just as . . . I don't know, it looked as if you were staring at something."

Surjan grunted. He stooped to hoist the creature up and sling it across his broad shoulders. Then he turned and jogged back to join the others.

Marty was impressed at Surjan's stamina, but he was also impressed with his own. He felt much less fatigued than he thought he should, for all the climbing and walking and even running he'd done this day. Was this evidence that the entire experience was, after all, a dream?

Two of the baskets were full of roots when they rejoined the others. Abdullah and Kareem were tending a small fire.

Surjan laid the antelope carcass down. François whistled.

"I see you did use the knife, though," Gunther said. "Hardly sporting."

"It isn't sport," Surjan rumbled. "I'm about to skin and butcher the carcass, and do you know what? That isn't sport, either. I want to eat."

Lowanna stood and walked away from the light of the fire into the gathering gloom. Marty followed her.

"Are you okay?" he asked.

"I feel suddenly nauseated." She bit her lip and stared westward as the first stars began to appear.

"I feel totally disoriented myself," Marty said. "And sort of embarrassed, that I'm so sure that this is Jebel Mudawwar, even though . . . even though that doesn't seem to be right. And confused. But I'm pretty sure this isn't a dream."

"It isn't a dream." Lowanna sounded frightened.

"I'm starting to see stars," Marty said. He turned right to look north. "There's the Big Dipper, always the easiest to find. Follow the front two stars to Polaris, there we are, kind of low on the horizon." He held out his right hand, pinky and thumb both extended to form a span that, at arm's length, would reach fifteen degrees. "About two handspans off the horizon. We're definitely in the northern hemisphere, and near the thirtieth parallel."

"You say it so lightly," Lowanna said. "Why do the words feel so heavy to me?"

Marty sighed. "I guess you're one step ahead of me. You're thinking through the consequences, and feeling their weight. We may be at Jebel Mudawwar. Which means something strange happened to us, and we're pretty far from Egypt."

Why wasn't he more shocked?

Was it because he was experiencing this after reading a predynastic text, and then seeing a text written in his own personal hieroglyphs but in a sealed and ancient Egyptian tunnel?

With that buildup, a sudden transition to Morocco somehow didn't seem like the strangest thing that could happen.

"Something strange," Lowanna murmured. Something was distracting her.

"You've probably got more wilderness experience than I do," Marty said, trying to bring her back into the conversation.

"Because I grew up Arrernte?" she pushed back.

"I did say 'probably,'" Marty added. "In any case, I'm asking for your view. What do we do now?"

"Prepare the antelope meat, like Surjan said." Lowanna leaned forward and vomited into the grass. She stood, wiping her mouth. "Excuse me. Cook it if we can. Or slice it and wrap it. Ideally, I'd like to salt it. But it'll keep for a day or two if we carry it with us. We should use the hide, too. Make it into water bottles, so when we get to an oasis, we can carry water with us."

She leaned forward, resting her elbows on her knees and breathing deeply.

"There will be people at the oasis," Marty said.

"Except what if there aren't?" she asked.

Marty remembered the town of Rissani, with its thriving bazaar and its whitewashed houses in rows. "Okay," he said, "better safe than sorry, so we take the time to make waterskins just in case. I assume that's something you can do."

She retched again, though nothing came up this time. "Maybe someone else can do it. I can give instructions."

"I think we better not drink any more water from those radishes," Marty said.

"It's not the water," she said. "I'm throwing up at the thought of meat."

"Have you always felt nauseated at the thought of meat?"

"No." Lowanna stood, inhaling deeply.

"Are you . . . ? Look, this is awkward, but if we're going to hike across the prairie through the night, I have to ask. Are you pregnant?"

"Not a chance." Lowanna walked back to the fire.

He felt relieved.

The antelope was butchered, various cuts skewered or lying on stone to be held close to the fire. Marty's mouth watered at the smell, but Lowanna turned her head aside.

Kareem had already started working the addax's hide; he had neatly laid it out on the grass and was scraping flesh and blood with a large bone. He had set aside other bones and the addax's entire head.

As Marty entered the circle of firelight, Abdullah slapped his nephew on the shoulder and pointed to his work. "Look what Kareem is doing, by God! He learned this at my brother's factory, they make sandals and bags!"

"He's a good worker," François said.

Abdullah beamed.

"Don't we need to cure the hide?" Marty asked. "I mean, before we do anything with it?"

"We can use it like this, but it will stink. Water will taste funny if you make a water bag." He shrugged, then reached over to tap the addax's skull with his scraper. "We can . . . cure the hide. We can prepare it with brains. It's how the Bedouins do it."

"We need to build shelter," Gunther said. "We can scout the cliffs for a cave we might start with, but first we should make woven mats and maybe stretch the addax hide over a frame, to shade us from the sun."

"You want to stay here?" Lowanna asked.

Surjan seemed to be biting his lip.

"If we go east . . ." Marty began.

"We're not where you think we are," François said. "Obviously."

"You think I'm *obviously* mistaken?" Marty felt irritation, and tried to keep his voice level.

François spread his arms. "Where's the wall, Marty?"

Marty nodded glumly.

François grinned. "So we build a shelter, secure food and water, and then we think about our options. If food is abundant, maybe we even wait until someone comes along who can tell us where we are."

Surjan had turned his back on François, busying himself with tending the roasting meat.

"That's the money vote," Lowanna muttered.

"It's *my* vote," François said. "If you don't respect that I paid for this expedition, at least you might respect that I'm a member of it."

Kareem was shaking his head as he knotted together grasses into a cord.

"Please, sir," Abdullah asked. "Which way is Cairo?"

"Okay," Marty said. "There are good arguments for what François suggests. We potentially avoid making a big mistake, going off half-cocked. Maybe we avoid attracting unwanted attention, or getting more lost. What are our other options?"

"We could go east," Lowanna said.

"Well, that certainly seems like a good idea to me," Marty. "If something, ah . . . strange has happened and we're in Morocco, which is where I think we are, we'll find out in a short march."

"No wall," François said. "Not Morocco."

"No cave," Surjan said. "Also, no Nile, no airport. Instead, this big rock. Not Egypt."

François harrumphed.

"We'll take water and food with us," Lowanna said. "If we don't find this Rissani in ten miles, we can even come right back, if we want to."

Marty met her gaze and they shared a brief smile. Did she actually agree with him? Or was she supporting his idea because she didn't like agreeing with François?

"This is silly," François said. "Marty has a teleportation fantasy, and you all want to hike out into the desert. I'll have you know the last Jew I read about wandering into the desert leading folks got lost for forty years."

"Anyway, if we're near the dig site," Marty said, "no teleportation and we walk east, where do we end up?"

"The Nile," François said.

"So it's a good test of the possibilities," Marty said.

"God willing, we are near the Nile," Abdullah muttered.

"We should vote," Marty said.

François grunted in disgust. "Fine. All in favor of making shelter, to protect ourselves from the sun." He raised his hand. No one else did.

"All in favor of hiking east tonight." Marty raised his hand.

The others all raised their hands.

"God willing, we will see the Nile in the light of dawn," Abdullah said.

"I don't like standing still," Surjan muttered.

"No one has to come," Marty said. "If anyone prefers to wait here, we'll figure out where you are and come back for you."

"Like hell I'm waiting here alone!" François snapped.

"Good," Marty said. "Then we ought to take an inventory."

Everyone pulled from their pockets whatever they had and Marty scanned the group's possessions.

"I guess I didn't exactly plan as well as some of you did for this event." Marty grinned. "A bunch of wallets with some plastic cards in them, cash that will have to be exchanged, probably at a bad rate, some house keys, three pocket knives, Surjan's hunting knife, and Kareem's fire starter."

"Everyone has one ankh: sharpen it, and we're armed," Surjan suggested.

"What about skills?" Marty asked. "We're out in the real world with just what we're carrying and whatever skills we've got. Anybody have any particular skills that might be useful?"

"What are we doing, filling out a dating application?" Gunther grinned. "I'm pretty good at poker, but I'm reasonably good at a hundred other things, too, and there's no way I can think of them to list them all right now. I can snorkel; do you think that matters?"

"Marty's right. We all probably have some possibly relevant skills," Lowanna said. "I can ride. I have some pretty good survival and orienteering sorts of skills. I know a lot of primitive crafts. Baskets, pots, leather."

"Survival and orienteering," Surjan said. "Hunting. Tracking. I can fight, with any weapon or no weapon. Marty can fight."

"Yes, I suppose I can," Marty said. "And I know a handful of languages, both old and new."

"I can do a million things," François said. "Most of them badly, but with no fear. I was a career university student, learning whatever caught my interest, especially when it came to the sciences and engineering."

"We can work and fight," Abdullah said, his arm draped over Kareem's shoulder. "Bargain. Work with beasts of burden. Kareem can skin an animal. Drive a car."

They all looked at Gunther.

"I can snorkel and play poker," he said, his jaw set stubbornly. "And I suppose, back in the day, I was an Army medic. I can do some first aid if it comes to it."

⤜ CHAPTER ⤛
SIX

I think that one can hear us.

Can you hear us, Two-Legs?

Lowanna felt ill.

It wasn't just the smell of the blood and the roasting meat, or the sight of the addax's head and the knowledge that Kareem intended to pound brains into the creature's own hide to help with the curing process, though those things bothered her.

But why should they bother her? They never had before. She was no vegetarian.

Was she?

It was also the voices. Was she going crazy? She glanced at Marty and wondered when she could tell him about them. She wasn't quite sure why, but she felt she could trust him. But on the opposite side of the campfire was François, he was staring at Marty, and the last thing she was about to do was to admit to anything around the banker.

Shifting her gaze from the others, Lowanna focused on roasting some radishes while the others roasted meat and made small talk. Again, she heard voices calling to her from the darkness.

Fire! Fire? But I saw no lightning!

Ah, it is a party of the Two-Legs. They brought fire with them, or they made fire. Look, they are eating a Curved Horn. They will leave us alone.

They only eat us when they have no bigger meat.

She ate the radishes before they had fully cooled, to distract herself from the chattering of the voices. She burned her lip, but the painful sensation passed quickly. Perhaps the joy of eating lifted the pain from her. It also eased the burn of her hand, from grasping the ankh.

Marty was probably right about where they were located, she thought. But Marty didn't see the whole picture.

And the whole picture was so much worse than just being in Morocco, which was bad enough. How had they been transported, instantly, two thousand miles, from Egypt to Morocco in a heartbeat?

Her fear was not that she was in a dream. Her fear was that she had gone insane.

While Marty and Surjan had been gone, she had heard screaming. No one else had batted an eye, but she had heard a voice crying of death and fear and solitude, drifting to her on the wind.

She watched Marty move around the fire. The others watched him, too. He had the confidence and the unselfconscious air of a natural leader, and everyone responded to it, whether they realized it or not.

François watched Marty through slitted eyes.

The first cooked steaks were ready. Marty offered her one, gently, and she only turned away and tried to sleep. She had a half-eaten roasted radish, but the nausea made it hard even to think of eating it, so she just clutched it to herself, closed her eyes, and breathed deeply.

She had the drifting sensation of sleep, and with it, the growing certainty that whatever was happening to her on this savannah was not a dream.

Take the food.

Now, she is sleeping.

Lowanna felt a tug at the radish in her hand. She opened her eyes; she was facing away from the campfire into the darkness. The light spilling over her shoulder illuminated two creatures, the size and shape of prairie dogs, within arm's reach. One had its front paws and teeth sunk into her roasted radish, now growing cold, and was trying to pull it from her.

The other lingered slightly behind, watching Lowanna intently. When she opened her eyes, they both began to chatter.

The Two-Legs is awake!
Run!

Feeling pressure in her bladder, Lowanna sat up and looked around. Kareem slept. The others were wrapping the last of the butchered and uncooked meat into grass envelopes and placing them into their baskets. Abdullah stood patiently waiting and keeping an eye on his nephew; he had the dirty addax hide rolled up over one shoulder, and a grass basket full of radishes over the other.

She rose and walked outside the reach of the campfire's flickering light.

As Lowanna finished relieving herself and stood, adjusted her pants, she caught sight of a silhouette walking in her general direction.

It was Marty.

He must not have seen her in the darkness, because he unzipped and quickly began relieving himself.

Do you think the Two-Legs can see us?
I don't know. But the dark one almost collapsed our burrow.

Lowanna turned in the direction of the furry creatures' voices and whispered, "Sorry."

Then she clapped both hands to her mouth.

It can see us! Run!

"Lowanna?" Marty's voice cut through the night.

"Just contributing to the topsoil." Lowanna winced as she turned to Marty, who quickly zipped himself, and walked to within arm's reach of him.

"Sorry about what?"

Lowanna felt heat rising up her neck and into her cheeks. Would he think she was an idiot?

"Can I tell you something in confidence?"

"Sure." Marty stepped closer. "Are you okay?"

"I don't know." Lowanna hesitated for a moment. "I'm hearing voices."

Marty was quiet for a moment. "I'm going to ask a question. It's a serious question, though I know it might not sound like one. What language were the people in the vision speaking?"

"No, it's not like that . . . it wasn't a person speaking." Lowanna's throat tightened. "And there was no vision."

Marty raised his hands and then dropped them. "What do you mean, then?"

"I think I'm going crazy." Her voice cracked. "I hear animals talking. I actually just apologized to a set of groundhogs because I heard them say I almost collapsed their burrow."

"Oh, okay . . ." His voice had a warm, comforting tone, and then he put a hand on her arm. Surjan was right, he had calluses, but the touch was reassuring, anyway. "You know, that chamber we were in probably hadn't been opened for thousands of years. Maybe you breathed in some dust and it . . . it had a mild hallucinogenic effect. You hear or see anything else unusual?"

"I don't think so." Her mind flashed back to the underground tunnel and the dusty chamber they'd entered. He might be right. "I saw an ankh and took it. I think everybody did."

"I wouldn't get too hung up on it, whatever effects it's having on you are almost certainly temporary." Marty grinned and tossed her a wink. "But in the meantime, if those groundhogs give you any good intel, let me know."

She had something else on her mind, but the wink disarmed her. She couldn't say what she wanted to tell him when he was being charming and cavalier.

Lowanna impulsively gave Marty a quick hug. "You don't need to tell anyone this."

"I don't. Also, I . . . I won't tell anyone." Marty motioned in the direction of the campfire. "Shall we head back?"

Lowanna shook her head. "You go ahead. I think I have to pee again."

"I have that effect on women." Marty chuckled and walked back toward the campsite.

A cooler breeze blew across the grassland, raising goose bumps on Lowanna's skin. Feeling a prick of pain on the back of her arm, she reached across and felt something hard on her skin. She scratched at it and managed to pull out what felt like a thin sliver of plastic from her arm.

What the hell?

She stared in the darkness at the thing which was just a bit over an inch long and looked like a tube of some kind. Lowanna groaned, realizing what it was.

"Oh damn. That's all I need at this stage."

Pocketing the plastic for later disposal, she returned to the fire.

"You slept a couple of hours," Marty said to Lowanna. "We're going to head out now and make for Rissani while it's still dark and cool."

"The oasis," she said.

"Well, the town," he said. "But yes. We should get there in four pretty easy hours. And we have food and water, in case I'm wrong."

Kareem awoke yawning and stretching when Abdullah prodded him, but scrambled quickly to his feet to shoulder not only a basket, but also, against his uncle's protests, the antelope head and the hide. Then they set out walking.

They all moved differently; Abdullah walked with the strong plodding step of a man who had carried many burdens, Surjan prowled like a cat, François clumped as if every step was a plea for someone to pave the road before him, and Kareem skittered across the prairie like a drop of water scrambles across a hot skillet. Marty seemed to float, as if he were parallel to the ground but not touching it. His mere steps looked like the motions of a kung fu master, graceful and effortless and almost inhuman. The basket hanging from his shoulder floated at his side.

They circled around the massif to get onto its east side. It was easy to steer by the stars, but Lowanna left that to Marty and Surjan— every time she looked up at the sky, she shuddered at its wrongness.

At least, while they were moving, the voices receded into the darkness. If she didn't listen for them specifically, she couldn't hear them anymore.

"We'll hit a jeep trail, any minute now," Marty said, four or five times.

At the southeast corner of the rock formation, Surjan raised a hand to stop them. He was clearly visible in the starlight; once they'd banked their fire, the sky was so dark, there might not have been an electric light within a thousand miles.

Suddenly Lowanna couldn't bring herself to look eastward, either. She stood still and stared at her feet.

They're stopping.

Do they see us?

"There's a trail here," Surjan called. "And it goes east. Only . . ."

"Only what?" Marty walked up to the front of the line to join the Sikh.

Marty and Surjan looked at the trail together. Lowanna trudged forward to join them.

"Not a jeep trail," Surjan said.

A distinct track cut through the grasslands, heading east. But it was a single track, pounded deep into the sandy soil and maybe four feet wide.

"I'll be," Marty murmured.

"Camel," Surjan said.

"Camel? What do you mean?" Marty peered down into the shadow of the trail.

"Camel tracks and sandals." Surjan shrugged. "Can't you see them?"

Marty shook his head.

"Are you taking the Michael?" Surjan pressed.

"I have to tell you something," Lowanna said, "and it's awful."

Everyone turned to look at her.

"How are you feeling?" Marty asked.

"This is not about how I'm feeling." Lowanna took a deep breath. "I think you're right, Marty, we're at Jebel Mudawwar. And of course, we're not in a dream, anyone who's still saying that needs to shut up, or I'll slap you."

The general murmur that ran up and down the group told Lowanna that others had come to the same conclusion.

"We'll get to Rissani," Marty said. "From there we'll get a bus or hire someone to drive us, and we'll fly back to Egypt. I know this is all strange, but of course there's some explanation. We'll get back to the site and figure out what happened to us."

"Or we won't figure it out." Gunther shrugged. "And we will have a strange mystery to tell our grandchildren. Like stories of rains of frogs, or people who saw armies marching in the night sky."

"There's no Rissani," Lowanna said.

"Sure there is," Marty said.

"Here's what you're not seeing." Lowanna shook her head. "We're in the past. We didn't just travel in space, we traveled in time. I don't know the exact date, but my guess is that we're somewhere between two thousand and five thousand B.C.E." Her head whirled. "Or maybe much earlier than that."

They stared. Their stares were so heavy, she had to set down her basket.

"That's a big jump." Marty's voice was soft.

"Big jump? You think we moved from Egypt to Morocco in the blink of an eye and that doesn't bother you at all."

Marty flailed his arms like a struggling bird. "Yeah, but . . . what evidence is there? I mean, there's the grass, that's strange, I'll grant you."

"And the path," Surjan muttered. "Camels?"

"We'll find the jeep roads." Marty's voice was confident.

"And the ruins?" François asked. "The twenty-five-foot-tall walls that aren't there?"

Marty opened and closed his mouth without saying anything.

"There's something else," Lowanna said. "What day is today?"

"March twentieth," François said instantly. "At least, that's what day it was in Egypt."

"And the grass." Lowanna pointed at the dark prairie around them, rippling silver under the stars. "Tall and green like this, that suggests it's still spring, right? Still March twentieth, or something really close to that. Spring equinox?"

"Sure," Marty conceded. "It's clearly spring."

"The precession of the equinoxes," she said.

They all stared. None of them understood.

"Look, here's the deal," she said. "For about the past two thousand years or so, on the day of the spring equinox, the sun is in Pisces. Sometime around the twenty-first century C.E., our time, it will move into Aquarius. That's what the Age of Aquarius is all about. We live—we *lived*—at the end of the Age of Pisces and at the beginning of the Age of Aquarius. For the next two thousand years or so, the sun would be in Aquarius on the day of the spring equinox."

"I think I'm following." Marty had a look of intense concentration on his face, his eyes visible only as black pits in the starlight.

"Let's make it round numbers, because each age really lasts something like twenty-two hundred years," Lowanna said. "But let's call it two thousand, for simplicity's sake. From two thousand B.C.E. to year zero, on the spring equinox, the sun was in a different sign still."

"Aries," François said immediately.

"You're saying that the sun moves through the Zodiac over the course of the year," Marty said, "but it also slowly moves so that what sign the sun is in each month gradually changes. Over thousands of years."

"One rotation all the way around the Zodiac is something like twenty-six thousand years." Lowanna felt exhausted. "That slow movement is called the precession of the equinoxes."

"And?" Marty's voice held an ominous edge.

"I saw the sun set last night," Lowanna said. "Once it was down, I saw the edge of Gemini and I saw Cancer. They were pretty clearly visible. Which I think means that the sun is in Taurus. At or near the spring equinox."

"What you're telling me," François said slowly, "is that I am no longer a Leo."

Surjan and Gunther chuckled. Abdullah and Kareem looked baffled.

"I call cheating," Gunther said. "You didn't list astronomy as a skill."

"You think we're in the Age of Taurus," Marty said. "Which is to say, between twenty-two hundred and forty-four hundred B.C.E."

"Give or take," Lowanna said. "Not sure how close we really are to the equinox. And those are approximate numbers. But yeah."

"Which is to say," Marty continued, "at the very beginning of Egypt's written history. Or earlier."

"About the time of the tablet?" Gunther murmured.

"Possibly," Lowanna admitted. "Although two thousand years is a long time, so we could be in the Age of Taurus, and Egypt could still be a thousand years in the future."

"In fact," François added, "we could be *twenty-six* thousand years before the birth of unified Egypt. Or *fifty-two* thousand. Right? This is a cyclical phenomenon."

"Yes." Lowanna felt very small.

"Does anyone know what the climate of north Africa was in 30,000 B.C.E.?" Marty asked. "Or 55,000?"

"I would have said this was all insane twelve hours ago," Gunther said quietly. "And frankly, it all still sounds nuts."

"We're heading straight for a test of the hypothesis." Lowanna pointed eastward. "I think we should see the lights of Rissani, if we're within ten miles of it. I think we're going to follow this track, and we'll come to the river you're talking about, but we'll never see Rissani. No town."

"If you're right," Marty said, "I don't think we'll find Sijilmassa, either. That's a medieval town, way too late."

"No buses, no rental cars," Gunther said.

"No airplanes and no ships," Surjan added. "Bother."

"And then what?" Lowanna asked.

"Come to think of it," Surjan muttered, "I haven't seen a single jet trail all day."

"We'll do whatever François decides, by God," Abdullah said. "This is his expedition."

François cleared his throat but said nothing.

"I think there's something I need to tell the rest of you," Marty said. "I had a vision on the way here."

"You mean, besides the vision we all had?" Gunther asked. "A light and an ankh?"

"I dreamed of a journey," Marty said. "Between the moment when I grabbed the ankh and the moment of finding myself standing at the top of the cliff on Jebel Mudawwar, I dreamed of a long journey overland to the east, and I dreamed that we needed to hurry. Did anyone else have that dream?"

There was a round of muttered negatives.

"I dreamed of a journey," Marty said. "And I got the sense there was a time imperative, a countdown, so to speak."

"You're saying that if we get to the oasis and there's no town," Gunther said slowly, "we just keep going until we get to Egypt."

"Two thousand miles, give or take," Surjan said. "A long journey overland, indeed."

"I just want you all to have all the information when we make a decision," Marty said.

François grumbled wordlessly.

"I've been hearing animal voices," Lowanna said. She looked at Marty as she said it, and he nodded. "I'm pretty sure I'm not crazy."

"In the interests of everyone having all the information," Marty said. "And I'm also pretty sure Lowanna isn't crazy."

"I hope you're confident I'm not barmy, either," Surjan said. "When I killed the addax, I saw a light."

"Maybe our . . . situation . . . is causing us to experience sensory malfunction," François said.

"I didn't experience 'sensory malfunction,'" Surjan objected, "because I am not a robot. *I saw a light.* It came out of the addax and went into me."

They stood together silently for a minute.

"Well." Gunther took a deep breath. "I guess we need the data. And I think that means we go east to the river and find the oasis. Hopefully, we also find a town there, and people who drive automobiles. But if not . . . going on to Egypt might at least help us know whether we're in the fourth millennium B.C.E. or the thirtieth. I, for one, wouldn't mind a shot at watching them build the pyramids. Maybe scratch my name on one of the stones."

Marty flinched visibly.

No one objected, so Surjan turned and marched toward their objective.

They walked through the night. Lowanna heard whispering in the darkness from time to time. It bothered her a little less now.

She did look up to the horizon ahead of them, watching for the lights of a town. They didn't appear. She told herself that maybe Rissani was poor and didn't have electric lighting, or had so little electric lighting that it wouldn't be visible from a distance. But the farther they traveled, the more convinced she became that they'd fail to find Rissani.

There was no jeep trail, but the camel track continued eastward.

Sometime in the predawn hours, the vegetation around them began to change. In the darkness, Lowanna couldn't tell the species, but she recognized that they were now walking through trees.

She heard more voices.

Here come Two-Legs.

Hide! Into the burrow!

She ignored them.

The grassland abruptly dropped into a riverbed. Lowanna smelled the water and then felt the humidity on her skin. She also smelled the sweet, tangy aroma of fruit on the tree, and something else.

"Melons," she said. "I smell melons on the vine."

They reached the river, snaking back and forth around a rugged fin of rock.

"No Rissani," Marty said. "No Sijilmassa either, as far as I can tell. But this is the river."

Surjan muttered something under his breath.

"That tears it," François said. "We are no longer in the twenty-first century."

⇐ CHAPTER ⇒
SEVEN

The horizon was showing the first hints of dawn. Marty lunged at an unseen opponent, blocking hits that never came, and then launched a roundhouse kick that would have smashed into the side of his attacker's head.

Marty stood alone on top of a rocky escarpment to the east of the river. Farther east rolled unending grassy plains. Down in the river and on the other side stretched the patches of melons, berry brambles, and other water-guzzling plants that filled the oasis.

For nearly half an hour, he worked through a series of forms and exercises that he'd been doing all his life. He needed to clear his head. Also, the ritual workout gave him a sense of the familiar, something that he needed more than ever since the world around him had been turned upside down.

So much around him had been twisted up and had no explanation, but at least one thing had improved: his fatigue. Marty felt like he had before the bouts of fatigue had set in, so if nothing else, that was a boon he was grateful for.

The idea that some*how* he'd been transported both some*where* and some*when* unexpected was the stuff of nightmares. It was impossible. As far as he knew, the giant three-sided rocky massif was unique to Morocco. He'd been there before, and he'd also seen the massif in movies—distinctive as it was, it was a favorite of Hollywood location scouts.

As he continued working through his morning exercise, his mind raced with the improbability of it all.

So Lowanna was right and they really were in the distant past. Say, 3,000 or 4,000 B.C.E. When global climate was changing and the last of the glaciers were receding.

Being in the ancient past would explain why the ruins weren't where he thought they should be. The ruins of Sijilmassa hadn't even been constructed yet. Being in the distant past explained many things.

But it bothered Marty. They couldn't be in the past, that was a thing of science fiction, not science fact, and facts were what he lived and breathed.

Still, he'd long ago learned the phrase "disagree and commit." Despite his inability to wrap his head around the idea that time had flip-flopped on him, he was willing to just leave it be and move on. Just because Lowanna was sure about them being in the past due to the position of the stars, he wasn't there yet.

Not entirely.

His academic training didn't let him accept some of the things he was experiencing at face value. There had to be a better explanation.

He tried very hard not to think about the English-language sentence he'd read in the ancient tunnel, written in hieroglyphs of his own devising.

He wiped sweat from his forehead; his muscles had warmed and he felt good. As he snapped a front kick into the air, he heard the slap of his pants leg against his shin and immediately swung around, slamming a backfist into the imagined opponent, and then finishing the movement with a leg sweep.

Despite their march to find the ruins and his restless, dream-filled sleep, he felt more alive than he remembered ever feeling. It was as if the sun beating on him had oiled his joints, making every motion feel smoother, faster, and hell, maybe even stronger.

If only he had a heavy bag to pound against . . .

"I assume you're a black belt?"

Marty turned to see Lowanna approaching from the river. Below, he could see the rest of the crew stretching and preparing for the day.

"Every time I clear my head," he told her, "I find you there."

"Some kind of sign, maybe. You said you were having visions."

"I learned kung fu at home, from my grandfather. He was a monk at the Shaolin temple for twenty years before leaving China. I don't think they do belts in any formal way." He grinned. "It's like Mr. Miyagi said, 'Belt mean no need rope to hold up pants.'"

Lowanna laughed. "You never sparred at a dojo or anything?"

"Nope. Forms on my own, fighting when I had to."

She shook her head and smiled faintly. "So dorky."

"Marty!" François waved a greeting as he ambled up the slope. "Is your *vision* still saying we should head east, now that this ruin of yours didn't pan out?"

"We should discuss," Marty said.

"In the alternative," François said, "you could admit that you were wrong and we could now do a reasonable thing."

"In the first instance," Marty said, "the reasonable thing to do right now is to discuss with the entire party."

"The entire party—" François said, but Lowanna cut him off by simply walking down the slope.

Marty trudged back to the camp on Lowanna's heels.

The rest of the crew stood around last night's fire, looking back and forth between Marty and François. Several of them had been sharpening their ankhs on a large rock, following Surjan's example and direction, and now held pointed ankh-daggers.

"So here we are," Marty said. "Ancient Earth. How ancient, we can't be certain."

"It's possible we're here pre-*Homo sapiens*," François added.

Abdullah blinked. "Before *Adam*? What was there before Adam?"

"Desert, old chap," Surjan said. "In the beginning was the sand. But something made those trails we followed last night, and it wasn't addax."

"I think there's no end of speculation we could get up to," Gunther said. "None of it will substitute for actual experience of our . . . new environment, and none of it is as important as the practical question."

"Should we kill Hitler?" François suggested.

Marty chuckled. "More broadly than that, what do we do?"

"Get back home," Lowanna said.

"Agree," Marty said instantly. "Does anyone have any ideas about how to do that?"

"About the whole killing Hitler thing," Surjan said. "If we're in the past, how much do we worry about changing the future?"

"That's an argument for getting home as soon as we can," François said.

"But also," Lowanna added, "it's an argument that can't go anywhere, practically speaking. We can chase our tails down theoretical alternate universes all night long, but at the end of the day, unless we commit group suicide right now, we risk changing the future. We just have to live with the risk. Heck, we might make the future better."

"If we make a future in which we ourselves can't be born," Marty said, "theoretically we have a paradox problem. Which, I don't know, theoretically, maybe that destroys the Earth."

"You ready to kill yourself, then?" Lowanna challenged.

"No," Surjan said instantly.

"No." Marty's voice was softer.

Silence.

"About getting home," François said slowly. "If some sort of spatiotemporal anomaly moved us from future Egypt to past Morocco, we should first of all feel grateful."

"A what?" Marty asked.

"He means a glitch in the matrix." Lowanna waved dismissively. "Why in the world would we be grateful?"

"That the Morocco end wasn't ten miles removed, or even a hundred yards removed, in one direction or the other. We could have been thrust into outer space, or under the Earth's crust."

"We are alive, praise God," Abdullah said.

"And then?" Gunther asked.

"Doesn't it seem likely," François continued, "that if the spatiotemporal anomaly continues to exist, or if it is likely to repeat itself, that the most likely way to encounter it again, and therefore to get back to the twenty-first century, is to stay at the Jebel Mudawwar?"

"You want to go back," Marty said.

"It was a mistake to leave," François said. "We should return to the massif, find water, build shelter, and look for the road home."

"That sounds wise, by God," Abdullah said.

"I don't want to die before Adam," Kareem added. "It feels like a cursed fate if it happens."

"Or, second best," François said, "make our shelter here where there is water and abundant food, and take regular expeditions back to the massif."

"I take it you forgot to mention your background in theoretical physics yesterday?" Marty asked. A chuckle ran through the group. "Okay, so that might be right, François. And we should put it to a vote. But here's where I worry. What happened yesterday wasn't some normal, or even unusual occurrence. As far as I know, it was a unique occurrence in the history of the planet."

"As far as you know," François said. "But the history of the planet is almost entirely unrecorded."

"True. But the most likely outcome of sitting around and waiting for the . . . spatiotemporal anomaly, as you say, to reoccur would mean sitting around and getting old on a desert rock. I'd further argue that the glitch might not really be a glitch, but a doorway. A doorway that's maybe still open and accessible back where we came from, which would also be east of here."

"If we encountered the anomaly again," Gunther said, "there's no reason to think it would automatically send us home. It might send us farther into the past. This time it might place us in the Earth's core."

"I have no appetite for sitting around and waiting," Surjan growled.

"You want us to follow your vision," François said. "You want to march eastward. For some fifty days."

"It gives us direction, at least," Marty said. "If we're still near Aswan somehow, we should hit the Nile shortly."

"Immediately," François shot back. "We'd have hit it last night."

"If we somehow got turned around and on the other side of the Nile," Gunther said, "we'll hit the Red Sea soon enough."

"But neither of those is true," Lowanna said. "So in fifty-odd days, we'll reach the Nile."

"Perhaps at about the time that Egyptian civilization is being founded." Gunther's eyes lit up. "When the Badari pull the rip cord and go pharaonic. How exciting!"

"You want to follow Marty's vision?" François laughed. "Why don't we follow the animal voices Lowanna is hearing? Surely, they're just as likely to contain wisdom. Hey, little sparrow, which way to the twenty-first century?"

"I'm just as uncomfortable as you are at the fact that I'm having visions," Marty said.

"I'm not uncomfortable that you're *having* visions," François said. "I'm uncomfortable that we're seriously considering *following* them."

Marty could only shrug.

"Fine." François glowered at Marty. "Other plans?"

No one offered any, and François called for a vote.

The Egyptians voted with François. Everyone else voted to go east. François kicked the sand, but said nothing.

The crew took last drinks of water, hefted packs onto shoulders, and climbed back up out of the riverbed and onto the plains.

As Marty's gaze followed the path ahead, the vision replayed in his mind.

Ahead of him, according to what he saw, stretched fifty-four sunsets and an incalculable number of steps to walk. With all the insane and undeniable things Marty had experienced since coming to Egypt, he felt he couldn't deny the reality of his vision. And with all the bizarre things that had already transpired, Marty couldn't imagine what might happen next.

It had been three days since leaving the oasis. As Marty chewed on a piece of the bland-tasting meat, he felt a growing sense of concern. Food hadn't yet become a problem since François had had the idea to divvy up the meat and drape it over their woven packs. This let the sun do the work of drying it into a jerky-like consistency to help retard spoilage. As of this morning's inventory, each of them still had a few days' worth to gnaw on, but water was going to be a problem.

They hadn't found any radishes since leaving the oasis. No melons or anything else with water in it. No animals they had any chance of catching. And no signs of water.

Upon breaking camp this morning, François had taken it upon himself to lead the group's march eastward. Making a point of "leading" might be something the Frenchman needed for his ego or self-worth. All they were doing was following a faint trail in the grasslands that seemed to perfectly align in an east-west direction.

It was nearly midday when Abdullah whistled.

"Oh, excellent!" François called.

Marty increased his pace. His gaze followed the Frenchman, who'd veered off the trail at a jog, with Abdullah by his side.

There was someone ahead in the tall grasses!

The stranger wore a long loose-fitting robe with the hood pulled up. A djellaba, he'd have called it, seeing it on the streets of modern Cairo. François and Abdullah approached the newcomer, and Marty realized that the stranger was very tall and big, bigger than Surjan, NBA all-star power forward-sized. Marty jogged after the crew as François waved at the lone figure, yelling a greeting alternating between French and Arabic.

This was good. A person was a source of information.

The figure turned toward François.

He had a spear in his hand.

François slowed to a walk and began rattling off a series of questions, each in Arabic and then in French. Marty raced forward. He had an uncomfortable sensation in his stomach.

The giant in the djellaba lunged toward the Frenchman with his spear, and the world slowed down.

Abdullah jumped at François, knocking the banker to the side. The stranger plunged his spear into Abdullah's chest.

Marty jumped. He slammed into the robed man with a flying side kick, sending the stranger staggering. The hood fell back and time seemed to stop.

Glaring at Marty with malevolent yellow eyes was something out of a nightmare.

The head was shaped like a canine's. A long snout snarled at him with bared teeth and a silver nose ring. The ears stood straight up from the top of its head and were square at the top. This was no wandering Berber, it was no human at all.

It was a monster.

And before Marty could even register what he was looking at, the creature ripped the spear from Abdullah's collapsing body and lunged at him.

Muscle memory kicked in. Marty blocked the attack with one hand and slammed his palm into the back of the creature's elbow.

The bone cracked with a sound like a gunshot.

The creature howled. It lunged at Marty with clawed fingers extended.

Marty caught both of the creature's wrists, fell backward, and flipped the monstrosity onto its back. His shoulders screamed with the effort. Marty was tall, but this beast loomed over him and weighed twice what he did.

The creature recovered almost instantly, scrambling to its feet. It bellowed an ear-splitting roar that shot vibrations through Marty's chest, and charged, shoulder first.

Barely sidestepping the attack, Marty smashed a closed fist down on the end of the creature's snout, sending the creature staggering backward as its nose ring fell to the ground in two pieces.

Fumbling for something under its robe, it pulled out a bronze medallion. Marty swiped at it with a crescent kick.

A red beam flashed from it as the metal disc flew from the creature's grasp.

Looking stunned, the monstrosity wheezed and bent at the waist, reaching for something near its feet.

Marty grunted as he launched a spinning back kick.

His heel connected with the side of the creature's head and Marty felt and heard the neck snapping.

Surjan raced up, wielding the ankh like a sword just as the creature collapsed to the ground. "What the hell is that?"

Marty stared at what he'd done, his body tingled with the adrenaline racing through him. The world blurred and the sound of his heart thundered in his head.

François wept as he pumped Abdullah's chest, performing CPR on the injured man.

Gunther came to François's side, listened at the Egyptian's lips, and rested a hand on the Frenchman's shoulder. "He didn't have a heart attack, François. And he's gone. He died instantly."

François roared and punched the sand with both fists. It was a childish and impotent gesture, and Marty found it touching.

Marty jumped as Lowanna touched his arm. "Are you okay?"

He nodded. "I couldn't . . . I tried to . . ." Words were failing him.

"Marty, I saw what happened." She rubbed her hand across his back. "You were amazing."

"But I couldn't—"

Yanking on Marty's arm, Lowanna turned him toward her. With a stern expression she growled, "This wasn't your doing." She hitched her thumb toward François. "It was his." She leaned closer and spoke in a hoarse whisper, "If that bastard didn't assume everyone would bow to his every word, this wouldn't have happened."

"On the other hand," Marty said, "if we'd stayed at Jebel Mudawwar, Abdullah might be alive."

Suddenly the world flashed white and Marty saw in his mind's eye an image of the chamber that had sent them to into the past.

The crew was standing motionless, stuck within seven bluish-white beams of light.

The light bathing Abdullah's statue-like image flickered and blinked off.

Abdullah pitched forward. Before he even hit the ground his body exploded into a cloud of dust.

Marty gasped as the chamber blinked out of existence and he saw Lowanna's eyes widen. "Did you see that?" he asked.

She nodded, the fearful expression giving way to one of anger.

François sobbed.

Marty took a deep shuddering breath and gave Lowanna a quick hug. "None of that matters . . . we can't afford to lay blame. That'll drive a wedge into the group and will end up getting us all killed. Let's just focus on the next steps."

Lowanna turned to the Frenchman and narrowed her gaze. If looks could kill, François would have gone up in flames.

Marty glanced at their dead crewmate and felt a wave of sorrow. If he'd only been a few feet closer . . .

This crazy journey into the unknown had suddenly become very real.

⇌ CHAPTER ⇌
EIGHT

Marty stared at the bubbling remnants of what had attacked them. The body of the attacker only moments earlier had been a corpse like any other dead thing, with its jackal-like neck twisted at an unnatural angle. And just as Marty crouched down to get a closer look, its skin shimmered with a glow that coalesced into a floating ball of light.

Was that a will-o'-the-wisp?

He'd heard of such things, glowing balls of light, but never seen one. Marty had always understood they were either folklore or associated with the gases given off by swamps or garbage dumps.

The shimmering ball drifted toward him. Before he could move out of the way, it touched his hand and disappeared. A tingling sensation traveled up his arm, spreading throughout his body. It was almost as if he'd stuck his finger in an electric socket. Except it wasn't painful.

It was invigorating.

He felt goose bumps rise on every inch of his skin.

He looked over at Lowanna, who was watching François dig a grave with his ankh, still weeping, though now silently. She looked different. Clearer, as if his vision had improved. Something about her was suddenly more eye-catching.

Adrenaline?

Then he breathed in deeply, feeling a shiver of exhilaration run up and down his spine. Hanging in the air were the coppery scent of blood and the thick musk of sweat. He sensed the chlorophyll from the grass, the smell of the freshly turned soil, the musky odor of whatever it was that had attacked them, and even his own sweat—and every scent was intense.

The creature's body started to smoke.

Marty took several steps back. The monster's skin sloughed away and turned into a dark-gray sludge. The animal scents gave way to the combined reek of bleach and decay.

"It looked Egyptian." Surjan wore a look of disgust on his face. "What *was* that thing? Anubis, is that what he's called? The god of the dead?"

Marty shook his head. "Not Anubis. Anubis has a jackal's head, and that's all. Dr. Frankenstein randomly slapped this monster together, without regard to species."

But it wasn't random at all.

Marty had been too shocked during the encounter to even think straight, but now he knew what the monster reminded him of.

With the body decomposed and melted into the soil, he saw the sandals it had worn. The Egyptian-style kilt under the robes. Most of all, the jackal's head with the long donkey-like ears, squared at the top.

Not a jackal's ears. A donkey's.

For an Egyptologist, all of these things pointed to one thing and one thing only.

"Seth," he said.

This thing may not have been the Seth from Egyptian mythology, the brother of Osiris, the god of war and disruption, but it had looked exactly like what Marty had seen on tomb walls up and down the Nile.

And in the pictographs atop the Jebel Mudawwar.

"Seth?" Surjan frowned.

Marty's heart thudded loudly in his chest. He wondered aloud, "And when he's killed, all hints of him vanish?"

Surjan knelt by the remnants of the creature and with a stick dragged a woven basket from the sludge. He looked inside it and frowned. "Slabs of dried meat."

Lowanna walked around the remnants of the creature, took one look at the basket, and kicked it over, sending its contents flying.

With an expression of disgust, she looked back and forth between Marty and Surjan and said, "There's something about that stuff." She paused, seemingly at a loss for words. "It's . . . it's—"

"*Haram?*" Kareem staggered toward Marty with a somber expression. "Is it *haram?*"

Haram was Arabic for forbidden.

Lowanna nodded. "Yes, it's *haram*. I don't even know how I know, but it's not for us to eat."

Kareem handed a metal object to Marty and said, "I found this in the grass. It flashed a red light when you kicked it out of the demon's hand."

"Are you okay?" Marty put a hand on the young man's shoulder.

Kareem's lower lip was trembling. "My uncle was a good man. He died like a hero, praise be to God."

Marty looked down at the medallion. It was the size of his palm and bore an engraving of an infinity symbol, like the numeral 8, lying on its side. He turned it in his hand and frowned. Or maybe it was just an eight. It couldn't really be either, though; neither symbol had been invented by 2200 B.C.E.

Marty pocketed the medallion and moved to where François was trying to lift Abdullah's ruined body. "Let me help you."

"No!" François turned his back to Marty and staggered toward the shallow grave he'd dug. "This is my doing, I'll take care of it."

Marty watched as the sixty-something-year-old man carefully lay Abdullah into the freshly dug trench. The Frenchman was muttering something, his face wet with tears.

This reaction was not what he'd have expected from the money guy. He'd gotten the impression that François had always been rich, and that he looked at everyone else as a tool to use as he willed. And with enough money, he was probably not wrong. Such care over a corpse, such distress at the death of an employee, seemed out of character.

François made the sign of the cross and bowed his head. "I'm sorry, my friend. I wish that I could have helped you more in this lifetime. If the God of Abraham, the Gods of Egypt, or whoever might be listening, maybe this can help you in your next life." He pulled out his wallet and lay it on Abdullah's chest. Then he lay Abdullah's ankh in the grave beside him.

Lowanna walked up beside Marty. He put his finger to his lips and pointed at the grave site.

With one hand pressing down on the wallet, François sobbed silently and began chanting in Arabic. "O Lord, forgive Abdullah bin Rahman and elevate his station among those who are guided. Send him along the path of those who came before, and forgive us and him, O Lord of the worlds. Enlarge for him his grave and shed light upon him in it."

Surjan knelt beside François. "It's getting late. Should we make camp?"

François sat up straight, his eyes bloodshot and his expression vacant. He grabbed a handful of the soil he'd dug up and dropped it onto Abdullah's body.

Gunther and Kareem had also come to pay final respects as François continued slowly pouring soil back into the hole.

"François?" Surjan asked again.

Anger flashed in the Frenchman's eyes and he spoke in a hoarse whisper. "I don't care. I'm not making any more decisions and I am not responsible; no more, do you hear me?"

As François continued pouring one handful of soil after another into the hole, the rest of the crew turned to Marty.

They were looking for an answer.

Marty glanced to the west at the sun hanging low in the sky. "Okay, let's set up a camp. Kareem, you start the campfire. Surjan, you and Lowanna see if you can find food and water." He hesitated, because he didn't want to feel responsible, either. "Does that work?"

The crew nodded and went their separate ways.

Marty approached Gunther. He tilted his head toward François and whispered, "Can you help Kareem and also keep an eye on François? You know them both better than I do, and you're better at—"

"I got it." Gunther nodded. "What are you going to do?"

Marty looked over at the remnants of the monster. "You know what that thing looked like, right?"

Gunther nodded, and despite several days' exposure to the sun, he looked pale. "I was at a distance, but unless I was hallucinating, it sure as hell looked like you were scrapping with something that had come to life from Egypt's past. Its *mythical* past."

"It was Seth. Or at least something that sure looked like all the images."

"Like the images on Jebel Mudawwar."

Marty nodded. He pulled in a deep breath and his mind reeled with the myriad of faint scents he detected. "I have to try to figure out what that thing was."

Gunther glanced at François, who was still dropping one handful of soil at a time into Abdullah's grave. He put his hand on Marty's shoulder and gave it a squeeze. "If you need to talk, just let me know."

Marty walked over to the remnants of the creature, knelt down next to the sludge, and picked up one of its sandals.

He'd seen this style of sandal before, many times.

In burials that had been sealed shut thousands of years before the birth of Christ.

He'd never seen one this big before.

Surjan hefted the spear he'd taken from the monster. It was perfectly balanced and reminded him of the spear he'd trained with as a kid. He glanced to his right and found Lowanna digging around a plant with the sharpened end of her ankh. "You find something, love?"

"I'm not your love." Lowanna grabbed at the base of the plant, arched her back, and pulled with both hands. She grunted and fell backward with an explosion of dirt.

As the dust settled, she held up a web of roots with at least a dozen fist-sized radishes hanging from it. Suddenly she turned to the north. "I hear something."

Surjan crouched in the grasses and scanned the prairie. "What do you hear?"

Before she could respond, he felt a vibration in the ground followed soon after by the sound of hooves. He tightened his grip on the spear and Lowanna whispered, "I think those are impala. You don't normally see them this far north, but there's nothing normal about this place."

Keeping his head low, he spotted the animals racing across the savannah. They formed a herd of nearly one hundred deerlike animals racing across the savannah.

Lowanna pointed in the direction of the herd and said, "There are young ones and two injured animals at the back of the herd. Please don't aim for the young ones."

Surjan crept forward.

The wind was blowing toward him, which was perfect. They wouldn't catch his scent.

They turned and began to move slowly toward him.

He stretched his arm, preparing for the throw. Worrying that the injury to his forearm would impede his aim, he probed at it and felt no pain.

That seemed wrong, so he unwrapped the bandage to look at the wound, just in case.

And there was no wound.

He stared briefly, but then shook his head. This was a mystery for later, maybe to share with the whole crew. He tucked Marty's bloody shirt strip into his pocket and settled into a throwing posture.

He adjusted his grip on the spear and waited. As the herd raced from east to west, he spotted one of the larger animals near the back. Its hind leg was bloodied already and it lagged behind the others. Surjan breathed slowly as the thunderous sound of the herd rolled over him.

Just as the back third of the herd approached, he adjusted his stance and his vision focused on his quarry. He hadn't thrown a spear in twenty years, but the lessons from his childhood flooded back.

Wherever his fingers pointed upon releasing the spear was where the spear would go.

Even injured, the animal was likely running at forty miles per hour.

At one hundred feet, feelings of isolation and despair washed over Surjan. He'd felt sympathy with his prey before, but this was more distinct than he'd ever experienced.

He threw the spear, making sure to aim directly ahead of the animal.

The weapon sailed through the air. At the last moment, just before impact, the impala saw the incoming projectile and turned. The spear penetrated deeply into its chest, sending the animal tumbling to the ground.

The remainder of the herd veered away from Surjan as he stood and raced toward his quarry.

The spear had gone directly through the front shoulder, into the chest and out the other side, killing the animal instantly.

It was a clean kill.

And much easier with a spear than with a knife.

Surjan placed his hand on the neck of the animal and whispered, "Thank you, Lord, that with each breath, during moments of pleasure or pain, we are brought closer to you each day. Thank you for this bountiful gift and it will not go to waste."

As he pulled the spear from the animal, a ball of shimmering light leaked up from within the animal's body. His eyes widened and he struggled not to sully his just-finished prayer by blaspheming.

The glowing orb drifted toward him. The same thing had happened when he'd killed the addax, but this time he was ready for it, and he wasn't afraid. He reached forward and as his fingertips touched the edge of the light, a sense of pins and needles raced up his arm and spread through his body.

He felt a wave of odors wash over him as he suddenly detected the coppery smell of both the old and fresh blood coming from the corpse of the impala, the scents subtly different. There was also a musky aroma he didn't recognize coming off of the animal. A hundred yards away, he heard Lowanna digging in the dirt for more plants.

Through the soles of his feet, he felt the vibrations of the herd as they raced to the west.

He grabbed the impala by its horns and began dragging the hundred-plus-pound animal back to camp.

Lowanna joined him as she hoisted a bag of plants over her shoulder. She pointed at the impala. "The herd was better off with that one culled and it knew it."

"Did it . . . tell you this?" Surjan asked.

She shook her head. "It would have attracted other predators if you hadn't helped."

"Helped?" Surjan looked at her with a raised eyebrow. "Marty said you didn't like the idea of killing animals."

Lowanna made a huffing sound as she waved his comment away. "That's ridiculous. Some things need to happen for the good of the rest of us. We need food to live. That animal was a risk to the herd." Lowanna looked up at Surjan and frowned. "Are you okay? You seem troubled."

As they returned to the camp, Surjan sensed the rest of the crew's footsteps before they even crested the hill. The campfire was lit and for the first time that he could remember, he breathed in the scent of smoke and could tell that most of the smoke was still coming from burning grass and the wood had yet to fully catch fire. He hadn't even consciously been aware that the smell of burning grass and wood differed.

Surjan stopped for a moment and inhaled. Why was he suddenly aware of so many different scents all around him?

Lowanna looked back at him with a puzzled expression. "Hello? Are you okay?"

He opened his mouth to respond, shut it, and then shrugged. "I think so. It's just now hitting me how different this place really is."

"Better late than never." She smiled and motioned for him to follow her. "Come on, let's get back to the fire."

Surjan put a smile on for her. His mind was racing.

Something had changed about him, and it had happened after he'd killed that animal.

⇜ CHAPTER ⇝
NINE

It was midday and they'd managed to find an unlikely shady spot under a set of palm trees. No water was in sight.

There were forty-nine days left on their trek eastward, if Marty's vision was to be trusted. His "visions" might be the better word, because he awoke each morning from the same dream, with the same clock counting down to the same encounter with the same enthroned man.

His was a strange face. He wasn't handsome, with big ears and goggle eyes. He looked worn, like a statue that had once been handsomer, but had melted in the scouring wind.

Marty bit into his radish and savored the spicy sweet flavor of the starchy root vegetable. He'd never been a fan of cooked radishes, but they were refreshing and tasted very different raw. With a texture like a potato's, it served as a source of calories, vitamins, and liquid.

On the other hand, he'd have given a lot for a cool glass of water.

"Marty, aren't we now at the point of no return?" Gunther asked with a mouthful of dried impala jerky in his mouth. "It's been five days, hasn't it?"

He nodded. "We've been keeping a ridiculous pace without really slowing." He looked over at François, the eldest and least in shape of the group, and the man looked perfectly fine. In fact, he looked healthier now than when they'd started this journey; his chest was still a robust barrel, but his gut had almost entirely melted away.

"François, you're the one with the watch. How many hours a day have we been walking?"

"About sixteen."

Marty frowned. "Anyone know what the average walking speed is for—"

"Anywhere from three to four miles per hour," François said curtly. "With a small break during the midday heat, we're averaging fifteen hours walking time and I'd guess we're going almost fifty miles in a day."

"No blisters," Surjan said.

Marty hadn't had any, but it hadn't occurred to him to ask anyone else. He looked around the crew. "Is that true? No one's had a blister yet?"

Heads shaking.

"No sprains or strains, either. I think we heal too fast," Surjan said. "My wound melted off my arm in a couple of days."

Marty had an old trick, from many years of hiking into remote digs, to keep his legs working. He would lie on his back during rest stops, elevating his legs by resting his heels against a boulder or the trunk of a tree. That let blood flow from his legs back into his torso; over the course of a long hike, that kept his legs feeling light and his blood oxygenated.

On this entire walk, he hadn't felt the need to use his trick even once.

And Marty's fatigue had gone.

"And we're in a land in which the Egyptian gods walk in broad daylight," Gunther said.

Marty felt disquieted, but he didn't know how to answer. He turned to the east and stared at the never-ending expanse of savannah ahead of them. "Given that I don't think the Red Sea is more than two hundred miles east of the dig site, and I don't see any signs of seagulls or water ahead—"

"You were right, then," Gunther interjected.

Lowanna crunched on her radish and pointed to the east. "If we actually started somewhere near Morocco and are going east at fifty miles a day, that almost sounds like the schedule Marty's talking about."

"Marty's rock formation is only about two thousand miles from the dig site." François turned to Marty. "Didn't you say your vision had fifty-four days elapsing, so that should leave forty-nine currently. Right?"

Marty thought of the enthroned man with big ears. He nodded. "I don't have any better ideas. Do you?"

The crew shook their heads.

Surjan sniffed and turned his head, then pointed east. "I think I smell water."

"You can smell water?" Gunther asked.

Surjan pursed his lips and shrugged. "Ever since I killed that impala, my senses are working at a new level. I can't explain it."

"You as well?" Marty's eyes widened. "I can't smell what you're smelling, but I definitely noticed a huge change after killing that creature." He hesitated. "I saw a light, after I killed the Seth-person. Did you see one when the impala died?"

"I did." Surjan's expression suddenly matched Marty's look of incredulity. "A light of some kind leaked up from them both, but it was only at the second occurrence that I *felt* anything strange."

"When your senses improved?"

Surjan nodded.

Marty scanned the group. "Has anyone else experienced this kind of new level, or unusual perceptiveness, while we've been here?"

The group shook their heads.

"Let's all share whatever it is we experience. It could be important." Marty breathed in deeply and didn't detect anything in the air. He gathered his things and stood. "Well, it's time for us to get moving, anyway." He smiled at Surjan. "Let's test your nose."

Marty breathed in the scent of something in the air . . . his mind wanted to call it green, but it was grasslike in nature and maybe he was catching a whiff of what Surjan had detected.

"It's that way." Surjan jogged toward a rocky outcropping about a mile away.

As they got closer to the rocky formation, he now knew what Surjan had meant with regard to the scent of water. At this distance it filled his nostrils with smells that reminded him of slick algae-covered rocks. It was like being at the ocean shore but without the salty tang.

A fringe of palm and olive trees clustered around the rock. More importantly, Marty saw the glint of sun reflecting off water. "Surjan, from now on, we trust your nose."

The group picked up its pace. What unfolded in front of them was a shade-covered lake bordered with trees.

"Nobody drink the water yet," Lowanna called in a loud voice. "This isn't like the river, which was moving and had been filtered through sand, clay, and rocks. Trust me, none of you wants to get diarrhea from the standing water. Let's heat it first."

Marty pointed to Kareem. "Can you start a—wait a minute." He turned to Lowanna with a puzzled expression. "How do you plan on heating water?"

Lowanna scanned the shore and pointed at a fallen log, "Surjan, help me drag this thing up onto the grass."

Marty watched as Surjan walked into the water and helped shove a five-foot section of log to the shore.

Surjan, Kareem, and Lowanna together quickly rolled a section of an olive tree trunk up onto the grass.

"These are cultivated olives," Surjan said, examining a branch of a living tree as he passed. "Not well tended in recent years, maybe. But humans have lived here once."

"*Someone* has lived here once," François muttered.

Kareem gathered dried grasses and smaller sticks to start a fire while Lowanna began scraping the rotten bark from the tree. She turned to Gunther and motioned toward the shore. "Can you collect a bunch of fist-sized rocks? We'll heat those up on the fire that Kareem makes and then use them to purify the water."

Gunther nodded and walked over to the shore, and Surjan looked at what Lowanna was doing with a perplexed expression. "I don't understand. What are you doing to the—"

"Surjan"—Lowanna motioned for the tall man—"just come here and help me dig into this log."

"Fine," Surjan said. "But then I'm setting up a khazi. I know you're all grown-ups and don't need to hear this, but no relieving yourselves near the water."

Marty walked over to the cliff face. It was about thirty feet tall, not perfectly vertical but leaning back at a steep angle, and its edge ran from east to west. It looked like a fault line where a section of the earth had been shoved upward some time long ago.

It was strange to see, since to the best of his knowledge, there weren't any active fault lines anywhere in the Sahara.

As he walked along the shadowy bottom of the cliff, he spotted what resembled small steps cut into the rocky wall. A person with really excellent balance, he estimated, could walk straight up the face using just his feet. A person with reasonably good balance could go on all fours comfortably.

Moving back for a better view, he visually followed the cuts in the rock up to what seemed to be a crack in the cliff's face. Most of the crew was busy working with Lowanna on her water purification project, but Gunther was knocking sand out of his boots.

"Gunther!" Marty called. "Come join me. Or at least watch."

Gunther joined him. "The buddy system, eh?"

"It's what Mrs. Jones taught me in fourth grade," Marty said, and started up the rock.

Only the front half of his foot fit on the cuts into the cliff, so he was careful about his balance, leaned forward to use his hands, and slowly walked up the face of the cliff.

As he got higher, what he'd thought was a crack actually turned into an entrance to a cave. It looked like a crack from down below because instead of being an opening you could walk straight into, it required Marty to walk sideways into the entrance that ran almost parallel to the cliff face.

As Marty scooted his way into the opening, he realized that it wasn't a true cave, but a short natural fissure in the cliff face. It only went in about ten feet, but at the end of the ten-foot corridor he spotted a lidded ceramic container.

Someone had been here.

"Marty!" Gunther called.

"Come on up!" Marty answered.

But the pot wasn't what drew his focus. Marty found himself staring at the inner side of the rock wall about a foot from his face. A series of lines was scratched into the rock and as he backed away, trying to get a better look, the lines began to take the shape of a rudimentary map.

It showed various paths, but there were no hieroglyphs or language that Marty could make sense of. He turned his head and his eyes widened as he spotted an infinity symbol on a box.

Marty dug the silver-colored medallion out of his pocket and stared at it. Could the map be referring to more of these things? Or did the medallion and the map both refer to something else?

Nature almost never had a single instance of anything. It was more like cockroaches—if you saw one, there were at least one hundred somewhere nearby. Marty felt his hair stand on end as he wondered if this world was filled with copies of Seth running around everywhere.

They hadn't seen anyone yet other than that monster, but someone had clearly once occupied this oasis. Humans? Seth-people? His stomach gurgled with concern as he stared at the useless map. He had no bearings, no idea where he was, and no way to use any of the information on the map.

Gunther climbed in through the crack. "Invigorating," he said. "I feel like a boy again."

Marty scooted deeper into the corridor to make room. He stepped on a loose rock and one of his feet shot out from under him. As his grip inadvertently tightened around the medallion, a red beam flared to life, briefly painting a long line along the map.

Marty landed sitting on sand amid loose rocks. The light blinked off and Marty stared at the medallion, wondering what the hell happened.

He squeezed the medallion again. Nothing.

"What in the world is that thing?" Gunter asked. "And this map?"

"I don't know," Marty said, "but if that's a map to where to find more of those Seth-people, I don't want to go to where X marks the spot."

Marty stood and examined the rest of the chasm. No more maps or other markings in the stone, no further evidence of occupation.

"Marty! Where are you? Gunther?"

It was François's voice.

Gunther turned, leaned out slightly, and waved. "Coming right out!"

"What?" François called back.

Marty walked to the back of the hidden alcove and lifted the lid to the ceramic pot. It came away easily; the pot was filled with grain. He slowly edged his way back out of the fissure and followed Gunther out.

When he stepped back into the sunlight, Gunther was near the base of the cliff again. Marty saw several of his crewmates watching him.

François stood at the base of the cliff and yelled up at him, "How in the world did you get up there?"

Marty shifted the vase, which weighed about thirty pounds, and began carefully navigating the carved stairs downward. He leaned a little more on his knees this time, and found it helped him keep his balance.

François's eyes were huge as he watched Marty slowly descend the treacherous steps. "You're crazy. I can barely even see those sorry excuses for steps and you're climbing them by feel while holding something in your hands?"

Marty grinned. "It's not that hard if you—"

The ceramic vase suddenly broken open from the pressure of his one-armed embrace, sending grain, shards of ceramic, and Marty sliding to the ground.

By some miracle, Marty managed to land on his feet, but not without consequences.

His left forearm burned. Gunther raced to him and clamped his bleeding wound closed with his hands and yelled, "Someone get me something to bind his cut with!"

With the sound of his heartbeat thundering in his head, Marty stared at his bleeding arm. "Gunther, what's going on with your hands?"

The man was tightly gripping both sides of his sliced forearm so that the edges of the wound stayed closed, but in the shadows under the cliff's edge, Gunther's hands were radiating white light.

Marty felt a warm sensation pouring into his forearm. Not the warmth of his own blood, but warmth like you'd feel from a hot water bottle.

Gunther yelled and let go of Marty's arm.

The glow vanished. Surjan raced forward with a long cut strip of someone's undershirt, dampened.

Gunther grabbed it and also Marty's wrist, and then stared at Marty's arm. "How the hell . . . ?"

Marty's forearm was a bloody mess, but as Gunther wiped the blood from the wound, it became evident that the edges of the injury had stuck together. The wound was still visible, but it was stitched shut—albeit sans stitches.

"I wish we had some alcohol or something." Gunther began wrapping Marty's arm with the strip of cloth.

Marty whispered, "Did you see what I saw? The glow?"

Gunther furrowed his brow and nodded. "We're in the Twilight Zone."

"The old TV show?" Marty asked.

"These are grains of wheat!" François started picking up fingerfuls of the spilled grain and putting it in the intact upside-down pot lid. "I can grind this and make flatbread."

"You said jack-of-all-trades of science and engineering," Surjan pointed out. "Not arts and crafts."

"If you want to eat my bread," François said, "you're going to have to be nicer to me."

Gunther tied off the end of the bandage and worried over Marty's arm. "By some miracle, it doesn't look like it's bleeding anymore."

"It actually feels fine." Marty patted his friend's shoulder. He'd known the man for over two decades and seeing this mother-hen side of him come out wasn't a surprise. He motioned toward the log and said, "Let's go see how the water situation is coming."

Marty was impressed at how quickly Lowanna and Surjan had managed to dig a boxlike channel into the wood and fill it with a few gallons of water using her freshly woven baskets. The baskets leaked, but they were good enough to transport water the dozen or so feet from the shore to the partially hollowed-out log.

The wood-sculpting made him think of Carlos and Pedro. Had Pedro's wife given birth yet? Had the customer ever come by to collect the dining room set and pay for it?

Did those questions, really, even make sense?

He shook his head vigorously.

Now the entire team watched as Lowanna completed the operation.

Lowanna approached the large campfire with two sturdy sticks. She held them like chopsticks and with very little fumbling managed to pick up a heated rock, rushed over to the log, and dropped it into the water.

A sudden burst of steam whooshed up from the water as

Lowanna hurried between the campfire and the log, repeatedly adding hot stones to the water.

After several trips, she paused to check on her handiwork. Marty saw steam rising from the water and asked, "Is this to get rid of whatever nastiness might be in the water?"

Lowanna nodded. "I'm most worried about giardia. The last thing anyone needs in a desert climate is to be losing water because they get a nasty case of diarrhea."

"Don't you need to boil the water for that?"

"No." Lowanna dumped another set of rocks into the water with minimal splash and maximal steam. "We just need to get the water up to about fifty-four degrees Celsius—one hundred and twenty-nine degrees Fahrenheit—for about ten minutes. That'll take care of any live bugs and cysts that are in the water."

"Brilliant," Surjan said.

Marty smiled.

This motley crew seemed to have a reasonable set of survival skills. He liked to imagine that he would have thought about raising the temperature of the water, thus disinfecting it and making it safe for them to drink, but it was great that he didn't need to.

"You know, I accidentally made the Seth-like person's, uh, laser-amulet go off again," he said, thinking out loud. "I wonder if it could be used to do something useful. Like heat water."

"We should experiment," François said.

"I'm not sure I feel comfortable doing that," Marty said.

"I'm not sure I feel comfortable with Marty doing that, either." Gunther grinned.

François held out his hand. "Give it to me. As the non-technophobe in the party and, I will bet you anything, the owner of the best tech toys, I am clearly the one who should be doing the experimenting."

Marty shrugged and handed over the amulet. François immediately set himself to probing at the bronze medallion with his fingers.

Marty touched his bandaged forearm. As he pressed lightly on the wound, he couldn't feel the injury.

He successfully wiggled his fingers on his left arm and wondered if Gunther was right.

Maybe they really were in the Twilight Zone.

CHAPTER TEN

Marty was scouting ahead of the rest of the party. He and Surjan generally took turns, with the others bringing up the rear. Sometimes Lowanna scouted, and Kareem was also becoming quite adept at moving silently, so he got worked into the rotation. Gunther and François both made too much noise to be trusted with going first.

Marty found he could move quietly. Being out ahead of the others let him really enjoy his sharpened senses. The details of the flowers along the trail, or the variations and motifs of the birdsong he heard, sprang out to him in vivid detail.

And when he got far enough ahead, sometimes he would stop and practice his forms. The others trailed a half mile or so behind him, just visible as a clump of dark shapes when he looked west.

He heard a bird call, and knew instantly it wasn't made by a real bird.

He kept walking, forcing himself not to hesitate. If someone—or something—was waiting in ambush, perhaps if he didn't let on that he had noticed them, he might turn the tables and ambush the ambusher.

The sky overhead was cloudy and sporadic rain had fallen all morning, but the terrain consisted of gentle, rolling hills thick with tall green grass. The trail stretched more or less straight out ahead of him, and off to his right, a modest bump of a ridge rose about the surrounding grassland. There were no trees in sight. A dark spot lay on the south side of the ridge, just visible to Marty. Was it a shadow? But from what?

Could it be greenery?

If someone was lying in wait and watching Marty, he would find them in the grass.

Marty stopped. He stretched his neck and arms, and then he stepped to the right side of the trail and made a show of slowly urinating. While he went through those motions, he carefully scanned the prairie around him, without turning his head.

There, to his left, he saw two boys crouched in the grass. They were young and small, so Marty had longer legs. On the other hand, he'd been walking all morning, and they might be fresh.

He took to the trail again and walked in their direction. They didn't look ready to attack. Marty could ignore them—on the other hand, if he could talk to them, he might be able to get useful information out of them.

Of course, he didn't want them to run away and bring back a war band.

When he'd come as close to them as the trail reached, they were twenty feet off to his right, holding their breaths. Marty leaped after them, sprinting and covering the distance before they could react. The faster boy was rising from his crouch when Marty stepped on his foot and pushed him hard, knocking him to the ground. He grabbed the second one by the back of his neck and simply held him in place.

The boys squirmed, but went nowhere. Looking at them, Marty realized he'd underestimated their ages. They were teenagers, but they were small and thin. They looked undernourished. Their hair was dark, long, and ragged and they wore simple undyed woven tunics with no leggings. Their feet were bare. Their skin was a deep olive complexion and their eyes were dark brown.

Bedouin? Or Moroccans? Marty tried Arabic first. "*As-salamu alaykum,*" he said. *Peace be upon you.*

The one on the ground spoke. "Who are you?" he asked in English.

No, not in English. What language was that? Suddenly Marty, master of multiple tongues, spoken and written, wasn't sure.

"My name is Marty," he said. What language was he speaking?

He had no idea. The hair on the back of his neck stood up. "I'm a friend."

"We don't know you," the standing boy said. "You're not a friend."

"I want to be a friend," Marty said.

"Are you a trader?" the boy on the ground asked. "Traders travel this road."

"I'm like a trader," Marty said. "I'm a traveler. I'm a wanderer. I don't have anything to trade, but I want to meet new people and make friends." He gestured down at himself. "Look, I have no weapons."

"We're watching for traders. And for the Ametsu." The standing boy pointed back at the trail behind Marty. "Do your friends have weapons?"

"We are armed." Marty shrugged. "But as travelers, not for war."

The boys looked at each other.

"Our people are numerous," the standing boy said.

"They're armed," the boy on the ground added. "They're warriors."

"Good," Marty said. "Can you take me and my friends to meet them?"

He wanted information. The whole crew did. In an ideal world, he'd like someone who could tell him what year it was, but he also wanted geographical data and information about the Seth-headed men.

But what language were they speaking? And who or what was an Ametsu? Marty felt a nervous nausea fluttering in his stomach.

They stood and waited. Marty smiled. He remembered research he'd read about smiles, indicating that humans in multicultural societies smiled more. The researchers, at least, believed that this was because smiling was a nearly universal sign of benevolent intentions. You smiled at people not of your own tribe to reassure them that you weren't hostile, so in a society containing multiple tribes, people smiled a lot.

He smiled at the boys. "I'll give you a gift when my friends arrive. And then maybe we can trade with your people."

When Marty's friends caught up to him in ten minutes, he took two thick, thumb-sized strips of dried addax and impala and offered one to each boy. The meat was stretched over frames carried by

Kareem, Gunther, and François. Lowanna, at her insistence, carried a frame also, but it held the stretched and drying addax pelt.

The boys grabbed the dried meat, popped it into their mouths, and chewed heartily.

Surjan joined them last.

"I have asked these boys to take us to their village." Marty found that he was still speaking the unknown tongue. "We will trade peacefully, and I hope we can learn information."

"Very good!" François rubbed his hands.

"There may be many of them." Surjan frowned. Translation: *What if we get into trouble?*

"I think they're peaceful," Marty said, "as we are peaceful. If they don't wish to be peaceful, we'll leave." Translation: *If they attack, run like hell.*

Marty nodded to the boys, who led them away from the trail and toward the ridge on the south. Gradually a path took shape, as if this land was much-walked, but the people doing the walking tried not to make themselves too conspicuous.

At the southern edge of the ridge, Marty detected the scent of water ahead of them. Darker green of melon vines and fruit trees stretched into sight, like the belly fat of the rich oasis spilling into view over its belt.

Two men with spears stood at a small clearing. They wore undyed weave and each held a long spear in his hand. At the sight of Marty side by side with the two boys, one of the men stepped forward and lowered his spear into a position of challenge. He had long arms and large hands, with skin the reddish color of wet clay and a hooked nose that leaned slightly to one side.

"Badis," one of the boys said. "These men are traders."

"We're explorers," Marty said, though he wasn't really sure about the nuances of whatever word it was he was using for "explorers." The others in the group stared at him, obviously understanding his speech. "We're passing through and just want to trade information. We have gifts." He handed Badis two larger strips of antelope meat.

"Are you from the Ametsu?" Badis asked.

"We don't know what the Ametsu is." Marty smiled. "We're here on our own. We're a little lost, and could use some information."

Badis narrowed his eyes to examine the party, and focused on

Surjan as he joined the others. "The big one leaves his spear with me," he finally grunted. "And then I will take you into the village."

"Bloody hell." Surjan grumped but handed over the weapon. Then Marty followed Badis along the trail around the ridge, companions in tow.

Marty plied Badis with simple questions about the name of his people and where the nearest large water was and was met with stony silence. Once they were around the ridge, though, some of the answers became obvious: two visible springs fed a wide blue lake that was bearded with brilliant green forest and brambles. In a ring around the brambles, a band of land was hoed rudely into furrows, and was covered with ground-clinging vines.

In and around the trees squatted huts made of animal hide stretched over poles bent and lashed into frames. Perhaps a hundred people stood scattered across the scene, all turning now to watch Marty and his group approach. Their clothing was undyed, but many of them wore elaborate tattoos and jewelry of bright stones and ivory. Their skin was the color of sand, ranging from dull khaki through bright yellow to dark red, and Marty was surprised to see more than a few heads of blond hair among them.

Small goats grazed in the forest, surrounded by fowl that looked like stringy chickens.

Badis took Marty to a wide shelf of packed earth and pebbles, rising above the lake just beneath the western end of the ridge. Two men met them there: one tall, thin, and hunched over, with numerous long bones piercing his cheeks, and the second broad and muscular, with a wide nose and flaring nostrils. The four of them nearly filled the shelf, leaving Marty's friends standing in reed-covered marsh behind him. François grumbled and pushed himself to the front, joining Marty at his side.

Marty wasn't sure he was excited to have François's help, but he smiled and clapped the banker on the shoulder.

He began by handing strips of meat to the two men.

"These are the Speakers," Badis said. "Speaker for the gods"—he indicated the taller, thinner man—"and the speaker for the tribe," who was the man built like a bull.

"I am the speaker for our people." François tapped his own chest. Marty heard the faint chink of metal in the tap, and remembered that

François was wearing the medallion they'd taken from the Seth-headed creature. "I am also called François."

"And you?" Godspeaker pointed at Marty.

How to introduce himself? But Marty didn't have to worry about it long, because François stepped in and did the introduction himself. "He is called Marty. He is also called Doctor Cohen. As a doctor, he is master of many hidden lores relating to the earth and mankind. Further, he is a seer."

Marty felt embarrassed. He bit his tongue to avoid injecting that he was just a woodworker.

"Badis has brought you into the village," the Tribespeaker said. "He has judged you safe to deal with. Know that his life stands surety for his assessment. If you attempt to harm anyone here, he will kill you. If he fails, you and he will die together."

The hidden watchers on the path, the warriors with spears, and now this. These villagers were willing to trust, but they lived in a dangerous world.

Marty nodded.

"We come in peace," François said. "Does your village have a name?"

"The gods have called this place Ahuskay," the Godspeaker said. "These are the beautiful waters."

"We are looking for waters," Marty said. "We travel east, and we are looking for great waters."

The Tribespeaker raised an eyebrow. "A river?"

"A river so big you would call it a sea," Marty said.

"You mean the edge of the world," the Godspeaker said.

"Yes." François nodded. "How far until the edge of the world?"

The Tribespeaker shook his head. "Many days' walk."

"Ten days?" François suggested.

"A hundred. Or more. None of the people of Ahuskay has ever been."

Marty nodded. That put the edge of the world, which might be the Nile or maybe the Red Sea, somewhere between, say, fifteen hundred and two thousand miles to the east. Which meant that he had been to right to think they had arrived in Morocco.

"What other kingdoms do you know?" François asked. His facial expression was thoughtful. Was he looking for confirmation about the date? "As we travel eastward, what other people will we meet? Traders?"

"Traders." The Tribespeaker nodded. "Herders. And the Ametsu."

The Godspeaker spat.

There was something familiar about the word "Ametsu," but Marty couldn't put his finger on it.

"Where are you from?" The Tribespeaker asked.

"Our friends are from many lands," Marty said. "But we took an unexpected journey from the edge of the world. We lost our way in a great storm and traveled for many days, and now we're trying to return there."

"You will travel dangerous roads," the Tribespeaker warned them.

"Robbers?" Marty asked. Robbers were an endemic problem throughout most of the ancient world. Bands of armed men who simply killed travelers and stole their possessions.

The Tribespeaker nodded. "And worse."

"We're not too worried about bandits," François said. "We were attacked west of here by a monster. With our combined might, we defeated it easily."

"What kind of monster?" The Godspeaker eyed François warily.

"A giant." François was exaggerating a little, but maybe, in preliterate, mythological societies, that wasn't such a bad thing. "A giant with a head like a hound and with square ears."

The Speakers both froze, staring at François.

"So that's one less danger for your men to worry about," François said.

"You lie," the Godspeaker said. "The gods have told me no such thing. The gods would have warned us if they had left us so exposed."

"He tells the truth," Marty said. "Why are you distressed? Surely, this monster was no ally of yours."

"The monster you describe," the Tribespeaker said slowly, "is known to us as the Ametsu."

They had been worried about the Ametsu. The boys guarding the approach to Ahuskay were watching for the Ametsu.

"The Ametsu was your enemy," Marty said, taking a guess. "Why do you . . ." He didn't want to say "fear," which might be insulting. "Why do you hate the Ametsu?"

"The Ametsu takes men," the Godspeaker snarled. "A tax, they say."

"They say we are their farmers and also their crop," the Tribespeaker added.

So there was more than one Ametsu. Marty's heart sank.

"Slaves?" François was turning pallid.

"Food?" Marty guessed. "Do the Ametsu eat your people?"

"When the Ametsu comes..." The Tribespeaker spoke with a heavy voice. "He forces us to choose victims. A young woman and a young man. Healthy. He kills them in front of us. He takes their livers."

Just like that, the Ametsu was singular again.

And...livers? What would the Ametsu do with human livers?

François gasped and swayed on his feet. Marty grasped his arm to keep him upright. "Marty," he grunted. "Livers."

"What?" Marty asked.

"The bag of meat."

The strange meat that the jackal-headed giant had been carrying.

The meat that had so disturbed Lowanna.

Human livers?

"We killed the Ametsu on the road," Marty said. "This is a joyous day for the people of Ahuskay. We killed the Ametsu, he will trouble you no more!"

"Yes!" François regained mastery of himself and reached inside his shirt. He pulled out the jackal-headed man's infinity medallion and hung it visibly on his chest. "You see? We have a trophy evidence of his death. You're safe now!"

A loud groan rang across the lake. Looking about at the people of Ahuskay, Marty saw terror on their faces. Many fell to their knees. A few fell prone.

The Godspeaker spat.

"You fools!" Badis snapped. "There are many Ametsu, not just one. Now the others will come for vengeance, and they will kill us all!"

⪡ CHAPTER ⪢
ELEVEN

"Badis, kill them," the Godspeaker said.

Badis lunged forward with his spear. Marty felt the movement coming more than he saw it. He stepped inside the attack, so the spear slashed through empty space, and he caught the weapon by the shaft.

"We come in peace," he said.

"Hold." The Tribespeaker raised a broad-fingered hand and Badis stopped where he was. The warrior glared at Marty with intense concentration.

But not, Marty saw, hatred.

"The Ametsu will kill us," the Godspeaker murmured.

"Perhaps not." The Tribespeaker had a reflective look in his eyes. "Many hidden lores, indeed. Where did you kill the Ametsu?"

"Far from here," François said.

"West," Marty added. "Just this side of a river where melons grow. You may know it as the Ziz. The nearest river west of here of any size."

"I do not know the name Ziz," the Tribespeaker said. "But I know the river."

"Near," the Godspeaker said. "Too near. We are the closest village, and the death will be blamed on us."

"I don't see how that could happen." François spread his hands in a placating gesture that only made Badis growl.

"The land here is wide, O Speaker for Strangers." The Tribespeaker made a circling gesture toward the horizon. "The river you speak of is home to forests where my people hunt and trails my people walk. The Ametsu know this."

"And also that." The Godspeaker jabbed a finger at the medallion on François's chest. "They can follow that totem. It is well known."

"Your grandmother said it, at least," the Tribespeaker murmured.

"So did yours." The Godspeaker spat. "Were our grandmothers fools, then?"

Men and women around the edges of the lake were stooping into their hide huts and reemerging with spears, slings, and throwing sticks. Just how well did their voices carry?

Or was that perhaps the point? Were Marty and his friends forced to meet the Speakers on this shelf precisely so that the meeting would be public, in front of everyone? Which would mean that these people liked to share all their data and have open decision making, as Marty did.

As Marty mostly did. Though he hadn't told the crew about seeing his own secret hieroglyphs in the tunnel.

Because he felt . . . embarrassed.

Since the Ahuskay people looked fearful, Marty's instinct was to lower his voice. Instead, he raised it.

"We now understand that our actions may bring misfortune upon you. Tell us how we may avert the misfortune from you."

"A sacrifice," the Godspeaker hissed. "We will turn you and that idol in to the Ametsu, and they will punish you for your actions, instead of punishing us."

"No one will be punished." To his credit, François's nerve was holding. He still stood with arms open, smiling, not backing down. "We didn't attack the Ametsu, he attacked us, and he killed one of our crew before we defeated him. We do not deserve death. You have done nothing, you have killed no one, your people also do not deserve death."

"If you think you will cause the Ametsu to listen to your reasoned words," the Tribespeaker said, "it's clear that you have no experience of the Ametsu." His eye wandered to Marty. "Or did you have something in mind other than words?"

"Does the Ametsu come from a village?" Marty had no idea where such creatures would live. The beast-headed thing had looked like nothing so much as Seth, the Egyptian god, but as far as Marty actually experienced them, the Egyptian gods lived in books and tombs. "Perhaps a cave?"

"The Ametsu live in a fortress east of here," the Tribespeaker said.

"On the road?" François asked.

The Tribespeaker shook his head. "The road is a trade road. It goes east to the end of the world, wandering sometimes north and sometimes south to follow the best water and the richest herding grounds. The Ametsu live in a fortress with their servants, the Ikeyu. East of here, but also south."

"Ikeyu are men?" Marty asked.

"Ikeyu have the heads of cattle," the Godspeaker said. "They are fearsome and strong."

François nodded slowly. "The seer and I have spoken *for* my people. We will take action to protect this village. Allow me now to speak *with* my people, so that we may decide what action best to take."

"It is only to plan," Marty said. "A council of war. We invite Badis to be party to our counsels. He will be your eyes and ears, and we accept that our lives are forfeit if we do not raise this knife blade away from your necks."

"If you do not do as you say, your lives are forfeit," the Tribespeaker said. "The Tribe has spoken."

"Whatever your plan," the Godspeaker said, "you must remove the Ametsu totem from Ahuskay."

The Speakers both nodded.

Marty and François turned back to their friends and walked toward the forest, Badis following them.

"'Raise this knife from your necks'?" François said. "Gunther didn't tell me you were such a poet."

"Is it just me," Marty said, "or is your hair growing back?"

François ran his hand over his stubble-encrusted head, and shrugged.

Upon entering a clearing in the forest, the six members of the crew and Badis stood in a loose circle.

"What language is this that we're speaking?" Gunther asked. "It feels like Tuareg or something, and I don't speak Tuareg."

"We have bigger problems right now," Surjan growled. He fixed his eyes on Badis and got a reciprocal stare.

François opened his grass basket and was rummaging around inside for something.

"You all heard that," Marty said. "Apparently, the Seth-like creature we killed was one of a tribe. These people fear that if we don't help them, the Seth-people will overrun and kill them."

"Eat their livers." Lowanna shuddered.

"Let's agree to give these things a name," Gunther said. "The thing we killed wasn't human. They're Sethians."

Marty nodded. "Ametsu, in the local language."

"Obviously, the first step for us to take is to scout out this Sethian fortress." Surjan scowled. "Once we know how many there are and their disposition, we can decide whether it makes sense to attack them."

"Or whether they're open to peace overtures," Gunther said.

François set down his basket. He held up one of the flatbreads he'd baked earlier in his hand. He broke off a chunk and handed it to Lowanna, and then a second chunk to Badis. "I have a lot more where that came from."

The spearman sniffed it and took a nibble.

"Half of that is moldy," Gunther said.

"Oh, good," François said. He wrapped the moldy part up in leaves with visible delight and stowed it again in the basket.

"Really?" Gunther asked.

"Yes," François said. "If you get any more pieces with mold, let me know. Give it to me."

"Here comes the jack-of-all-trades in science," Lowanna grumbled.

"Experimentation doesn't hurt," François told her.

"Not everyone should go," Surjan continued. "Only people who can move quietly, and leg it if things go pear-shaped. I'll go."

"And I," Marty said.

"I'm going," Kareem said. When Marty looked at him, he nodded stubbornly. "I can move very quietly."

"We'll need guides." Marty turned to Badis. "Will you come with the three of us? Our other three companions will stay here, as the guests of your village, and to guarantee our good behavior."

He didn't say "hostage." He didn't want to encourage the Ahuskay to think that way.

"I know the way," Badis said.

The Ahuskay warrior returned Surjan's spear to him. The three travelers took their ankhs and their knives. Marty took the medallion back from François. At Badis's direction, they left everything else, but Badis supplied each a full waterskin and a light rolled blanket. Under the Godspeaker's cold stare and the Tribespeaker's more calculating, considered gaze, they left just after the sun went down.

"How far is the journey?" Marty asked as the firepit lights of the village disappeared into the shadow behind them.

"Are you a child, Seer?" Badis chuckled. "We will be there before dawn. They are in the canyon lands."

They walked, following Badis's directions. Marty marked the passage of time by watching the stars slip over the horizon—fifteen degrees made an hour, and he could neatly measure fifteen degrees with the span of a hand. For three hours, they rolled doggedly across gentle prairie.

And Marty didn't feel tired. At this point, he couldn't attribute it to adrenaline. Coming here, coming to this time, had affected him physically.

Marty didn't see the canyon lands coming, but Surjan did. Just before Marty slipped and fell into a chasm, the Sikh grabbed him by the shoulder and caught him. At his feet, the ground fell away in an abrupt and narrow stone chimney.

"This is not a secret passage," Badis said. "There are no secret passages. But this is a passage the Ametsu do not use."

Badis went first and Marty followed. Even with no light, he found it surprisingly easy to navigate his way down the sheer stone. He seemed almost to drift from point to point, finding solid purchase for his boots in cracks he would have imagined much too small to use. He had to hold himself in check to avoid overrunning the Ahuskay warrior.

Surjan's movements were more labored and muscle-intense, but the soldier grunted his way to the bottom and stood with his hands on his hips, as imperturbable as ever. Kareem found a crack he liked and leveraged both fingers and toes into it to descend like a spider, moving in a fluid, direct line straight to the ground.

"My uncle never told me that there would be so much climbing in an archaeological expedition." Kareem's voice had a note of pride in it.

"This is not a typical dig," Surjan growled.

"We are close." Badis held his voice down.

They followed the Ahuskay spearman along a narrow canyon choked with boulders and with thick, brown, gnarled vines whose bark scraped at Marty's and Surjan's palms and forearms and faces when they stumbled. Badis moved with more practice, one hand against the wall, and he stumbled rarely.

Kareem seemed never to stumble at all, but to step with perfect confidence and accuracy in the gloom. An ability gained from a youth spent navigating the alleys of Cairo? Or living in Egyptian villages that were poorly lit and haphazardly constructed?

"We're here," Badis whispered.

He crouched down on all fours and the others followed suit. They eased to the edge of a cliff and looked down into a broad, wet, green valley.

"I smell animals," Marty whispered. His eyes were adjusted to the changed light.

"There's a herd of cattle," Kareem whispered. "Opposite us, on a high shelf, there are two large buildings. They're rectangles made of bricks. Stone bricks, I think."

Marty's older eyes were adjusting to the gloom. "Mastaba. If this were a dig, I'd say that was a mastaba. Buildings shaped like sloped benches. Before the pharaohs built the pyramids, they shaped their tombs and temples like that."

"There's a wall protecting those buildings," Surjan said. "Is that a Sethian standing in the gate with a spear?"

It was.

"We need a count," Surjan said. "Could we climb to the canyon above and look down in?"

"We could examine the size of their trash heap," Marty said. "That would give us an idea of the size of their population."

"Spoken like an archaeologist." Surjan grunted. "Would you like to analyze it by layer? Look for seeds in the feces?"

"They have farmland, too," Kareem said. "I see furrows."

"We still have a couple of hours of darkness," Marty said. "A direct assault is obviously foolish; we need information so we can consider how to choose a battlefield to our advantage. Surjan, let's you and I creep up and try to climb that wall, see what we can see. Kareem, you and Badis stay here and call an alarm if you see any Sethians moving."

"I'm the better creeper!" Kareem protested.

"You also have the best eyes," Marty pointed out. "We can only use you in one place. Yell to warn us only if you have to."

"Stay with me and watch," Badis said to the young man.

Marty and Surjan lowered themselves down the cliff, which turned out to be only about eight feet tall. Surjan left his spear behind but carried the sharpened ankh in his hands as they dodged among cattle. They were the long-horned African cows that appeared in all the early Egyptian images. They lowed only a mild protest as Marty and Surjan dodged among them.

Marty looked back and forth as he moved, between the Sethian standing in the gate and the base of the wall, where he wanted to scramble over and look inside. The Sethian was immobile, standing in the shadow of the arch over his head. Was he actually sleeping?

Marty's foot found the plowed furrows Kareem had described. Despite the sudden irregularity of the soil, he didn't lose his footing. Surjan grunted, biting back a curse behind his big teeth.

There were cattle against the side of the canyon below the wall. They obscured the features of the land, but Marty thought he could make out a rugged slope turning into a smoother, horizontally cracked stone, a wall of sandstone whose natural crumbling made it resemble brick, and would give easy footholds and toeholds. The slope climbed some fifteen feet, and then there was another fifteen feet of canyon wall. Then the natural stone ended, and brick began. The gaps between the bricks looked deep, perfect for sinking fingers and toes into.

Marty squatted.

"This is easy," he whispered, once Surjan crouched beside him. "You watch from here and I'll climb the wall. I'll lie on the top, see what I can see and count what I can count."

"It would be stupid to go over the wall and into that compound alone," Surjan muttered. "You would feel like it was heroic, but really it would be stupid."

"When do I do stupid things?"

Surjan shrugged. "When you committed us to clean out all these monsters, for instance."

"I'll just look."

"You did hear me, right?" Surjan frowned.

Marty shot him a thumbs-up signal and moved to the wall. A breeze wafted by, carrying the scent of cattle. It was more than just cattle, it was as if someone had extracted the essence of a thousand years of the pharaohs' herds and distilled it into a single, explosively musky bottle, added a hint of cinnamon, and then shattered the bottle inside Marty's nostril.

He half-expected to black out.

Instead, he took a deep breath, shooed the cattle away, and stepped to the base of the wall.

A man stood up. He had been concealed, sitting among the herd on a small boulder and nodding, by the fact that his head was the head of a bull. He had the same long muzzle, the same wide, gently curving horns, and a ring in his nose.

A ring, just like the ring the Sethian had had.

But from the neck down, he looked human. Six and a half feet tall, muscular, but human. A broad strap over his shoulder held a large pouch at one hip, and in his hand, he held a spear that had to be twelve feet long. The intense bovine odor came from him.

Surjan reacted instantly. He sprang forward, sharpened ankh held low like a knife. But Marty's response was even faster. He leaped up against the stone of the canyon wall, feeling the boulders and the gritty sandstone beneath his feet. Pushing off the wall, he grabbed the bull-headed man by one horn and stepped with all his weight into the back of one knee.

The bovine man collapsed, crashing to the earth on his back. Surjan landed atop him, a knee on his sternum and the sharp tip of the ankh pressed to his throat.

"Who are you?" Marty whispered into the cow-shaped ear.

⇌ CHAPTER ⇌
TWELVE

"Your tongue is . . . hard." The bull-headed man grunted. "Do you ask my name?"

"For starters," Surjan said.

"Doath." The name sounded like the lowing of a cow.

"How many minotaurs live here?" Surjan pressed.

"Minotaurs?"

"With heads like cattle," Marty explained.

Doath chuckled, a low, rumbling gurgle. "I would have said that the cattle have heads like ours. I do not know this word . . . minotaurs. Here they call us Ikeyu. In the east, by the sea, we are sometimes called Hathiru. I am a Hathir."

Surjan looked up to find Marty's gaze in the darkness. "Your Egyptians know cattle-headed people."

Marty nodded, not wanting to say more. "How many Hathiru live here?"

"Twenty-three," Doath said. "If you're hungry, take a cow. I won't tell. We lose cows to the wild dogs of the prairie all the time. And to . . . cats. But leave me in peace." He chuckled again. "I would taste bad."

"What do you Hathiru do?" Surjan asked. "Are you all herders?"

"No," Doath said. "Some of us farm."

"You're just the working class of the Sethians?" Surjan shook his head.

Doath was slow to answer. "I do not understand those words. We work so that we can live. The work is hard. There are cattle to raise and protect and slaughter. There are crops to plant and manure and harvest. Is it not the same with your people?"

"Do you ever go to war?" Surjan inquired.

"Against wild dogs and cats, yes," Doath said. "Against mankind, no. There is land enough and water enough and sky enough for all."

"And the others?" Marty asked. "The Ametsu? How many Ametsu are there?"

"Here? Now there are four. Sometimes there are five, or six."

"Do they rule you?" Marty asked.

"They eat our food," Doath said. "They protect us, when it is needed."

"You're a giant with horns as long as my leg." Surjan snorted. "How often do you require defending?"

"Not often," Doath admitted. "Sometimes, they kill us for our organs."

"Livers," Marty said.

"Yes."

"And are there other kinds of people here?" Marty asked. "Mankind, or others?"

Doath hesitated. "Not here. The Ametsu have slave armies, but not here. In the east, by the sea."

"And you Hathiru?" Marty pressed.

"We have no use for you." Doath chuckled. "You are not very good workers, you are tiny, and you do not taste good."

"What would your people do if there were no more Ametsu?" Marty asked.

"Work," Doath said. "Eat. Live."

"Is that all?" Surjan pressed.

"Well," Doath said shyly. "Also, rut."

Marty managed not to laugh.

"Dr. Cohen?" Surjan said. The formality was a sharp reminder of their situation, and that Marty was in some sense in command.

Marty had to remind himself that he was not negotiating with a ruler. Doath was no ambassador, there was no reason to be certain his information was reliable or that his characterization of his people's desires and actions was accurate. He needed verification.

"Stay here," he said to Surjan, speaking very carefully and deliberately in English. "Guard this prisoner. I will creep up to the wall and count."

"Don't do anything stupid," Surjan said. "Dr. Cohen."

"Stupid turns out to be almost entirely a matter of context," Marty said.

"I don't know any of those words," Doath said. "Don't kill me."

"Don't move," Marty said, switching back into the instinctive human tongue of this millennium, "and we won't have to."

Surjan repositioned himself, tightened his grip, and reminded Doath that he was ready to strike with the ankh at a moment's notice.

Marty went up the wall.

The boulders were easy; he fairly ran up them. The sandstone was barely any more difficult, and his vertical crawl quickly shot up the rock face. Even the bricks scarcely slowed him down. They were of stone, rather than mud, so their edges were firm and didn't crumble when Marty put his weight on them.

In less than a minute, he was at the top of the wall. Looking down at Surjan in the shadow, he thought he'd climbed fifty feet, nearly straight up.

This sort of acrobatics hadn't been any part of his Egyptology curriculum.

Were years of martial arts and conditioning paying off?

Or was this facility with climbing another strange effect of his being in this alien world?

The top of the wall was rough, with no parapet or breastwork. From this vantage point, Marty could see clearly that the two mastabas were of equal size and almost identical in appearance. The name "mastaba" meant "bench" in Arabic, but they had never looked like benches to him. They looked like bricks of butter, flat on top, straight on the two long ends, and on the short ends cascading down as if melting, or like the early precursors of pyramids. They amounted to rectangular buildings, one story tall, with accessible roofs. The mastabas were both dark. The farther mastaba from him had a tower that rose an additional twenty feet, with its staircase around the outside. The tower's top was flat and open; Marty lay still, watching the tower until he was certain that there was no one on its top.

So they couldn't defend the walls as such, but if the Sethians could hold the gate, and fire missile weapons from the top of that tower, the wall would still be a formidable obstacle. Especially in an age when no one had yet invented the catapult, the trebuchet, or even, as far as Marty knew, the battering ram.

Could he build a trebuchet if he needed to? Or could François, or someone else in the party figure that one out?

Something stank. Reeked. It wasn't the cattle and Hathiru smell, which still reached him fifty feet off the ground, but something else.

Marty hesitated. He'd told Surjan he wouldn't do anything stupid. But now that he was up here, he'd learned nothing new from climbing the wall. Something smelled bad, and there was a tower. But was Doath's count correct? Were the Sethians armed? Were the Hathiru indeed nonhostile?

And he had also told Surjan that stupidity was a question of context.

In this context, Marty really needed more information.

He slipped down the wall. He climbed in the corner, where the brick met the cliff rising above the two mastabas and formed a deep well of shadow. The climbing was so light that after a couple of shifts from one hold to another, he simply ran down the wall.

Which, looking back up at it, was taller than he would have thought.

But he felt light and agile and alert.

He crept to the corner of the nearer mastaba. A closer look showed that each long side of the rectangle was pierced by a single monumental door. Marty sneaked to the door facing the cliff, which lay in thick shadow. He pressed himself against the cool stone and listened. He heard the loud breathing of many lungs, a rhythmic storm of wheezing bellows.

And the stink was worse. It was yeasty, and it had an oily reek. Was there something in it of beans?

How fast could he run? He'd had a lot of success climbing, and Marty had felt light on his feet since coming into the ancient world. Could he outrun a Hathir?

Probably, if they met each other by surprise, and Marty ran instantly.

Stupidity was always a question of context.

Marty slipped in through the door. He moved slowly into the first chamber and the sound of breathing sharply diminished. Bulky shadows loomed up on all sides of him, but they were completely still. Marty found himself virtually blind. He probed carefully with his fingers, discovering baskets that sagged heavy with things that felt like legumes and tubers and grains. He also found sealed jars that smelled of oil, vinegar, and even wine.

Doctoring an enemy's drink was a staple of ancient wars, or at least a staple of ancient-world stories about war, which was not exactly the same thing. Marty tucked away the knowledge of this storeroom in his mind.

In the second room, the rotting stink punched him in both eyes, and Marty almost vomited.

It took him some time to understand the layout of the room. It contained a single enormous stone bowl, as big as a jacuzzi tub. The bowl filled almost the entire room, leaving scant area around the edges to walk. Whatever stank was contained in that bowl. It also emitted, Marty thought, faint warmth, and he would have sworn he could hear the sound of it bubbling. It was also the source of a faint glow that allowed him to make out the few details he could within the rooms.

He wasn't brave enough to reach down into the gloop and touch it.

The structure consisted of three rectangular rooms, each connecting to the next in sequence. In the third and fourth rooms of the mastaba, he found sleeping Hathiru. He found too many to distinguish in the dim interior, heaped as they were over sleeping benches and in corners of the room and even in the middle of the floors. But Douth's count of just over twenty seemed about right. All breathed deeply in sleep.

Their scent clogged his nasal passages. Would they smell him when they awoke?

He stood in the doorway upon exit, waiting to be certain he heard no sounds of discovery or pursuit. Creeping from one mastaba to the next, he paused to look out through the gate; the lone Sethian sentinel still stood his watch. From this angle, it looked even more as if the guard were leaning against the wall, asleep.

Marty slipped into the door of the second mastaba. The layout seemed to be exactly the same, but there were two immediate differences. First, the stench—both of the vat with the unknown stinking contents, and of the Hathiru—was greatly diminished. Second, there was more light.

This time it came from the ceiling. Marty had to squint to puzzle out what he was looking at, and finally guessed that it was a phosphorescent stone, perhaps set behind a lens. It cast enough light that he could see more details than in the other building.

He heard breathing, but it wasn't as labored as the sounds the Hathiru made. He eased into the first room and found a chamber with a single large wooden bedframe raised two feet off the floor on four legs as thick as the pylons holding up Fisherman's Wharf in San Francisco; Marty didn't think he could wrap his arms all the way around one of them. Cushions were piled on the bedframe and a Sethian lay stretched out across it, snoring gently toward the glowing stone in the ceiling. Spears leaned against the wall beside a narrow chest, and Marty examined them.

Should he take a spear and impale the sleeping Sethian?

But if the Sethian made a noise and woke the others, he would be outnumbered three to one, by dangerous creatures who could have killed his entire crew. He'd kicked the Ametsu in the face and scored a lucky blow, but how lucky could he get against three of them?

He could stab one and flee.

But then Surjan and Kareem and Badis would all be taken by surprise. And the only way to flee seemed to be back up the canyon, pursued by determined foes with longer legs.

How much time remained until dawn? Could he bring back his three companions? Each could take a spear, and with a coordinated strike, they could kill the Sethians in a single instant. If Doath was telling the truth about the Hathiru, and every indication seemed to be that he was, then the cow-headed men might at best welcome their liberation, and at worst—

Marty heard footsteps.

He slid under the bed.

Heavy feet trod into the room. In the pale, bluish light filtering down from the phosphorescent stone, he saw the advance of sandal straps wrapped around enormous calf muscles, and feet that wore the sandals. A cloak drifted along the floor behind the calves, and the butt of a staff—or spear?—thumped beside the right foot.

The feet and cloak and staff all stopped beside the bed.

How good was the Sethians' sense of smell?

He heard a voice, deep and rumbling. He didn't understand the words. Then the voice again, and finally, the bed rattled. A second voice joined in, this one snapping and reproving. Two more feet touched the floor as the awakening Sethian sat up. The first Sethian then walked away.

Marty tried to breathe. He'd heard old stories from his grandfather about monks who could apparently go without breathing for extended periods of time because they had learned to inhale and exhale through their ears, their eyes, other bodily orifices, and even through their skin itself. It was mystical nonsense, of course, but in that moment, Marty pressed his lips shut and tried to breathe silently through the pores of his skin.

Was that the gray light of early day seeping in at the door?

The Sethian stood, snapped out wolfish noises that sounded like curses, and took something out of the chest. A cloak fell about his feet, and then he took up his spear and stumped out, following the first Sethian.

Marty slid out from under the bed as if he had wheels under his ankles and shoulders. Before he'd come to a stop he rolled, springing to his feet and racing for the door by which he'd entered. The way was clear, so he moved out into the courtyard, picking up speed.

He'd never tried parkour, but he'd seen some of those athletes climb the corner connecting two walls by leaping from one wall to the other and back several times, jumping higher each time. Marty was dizzy from breathlessness and fear, so he wasn't quite sure how he did it, but suddenly he was at the top of the wall, sitting astride it and preparing to drop down the other side. Had he climbed? Leaped? Parkoured?

Surjan was shaking his head in disapproval as Marty slid down the outer wall.

"Stupid," he muttered, when Marty reached him.

"I learned a lot," Marty said, "but now we have to run."

Surjan looked down at the Hathir. "You remember what I told you."

They raced across the fields and the pasture full of cattle. Light glinted off white horns and pelts now. Was Marty also visible? He didn't dare look back. With better light, he and Surjan now found an easier scramble up the short wall on the other side, rejoining Badis and Kareem.

"My bread is also moldy," Kareem complained. "It tastes terrible."

"Keep it for François," Surjan muttered. "He likes it that way. He's convinced it's science."

"But now we need to run," Marty said. "Fast."

⊰ CHAPTER ⊱
THIRTEEN

"Please tell me exactly what your grandmothers told you." Marty was keenly aware that he was talking to the two Speakers across gulfs of language, culture, and five thousand years of time. He tried to keep his voice neutral and he held his hands in his lap, fingers slightly curled and palms up. "About the medallion."

He sat with François and Surjan inside one of the largest hide huts. Across an empty firepit, they faced the Godspeaker, the Tribespeaker, and Badis. All sat cross-legged.

Marty and his companions had marched directly back from the Sethians' fortress, stopping only to drink and scan the horizon for signs of pursuit.

When they'd reached Ahuskay again it was midday. Kareem had stretched himself out on a thick bed of grass beside the lake and fallen directly asleep. Marty had collected the banker and brought the two older warriors into this conference.

"My grandmother told me that the Ametsu were sorcerers." The Godspeaker closed his eyes and nodded slightly as he spoke. "That their hearts were linked by the amulets on their breasts. And that every Ametsu always knew where all the amulets were at all times. For this reason, it is folly to kill an Ametsu. All the others of their kind already know who the murderer is."

"It wasn't murder," Surjan growled.

"And it is even greater folly to take anything belonging to the

Ametsu," the Godspeaker continued. "But especially the amulets. The Ametsu know where the amulets are at all times. They are likely already coming in numbers, to avenge their brother's death."

"We have learned valuable information on our journey," Badis said. The Ahuskay warrior spoke with bowed head, and slowly. "The Ametsu are not great in number. We saw four, and when we interrogated an Ikeyu herdsman, he said that there were four of them."

Though sometimes five or six. But the fifth could be the Ametsu the crew had already killed.

And the sixth . . . an occasional visitor?

"How many Ikeyu?" the Tribespeaker asked.

"Twenty-three," Badis said.

"Our warriors have never fought the Ikeyu," the Godspeaker said. "They are large, and have fierce horns. Twenty-seven monstrous warriors are more than enough to obliterate all our people."

"We believe the Ikeyu are peaceful," Badis said.

"The Ikeyu are herdsmen," Surjan added. "They will not attack you."

"And if they do?" the Godspeaker demanded.

Marty smiled. "Then we will keep our vow to defend your people."

"Have we not behaved honorably with you?" François asked.

The Speakers looked at each other silently.

"But I don't believe the Ametsu are coming to this village to avenge anything," Surjan said. "I don't think they're aware of the death yet."

Marty nodded. "They didn't seem to be organizing to go anywhere."

"They will!" the Godspeaker snapped.

"My grandmother told me a slightly different story." The Tribespeaker spoke slowly, chewing each word before he released it. "She said the Ametsu were sorcerers, yes, and their sorcery was in their amulets. She said the amulets were second hearts, and that you could kill a sorcerer by destroying its second heart. But also, she said she had once seen a wounded Ametsu. It had broken its leg in a flood and was trapped beneath a fallen log. Grandmother saw the Ametsu and watched it from hiding. She hoped it would die and she might find something of value on its body. But it made a terrible light with its amulet."

"Did that heal it?" Marty asked.

The Tribespeaker shook his head. "It didn't free the Ametsu, either. But six hours later, more Ametsu arrived, and they lifted the tree and carried their wounded fellow away."

Marty, Surjan, and François exchanged glances.

"It's a beacon," François said. "For remote signaling. I know how it works."

Marty raised an eyebrow, and the Frenchman nodded his confirmation.

"So it can call for help," Marty said.

"It can do more than that," Surjan told them. "One of your risks when you send someone out on patrol is they get stuck and need help. So this beacon allows the Ametsu to signal. But another risk is that your patrol gets wiped out, and you don't learn of it. So another thing you can do is arrange periodic check-ins."

"You're saying that maybe the Ametsu expect their travelers to report home by flashing their beacons every day," Marty said. "And when they don't, base camp knows something is wrong."

"Probably it isn't every day, or they would already have mobilized," Surjan suggested. "So maybe it's every three days or once a week or something. But yes, that's how I would do it. So I think yes, they're going to miss a signal and come out looking for the dead Sethian. And it will be sooner rather than later."

Marty nodded, against his will.

"Did your grandmother say anything else about the light?" Surjan asked. "For instance, did she say that the Ametsu flashed the light in a pattern? Or that he pointed at the heavens in a certain direction?"

The Tribespeaker shook his head.

"We have some advantages," François said.

"Numbers. The high ground may be defensible." Surjan looked at the Speakers. "If we wait for them on the ridge, is there water up there?"

The Tribespeaker nodded.

"We have another advantage," François said. "We have the amulet."

"If we knew how to use it," Marty murmured.

"Not all of us get to spend our days out ahead of the crew, enjoying the scenery alone." François grinned. "Some of us have been fiddling with alien technology as we walked instead, and learning how it worked."

"Alien?" Surjan asked.

"Well, think about it." François said. "These things obviously have some different kind of blood chemistry from what Earth animals have. What other thing directly converts from a solid to a gas without applying heat?"

"A mothball does." Marty grinned.

"Exactly my point. For all we know those things we're dealing with are made of some completely bizarre set of chemicals that are either artificially made or they came from somewhere else." François's eyes widened and his voice took on a more excited tone. "Holy crap, guys. Think about it. These things are just like images from Egypt's pantheon of crazy mythology. We *know* it's a myth because we've never uncovered an example of such a creature. Well, now we know why. These things just go poof after you kill them. Aliens, I'm telling you—it's the only thing that makes sense. What else would you call it?"

"You can make the beacon work?" Marty asked, wanting to avoid the pointless debate on something neither of them could prove.

François nodded. "Depending on how I twist the face of this medallion, there's several shades of light that come off of this thing, and an on-and-off switch. So I think if we stick to the shade of light that the Sethian had it set for, turn it on, and point it at the sky, that would have to be the Sethians' distress signal."

Marty tried to game out the possibilities in his head. "If we get the distress signal wrong—"

"Then we warn the Sethians that we have their beacon," François said, finishing his thought. "And that's not good."

"You might have thought about that while you were dinking around with the medallion on the trail," Marty pointed out.

"Yes, we all might avoid taking unnecessary risks," Surjan said.

"I only did it in the daylight." François sniffed.

"So we have to be prepared for the possibility that they come looking to rescue a comrade with a broken leg," Marty said. "And also for the possibility that they come intending to crush the humans who have stolen their device."

"Mostly, we have to be prepared for the inevitability that they will come," Surjan said.

"And we have to be prepared to kill them." Badis's eyes gleamed.

"Can we count on your other warriors to help us?" Marty asked the Tribespeaker.

The Tribespeaker was slow to answer. "I have been patient. You are strange and this situation is new, and my father told me that it was almost always wise to make decisions slowly, and rely heavily on the wisdom of my ancestors. But what comes on us now is a threat my ancestors have never known. Yes, my warriors will fight with you. So will the women and the children, if need be. But know this, seer Dr. Cohen: I will hold you to your oath. You will save my people. And for every one of my people who dies, I will kill one of yours."

Surjan growled without words.

François spread his hands. "You have never seen warriors as great as ours. We will kill the Ametsu and there will be no deaths from among your people. Thank you, Speaker for the Tribe."

"The Tribe has spoken," the Tribespeaker grunted.

The Speakers remained in the hut in deep discussion as the other four emerged. "Badis," Surjan said. "Gather the warriors. We'll need to give them instructions."

"We'll probably need the others, too," François. "Maybe not to stab with spears, but I think we're going to want to do some digging, or lay ropes, or such."

Badis hurried away.

"You have a plan to share with us, then?" Surjan asked.

"Well, no," François admitted. "But I've seen *Home Alone.*"

They hiked up onto the ridge to survey the land. The ridge had less grass than the surrounding plain. It was a blade of rock poking up through the dirt, carrying just enough soil to keep a thin green toupee going. Abundant boulders lay piled and tumbled about the stone. The shape of the ridge wasn't uniform—its sides had eroded into multiple steep, short, narrow gulches, ending in cliff faces or in rugged scrambles up to the top of the ridge. Two of the gulches had springs that fed into the lake; a third spring bubbled from the stone near the top of the ridge.

Marty turned three hundred sixty degrees, examining the lay of the land and asking himself, What would Hannibal do? How would he control the battlefield? How would he fool or approach the enemy, to get exactly the battle he wanted, the battle that favored him?

He trailed his fingers through the cool flow of the spring water. "If we were worried about a rival tribe, I'd say we build a fence and rely on having our own food and water."

"But the Sethians have laser beams," François said. "Who knows what else they might have?"

"It's a beacon," Surjan growled. "Don't get carried away."

"If they have laser beacons," François pointed out, "they might also have rocket-propelled grenades."

Surjan snorted.

Down in the village, Marty saw Gunther sitting within a circle of children, telling them some tale. Kareem still slept. Lowanna had been sitting alone at a finger of rock at the eastern end of the ridge. She now stood and made her way toward them.

"We need to burn the village," Marty said.

"Whoa!" François raised his hands in a calming gesture. "You might be a little short on sleep there, Doctor."

"He's right," Surjan said. "We need to use this ridge, there's no other terrain for miles around. But if the village is here and intact, with no sign of villagers, it looks like a trap. If there are burned huts here and the beacon is going off, then maybe it looks like there was a battle, and the Ametsu is calling for help." He paused. "You know there are many, many ways we can get this beacon wrong. And only one way to get it right."

Marty took a deep breath. "Yeah. But I think they'll come investigate, in any case. Wouldn't you?"

"I would," Surjan agreed.

François scratched his chin. "You're right. We need not just a burned village, but a scene. We need bodies. To make the whole thing look real."

"I wish we had the body of the Ametsu," Surjan grunted. "That would look real."

"Except they turn to oatmeal," François pointed out.

"Well, killing anybody is out," Marty said.

"Who said anything about killing anyone?" François grinned.

Lowanna reached them. Her eyes were sunken and her hands trembled.

"You aren't sleeping well," Marty said.

"I hear voices," she said.

Marty's heart sank. "I'm sorry."

"It's like you said." She swallowed. "It's better that everyone has all the data, right? So here's some of the data. I'm going crazy. You can't count on me."

"That's not the data," Marty said gently. "That's a conclusion. The data is that you hear voices, like I see visions." Visions of an unhandsome man, with big ears and staring eyes. "You're stressed. You're tired. I wish I had something to help you sleep."

"No one's going to prescribe her an Ambien, Marty," François said.

"Maybe the village has a little alcohol they can spare," Marty suggested.

François frowned. "Once in a while, a bird says, 'Hey, look at me'?"

"Constantly," Lowanna said. "Every animal we pass. Including, yes, every bird."

"Every animal is a lot of animals," Marty said.

"Far more than you realize." She fixed his eyes with her gaze. "We pass mice and snakes and little things I can't identify, like gophers, all the time. The rest of you don't see them. But I do. Because *they talk to me.*"

Marty hadn't given much thought to Lowanna's voices, because she hadn't talked about it very much. Now, suddenly, he saw that hearing the voices weighed on her.

"What do they say?" Surjan asked gently.

"Redrum, redrum." François snickered.

"Shut it!" Surjan bellowed.

François blinked and closed his mouth.

"What do they say?" Marty asked.

"Animal things," she said. "They call us Two-Legs all the time. They ask if we'll drop crumbs for them to eat. They warn each other to get out of our way. Or to hide from the predators."

"What do the predators say?" Marty asked.

"The predators are silent," Lowanna said. "At least while they're hunting."

"These voices," Marty asked. "Is this why the thought of meat started making you ill?"

"Maybe," she said. "Probably."

"We're all sleepless," Marty said. "And we're all stressed. It would be surprising if none of us were seeing and hearing things. But I don't think you're hallucinating."

"She is not hallucinating," Surjan said.

"We're all stressed and sleepless," François said. "And scared and confused and worse. Because we have all experienced and seen and even done things we never imagined we would. But we didn't hallucinate the Sethian, did we? We didn't hallucinate Dr. Cohen killing him with a karate kick."

"Kung fu," Marty murmured. "Kung Fu Cohen, remember?"

"Whatever. Did we hallucinate him dissolving into goo?" François pressed. "Did you hallucinate the other Sethians? The cow-headed ones, what did you call them? Hathiru?"

"They taught me the word themselves," Marty said. "Doath did."

"I hallucinated nothing," Surjan said.

"Right," François said. "Me neither. So I believe that Lowanna isn't hearing things that aren't there. The animals *are* talking to her."

Lowanna looked down, as if embarrassed by the support.

"Agreed." Marty nodded, immediately thinking of Dr. Dolittle. "But why? And why just her?"

"Those are great questions to ask," Surjan said. "But maybe we should ask them after we deal with the outpost of Sethians that we're pretty sure is going to come try to kill us."

"Agreed," François said. "And one more thing. All of you."

They all looked at him.

"If you jackasses ever want to be hired by me again," he said, "you need to learn to take a joke."

⪢ CHAPTER ⪡
FOURTEEN

Lowanna lay on her back, feigning death. François had wanted to smear her with blood, and even drape a goat entrail artistically over her shoulder, as he had done to several of the villagers, but the mere thought had made her vomit. Instead, she had smeared dirt on her face and limbs conspicuously. Gunther lay at the bottom of the ridge, very visible against the grass-furred stone, with blood spattered all over his chest and face and a goat lung stuffed into his shirt pocket.

Lowanna lay still and tried listening to the hens.

She couldn't quite shut out the sound of the goats, but the goats were more complex. They followed the movements of the humans of Ahuskay village, hoping the women would give them handfuls of seeds or melon rind, or the children might give them unwanted gruel. They monitored the movements of the men mostly to stay out of their way, to avoid being kicked. In the bleating of the goats, Lowanna heard warnings, threats, and the sharing of information.

Fat Head smells like melon.

I found sliced tubers in Wobble Bottom's hut.

Stay away from the females!

This chopped vine is tasty.

It was distracting, it was too much. It drew her in, and the chaos of voices felt painfully like madness.

She tried instead to listen to the hens. They were simpler, stupider, more focused creatures.

Food, food, food, food, food, mine! Mine!
Food, mine! Food, food, food.

If Lowanna listened to the hens long enough, their words disappeared, and the animal sounds came very close to returning to being simple white noise.

Very close. But not quite.

Villagers—mostly women, a few older children, and all of the men—lay bloody and pretending to be dead. Three huts had been burned, and lay still smoldering; the others had been knocked down, the pieces scattered to look like vandalism rather than deliberate deconstruction.

The villagers had resisted the idea of burning all the huts, even after Marty explained the intent. But once the Tribespeaker became convinced, he had announced, "The Tribe has spoken," and down the huts came.

Goats had wandered away with hides and poles in their mouths, and the villagers, following their Speakers' instructions, lay still and let it happen.

Every adult of the tribe had a spear hidden in the underbrush, close at hand.

The few women missing from the scene, and the rest of the children, had crept away south toward a hiding place in the prairie, with food, water, and weapons, before François had activated the beacon.

The beacon shone now, a laser beam pointing up into the sky like a klieg light. It was tilted to shine to the south and east, where the Sethians lived. It shone out a narrow gully on the ridge's flank, where the amulet lay on the chest of Surjan, cloaked and covered and made to resemble the Ametsu as much as possible.

Which was not very much. The head was the wrong shape, and for all his size, he was a little short. But maybe in the darkness it would be good enough.

Lowanna lay on the southern edge of the forest, farthest from the decoy. Marty and the Ahuskay warriors were closer to where they hoped to trap the Sethians, armed and waiting. François lay on his back a few feet from Lowanna.

That was by his own choice. And he was absolutely covered in goat entrails.

Probably, he was doing it to goad her. She was determined not to react.

"You know," François said suddenly, "there are many thinkers who believe that Earth life is all a simulation, anyway."

"What?" She wanted him to shut up, but focusing on his whispered voice was another way not to pay attention to the goats.

"Life as we know it. Life in twenty-first-century Earth. If life were a simulation, that could explain a lot of oddities. Cryptids, like the Loch Ness Monster and Bigfoot. UFO sightings. It could also help explain the Placebo Effect. Why do people's brains apparently have the power to heal them? Well, because all we really are is a brain, in a simulated world, and the apparent healing is only perceptual anyway."

"Is this the kind of thing you talked about while you were smoking pot at those private prep schools you went to?" she asked.

"Yes. And the Fermi Paradox. Given all that we know about the probability of intelligent life and the size of the universe, we should be seeing aliens all the time. We don't. Why is that?"

"Because it's really a simulation," Lowanna said. "And the contradiction is just bad story design by the programmers."

"Bad worldbuilding," François said. "Yeah. And so I'm thinking—"

"Being in a simulation would also explain why we seem to be in the fourth millennium B.C.E.," she said. "Marty's vision. The voices I hear. The wrong stars. The blobs of light. The Ametsu and the cow-people."

"Yeah," he said.

"I'm going to try not to be an ass when I say this," Lowanna said. "Shut up."

He shut up.

Unfortunately, that brought back the sounds of the goats.

Maybe these big Two-Legs have food.

Ouch! That hurts!

Stay away from these big Two-Legs.

Lowanna stiffened. Had the Sethians arrived?

She heard the heavy crunch of footsteps. Her eyes were closed, but she couldn't escape the panicked squeals of chickens as they flowed past her, seeking to flee from something that was enormously heavy, but walked like a man. She squinted through her eyelashes and saw only the dark outline of a head against the stars above her.

But it was a monster's head, with a long snout and long, square ears.

She held her breath, and it passed.

She heard goats bleating to the south, on the grassland beyond the forest.

Is the big Two-Legs a predator?

Will it eat goats?

François whispered in a voice so soft it sounded as if he wasn't moving his mouth at all, but exhaling words directly from his lungs. "It's going toward Surjan."

Lowanna said nothing.

Her role in the plan, with François and the women lying in the village and around the edge of the lake, was first of all to look dead. And second, when the warriors sprang their trap, she and the others were supposed to rise up with their weapons and stop the Sethians from running away through the village, trap them against the ridge.

But only one Sethian had come. Would they have to repeat this three more times?

Big Two-Legs are bad.

Big Two-Legs is hunting the children. Stay away!

Lowanna almost laughed, despite the tension. She was in some twisted intersection between George Orwell and Rudyard Kipling, being warned about the evil of Two-Legs by talking goats. Lying on her back, playing dead, on an African savannah.

Five thousand years before her own birth.

"Shhh," François urged her.

Big Two-Legs is hunting the children.

Lowanna sharpened her ears to focus on the goats. They had gone back to nattering about melon rinds and stray seeds, but there were other voices.

Stay away from Big Two-Legs!

Run! Run!

They were the voices of prairie mice and snakes and ground birds. And they all came from the south.

"François," she whispered. "There are other Sethians."

"We know there are," he whispered back. "Shh."

"They're going after the women and children."

He raised himself up on one elbow and looked at her. "Animals are telling you this."

She nodded.

He picked himself up off the ground, shook off the bloody guts, and grabbed his spear. They were at the edge of the forest and far from the ambush spot. Lowanna climbed to her feet and looked across the woods and the lake, seeing there a single Sethian, tall, beast-headed, spear-carrying, and walking into a trap.

And she saw all the men and women who were about to lose their children and didn't know it.

She hadn't taken a spear, because she hadn't thought she'd need one. Rummaging through the knocked-apart skin and bones of a nearby hut, she grabbed the curved throwing stick. It was heavy, a hunter's weapon. She knew from experience that it would kill even large animals with a single throw, if you hit them just right in the head.

And she knew how to throw it.

As she and François turned to creep from the forest, a woman lying on the ground reached up to grab Lowanna's hand. "What?" the woman murmured. Lowanna recognized her as a young mother named Zegiga.

A young mother whose two young children were maybe now being stalked by the Sethians.

"There are Ametsu hunting the children," Lowanna whispered. "Shh. Get a spear and come with us."

She led, tiptoeing out across the grassland and looking back at the same time, making sure that the Sethian at the lake hadn't noticed her movement. It would be a disaster if she tipped off the first Sethian, just as it would be a disaster if the Sethians killed the Ahuskay children.

François followed. Zegiga came after, with three other women whose names Lowanna didn't know. They were all young. Were they all mothers? Had they chosen to lie at the edge of the forest to be near their children?

Were they all now panicking?

Goats loped toward Lowanna out of the darkness.

Melon rind is delicious.

I want water.

Lowanna stooped and grabbed the foremost goat by its horns. It was a big old billy with a wise face. "Big Two-Legs," she whispered fiercely, staring it in the face. "Big Two-Legs with the beast face. Are they hunting the children?"

The billy bleated. *One Big Two-Legs. It's almost to the children.*

Lowanna released the goat and ran.

François ran after her. "That was insane! I mean, bad word choice...but...were you just talking with a goat?"

The children and many of the women, especially the older women, had been sent to a small lake two miles away from Ahuskay. The lake wasn't hidden and it wasn't especially sheltered, just a depression beneath three large standing stones where a stream flowing from Ahuskay's lake gathered into a large pond. The depression was deep enough that Marty and the Speakers had decreed that the children could have a fire there. The fire would cook food, drive away wild animals, and keep spirits up.

Had it also attracted the attention of the Sethians?

Or had they tracked the party of the children to their hiding place?

She ran faster. Her lungs pounded, but she knew to a dead certainty that she had never run this fast in her life. She was surprised that François managed to keep pace with her, and exulted to hear the footsteps of Zegiga and the others falling behind.

Which was perhaps a little foolish, since she raced to battle.

A low rise separated her from the depression containing the lake. She splashed across the stream that crossed from her right to her left side, flowing around the mound of earth. She didn't see the Sethian yet, which meant it had to be down in the actual depression. She remembered his height and the muscle mass of the beast that had killed Abdullah, and the fierce primitive look of his fire-hardened spear.

François bent his course and ran around the right side of the depression. Lowanna raced straight as an arrow, up onto the low headland.

She skidded to a stop at the crest, heart pounding. Below her she saw the village's old women huddled in a defiant knot. They held spears upright defensively, and they knew how to use them, but they were small. Before them, back turned to Lowanna, loomed a muscle-bound Sethian with its own spear. Its erect ears made it look eight feet tall, and its head made it look like a monster.

Its kind *were* monsters. Abdullah had died on a spear just like the one Lowanna was looking at now.

Behind the women, the children cringed and wept beside a large fire. There were maybe thirty of them—they were dirty, and wore ragged little tunics like shifts in some Dickensian orphanage. The oldest might have been ten or twelve years old, and they were all thin and tiny.

"Hey, ugly!" she yelled.

She threw her stick.

The Sethian turned at the sound of her voice, raising its muzzle to look for the source of the cry. Her throwing stick struck it in the side of the head. In the shadow, she thought she saw blood on its face and shoulder. Its right ear sagged and it staggered briefly to one knee.

The stick, of course, didn't come back. Real throwing sticks didn't return to you when you threw them. It skidded off the side of his face and disappeared into the darkness.

Lowanna had the initiative, and she wanted to keep it. She hurled herself down the hill, taking the slope in ten-foot bounds that risked breaking her neck or an ankle at each step.

The women behind the Sethian wasted no time. They stabbed the Sethian in the back with their spears. If they were penetrating its skin, Lowanna couldn't tell.

It roared in pain and rage. Spinning around and rising to its feet in one motion, it knocked the weapons from their hands and sent them flying. It strode toward the children, legs covering five feet in a single step.

An old woman stepped into its path. She had lost her spear, but she stood before it with chin turned up and hands raised, yelling at it to stop.

It grabbed her by her hair and spun her in a single violent motion. Lowanna heard her neck snap.

As the other old women scrambled to recover their spears, the Sethian stooped. It took something from its belt and slashed at the dead woman's body.

Lowanna kept running. François burst into view again at her right, still clutching his spear.

The Sethian spun around, hands raised. In one, it held a short, curved knife. In the other, it had a small bit of bloody meat.

The woman's liver.

It sank his teeth into the liver, slurping it quickly into its gullet. Its teeth gleamed red with blood and it emitted a bellowing, bass laugh. The children shrieked and scattered away from the fire, toward the edges of the depression. The women wailed.

François broke out ahead of Lowanna and struck at the Sethian's chest with his spear.

François moved fast, surprisingly fast for the boxy-looking banker he was.

But the Sethian smashed aside the spear with a flick of its wrist, and the weapon flew into the pond. As François charged forward, hands suddenly empty, the Sethian punched him in the face.

François fell to the ground.

The Sethian stepped forward over François's body, blood on its teeth and blood on its knife and a predator's grin on its lips. "Come here, little humans!" it roared to Lowanna and the old women. "Come to me now, all of you. I have belly enough to fit you all, and I have a hunger to end the world!"

CHAPTER FIFTEEN

Marty's eyes blurred. He felt bone weary from having stayed awake for almost two days straight. It was all he could do to focus and keep himself on the path. The green grass to either side rose nearly to the height of his waist. The sky was a deep lavender bruise, mottled with the last, largest stars of the night, and as Marty stared along the trail, the sun rose at its end. For a perfect moment, the sun's golden light poured out across the sky. The light relieved the heaviness of the night, it burned away all the stars, and it blazed at the end of the straight path like the flaming head of an ignited arrow, for a long, perfect moment.

Then the sun and the path both disappeared, and Marty was lying in a dirt trough on a cold hillside.

He had fallen asleep.

He was about to shake himself to chase away the last shreds of sleep when he heard a heavy footfall on the slope below him. Sleepiness vanished.

Marty raised his head slightly from the trough, peering around a large rock. His body was covered by a sheet of rough cloth that had in turn been buried under a thin layer of sand, creating a hiding spot for him, a little like a hunting blind.

He looked down into the ravine. For a moment, he was blinded by the laser, angling up into the night sky. Then he recovered his vision to see Surjan, who lay against the gully wall mostly covered by his cloak. He was a little too short really to pass as a wounded Sethian, but he was taller than most of the others, and he had insisted. His face and feet were hidden, and one arm gripped the Sethian's spear that Surjan had taken. His chest was exposed; the amulet lay on it, firing its beam to the cloudless night sky.

Then Marty saw, just beyond Surjan, an approaching Sethian. This monster, too, was the height and build of an NBA power forward, with broad shoulders and narrow hips. It carried a spear, and a cloak fell from its shoulders to its ankles.

But it was alone.

On the one hand, that should make the battle easier. Marty hadn't relished the thought of battling four of these beasts simultaneously. On the other hand, it meant that there were further battles to be fought beyond the present one. And where were the other Sethians, anyway?

The Sethian called out, words Marty couldn't understand.

As planned, Surjan groaned in response.

The Sethian entered the mouth of the ravine. It slowed its steps, halted, and turned to look behind it. Men lay on the ground, tents burned, and herd animals roamed free. It was a scene carefully set to convince the Sethian that its fellow had come to the village, had a fight, and wreaked great carnage before activating its distress beacon.

The Sethian turned back around to look at Surjan. It raised its spear, couching it like a lance in its elbow and stepping forward as if it intended to poke Surjan.

Then Badis and his men rose up from their fake deaths and yanked the rope.

The loop, hidden like Marty's body under a carefully placed layer of sand and pebbles, closed up around the Sethian's ankles and then snapped tight. The rope was woven; Lowanna had made it, together with a number of the Ahuskay women laboring under her guidance, and it was as thick as a human wrist.

Badis and his men gripped the line with all eight of their hands and dragged the Sethian toward the lake.

Surjan leaped forward. Without bothering to remove the amulet, he attacked repeatedly with the spear. Stabbing overhand, he brought the sharpened point down over and over onto the monster's skin.

The Sethian raged and thrashed, and its skin did not break.

Marty scrambled down the side of the ridge with other warriors at his side. Gunther and others rose and attacked the Sethian. Gunther smashed a rock against the side of the beast's head, and Ahuskay warriors stabbed with stone knives and wooden spears.

The Sethian roared but did not bleed. Rolling onto its back, it lashed out with one hand and grabbed Surjan by the ankle. It dragged the Sikh into a wrestler's embrace and squeezed.

Surjan bellowed, his voice pitched to the same note of rage and hatred as the Sethian's.

They knew—the villagers had warned them and they knew from their own experience—how hard it was to break the skin of one of the Sethians. Water was their second plan; they would drown the beast. Badis and his men sloshed through waist-high water, trampling reeds and churning up mud as they dragged their burden. The Sethian bellowed and rolled again as it hit the lake, thrusting Surjan under the surface.

Gunther threw rocks, hitting the Sethian in the chest and shoulders to no effect. Ahuskay warriors stabbed and slashed, and nothing happened.

The Sethian stood, hauling on the rope. Badis and his men fell into the water. Surjan got his head above water to take another gasp of air and then the Sethian refocused its attention, pushing the Sikh back under.

Surjan had lost his spear in the fray. He thrashed under the water as the Sethian held him down, and Marty finally caught up. He wanted to kick, knowing that his power was in his legs and feeling some confidence in the fact that he'd killed his first Sethian with such an attack. In the waist-high water, though, he couldn't jump, and he couldn't raise his legs to attack quickly, either.

He punched the Sethian in the ribs and in the kidney. He slammed his fists as hard and as fast as he could, landing a flurry of blows such that would have dropped any ordinary man in his tracks.

The Sethian grunted, and didn't fall.

Surjan still thrashed, churning the water, but bubbles weren't coming up anymore. If his lungs were empty of oxygen, he didn't have much time left. Marty grabbed the Sethian by the elbow and stepped on its knees. He planned to lever himself into the air and attack the Sethian's face.

Instead, the Sethian batted him away, sending him flying ten feet. But that action required an arm.

With that one limb pulled away from its task, Surjan broke free. He surged up from the water gasping and grunting, and in his two hands together he held his sharpened ankh.

The Sethian punched Surjan in the face, and in the same moment, Surjan stabbed the Sethian under his ribs with the sharp tip of his ankh.

The ankh penetrated and sank all the way to the crosspiece in the alien flesh.

Surjan spun about with a crack and a splash, and collapsed into the water.

Badis and his men thrashed forward in the lake, trying to regain their end of the rope. Gunther raised a large rock over his head and stepped forward. Marty struggled in the mud to regain his feet and rejoin the fray.

But the Sethian stood still. Blood poured down its side and it stared at the wound. It opened its mouth and blood poured out, sloshing into the churned mud of the lake. Finally, without a sound, it collapsed forward into the water.

Marty rushed toward Surjan. He heard the victory holler of the Ahuskay warriors, and then he saw that the Sethian's skin was shimmering. He dragged Surjan up from the water and saw that the Sikh was breathing, and then a blob of light rose from the Sethian's body.

It drifted into Marty, sending a tingling sensation through him.

The Sethian, floating on its face on the lake, began to melt. Skin sloughed away and disintegrated, the firm and too-muscular flesh seemed to dissolve into sludge before Marty's eyes, and the bleachy-smelling sludge, diluted by the waters of the lake, drifted away in slow, greasy curls. Within moments, the terrifying apparition of the Sethian was entirely gone.

Surjan stirred. "What happened?" he murmured into Marty's shoulder.

Badis knelt, patted around on the bottom of the lake with both hands, and came up with Surjan's sharpened ankh. "You had a magic weapon, my friend," he said. "You didn't tell me."

✛ ✛ ✛

Lowanna scooped the throwing stick off the ground and charged.

The stick was not made to be thrown at this close range. But she could slash with it, and she did, hacking the Sethian in its rib cage.

It responded by slashing at her with its dagger. She managed to throw herself out of reach, and while she lunged a few steps to one side, François was dragging himself to his feet.

"If any of you wishes to flee," the Sethian rumbled, "do so now. I will not pursue you."

Zegiga shrieked and hurled herself forward. Lowanna expected an awkward and untrained lunge, but the woman had clearly used a spear before. She caught the Sethian by surprise, too, and struck it under the arm with the point of her spear.

It clamped its arm down, trapping the spear point. Turning to face Zegiga, it roared at her. It opened its mouth shockingly wide, and Lowanna could see the bloodred flesh of its tongue and the bloodred tissues inside its mouth.

Zegiga didn't let go. She held onto the spear with both hands. The Sethian pivoted, dragging Zegiga sideways across the ground. The movement skinned her knees raw instantly and she left a pink smear of blood on the grass and soil.

And then a second of the young mothers charged with her spear. The third sprang after her at the same instant, and they poked the spears into the Sethian from two different sides. It hissed and spat. "Look!" it bellowed. "You cannot harm me!"

It was true. Its flesh was scratched, maybe, but it wasn't bleeding.

"Help me!" Lowanna cried. "Attack!"

François stared at her and she charged. She leaped and grabbed the Sethian by a long, square-tipped ear, and threw all her weight into it. The monster staggered and slipped to one knee. The women with spears pressed forward and forced it back a pace before it caught his balance.

Then the old women swarmed the Sethian. They issued a ululating war cry, a shuddering vibrato sound that pierced Lowanna's heart, and they grabbed it with their bare hands. Spears abandoned, they tore at its belt and kilt and shoulder band. They tugged at its ears. They took wounds from its jaws and from its swinging fists, but where one fell, there seemed always to be a second.

"The fire!" Lowanna yelled. "Onto the fire!"

François charged back into the fray. "What on earth are you saying?" he demanded.

He stabbed the Sethian with a spear, not breaking the skin again, and then got knocked down for his trouble.

"I'm telling everyone to attack!" she yelled.

The women were swarming the Sethian, but it had regained its balance. It stood just a pace or two from the fire at its back, but now it flung the women away. It hurled Zegiga into the pond and knocked two old women senseless with one swing of its fist.

"Who are you even talking to?" François asked.

We are here.

What?

Lowanna looked around the low depression. The children had vanished, slipping off into the night to escape. But a herd of goats stood arrayed on the low depression, staring down their long muzzles at Lowanna. In the center of their line stood the wise old billy she had spoken to minutes earlier.

"Knock it into the fire!" she cried again, to the wise-faced old billy goat.

The goats charged.

The Sethian stood its ground. Snatching a spear from the earth, it impaled the foremost of the goats, skewering it entirely and sending Lowanna to her knees with a violent wave of nausea. The goat wailed as it died, a human sound that ended in gurgling.

But the second goat butted the Sethian and rocked it on its heels. The third knocked it back a step. And the fourth knocked it over.

The Sethian crashed back onto the fire, sending sparks and small coals flying in all directions. Lowanna jumped onto its chest with both knees. She felt the air leave its lungs just as it tried to howl, and then it and she were both sucking in smoke.

François joined in, poking the Sethian in the belly as if to pin it in place.

Then the women pounced on it again, ululating and shrieking, and this time they hurled stones. Dragged up from the pond or snatched from the sides of the depression, they tossed rocks onto the Sethian's arms and legs and cracked them onto its skull. They seized Lowanna and tried to pull her off, but she refused. Seeing the fleeing children in her mind's eye and hearing the final screams and choking of the impaled goat, she struck the Sethian again and again. François helped, kicking the monster and stabbing it with his spear, and the flailing and grabbing arms thrashed, then became groggy, and finally went still.

A charnel stink of burning flesh rose from the fire and the Sethian's body.

François finally pulled Lowanna away. She fell to the ground and vomited.

She looked up just in time to see the Sethian's body begin to shimmer. The fire was almost entirely buried beneath rocks, only cracks of orange light escaping here and there, but its skin suddenly seemed to glow.

And then a white light distilled itself from the body of the dead Sethian. It drifted toward her, and blinked out of existence the moment it touched her, leaving only a slight tingle in her leg as evidence that it had even been there.

Most of the women were no longer watching. They had already rushed to the edges of the depression to gather up and reassure the children, and to look for further threats.

One woman turned and faced the three standing stones that watched from above. "The gods!" she shrieked. "The gods have delivered our children!"

François laughed. "The gods, and Lowanna Lancaster."

The wise-faced billy licked Lowanna's face and bleated.

Not many Two-Legs speak our tongue these days.

"No, indeed," she said. "Not many. Are there other Big Two-Legs here tonight? Here or at the village?"

Not tonight.

Eventually, François and Zegiga helped her to her feet. She passed the shuffling walk back to Ahuskay in stunned silence, and when she arrived, someone she couldn't see made her drink cold water. Gradually, she found herself standing in a small circle with the Godspeaker, the Tribespeaker, and Marty.

"I failed," she said immediately.

Marty put a soft hand on her shoulder. She wanted to lean against him and wrap herself in a comforting embrace, but kept her feet.

The Godspeaker spat on the ground. The bones pushed through his cheeks quivered with emotion.

"No." The Tribespeaker shook his head. "We killed one Ametsu here at the village. You and your speaker killed the other one at the hiding place of the children. You saved the lives of all our children. You did not fail."

"A woman died before I could save her." Lowanna flinched, remembering the sight of the Sethian slurping down her liver. "I didn't learn her name."

"Her name was Kahina," the Tribespeaker said gently. "She was my mother."

"A life is forfeit." Lowanna found she was crying, and she swallowed, trying to dam the tears. "Let it be mine."

"I knew about my mother's death," the Tribespeaker said. "I heard it from Zegiga. Is Zegiga's a name that you know?"

"Yes," Lowanna said. "She was very brave in rescuing her children."

"Zegiga told me about your reckless courage," the Tribespeaker said. "She told me also that you summoned the animals themselves to fight the battle with us. She told me that you are worthy of my esteem, that you all are. And do you know why I place so much weight in what Zegiga tells me?"

"Because she's fierce and loyal," Lowanna said.

"Yes," the Tribespeaker agreed. "And because she's my wife. There will be no more deaths tonight. The Tribe has spoken."

"Except deaths of Ametsu," Marty said.

The Tribespeaker looked surprised. "You have appetite for more blood, Seer?"

"No," Marty said. "But if we wait, the other Ametsu will realize that we've defeated these two. We can retain the initiative, and maybe catch them by surprise, if we attack tonight."

CHAPTER SIXTEEN

The night was quiet. Marty peered up from the fields just below the Sethian outpost. With the crescent moon now hidden behind clouds, the canyon was shrouded in gloom. He could barely see the ground, much less the two mastabas behind the wall. He turned to Kareem and whispered, "On top of the mastaba on the right, there's a watch tower. Is anyone patrolling, or maybe watching from the tower?"

Kareem craned his neck and frowned. "I see one on the tower."

"A Sethian?" Marty stared up into the darkness and saw absolutely nothing on top of the fifty-foot escarpment.

"I think so." Kareem gasped. "It's wearing a hooded robe."

"Wide horns, or tall ears?"

"I can't tell."

A Sethian. Marty doubted it was one of the cow-headed Hathiru. Either way, it didn't matter. Getting up there without being spotted would be nearly impossible.

Somewhere in the darkness, he heard a low grunting noise. Before he could ask what it was, he heard Lowanna's voice. "Marty, I'm approaching with a couple of friends. Don't make any sudden moves."

It took all of Marty's self-control not to take a step back as a full-sized pig approached. "What the . . . ?" As she came closer, he spotted a few more shadows. She had brought an entire pack of wild boars, tusks and all, with her. "I thought you were going to be back on the other side of the creek with François."

Lowanna stopped with her face less than a foot from his and whispered, "Change of plans. It turns out that the Sethians occasionally like to kill and butcher wild boars. This one"—she turned and patted a large boar's head—"wants to know if we plan to kill the Sethians."

Marty looked back and forth between his crewmate and the one-hundred-pound-plus animal with sharp tusks. "Sethians aren't the only ones who eat pigs, you know."

Lowanna shrugged. "When I hear the pigs are planning to attack *our* camp, I'll let you know."

Gunther whispered, "Twilight Zone, I'm telling you. We're in an episode of *The Twilight Zone.*"

Marty shook his head. "Is that all they played in Germany when you were growing up?"

Gunther shrugged.

Marty took a deep breath and let it out slowly. Then he shifted his attention back to Lowanna. "Okay, Dr. Dolittle, of course we're planning on killing them. The Sethians, I mean."

Lowanna put her hand on his shoulder and gave it a gentle squeeze. "It's okay. They want to help."

"Help?" Marty stared at the creature as it scraped one of its tusks on the ground, digging a deep furrow. "What do I do with wild boars?"

"Keep the plan simple, for starters," she suggested.

Marty considered. Boars were infantry, and melee fighters. You couldn't really hide a mass of them. On the other hand, their first attack would likely be a complete surprise, and could be really demoralizing for the target.

"Can you tell them to spread out down here below the fortress?" he asked. "Then once we get those Sethians to come out, the boars can attack. Or, at the very least, distract them."

"I can ask them," she said. "I talk to animals. I don't command them."

"Brilliant." Surjan piped in from somewhere behind him in the dark. "As long as we humans are focused on the battle and ignore the oinking."

Marty scanned the rest of the crew. "Remember your ankhs. That seems to be the most effective weapon against the Sethians. There's a set of steps going up the outpost gate. I'd expect these things to come rushing down it. Kareem, Surjan, and I will approach the base on either side of the stairs. Lowanna, we don't know how well our targets can see in the dark, but assume they're eagle-eyed like Kareem is, so stay out of sight and do whatever it is you need to with these friends of yours. Gunther, you go back to François and tell him to count to a slow thirty before setting off the light show. We should all be in position by then. Any questions or concerns?"

"What if they stay up there?" Surjan asked. "What's the contingency plan?"

Marty turned to Kareem. "How are you at climbing?"

"Very good."

"If they don't come down, we'll have to go up and get them," Marty said. "Kareem and I will climb the walls on either side. Let Kareem or me start a commotion up there before you try anything else. Make sense?"

Surjan nodded.

Kareem grinned, his crooked teeth glowing in the darkness. "I like this plan, by God."

"Good." Marty took a deep breath.

Marty heard the sound of a cricket to the east and knew Surjan was in position. He turned in the direction he thought François was and waited.

Somewhere in the darkness, he heard a grunt. Then another in a completely different direction. Lowanna was moving boars into position.

A bright red beam of light speared upward. Marty's heart raced as he listened for the sound of any Sethian response.

There was a scraping sound high overhead.

No footsteps.

The light from the beam had its origin in the darkness across the canyon, opposite the fortress. It shot straight up into a cloud, illuminating it with a surreal reddish tinge that cast weird shadows across the ground, and Marty saw moving boar silhouettes trotting in various directions.

He pressed himself against the rocks at the base of the outpost, not sure what to expect, and waited.

Thwack!

A ball of fiery light flew from the fortress in the direction of François's red beam.

Several seconds before impact, the beam blinked off.

Thwack! A second fiery ball was launched from the outpost.

The first projectile crashed into the ground, splashing fire in all directions. Marty shuddered.

Marty grabbed the rough rocks that formed the base of the outpost and scrambled up.

Another *thwack!* and a third projectile.

Killed. Burned to death. All Marty could think of was how he might have just gotten more members of the crew killed as the glow of fire cast dancing shadows on all the canyon's walls.

He was past the rocks and gripping the sandstone slabs that made up the middle portion of the outpost. He was almost thirty feet aboveground, and rushing upward, when he missed a foothold and fell.

He caught himself on a rock with one hand and dangled.

Focusing on one task and only one task, he swung himself around, caught the edge of the sandstone with his other hand, and then got his feet back under him.

More slowly, forcing himself not to worry about François and Gunther, he finished the climb. As he finally reached the top and reached over the wall, he heard a howl of pain.

With his toes firmly planted in the seams of the outpost's wall, Kareem peered up and spotted a Sethian scampering down from the watch tower. Stairs wound around the outside of the tower, he could now see, and more stairs took the Sethian down the side of the mastaba.

Could he really do as he had been asked, could he do as he planned? He was a runner of errands, a motorcycle messenger, a lifter of crates, and a digger of holes. In lean times, and with many prayers for forgiveness, he might even be a picker of pockets.

But a warrior?

With his ankh secured in his belt, he climbed up to the top of the wall. François's red beam of light turned off. The Sethian that had climbed down from the watchtower was less than ten feet away. He was below Kareem, and he looked to his left; he stared up at the cloud that had suddenly gone dark.

This was exactly such a devil as had murdered his uncle. Abdullah had approached the demon in peace and the demon had murdered him with no remorse and with no hesitation.

Now Kareem would kill the devil with no remorse, too. He took the ankh into his hands.

He was no errand boy.

Kareem crouched on the top of the wall. He felt his heartbeat in his thighs as he gathered himself, the ankh gripped tightly for a downward strike.

He would see Abdullah's family again. If not here, then in the world to come, where he would see Abdullah, as well. And he would not be ashamed to hold his head up in the presence of his uncle's family, by God.

The Sethian looked away, toward another demon, this one at the center of the fortress's enclosure. Kareem jumped.

Kareem slammed the sharpened tip of the ankh down into the point where the Sethian's neck and shoulder joined.

The creature let out an earth-shaking bellow of pain and spun around to face Kareem.

But Kareem had expected the monster to react. He remained gripped onto the ankh as his legs were flung outward due to centrifugal force. The force of the motion caused the ankh to slice across the side of the creature's neck, spraying a fountain of blood in all directions.

The demon fell to one knee and Kareem landed on his feet. Other devils would come; he must act fast. He raked the razor's edge of the ankh deeper into the Sethian's neck and then danced back, barely avoiding a swipe from the wounded creature.

As the monstrosity collapsed to all fours, Kareem pulled his ankh-dagger from its shoulder and shoved it into the base of its skull. The snap of bone shattering echoed in the air. He jumped clear as the Sethian's body convulsed.

"For my uncle!"

Kareem spat on the monster. His body tingled and his throat tightened.

It was his first kill of any kind.

It felt good.

He wanted to do it again.

He was a warrior.

Then he saw light beginning to gather on the Sethian's corpse.

Across the outpost, Marty saw Kareem on top of a writhing Sethian, his ankh buried deep into the creature's back.

Carrying a ceramic pot filled with writhing flames, a second Sethian rushed toward his fallen comrade. Marty heard the scraping of hooves on stone.

A compact figure launched itself from the shadow of the fortress gate and slammed into the Sethian, sending the creature and its fiery possession flying back.

The pot crashed to the ground, spewing flaming liquid in an infernal cone.

Marty felt the heat despite the distance. The boar squealed and raced briefly in circles before zooming out of sight, back down the stairs.

The Sethian screamed and thrashed. Liquid fire covered him from his head down to his waist.

Surjan rushed up the stairs and then backed away from the flames. The Sethian lurched to its feet and staggered toward him. He moved back, ankh held before him, to defend Kareem. The burning Sethian fell to its knees and finally toppled forward and lay still.

Marty smelled oil and charred flesh.

Outside the fortress, he heard squeals and more grunting.

Marty rushed past the conflagration just as Kareem hopped off the still body of the Sethian. Kareem stepped away from the corpse, which promptly began to dissolve.

Despite being covered in gore, the young man had a huge smile on his face.

Marty felt a twinge of guilt; he was putting the young man's life at risk, and leading him to commit extreme acts of violence.

But he didn't think he really had much choice.

And was the violence, after all, extreme? Or were Marty and Kareem both acting in defense of the human race?

"Are you okay?" he asked.

Kareem wiped the gore from the ankh on the Sethian's kilt and cape and shot him a thumbs-up.

"Marty!" Surjan called.

Marty turned and saw Surjan, his ankh held up before him, facing off with a dozen of the large cow-headed people now emerging from their mastaba. Marty raced past the flames and the smoking corpse with his own ankh at the ready. "Hold up! Doath—is one of you Doath?"

One of the taller cow-headed people with very widely set horns stepped forward. "I am Doath. Do you remember me? You are the man who climbed the wall. We do not wish to fight. We are watching."

"Watching?" Surjan growled.

"This is their home, too," Marty reminded him. "I remember you," he said to the Ikeyu.

"Marty!" Kareem yelled from the other side of the flames. "Look at the beam."

Marty looked at the place in the eastern sky where Kareem was pointing and saw nothing.

He turned to the cow-people. "Are there any other Ametsu here? We killed four tonight. Two here and two on the prairie."

Doath dipped his horns from side to side, a bit like an Indian head bobble, but slower. "There are two others. They are traveling."

One of those two was likely the first Ametsu they had killed.

But that left one.

"Damn it!" Marty raced toward the stairs. "Surjan, check on François and the others! Kareem, I didn't see that beam! Can you—"

"I'll lead you!" The short young man hopped over the edge of the fire and raced through the gate.

Marty, Surjan, and Kareem spent an hour hunting for the fifth Sethian. Kareem found recent tracks heading eastward along the muddy sections of the creek, but none of them had managed to spot the Sethian, and the tracks eventually disappeared on a broad shelf of stone.

Kareem seemed increasingly fidgety and agitated during the search.

The crew had come out of the encounter unscathed, and had even gained a few baskets of dried beans from the outpost's stash. One of the boars had gotten burned, but Gunther gave it first aid.

No repetition of the glowing Gunther-hands incident.

As Marty relaxed beside the stream, Lowanna sat down beside him. "You did great."

Marty snorted. "I didn't lay a finger on anything. It was one of your pig friends and Kareem who did it all."

"You were the leader." Her voice was soft.

Marty shrugged. "Stop arguing."

The sun rose during their journey back to Ahuskay village. Marty felt tired, but triumphant, and his crew walked with heads held high and steps crisp. It was early morning when Marty and the rest of the team arrived.

Zegiga and Badis met them at the edge of the village. "The Ametsu?" Zegiga asked. "They're dead?"

Lowanna nodded. "Your children are safe."

Zegiga let out ululations of joy. Badis nodded, catching Marty's gaze with a look of grim satisfaction.

Others emerged from their tents and Marty caught sight of the Tribespeaker. He approached the crew with a pleased expression. "So, it is done?"

Marty was careful not to shrug. "We killed two more Ametsu. We believe that all the Ametsu who live in that fortress are dead, save one."

"Then we are not completely safe," the Tribespeaker said.

"The survivor fled eastward," Marty said. "We also travel to the east. We shall try to find that survivor."

"There must be more Ametsu in the east," the Tribespeaker mused.

"Can mankind ever be safe, as long as such creatures walk the Earth?" Marty asked.

The Tribespeaker looped his arm over Marty's shoulder and motioned for the crew to follow. "Come. You all need rest. Tonight, we shall feast."

François walked with Kareem, away from the others. "You seem upset, young man. Is there anything I can do to help?"

Kareem spoke very quietly. "Perhaps I have lost my soul."

"Your soul?" His eyebrows rose. "How so?"

"Killing is forbidden—"

"*Murder* is forbidden," François said. "You have not committed murder."

"I stabbed a man in the back."

"A man?"

Kareem hesitated.

"Not a man," François said. "A monster. A beast. Yes?"

"Yes." Kareem nodded slowly at first, and then eagerly.

"Worse than a beast, a demon. A demon such as the one that came here and tried to murder the tribe's children. A demon such as the one that murdered your uncle, my friend Abdullah. You killed a demon, and you killed it in defense of human life. Had you not killed it, it would certainly have harmed you or others in our crew. Or villagers. Agree?"

"Yes, but . . ." Kareem's voice took on a panicked tone. "I felt good doing it. That makes me wicked."

François smiled and draped his arm over Kareem's shoulder. "Kareem, it does *not* make you a bad person to be pleased that you're helping those who need help. Everyone has a role in life. Some are scholars and their goodness is embodied in their teaching of others. Others are carpenters who make sturdy homes of high quality so that they can be safely sheltered from the sun and the weather. Some people are warriors. You, my friend, are only just now learning your role. It isn't me who will determine your role: follow your skills, do what you're good at, and improve such things through hard work. And the test you can give yourself is a simple one: Is what you're about to do a benefit to a greater number than your not having done it?" He smiled and Kareem smiled back. "You protected Ahuskay. There's no need for guilt. And of course, if you have doubts, I'm always here to talk to."

"My uncle got me this cursed job—I mean, this job. I only have this job because of my uncle. And with him gone . . ."

François stopped and looked Kareem in the eyes. "You're not wrong to think that your position was gained because of the good word of your uncle." He tapped his index finger on Kareem's chest. "But it was *you* who earned the right to stay on the team. And with the way Dr. Cohen described how you dispatched that giant creature, I'd say you've doubly earned your place."

He managed not to laugh as he spoke. Did the young man imagine that François was going to *fire* him?

Kareem looked up at François and grinned. "The demon I killed was pretty big."

François turned Kareem around and they headed back toward the village. "Let's go back before they come looking for us. There may be young women who are anxious to express their gratitude to you. That's one of the occupational risks of being a hero."

François ruffled the young man's hair and grinned. Sometimes he regretted not having a child of his own.

Marty's mouth watered.

On a circular woven mat about ten feet across was a steaming mound of what looked like grains of whole wheat, and a variety of roughly chopped root vegetables. One of the villagers poured a sloshing mound of meat and thickened juices onto the grains. The chunks of fatty meat were roughly chopped into fist-sized portions.

On the other side of the mat, he spotted Lowanna struggling to keep a nauseated expression from her face. He managed not to laugh—she did, after all, look funny. Meeting her gaze, he jerked his head to suggest to her that she leave.

She nodded, took a deep breath, and excused herself.

The Tribespeaker sat next to Marty. He ripped a large chunk of flatbread in half, handing Marty the other half. With a practiced hand, the leader of the village took a smaller piece of the bread, leaned forward and scooped up some of the wheat and a jiggly piece of roasted fat. He turned to Marty and motioned with the food in his hand. "Please, Seer. Enjoy. This is for you and your people."

Marty emulated the Tribespeaker, scooping up what might have been a chunk of potato along with the wheat.

The elder motioned for Marty to eat and he popped the food in his mouth. His eyes widened with surprise as he bit down on the vegetable and it immediately squished into mush. It was an eggplant; Marty loved eggplant.

The Tribespeaker leaned close. "Good?"

Marty nodded as he chewed on the rubbery wheat grains and smiled.

The Tribespeaker popped the fatty morsel into his mouth and motioned for everyone to eat.

"What kind of meat it this?" François asked. "Did you sear it . . . roast it at all first, or just put it into the pot?"

Everyone else dug into the food as Marty went in for another helping. This time he tore off a stringy morsel of meat and popped it into his mouth. It was tender and had a gamey taste to it that reminded him of wild goat or maybe an old sheep. There was no seasoning that he could discern, yet it was the best-tasting thing he'd had since starting this crazy adventure fifteen days earlier.

The Tribespeaker motioned to a group of about ten villagers standing several paces away and turned to Marty. "We are all grateful for your ridding us of the Ametsu, Seer." He motioned to the villagers. "These are members of my tribe who want to help you in your travels."

Marty stared wide-eyed as seven smiling men and three women approached and seated themselves among his crew, joining in the feast. He knew all their faces, but the only one whose name he knew was Badis.

"I don't understand," Marty said.

The Tribespeaker grunted. "For a seer, sometimes your vision is quite dim. My people are grateful, and wish to speed you on your travels."

"Thank you," Marty said. "I think we can defend ourselves."

"There is one Ametsu left to kill," the Tribespeaker said. "At least. Any Ametsu who may live in the east must be discouraged from coming here for vengeance."

The Godspeaker spoke. "Also, we believe that we must tell the tale of this victory far and wide."

"To . . . enhance the fame of Ahuskay Village?" Marty suggested.

"To inspire other men to take up the fight," the Tribespeaker said. "If all men fight, then the Ametsu of the east will not see Ahuskay as a lone rebel to be suppressed. And if all men fight, the Ametsu cannot win."

Badis's eyes gleamed in the firelight. "We do not wish you to have all the fun."

Marty's first instinct was to decline the offer; what would he do with ten warriors, ten more mouths to feed? But the villagers all smiled and their young faces reminded him of undergraduate students.

Marty glanced across the mound of food at François, who nodded. He turned to the Tribespeaker and returned his smile. "That's a very kind offer."

"The Tribe has spoken. The Seer's host has grown by ten."

The Godspeaker leaned over Marty's shoulder to whisper. "Don't worry, they will be well-equipped."

"And we have one more gift for you." The Tribespeaker raised a hand and beckoned.

Zegiga approached, holding a folded cloth. Bowing, she opened it, revealing a long strip with loops at one end. The cloth was undyed linen, but neatly stained into its upper center were two circles, side by side.

"A banner," Marty murmured.

François laughed and clapped. "The symbol is perfect!"

Two circles? How were two circles perfect?

Not two circles.

The banner showed the infinity symbol of the Ametsu, broken in half. Marty chuckled. "It is a fit banner for those who would march to war against the liver-eaters," he agreed.

One of the women in the group had sat next to Surjan. She was tall and muscular, with a high forehead and wide-set eyes. Now she looked up at the big man. "I have seen you . . . you are the warrior. I am Tafsut, and I will fight beside you."

Surjan furrowed his eyebrows and shook his head. "You can't be serious." He glanced over at Marty and then shifted his gaze back at the woman, who was probably in her early twenties.

The woman's nostrils flared and she boldly returned Surjan's scowling gaze. "Do you want a contest of spears to prove I am worthy?"

"Contest of spears . . ." Surjan's scowl was overtaken by a beet-red blush. "Oh, bollocks."

The woman smiled and patted his arm. "I will not hurt you." She reached down to a tray filled with flatbread, grabbed one of the pita-like items, ripped it in half, and handed a piece to Surjan. "We have a long trip. Eat, you will need your strength."

Marty probably turned purple as he tried not to laugh. But as he watched all of the new members of the extended crew eat and attempt some amount of small talk with the others, he worried about what lay ahead.

There were thirty-nine days left before his vision came to an end. And in the end, hopefully was a return back to civilization, though he had no idea how. But if he was taking these people away from the village that he presumed they were born in, what about them? Things had suddenly become more complicated.

There was likely at least one Sethian out there or more that wanted them dead. The hairs on the back of his neck stood on end at the thought.

It was pointless to worry about the end of the trail, especially since Marty knew there were dangers lurking out there . . . and with a larger group, they were now a larger target.

As the feasting broke up for the evening, Marty saw Kareem slinking off into the trees with a young woman. Surjan's new acquaintance Tafsut led him in a different direction. François sat at a smaller fire with three women, telling them some story that provoked repeated gales of laughter.

"Good," Gunther said, appearing at his shoulder. "Let people unwind." The German sipped something fruity-smelling from a skin.

"I was thinking the same thing," Marty said. "What about you?"

"In this day and age?" Gunther laughed softly. "No, I don't think so. No need to call attention to myself. I'll unwind with a little wine and a good night's sleep."

"That sounds good," Marty agreed.

"Does that sound good to . . . Lowanna?" Gunther asked.

"What? Ah . . . Lowanna is great, I just . . . that would be very awkward."

"Would it?" Gunther drank a little more wine. "None of my business."

The German wandered away into the night.

CHAPTER SEVENTEEN

It had been five days since they'd left the village and Surjan worried about the Ahuskay warriors who'd joined them. They were deadly enough—they all had spears, and some had bows or slings, too—but their presence didn't make him feel more comfortable. The villagers who had joined them were all in their physical prime, late teens through mid-twenties, but they were having trouble with the pace that the crew set.

Even François, a man in his sixties, was putting the recruits to shame.

It was late in the day and Kareem was lighting the evening's fire while the rest set up camp and the newcomers groaned about their legs.

Marty stood watch apart from the group on a short rise, kneading his new banner. He carried it himself, folded up and out of sight, and wouldn't let Badis raise it on a pole for him.

Standing with his spear in one hand, Surjan watched over the group and their immediate surroundings. He shifted his gaze in François's direction and listened to the man sing some folk song as he prepared the group's evening meal. The sound was compelling, though the words were strange.

"That's not French," Surjan said.

François shook his head. "Breton. My grandmother only ever spoke French to policemen and tax collectors, and she always spat on the ground when she was forced to do it."

The banker had hired him to see to the crew's security, and Surjan still felt an obligation to carry out that mission. But the man he'd considered his boss was not the same person he'd first met a few months earlier.

At first, he'd thought it was his imagination tricking him, but now it was undeniable. Nobody would believe now that François was a man in his sixties. The wrinkles on his face, the jowls along his cheek line, they were gone. His belly was gone. He'd regrown hair, and it was blond. He looked at least twenty years younger.

His temperament had also undergone a marked shift. After Abdullah's death, François had become quieter. Initially, he had seemed morose, which was understandable since the man had lost someone he'd evidently cared for, but now his entire demeanor was different. He was still a font of random pieces of information and wasn't shy about sharing it, but he always took a step back. He was less assertive than he had been, and preferred to do what many might have considered to be the thankless jobs.

Cooking was one of those. He'd adopted the role of the group's cook, without invitation.

Had he given up the idea of being leader, and found something else to take its place?

Tafsut approached. She leaned her spear on her shoulder.

"Surjan, let's fight."

Surjan stared at the young woman and showed no reaction. The others, or at least some of them, had caroused with the villagers on their last night at Ahuskay. Surjan had caroused also, but then his carousing partner had come with them.

It felt like a breach of discipline.

"Not a love fight, you fool. Spear practice." Tafsut walked within arm's reach and looked into his eyes. "Well? Don't just stand there, let's fight."

He had a foot of height on her and was twice her weight. As she swapped her long spear from one hand to the next and back again, she maintained eye contact, showing no fear.

It felt like a breach of discipline, but it was an exciting breach.

"No wounding," he said. "Only spear-to-spear contact."

Tafsut took two steps back and twirled her spear like a baton. "I'm ready when you are."

Surjan swung the butt end of his spear at the woman.

With a loud wooden *thwack*, their spears met.

With a practiced swirling motion, she pushed his spear away and attacked with an unexpected ferocity.

He found he was smiling, and pressed his attack in turn.

The sound of the wooden spears slamming into each other at an ever-increasing pace began to attract attention from the others.

Using footwork that he'd practiced for many hours on the hot, hard-packed dirt of his family's yard in Chandigarh as a kid, Surjan pushed Tafsut back. She was as skilled as he was, and maybe more. But he was a little faster and a lot stronger and he had much longer arms. After she tapped him with the butt of her spear on his shoulder, he decided that he wanted to win.

His attacks grew fiercer and harder. When they made contact, she was knocked back.

Men gathered in a loose circle around them to watch.

Tafsut's eyebrows furrowed with a look of concentration as she worked her spear low and then high, pulling back just enough to block Surjan's attacks. She began to slow down. The effort was taking its toll.

Then her offense disappeared. Without the reserves to press him back, she was solely on defense, and began steadily to retreat.

After five minutes of constantly fending off his sweeping attacks and having to block his never-ending barrage of slashes, the young woman's face was beet red and drenched in sweat.

Surjan stopped and stepped back. "Enough."

She panted for breath, but smiled. "Enough for now."

Some of the warriors cheered. Marty clapped.

"Well done, you two!" Gunther yelled from across the camp.

The woman kicked at the dirt and looked away.

Surjan extended his hand toward Tafsut and smiled. "You fight almost as well as a man."

She clasped his forearm with a sweaty grip and grinned. "So do you."

Marty smiled as François sprinted toward the palm trees a quarter mile ahead. Since having arrived in this version of reality, each of the crew members had undergone changes. For some the changes were subtle, but for others, like François, it was as if he'd turned back time on himself. He looked like a man half of his sixty-something years.

And even though Marty didn't have a mirror, he felt like a younger—no, not younger, a *better* version of himself. He couldn't remember a time when he'd felt as strong, as clearheaded, and as full of energy as he did now.

But he wasn't sure his newfound energy was up to the burden of his responsibility. Regardless of whether he wanted it or not, he found himself the leader of this growing group of people, and they were on a mission. Every morning he woke to the same repeated dream, and if it was to be believed, they had thirty-three days left before coming to the end of that vision.

What might happen afterward was a question he'd pondered since the moment they'd arrived.

"Woo-hoo!" François jumped up and plucked something from one of the trees.

Marty jogged toward the palm trees as the others began clearing a space for the evening's camp. "What's got you so excited?"

François jumped again and snagged a low-hanging branch. "Dates, Marty." He plucked a wrinkled fruit from one of the branches he'd pulled down and popped it into his mouth. He made a moaning noise and his eyes rolled up into his head. "Oh my word, it's been so long since I've tasted anything sweet." He handed one to Marty.

The shriveled brown fruit was large, about the size of Marty's thumb. As he bit down carefully on the end, his teeth pierced the rubbery skin and he tasted what reminded him of a mixture of brown sugar and caramel. It was decadent beyond words.

François continued collecting dates as Lowanna approached.

Marty rolled the pit around in his mouth, trying to extract every last ounce of goodness. Lowanna wrinkled her nose.

"I think Surjan's right." Lowanna veered away from the trees and aimed for a particularly lush patch of the grassland, sniffing the air. "He said there's water somewhere near the surface and now I can smell it, too."

Lowanna began picking through the grasses, examining the ground. One of the warriors broke away from the group at the campsite and headed in Marty's direction.

"Marty," François called, "you need to take a look at this stone."

Marty turned to see François heaving an armload of date-laden branches over his shoulder.

He began walking toward François when the villager jogged forward and called out, "Seer, is there anything I can do to help you?"

Without looking back, he pointed in Lowanna's direction and said, "Go help her with whatever she needs."

Marty fast-walked over to François as he pulled down one more branch filled with dates. The Frenchman tilted his head toward the base of the palm tree. "I figured you might be able to get something out of that. I'm going to go prepare the meal and see what I can do with these dates."

François adjusted his unwieldly load and walked away. Marty knelt at the base of the tree to study a boulder with a flat vertical surface that looked like a slate chalkboard, marked with glyphs.

As Marty focused on the markings, he heard a shout followed by a splash. He turned in the direction of the noise and saw Lowanna helping the soaking wet villager scramble out of a pool of water. The pool had been concealed by a thick layer of underbrush until the Ahuskay youth had stepped through it.

Lowanna caught his gaze and with an amused expression yelled, "Munatas found the water!"

He shot her a thumbs-up and turned his attention to the markings on the stone. Some of the marks were etched into the stone, while others looked as if they were written with chalk.

The markings struck him as comprising a map.

On it were two deeply etched intersecting lines and radiating outward from that intersection there was a spiderweb of thinner etched lines, each of which led to a symbol. Some of the symbols looked like trees, so maybe they indicated oases, but other symbols were indecipherable. Next to the unfamiliar symbols were a varied number of slashes that looked to be . . . Marty touched one of the white markings on the gray slate and it wiped off easily.

It was definitely chalk.

Marty looked up as several Ahuskay warriors approached, each carrying a pair of clay jugs. "Munatas! Can you come here?"

The young warrior jogged over, sandals sloshing. He was gangly and big-eared, with a grin that rarely left his face. "Yes, Seer?"

Marty pointed at the rock. "Do you recognize this?"

Munatas crouched low and tilted his head as he studied the stone. "Yes. This is a merchant's tally." He leaned over and pointed at one of the symbols near the edge of the map. "This is our village. And we are now near the crossing." The young man turned and pointed to the east. "About two hundred paces that way is a north-south road. I've been to the village north of the intersection once when I was young."

With a surging interest in what the young man knew, Marty pointed at the chalk marks. "If the symbols are villages, what are these markings for? Some villages have none, some have multiple."

"Oh, that's the tally. They are marks for other merchants to know whether or not a village has been visited recently. This stone tells merchants where to go next, otherwise a merchant would waste a lot of time going to villages who don't yet need his products."

Marty stared at the map, noting which villages had more marks than others. "So, when a merchant decides to visit a village, he places a mark on the stone?"

"Yes. Merchants talk, Seer. How else could they be merchants? Do they not talk in your land?"

"They do." Marty nodded. "What if it rains? Or animals rub against the stone and erase the marks?"

The villager shrugged. "I'm not sure. I guess they just have to visit the village and risk wasting some time. But some talking is better than no talking."

Marty grinned at the creativity involved in solving such a basic problem. How do you know what village is most likely to need a merchant's attention without being able to reach out and call them? Such a simple thing had to be a huge boon to a merchant's daily travel.

He pointed at the tablet, dragged his finger from west to east, and asked, "Do you recognize any of the places ahead?"

Munatas shook his head. "Other than the one village I visited as a child, I've never been farther from home than we are now."

Marty motioned toward some of the others who were filling jugs with water. "Have they?"

The villager shook his head. "I doubt it. My father's uncle's wife's brother is a merchant and we were visiting him. The rest of my people are all farmers. They only travel long distances to get a bride, or to visit a holy place."

"Well, thank you for the help." Marty pointed at the jugs the young man was carrying. "That's all I needed, you might want to put those jugs to good use."

"You are very welcome, Seer." Munatas smiled and walked to where Lowanna was directing the villagers on filling the jugs.

Marty looked down at the tablet, examined the markings of a few villages ahead, and wondered what they might run into.

Marty nibbled on the freshly baked date bread that François had prepared and savored the chewy bits of sweet dates. The tiny pieces of chopped fruit reminded him of a hearty, full-bodied raisin. It was almost sunset and the shadows were growing ever longer as the group finished their meal.

Looking across the camp he spotted the tall Sikh sitting cross-legged with his food bowl in his lap and wiping up whatever was left with a piece of flatbread.

Sitting next to him was the female villager who'd taken an interest in the ex-soldier. Marty chuckled as he watched Surjan stand, the woman mimicking his every move.

With his stomach full, Marty opened his pack and removed the bundle of flatbread he'd saved for traveling. He probably should have eaten it instead of the fresh date bread, but the temptation of eating something with a little sweetness had been too much.

Unwrapping the bread from his pack, he found mold on one of the pieces. With a sigh, he pulled that one out and inspected the rest. They seemed fine and he rewrapped both the fresh and semi-stale bread.

Marty picked up the moldy bread and scanned the camp until he found François fumbling with something in one of the two packs he carried.

He walked over to the Frenchman, sat next to him, and handed him the bread. "You still using the moldy bread?"

François tilted the bread at an angle and looked closely at the mold. With one hand he held the bread; in the other was a small stick that he used to rub away a layer of the mold.

"What are you looking for?" Marty asked.

"Well, since we don't exactly have a microscope or any of the normal ways to isolate the penicillium mold, I'm scraping away the stuff that doesn't look right, leaving just the bright green or blue-green mold."

"And that's the color of what turns into the antibiotic we all know and love?"

François made a so-so motion with his hand. "It's the best I can do given the circumstances. I'm trying to concentrate some of this and I'll do some testing later to see if I can isolate the right strain of the good mold." He opened a smaller pack—inside was a collection of bread, all of which was covered with greenish mold.

"Do you think what you're doing could work?"

"Of course." The Frenchman carefully deposited Marty's bread into the pack and closed it once again. "I've actually done this before, ages ago . . . or ages from now, if you prefer. Let's hope we don't need it, because I'm sure it'll taste horrible."

Marty stared at the financier and shook his head. "You've *made* antibiotics before? How? Why?"

François looked over at him and smiled impishly. "I wasn't always digging in the dirt, you know."

"Gunther said you spent some time at school before becoming a banker. Where did you study?"

"Ah, well that's a simple question with a complicated answer. I did my undergraduate work at the California Institute of Technology, mainly focused on astrophysics."

Marty stared dumbfounded at the man. "You studied physics at CalTech? So, how did that lead you to growing antibiotics?"

"Astrophysics, to be precise." François wagged a finger in his direction. "And to be honest, I've lived a privileged existence, so for me school was an escape from being a responsible adult. I was sort of a professional student from the time I was eighteen until I was about forty. Somewhere along the way I dabbled in the biological sciences."

"Twenty-two years? Good lord, how many degrees did you end up *dabbling* for yourself?" Marty stared.

"I didn't earn nearly as many degrees as you might think. I wasn't really looking for the degrees themselves, I was looking for knowledge. You know, audit this seminar, enroll in that class . . . In some cases, the school wouldn't let me take certain courses without taking a list of prerequisites. So, I suppose the degrees came more by accident than on purpose. Unlike you, *Dr. Cohen*, I never got a PhD in anything. Did a bunch of business school courses, which eventually led to me becoming an investor. Several bachelor's level degrees, a master's in chemistry, and I suppose I'm ABD in astrophysics as well."

ABD was shorthand for "all but dissertation," which meant that François had taken all the coursework necessary for a doctorate, but hadn't completed the requisite dissertation.

"I suppose in that mix was a biology class or two?"

François grinned. "Probably. Oh, and a few metallurgy classes. That was a lot of fun. I have a nice forge at my home outside of Paris. I know this all sounds eccentric, but I was enjoying myself, and I figured what better thing is there but to learn as much as you can and then try to use it."

"This is what you meant by jack-of-all-trades in science and engineering," Marty said.

"That, and I can cook." François leaned closer to Marty and whispered, "I never thought I'd get a chance to do what we're doing now. I have so many thoughts about what we might be going through . . . there's something very wrong about what's happening to all of us. Marty, I'm sure others have told you, but you look fantastic. You easily look ten years younger despite all that we've been through. And I know"—François raked his fingers through his blond hair—"I can't see myself in a mirror, but you all tell me I'm looking like a kid again. Hell, I've got more hair up top now than I did when I was forty."

Marty frowned at the thought he looked younger. Nobody had told him anything, but he certainly felt better in almost every conceivable way than he had in years. "Do you have any theories about what we're going through?"

He shrugged. "Somehow our bodies are repairing themselves." François held up his hand as Marty opened his mouth. "An example I haven't already shared. Ages ago I tore my meniscus in a skiing incident. It never fully healed and it hurt like a bugger. But that ache is gone. In fact, it was gone within a day or so of us arriving to this crazy situation we find ourselves in. Given the short period of time that it took for me to feel the difference, it's not what we're eating. And I fail to understand how it could be the air or the water."

"I suffered from fatigue," Marty said. "Vanished."

"You see?"

"Well, what could it be?" Marty had been pondering the same question for a while.

François opened and closed his hand and then showed the palm of his right hand. "Do you remember that burn we all had?"

"The one from the ankh? It went away pretty quickly." In fact, Marty couldn't remember the burn bothering him after the first few minutes.

"Yes. And how it looked like the gold had drained from the ankh into our hand? Anyway, I suspect that some of the symptoms we're experiencing are probably from whatever that gold stuff was." François took on a serious expression. "Think about it. We all saw the golden ankh. We all felt it do something to us. And we're all seeing changes." François leaned back and looked up into the darkening sky. "But this is all for the best?"

Marty laughed, a hollow sound. "It seems pretty premature to make that call."

François shrugged. "I've always believed in God, but it was almost as an academic thing. I chose to believe because there are some things I don't want to be left to chance. Either way, I'm a believer in a higher power, and I don't think he or she or it would have put us into this situation without a reason."

"You believe in destiny?" Marty asked.

"Maybe. Also, I believe in purpose, which is not exactly the same thing. Remember the tablet you read? It talked about a battle. That maybe we're being tested."

"To what end?" Marty frowned. "It certainly couldn't be the fate of humanity . . . I know the tunnel made it sound like the Apocalypse, but how could that even be possible?"

"It could be the fate of humanity," François said. "That might be exactly what's at stake. These Sethians, why do we fight them?"

"They fought us first," Marty said.

"And?"

"They're evil," Marty said. "They enslave humans and eat our livers."

"And in this world, if they're not stopped . . . might they destroy the human race?"

Marty hung his head. "They might."

"There you go, then." François shrugged. "We're saving the human race, we the dig crew together with this little host we accidentally recruited. And something important to that quest is supposed to happen in thirty-three days."

Marty snorted. "They're not much of a host."

François nodded. "Not yet."

⪡ CHAPTER ⪢
EIGHTEEN

Marty focused on the mental image he'd captured of the merchants' map-boulder. In the intervening three days, they'd walked past two villages that had been marked on the map, and were completely abandoned. Aside from empty mud-brick homes and farmland that had been almost taken over by encroaching sand dunes, there was nothing to see. No food. Not a single piece of unbroken pottery or any valuables that might be usable for trade.

As they walked farther east, the terrain had become noticeably drier, which was a concern. They'd found food by hunting and managed to preserve a few hundred pounds of meat for their journey. Marty worried they'd run out of water.

As the group crested a shallow rise, Marty spotted a few palm trees in the distance. This wasn't listed on the map. They were past the map, and beyond the personal knowledge of the warriors of the host.

Surjan walked up to Marty and spoke with a hoarse whisper. "I smell trouble up ahead."

Marty gave the tall Sikh a sidelong glance. "Literally? What is it that you're smelling?"

"I smell blood."

A cold sensation washed over Marty and he focused on the terrain ahead.

"I can smell the copper in the air," Surjan continued. "Something is dead, and it bled out recently."

"Could it be antelope?" Marty asked.

Surjan hesitated. "I don't think so."

Marty crouched low and everyone stopped. "Surjan, tell everyone to back up and stay behind the rise. Let's not make anyone aware of our presence yet."

As the Sikh herded everyone back, Marty scanned the group and settled on his Egyptian companion. "Kareem." He curled his finger at the young man, who approached. "You've got better eyes than I do, tell me what you can see."

Kareem's focused on the land ahead of them. After about ten seconds, he frowned. "I see movement near the palm trees. Looks like people and . . ."

"Sethians or people people?"

Kareem shook his head. "I think I see six people and a camel."

Marty looked over his shoulder and motioned for Surjan to come back.

The tall man bent low and scrambled forward, crouching beside Kareem.

"Can you tell what direction you smell the blood coming from? Is it from the direction of the oasis?"

Surjan took a deep breath and shrugged. "The wind has changed. I don't smell it anymore." He pointed to the east. "But the wind was coming from that general direction before. It could be the oasis, or somewhere else in that general direction."

François walked forward and said, "Are we going around them or trying to meet with them? I guess I don't understand why the sudden concern. There are sixteen of us, they should be the ones who are nervous."

Marty sighed. "Let's approach, but be ready for anything."

Tafsut, standing next to Surjan, turned and made a cutting motion with the tip of her spear.

Two Ahuskay warriors strung their bows and moved to the wings as the group began moving forward.

Surjan hung back a bit and began giving instructions to the group. "Spread out. If there's trouble, we make an easier target if everyone is standing next to each other."

As they got closer, Kareem walked up to Marty and whispered, "It definitely looks like six people. I don't think they're Sethians, praise be to God . . . unless these are short, fat Sethians."

Marty focused on the scene ahead as they walked toward the oasis. At about one hundred yards, it was clear that his group had the undivided attention of the people standing in the shadows of the palm trees.

All six ragged-looking men were armed, with spear, sword, or bow. In fact, two of them had strung their bows and nocked arrows, and appeared to be aiming in Marty's general direction.

François's greeting boomed across the sandy plains. "Greetings, fellow travelers, we come in peace. Lower your weapons so we can talk."

Something about the Frenchman's voice had a profoundly soothing effect on Marty. So much so that it took all of his will to keep his eyes on the men ahead of them instead of looking in François's direction.

However, three of the men at the oasis lowered their weapons and did turn to face François.

One of the others yelled something unintelligible and whipped something in the Frenchman's direction. Immediately, two arrows flew from Marty's group directly at the attacker.

One of the men tried pulling at the camel, which bellowed in protest and refused to move. Then he shoved his own spear through the camel's neck.

The camel collapsed in a fountain of blood. The camel driver and the other men raced south away from the oasis and Marty's group.

Some of the villagers began chasing the men. Surjan yelled at the top of his lungs, "Do not follow them!"

The warriors halted as the tall Sikh took charge.

"That may be exactly what they want. There may be traps. There may be others out there. Do *not* give them the advantage, do you hear me? Secure the oasis!"

Over the cacophony of voices, Gunther yelled, "François!"

Marty turned and a chill raced through him.

François was holding his arm as blood streamed down from the tips of his fingers.

He'd been hit.

Gunther raced to François's side as the Frenchman sat down on the ground, staring wide-eyed at the sudden appearance of his own blood. "It'll be okay." Gunther knelt, cutting open François's sleeve with his ankh.

François's voice quavered. "I barely felt anything, it happened so quickly."

Tearing open a wider hole in the sleeve, Gunther felt for the source of the bleeding and found a short metal spike buried in François's upper arm.

The smooth metal shaft practically fell out of the wound as soon as he touched it and the blood gushed from the pencil-diameter wound at an alarming rate.

"I'm starting to feel nauseated," François said as he closed his eyes.

With his right hand, Gunther squeezed just above the wound, trying to stanch the flow of blood as his heart raced with worry. As a medic in the German army, he'd seen similar wounds. With such a seemingly minor wound gushing blood in spurts, the spike had undoubtedly pierced the brachial artery. François would bleed out in a matter of minutes.

Focusing on the wound, Gunther fumbled for the strip of cloth he had in his back pocket, all the while squeezing François's upper arm as hard as he could. The German's heartbeat thundered in his ears as his skin tingled and his mind flashed back to that moment when Marty had cut himself at the rocky outcropping. He'd gripped Marty's cut, just trying to hold it closed until he could seal the wound, and then warmth had connected him to Marty . . . and the cut had shut.

Gunther felt the hairs on the back of his neck stand on end as a strange tingling sensation washed over him, and he tried not to panic as he focused on François's arm. He touched the gushing wound and the tingling in his body intensified. Heat flooded through his chest, down his arm, and into his hand.

Through the thundering sound of his heartbeat, he saw his hand glow with an eerie incandescence.

Gunther slid his grip down to the wound and wondered . . . how was it possible?

He willed the warm sensation flooding through him to go into the wound.

He had no idea what he was doing, or how it worked. But he had confidence that he could heal by touch, that his healing gift was part of some new skill almost seemed natural, as if it was meant to be.

François's bleeding slowed and then stopped.

The glow faded and a wave of exhaustion fell over Gunther.

François looked at his arm and grew pale. "What did you do?"

Gunther blinked his eyes and shook his head. He wiped the wound with a clean cloth from his back pocket and smiled.

He stood. He chuckled and shook his head, short on words.

"What?" François looked at his arm and flinched as he pulled out the projectile that had fallen down to the end of his sleeve. He held up the six-inch-long metal dart. "It was this that hit me?"

Marty rushed over and knelt by François. "Do we need a tourniquet?" He unbuckled his belt and Gunther put his hand on Marty's. Gunther laughed almost hysterically. "What?"

"It's healed," Gunther said.

Marty's face held a surprised expression. He leaned closer and probed François's arm for a full ten seconds before he looked back and forth between the Frenchman and Gunther. "I can't find a wound. All that blood and stickiness, but no wound."

Gunther helped Marty and François stand.

Surjan raced to them, wide-eyed. "François—"

"He's going to be fine." Marty motioned toward the oasis. "What's the story with the blood you smelled?"

Surjan continued to focus on François. "Are you sure you're okay? Your sleeve is a mess."

François smiled and patted the big man on his arm. "I'm a little woozy, but Gunther managed to patch me up. I probably need to get started on the meal—"

"Gunther didn't patch you up," Surjan said.

"No," François said. "Apparently, Gunther can heal by the laying on of hands. Of all your gifts, the most useful. No offense to the rest of you."

"You need rest, someone else will cook." Surjan shook his head and raised his eyebrows in surprise. "Some of the warriors are butchering the camel, so there'll be kebabs." He turned to Marty. "As to what I'd smelled, we found a body. I think that group came upon some hapless traveler and murdered him for whatever valuables he possessed. I'd wager that one of those possessions was that camel they ended up killing." He offered François his arm. "Let's get you by the fire."

Gunther watched as the head of security escorted the wobbly financier toward camp.

Marty scanned the blood-spattered dirt and turned to Gunther. "I don't understand. It looks like he spilled pints of blood, but you managed to heal him." He snapped his fingers. "Just like that."

Drawing the ankh from his makeshift holster, Gunther pressed his index finger against the tip hard enough to draw several drops of blood. "I'll show you."

Sheathing the ankh, he used his other hand to press on the cut finger and tried summoning that warm tingling sensation. As he focused on the cut, a few drops of blood dribbled down his finger. He felt a dull ache bloom at the back of his head as he continued trying to summon the glow he'd just recently willed into existence.

Marty furrowed his brow, but he remained silent.

After a full minute of trying to pull something out of the same well and only getting a headache for his trouble, Gunther harrumphed. He stuck his finger in his mouth to suck on the wound. "I don't know. I felt really tired after healing him. Maybe I'm drained. Maybe I used it up."

Marty smiled and draped his arm over Gunther's shoulder as they began walking toward camp. "Lucky for François, that you had it to use up. Lucky for all of us, that Kareem has eagle eyes and Surjan has the nose of a bloodhound and Lowanna hears animals talk."

"And you know kung fu."

"Well, I always knew kung fu."

Gunther nodded. "You know, once I left the Army, I didn't think I'd be fixing up patients ever again."

Marty laughed. "We have thirty days left on this journey. I'd be surprised if we *don't* have occasion to call on your gift again."

Gunther nodded. That was what he was afraid of. Was the healing a fluke? Could he do it again, on command? And if he could, what if when it was needed, it wasn't enough?

Lowanna was missing at the campfire, so Marty went looking for her. He found her a hundred yards away, staring into the darkness alone.

"You missed the excitement," he said. "Gunther laid hands on François and healed him. Neat as any serpent handler."

Lowanna turned and looked directly at him. In the reflected glow of the lights of camp, she looked like a woman made of gold. "Is that how François ended up a bloody mess, but didn't seem any worse for wear?"

Marty leaned closer. "You don't seem surprised. I mean, it looked like a dart had punctured one of François's arteries. That man should be dead, yet somehow, without even a tourniquet, Gunther managed not only to stanch the flow but François looks like nothing happened. Not a hole in his skin, not a scratch, not even a bruise. Just the bloody mess. Don't you think that's a bit nuts?"

Lowanna shrugged.

What mistake had Marty made?

"I'm not saying it's more impressive than what you do," he said. "I mean, even without the talking with animals stuff. Your wilderness skills alone have saved us many times. And yes, you have gained some undeniable . . . special . . . powers. I'm jealous."

Her expression stayed distant. He didn't seem to be digging his hole any deeper, he was just digging on a completely different planet from where the hole was.

"What's wrong?" he asked.

"I'm sorry." She grabbed his calloused hands. "I have mixed feelings about Gunther saving François's life."

"I don't think you really mean that."

"I only joined this dig for the money," Lowanna said.

"Yeah," Marty said. "Me too."

"It wasn't even to get rich, though," she pressed. "My family . . . needed the cash. This was the only way I could help."

Marty resisted the temptation to tell his own story. "You did a good thing."

"And he's lorded it over me." Lowanna sighed and squeezed his hands. "He did it more before you had joined the team. The guy's a total wanker. He always treated me like a lesser part of the team. He felt it was my role to make tea and coffee whenever he wanted it, and I'll be damned, I actually did it."

"You did that for your family, too."

"Yeah."

"He didn't ask anyone else?" Marty didn't doubt Lowanna; he had confidence in François's ability to be a callous jerk evenhandedly to the entire crew.

She shook her head. "Snide sexist comments all the time. I'd lose my girlish figure if I ate too many of those hard candies in the break room. How lucky I was to be hanging out with a bunch of men. Which did I find sexier, his money or Surjan's muscles."

"Maybe it's not so much that he's sexist," Marty said, "as that he's French."

Lowanna laughed. "I'm embarrassed because I let him treat me like that for a paycheck."

"You didn't do it for a paycheck." Marty gave Lowanna's hands a squeeze and felt himself flush with warmth as she stepped closer.

"So I guess I'm not especially excited that Gunther healed him. I mean, yay, Gunther . . . but . . ."

She was tall, and she stared directly into his eyes.

They were alone. She was beautiful.

The two of them were so close, they were breathing each other's air.

"I understand," Marty said. "I should have objected back at first. I noticed that he said a few things that might have been off-color. I'm sorry."

Lowanna slid one hand up onto his shoulder. "You noticed? You pay attention to me?" A sly expression bloomed on her face.

She slid her other arm around Marty's waist and pulled him in for a kiss.

The world stopped.

Her supple lips, the probing tongue, the primal urgency as she pressed against him . . . she took Marty's breath.

And just as quickly, Lowanna pulled back. "No. I can't do this."

Marty blinked.

Lowanna cupped his chin with one hand and smiled. "I'd take you right here, right now, but I can't risk getting pregnant in this place."

Marty nodded dumbly. She leaned her head against his shoulder and spoke softly.

"This place is completely bonkers. I had an implant put in just before coming to Egypt, a girl can never be too prepared. And that damned thing somehow wormed its way out of my arm after being here only a day or so. They're not supposed to do that."

"Implant? I don't understand."

Lowanna chuckled and gave Marty a hug. "A contraceptive. They last two or three years and are implanted just under the skin. Mine was in for a solid two months and out it came."

She took a step back and stared at Marty with dark eyes. "I'm not one for public displays of affection, if you know what I mean . . ."

Marty laughed. "It's dark, I don't think anyone can see."

Lowanna grinned, then looked down at her feet. "Maybe we should check in with the team again. On what everyone's experiencing, I mean. Gunther can heal . . . what else has happened?"

Marty tried not to frown. "You're not going to tell people about your contraceptive . . . or that we kissed . . . are you?"

Lowanna pinched Marty's cheek. "That's what I like to see, a man off balance and uncertain. Let's head back and talk with the others."

As most of the villagers lay on reed mats to sleep, the crew sat in a circle away from the campsite, sharing new developments in their experience.

Lowanna shared what she'd been hearing from animals recently.

"Woah!" Gunther shook his head. "That still amazes me."

"Says the guy who healed François by touch." She laughed. "Sadly, they don't tend to say much of interest, most of the time. They're tactical and immediate, they have short horizons."

Marty motioned to Kareem. "How about you? Any new abilities, sensations, anything out of the ordinary?"

The youngest member of the crew shrugged. "My vision is good." He tapped at the corner of his eye. "At night, too, praise God."

"At night?" Marty pressed.

"As good as by day," Kareem said. "Different, but just as good."

"Nothing you don't already know about me." Surjan shrugged.

Marty shifted his gaze to François.

"You have all gained powers." The Frenchman rubbed the top of his head. "Unless growing hair is a skill, I don't think I have anything new going on with me. Unless, of course, Gunther's success was due to my power to be healed."

"François, you're not seeing clearly." Marty stabbed the sandy soil with a stick. "Or hearing, rather. There's something going on with your voice."

"Eh?" François said, sounding for all the world like Snidely Whiplash.

"Yes," Surjan agreed.

Lowanna looked surly, but nodded.

"When you sing," Marty continued, "your voice is like a jackhammer."

"I'm flattered," François said.

Marty shook his head. "It's not that you have a good voice or a bad one, it's something about the tone of your voice lately that kind of forces me to look in your direction."

"I noticed that as well," Gunther affirmed.

Marty panned his gaze across the team. "Everyone is still physically in top form?"

Everyone nodded.

"Not a blister," Surjan said.

"I used to always get a stiff neck by the end of the day." Gunther rubbed the back of his neck. "That's gone."

François frowned. "I've been thinking about that. At first, I thought it might have been the ankhs. Now I'm wondering if it could have something to do with those blobs of energy we're picking up from our kills?"

"I have a question about that," Kareem asked. "What are those cursed things? Are they the souls of the dead?"

"I hope not," Surjan growled.

"It's energy," Marty speculated. "Vitality, power. It seems to come along with our . . . new abilities. And . . . I don't know about the rest of you, but did you have a euphoric experience after contact with the light?"

The crew nodded.

Kareem hesitantly raised his hand. "But is it a sin? To experience this . . . this . . ."

"Orgasm," Lowanna said.

Marty coughed involuntarily.

"Let's face it," she said, "it almost feels like a small orgasm, and anything that feels like that can't be bad."

"Where there is orgasm, there can be no sin," Surjan said. "The Book of Lancaster, chapter one, verse one."

"My boy." François spoke with a warm tone as he addressed the young Egyptian. "We aren't killing to achieve such a . . . thrill." He shot Lowanna an exasperated expression. "Or to gain . . . powers. Yes, the collection of this energy has some beneficial effects, but we aren't killing things for that goal. We fight and we kill to save ourselves, to save each other. Ultimately, that cannot be a sin. Do you understand?"

Kareem nodded. "And the people of Ahuskay? Do you think they experience the same thing?"

Marty shrugged. "It really doesn't matter—"

"It does, though," Gunther insisted. "They may be able to tell us what this is about. These energy blobs, as you call it."

"Why does that matter?" Lowanna asked. "What would we do with that information? We're here in this bizarre timeline just to get back to where we came from."

"It could be very important to know," Surjan said. "If we are fighting a battle, and our enemies might potentially have superpowers . . . or worse, might potentially *gain* superpowers *during the fight* . . . I'd want to know."

"They get blisters," Gunther said.

"Eh?" François again.

"The people of Ahuskay get blisters," Gunther said. "I bandaged a few for Munatas today. Maybe that suggests no powers."

"No guarantee the two things are connected," Surjan pointed out.

Gunther shrugged.

"Guys, we need to be careful," Marty interjected. "As it is, with our clothes and our . . . ways, we stand out. If we start asking questions that maybe give away that we're not from this place, or maybe from this time, or worse, questions that make it seem like we're not like them . . . that can only hurt us. Let's stick to what we need to know, and continue onward. We've got a long way to go, and who knows what dangers are lurking ahead of us?"

"Agreed," Lowanna replied and then the others all nodded in agreement.

"I think, for now," Marty said, "our working hypothesis is that the natives of this time don't experience the blobs of light and don't gain the special abilities."

"And the Sethians?" François asked.

No one had an answer.

⇒ CHAPTER ⇐
NINETEEN

"We don't have much water left." Gunther shook his waterskin, evoking only scant sounds of sloshing liquid.

Marty nodded. He didn't need the reminder. He'd given the last of his own water to Munatas.

He himself was sucking on a small pebble. It was one of Lowanna's trick-your-own-saliva-glands techniques, and it worked to keep his mouth feeling less parched. He also tried to breathe in, but especially out, only through his nose, because Lowanna said that if you breathed out, your nose hairs acted as a natural filter and helped retain water. She also said it resulted in a more noble shape to the head, but that wasn't really Marty's concern. He talked little, and kept his mouth shut. He tried imagining he was some ancient Shaolin monk who not only could breathe in and out through his skin, he could wick moisture from the air. Psychologically, maybe it helped. At least, it distracted him.

But none of those things stopped the fatigue and the lightheadedness that came with slowly running out of water. His skin felt like heated paper, and he thought he was starting to lose the ability to sweat. That couldn't be a good sign.

Twenty-three days left.

But twenty-three days until what?

As they moved into the summer and hiked east, the ground had slowly parched. It was still prairie, not the rolling dunes that it would later become when the Sahara swallowed it, but the grass became dry and brittle and yellow. It had been days since they'd last crossed running water, and the melons and fruit they'd gathered there were eaten.

Marty walked at the head of the main body. Lowanna and Badis brought up the rear, and Surjan and Kareem scouted ahead. Gunther unstoppered his waterskin, apparently seduced by the faint sloshing of the liquid, and then thought better of it and replaced the cap. Surjan came striding back.

"Water," he said. He turned and pointed at the northern horizon, where Marty saw a slightly darker yellow-brown smudge against a field of slightly lighter yellowish brown.

"We don't know that's water," Marty said. "It could just be a different color of stone."

"Or weed," Gunther said.

"I can smell the water," Surjan grunted. "It's so strong. Can't you?"

Marty shook his head. "But I know your nose is better than mine. How far away is it?"

Surjan looked and considered. "Two miles. It's a detour, but it's a detour we have to make."

Marty looked back at the group. His natural inclination was to have a discussion, but two of the younger spearmen were bright red, and Gunther's lips were cracked and bleeding. They needed water, and they needed it now.

He nodded to Surjan.

Surjan and Kareem turned from the path and led them north. The prairie looked flat here, but that turned out to be an illusion caused by the sameness of the yellow grass in all directions. Marty soon found that he was walking quicker to catch up to his two scouts, who otherwise threatened to disappear into a maze that started as depressions between gentle swells, then sank into wide ditches, and finally dug itself into proper canyons. But Surjan and Kareem had many days of practice leading the company now—between the young man's eyesight and Surjan's sense of smell, not to mention the Sikh's fierce combat prowess, Marty liked having them go first—and they left a trail of small rock cairns that was easy to follow.

One of the Ahuskay men tugged at Marty's elbow. It was Udad. He was young, with blazing eyes and a long nose that bent slightly. "I have been to this place, Seer."

Marty was startled. He'd been told the Ahuskay were pastoralists who mostly didn't travel long distances.

"Is there water?" he asked.

"There is a cave," Udad said. "In this cave, the sick are healed. I was brought here as a child, all this great distance from the village, because I was lame. I was brought into the cave and made to sleep there overnight. The power of the cave straightened my legs and I walked again."

"And water?" Marty pressed. Healing caves sounded nice, but if the host walked two miles off the trail and found no water, some of them might not make it back.

"I believe so."

When Marty finally did catch up to his scouts, half an hour later, they were standing beside a pool.

The pool was aquamarine in color and crystal clear; Marty saw the soft sands of the bottom. Water gushed from the ground a few steps from the pool and fed into it. The pool lay at the base of a dark orange cliff, the brow of which had provided the smear of color visible two miles away. All around the water lay a thick, tangled green grove, and Marty saw dates and figs as well as rustling branches that indicated animals.

Surjan and Kareem stood beside the spring and stared at the cliff.

"How's the water?" Marty asked.

"Sweet," Surjan said. "The water coming out of the ground is filtered by the Earth and doesn't need to be boiled."

Marty urged Udad to drink first. Then he lay on his belly to slake his own thirst. "What are you looking at?" he asked Kareem.

The young man pointed. A cracked shelf of rock angled from the corner of the pool up the face of the cliff. Fifty feet over his head, and directly above the pool, Marty saw that the cliff jutted out slightly, creating an overhang. Beneath the overhang, sinking into the cliff face, was a crack in the rock.

Then Marty whistled in surprise.

The crack was not a simple slash in the stone. It had the definite shape of an ankh.

"You see it," Kareem said. "What does it mean?"

"Well," Marty said, "it could be a trick of nature or it could be significant." He stared at the stone structure's unmistakable resemblance to an ankh and felt a chill race up and down his spine. Such a shape being a coincidence of nature was hard to imagine.

Kareem looked up at him expectantly.

"Does it have a meaning?" Marty shrugged. "It's a good question, but it's not one I'd ask yet. We have to collect more data, and we don't want to judge anything before we've done so. It's how, as a scientist, we can maintain objectivity. We must always be open to the possibility that there is no meaning or there may be profound meaning."

Surjan laughed. "What he means is, maybe it's just a hole in a stone wall. In your heart, you really expect to reach Egypt and find the archaeological site still waiting for us, don't you, Marty?"

Marty gave Surjan a wink. "I'm not prepared to make any kind of preternatural assumptions about anything without hard evidence. I'm weird like that."

"With respect, Seer," Udad said, "I was taken into that cave as a boy."

"I'm going to go get some evidence, God willing." Kareem started toward the crease in the rock.

Marty followed.

Kareem easily hoisted himself up onto the rock shelf. He offered Marty a hand, but Marty waved it away and sprang up unaided.

He heard thrashing in the woods behind him, and it was François. "Hand?" the Frenchman asked, reaching up. Marty hoisted him up to the ledge.

From this vantage point, he saw Lowanna and Badis finally reach the oasis. She said a few words to the men, and then they all lay on their bellies to drink and to fill waterskins. Udad alone stood, watching Marty.

"You're not thirsty?" Marty asked François.

François snorted.

The shelf was wide as a bike path, but it rose at a steep angle. Kareem and François went up on all fours, but Marty found that he could balance on the balls of his feet and walk straight up with ease, if not quite in comfort.

After rising several stories' worth, the ledge widened and flattened. It lay under the rock overhang, and the stone of the shelf was heaped with bat guano. From here, Marty could see that the opening did indeed lead into a cave, and it went back far enough that it eventually disappeared in shadow. From this perspective, also, the cave opening did not seem to be shaped like an ankh.

"You see?" Marty said to Kareem. "Maybe it's a coincidence that the opening looked like an ankh from below. From here it just looks like an irregular hole."

"Oh my, yes," François said. "At last!"

"Well, don't get *too* excited about it," Marty said.

"No, look!" François rubbed his hands. "Bat guano!"

"Okay, then."

Kareem was staring into the cave. Marty stepped near the edge of the shelf and looked down—his people were harvesting dates and relaxing in the shade, already appearing greatly refreshed. Udad still stood apart, gazing up at him.

"I'm going to go in," Kareem said.

"Wait," Marty suggested.

Kareem grinned at him. "We need data." He loped into the cave.

Marty followed. The floor was soft sand and the passage sank straight back, dropping slightly. Then it jogged left, and then right, and suddenly he smelled a strong, bitter reek. It was familiar—was it the same stink he had smelled at the Sethian outpost, inside the quarters of the Hathiru?

He clearly detected whiffs of petroleum.

And surely, that yeasty, oily-smelling substance in the Ametsu compound was the same stuff they had ignited and thrown, the sticky liquid that had burned like napalm.

Kareem disappeared into darkness.

"Kareem?" Marty called. "Kareem?"

The world had gained strange new colors for Kareem. He didn't have names for them, but they seemed vaguely reddish. He had noticed this since the moment when the company had found itself on Jebel Mudawwar, but it *really* manifested itself in the darkness. At night, the strange colors somehow made it so that Kareem could see the ground at his feet, and objects in the dark that should have been invisible to him—plants were one shade, animals another. And the colors of some objects, especially, for instance, stone, and the earth, changed color over the course of a night.

Here again in the cave, he found the strange new colors meant that he could see the cave walls and floor even after Marty was forced to stop. He saw the bats as bright reddish clumps, firmly gripped to the ceiling of the cave. Kareem kept walking. He heard Marty calling after him, but he was too excited at the strangeness and newness of what he was doing to stop.

Perhaps the foreign archaeologists felt like this, when they stumbled upon the tombs and treasures of Egypt's kings. And what mysterious treasures might Kareem find in this cave shaped like the ancient pharaonic cross? He envisioned gold coffins and heaps of jewels.

Or heaps of data for Dr. Cohen.

Thinking of Dr. Cohen, Kareem turned back. His heart leaped with delight at the fact that he could see his own footprints, painted in the strange colors behind him. But they were fading slowly, and he worried they might not last long enough for him to find his way back. From the corner of the room, he collected a heap of pebbles. He filled his pockets with them and also his hands.

"Don't worry!" he called back. "I'm only looking!"

"*Whatever you do, don't light any torches or make any sparks. I smell oil in here.*" Marty's voice was distant, with an urgent tone. Luckily, Kareem could see just fine. He hadn't thought of using his firestarter.

He left a slow, steady trail of pebbles. He found that, if he looked closely, he could see old footprints on the floor. They weren't noticeable for their color, so they must not be recent, but he could see dimpled sand that showed which passages had been walked in and which had not.

The air grew thicker the farther he went. It smelled like his cousin Ahmed's garage, which stank from the decades of oil stains on the floor, as well as from the sweat of the men tugging and hammering at the automobiles inside.

He followed the dimpled sand past large galleries, tall chimneys, thunderingly deep pits, and narrow cracks. The colors shifted the deeper he went, but he could always see.

And then, abruptly, the chamber ended. A smooth wall confronted him, with a mottled appearance. At the base of the wall rested a rectangular stone box, something like a crude sarcophagus. Elsewhere in the room lay blankets and other piles of bedding.

Kareem examined the wall. When he looked closely, he realized that the mottled shapes looked like hieroglyphs, only he couldn't make out the details. He could see a kneeling man, and a feather, and a man with raised arms, and the ankh.

The ankh appeared many times.

But many of the hieroglyphs were too confused for him to puzzle out, and he couldn't read them in any case. Maybe with more normal light, using his ordinary powers of vision, he'd be able to see the images. Maybe Dr. Cohen would be able to read them.

But the treasure wasn't in painted walls. Tomb treasures were to be found in coffins. Kareem examined the rectangular shape.

He tugged gently at the top, and it didn't budge. It was difficult to see with the strange-colors vision, but either the top was cemented onto the other stones or it was really just a single stone. He tugged at the front and sides to be sure, and they also didn't budge.

But when he pressed on the stone at the back of the box, it moved.

The flat rock slid sideways, opening to reveal a space within the box. Kareem pressed himself against the wall, trying to peer inside, but he couldn't see anything. He had heard many stories of curses and traps on ancient tombs, but his uncle Abdullah had assured him that that was all nonsense. Finally, he took a deep breath and reached inside.

And found a smaller box.

This one was made of wood, three times as long as it was wide, and nearly flat.

He took it.

No curses.

Curses were all nonsense.

But there was also no reason to linger in the cave. Kareem hurried toward the surface. His trail of pebbles glowed red before him and his return journey was much faster than his descent.

When he emerged into ordinary light, François and Dr. Cohen were where he had left them, except that François was now scraping bat dung together and bundling it into a leather bag. Had he sacrificed a waterskin for the purpose? It seemed like foolishness.

But Surjan and Lowanna and Gunther had joined them. When Kareem rejoined them all on the shelf, he smiled his best movie star smile and showed the box.

"I found writing," he told them. "Hieroglyphs. And this."

"Writing?" François asked. "In there? How did you even see?"

"He has pretty good eyes," Dr. Cohen said. "Even at night, remember? Maybe there was an airshaft or something."

"No, it was dark. But I can see in the dark." Kareem hesitated, trying to think how to explain it. "Even in total darkness. Cold things are different colors than warm things, I think."

François looked at Lowanna and shook his head. "And I get a jackhammer voice," he muttered.

"What's in the box?" Dr. Cohen asked.

Kareem shrugged, and then opened it.

Inside lay a gold ankh, looking exactly like the ankhs that each member of the company who had come from Egypt had. It gleamed, even in the shadow of the overhang.

"Don't touch it," François said.

Dr. Cohen reached a hand forward. "Why not?"

François grabbed the two sides of the box and slammed it shut. "Think about it, Marty. You and I are old men, aren't we? Well, I'm old, you're ... getting into middle age. But we work through the night, we walk all day, we go without water, and how are you holding up?"

"Pretty well," Dr. Cohen admitted. "Surprisingly well."

"You're outwalking and outworking those young Ahuskay bucks, and they're from this climate. Better than pretty well, I'd say. Something has put you into peak physical form." François arched his eyebrows. "It's put us all in top physical form."

"Clean living," Lowanna suggested.

"Hard exercise," Gunther added.

"Nonsense." François shook his head. "I think a good hypothesis is still that it's the work of the ankhs. Because all of you have felt these effects, right? It might be the ankhs. You young, strong types are younger and stronger!"

"I'm surprised Kareem isn't right back in diapers already," Lowanna cracked.

Kareem felt himself blushing.

"Go ahead and laugh," François said, "but it might be that the touch of the ankh is rejuvenating. At least to us, to humans. And, you know, to people who aren't actually getting *impaled* on the ankhs." He shot Surjan an amused look. "Also remember that our ankhs were gold when we first touched them and the color drained into us when we touched it. At least that's what I experienced." He turned to the others.

Marty nodded. "Me too."

Surjan and Lowanna both nodded.

"Anyway," François continued, "until we've worked out the significance of the ankh in all of this, let's not waste that healing energy by touching the ankh."

"You said you thought it was the glowing lights," Dr. Cohen said.

"This is science," François said. "Multiple possibilities. Could be this, could be that. Let's not take any chances."

Dr. Cohen looked lost in deep thought. "Udad said he was brought here to be healed."

Lowanna tousled François's hair. "I see what's really going on. Your hair's coming back. You've found a magical Rogaine, and you want to keep it all for yourself."

Dr. Cohen frowned.

François ground his teeth. "We leave it in the box. Do we need to debate this, really?"

"He's right," Dr. Cohen said.

"What about the hieroglyphs?" Gunther asked. "Aren't you curious to go in there and try to read them?"

"After the first turn or two the way passage goes completely dark," Dr. Cohen said. "And this place reeks of oil, likely from some natural fissure. I'm afraid if I took a torch in, it might be a really short reading session. I say we camp here tonight, fill up on water, and then hit the road in the morning."

François sat apart from the camp and studied the two scratches he'd gotten on his arm, both inflamed by a mild infection. He'd applied his "penicillin" mold treatment to one of the scratches and he'd left the other alone.

Marty looked over François's shoulder. "What are you up to?"

The Frenchman frowned as he ran his finger across the inflamed scratch. "I was testing out my antibiotic."

"You only treated one of the scratches?"

François nodded.

"That looks promising. The one closest to your wrist looks like it's almost completely healed."

François sighed. "Unfortunately, that's the one I didn't apply my treatment to."

Marty winced and patted François on the shoulder. "There's no such thing as a failed experiment, as long as you've learned something from the results."

"Oh, I learned something." François muttered. "This mold experiment isn't going to help us much. If at all."

"Fortunately, we're good healers," Marty said. "And we have Gunther."

⫷ CHAPTER ⫸
TWENTY

Four days later, Marty and the group arrived at a market town.

The town was laid out around a central well in a flat, hard-packed earth square. Standing on a low rise and looking down on the town, Marty could see a caravanserai with camels, and a building that looked like an inn, with beds drying in the sun on its rooftop, and a pottery on the square. Along with those permanent businesses, he saw many tents and awnings, displaying wares on blankets laid out on the ground, or surrounded by large baskets heaped with dried beans and currants and other portable trade goods. People walked from tent to tent, shouting out offers and counteroffers.

"It could be a village on the Nile today," Kareem said. "Or, I mean, tomorrow. In the real time. In the future."

"Some things change really slowly," Marty said. "And maybe some things never do."

"Assume the average household is five people," Gunther said. "Lots of children, but a high mortality rate. I make it about three thousand residents in the town. But there are far more than three thousand people down there."

"It's a market town," François said. "As in, this little piggy went there. Maybe it's even a market day. Excellent!"

"Excellent?" Lowanna asked. "Why is that? Are you in the market for something?"

"Oh, my dear," François said, "*everyone* is always in the market for *something*."

"I wouldn't mind having camels," Marty said. "Or whatever these people use as beasts of burden. It would be great to be able to carry more water."

"I bet we can trade archaeology lessons for that." Gunther grinned. "Teach them about life in ancient Egypt."

"Teach them your kung fu," François said. "Based on my experiences in this place . . . time . . . so far, I'd say they could all use it."

As they entered the market square, their modern, Western-style clothing drew stares from merchants who mostly wore burnooses, brightly dyed to show their owners' prosperity. Marty smiled and nodded greetings, but the stares were all abruptly averted when a wailing arose at the market's far end.

"The king is dying, the king dies!" the wailing went. It was melodic, with a fast-moving succession of short notes, and without accompaniment. A single woman, Marty thought, was the singer.

The king is dying, the king dies!
An evil spirit assails him!
A foul disease steals his breath!
Who will defend the king who has long defended Jehed?

"King?" Marty murmured.

"Being king isn't about the size of your kingdom," Lowanna said. "It's about your role in society. I've known tribes of fifty people that have kings."

"I guess we know the town is named Jehed," François observed.

The singer appeared. She was in her thirties, a dark-haired beauty with dark-olive skin and light-colored eyes. She wore a white burnoose and a bright red sash and she was followed by two bare-chested men, each carrying an upright pole. At the top of each pole was a straw figure, neatly tied and dressed in a little white cape. The figures were identical except that one wore a circlet of gold on its head and the other wore a tarry black blob. Behind them all came a man in a black burnoose, wearing a black skull cap. He held a small leather box in front of him with both hands. The woman continued her song.

Behold the king, behold the king's illness!
This is the thief of air,
This is the eater of the king's lungs!
Who will defend the king against this foul demon of pestilence?

"I have a good idea it's going to be that fellow back there, in the black," Gunther said. "Court physician, would you say? Or court wizard?"

"In the fourth millennium B.C.E.?" Marty snorted. "There's no difference."

François crossed his arms over his chest. "I have a better idea who's going to help the king."

"I don't think the king wants lessons in martial arts," Marty said absently.

The men in poles marched in a circle around each other creating, Marty noticed, something like the looped links of the infinity symbol. Coincidence? They rattled the two straw figures against each other as if they were fighting.

Behold the king's physician, behold the king's flame!
This is the thief-killer,
This is the healing of the king's lungs!
Wagguten will defend the king, Wagguten will save Jehed!

The king's pole-bearer, assuming that the figure with the gold circlet was meant to be the king, struck the other man's pole hard. The pole-bearer of the demon, or disease, dropped to one knee and shrieked a cry of defeat. The man in black stepped forward, opening his leather box. Inside the box, Marty saw the glow of hot coals, and the man in black, who must be Wagguten, touched the coals to the demon's straw.

The demon figure burst into flame. Soaked in oil, no doubt. Marty noticed that the sheer theater of the moment had overwhelmed even his hardened, academic companions.

Behold the dying demon, behold the ended curse!
This is the beast who ran,
Thus may all illness flee the king!
Wagguten has saved the king, long live King Iken of Jehed!

The demon's pole-bearer shrieked again. Then he rose and ran. "Long live the king!" the crowd shouted as he went. The fire streaked across the market and the man continued running right out beyond the edge of town. Out into the plains he ran, and the crowd continued to shout good wishes for the king, until the flame finally vanished.

"So . . . much . . . to say," Lowanna murmured. She stared at the singer and magician, who now retreated to a large building just beyond the edge of the market, the only building in the town with a second story. "That's the scapegoat ritual. The Greek pharmakon. The embodiment of evil in order to cast it out."

"It felt a little on the nose to me," Gunther harrumphed. "Straight out of *The Golden Bough*. Very 1960s."

Lowanna slapped him on the shoulder. "You stuffed baboon! You're going to criticize what you just saw because you don't like its *academic theory*?"

"I just mean . . ." Gunther hesitated. "I mean, didn't it seem rather *obvious*?"

"You fool." She laughed. "That wasn't some play put on by imaginative grad students. That was the real deal, and you just saw it almost five thousand years before *The Golden Bough* was written."

"Er . . . right." Gunther looked embarrassed.

"I have not read *The Golden Bough*," François said. "But why do you think that little performance was news? It seemed like a play to me."

"You're correct, it was not news. It was indeed a play," Lowanna said. "The purpose of the play was to drive evil out of the town."

"Specifically," François said slowly, "the evil affecting the king's lungs."

"Which could be many things," Gunther pointed out.

"Fortunately, we have more than one remedy available, don't we? For starters, I'm thinking you should try to Twilight Zone this bad boy." François wiggled his fingers in Gunther's direction, pivoted, and headed after the singer. "Follow me, folks."

"Wait, wait, wait." Lowanna rushed and caught up with François. The others struggled to catch up. "We need to think this through."

"Healing the king is worth a lot of camels, don't you think?" François's eyes gleamed.

"Yes," Lowanna agreed. "And the palace just committed to an act of magical healing, performed by one Wagguten. Which I think is that guy we saw. Or if that's not him, that was an actor playing him. And if we now show up and heal the king—"

"We make an enemy out of the king's wizard," Marty said. "She's right."

"Duh," François said. "Which is why we go offer our services to Wagguten, not to the king. And he will *absolutely* hire us."

"Why are you so confident?" Lowanna asked.

François beamed. "Simple. If we heal the king, he takes the credit. And if we fail and the king dies, then he makes us the scapegoats. It's no risk to him, and all upside."

"We just saw what happens to scapegoats around here," Lowanna said. "They get lit on fire."

François tapped a finger to his temple. "So let's not fail."

They had reached the large building, a minute behind both the singer and the magician. Two burly men with spears stood before the door. Each wore a white sash from shoulder to hip, and one raised his hand to stop them.

"Strangers do not enter," the spearman said.

"We aren't strangers," François said. "We're magicians, come from a great distance to heal the king."

The spearman looked François up and down. "Your clothing is odd enough to make you a wizard, but any fool may wear ugly clothes. By what token do I know that you are magicians?"

Badis pushed forward, eyes blazing and voice suddenly booming. "I am Badis of the Ahuskay. My home is three weeks' journey to the west. These people came to us from the wilderness, and I have seen their magical powers. They are warriors and healers. They command the beasts. They keep their word."

The spearman squinted at Badis. "What did they do in Ahuskay, with these magical powers they possess?"

Badis drew himself up to his full height and threw out his chest. "We were oppressed by Ametsu. These people slew five Ametsu and set us free."

Udad stepped forward. "I am Udad, also of Ahuskay. Badis speaks the truth."

The spearman frowned and nodded. "Wait here."

He disappeared into the large building. François turned and eyed the market, which had returned to its previous bustle and hubbub. Gunther was cracking his knuckles and rubbing his own fingers. Did he feel pressure?

Marty certainly did. He was happy to try to help this king heal in any way that was possible, but he didn't relish the thought that the penalty for failure might be, say, stoning, or death by fire.

"Why are you pushing to help this king?" he murmured to François, careful to speak in English.

"Because we're here and we can," François said. "And maybe he'll give us the camels you want. And besides, you were the one who volunteered us to go fight the Sethians last time. This is a much smaller risk."

"You're not going to try to use that . . . bread mold . . . on him, are you?"

The spearman emerged. "Dr. Wagguten will see you now."

Marty almost laughed. Surely, there was a better translation for whatever the spearman had said—but that was what Marty had understood. "Badis," he said. "Thank you. Perhaps it is best if the warriors of Ahuskay stay outside here, and stay out of trouble."

Badis nodded and he and the host withdrew.

The spearmen looked at the remaining people. "Are *all* of you magicians?"

"I'll stay outside," Surjan said. "Kareem can stay with me."

Marty, François, Lowanna, and Gunther followed one of the king's warriors inside. Within, Marty saw that the building was a complex structure with several mud-brick buildings, one of which was a stable, around a central enclosed courtyard. Three young children stopped their play in the courtyard and turned to stare at the crew; two women rushed from an open door to whisk them out of sight.

"The king's wives?" Marty murmured, thinking out loud.

"His maids," the warrior said. "Lunja is his wife."

Marty and François climbed steps to a room on the second story, their companions following.

Knotted leather strings formed a rude curtain in the room's doorway. Behind was a simple chamber with wooden stools, two windows that looked out over the town, and niches in the clay walls that contained an assortment of objects. Skulls, feathers, colored wax, jars, glass beads, a chunk of meteoric iron, an obsidian knife, and other knickknacks reminded Marty of the shelves of some kind of protohistoric general store.

The wizard stood at the far end of the room; with a wave, he dismissed the spearman.

Now that they could focus on Wagguten, they saw him to be a small man, with skin the color of bleached ochre and a thin graying beard. He had set aside his burnoose and wore a simple tunic. His face looked drawn and tired.

"Are you really magicians?" he asked.

"We have knowledge of healing," Marty said. He looked at Gunther, and Gunther cracked his knuckles. "My companion here has great skill." He thought of the extra ankh, which he was carrying in his basket. "And if his talents fail, we have another . . . tool . . . that may be able to help."

"We have a few other tools that may help." François smiled.

"Now you will tell me that you only want the king's weight in gold," Wagguten said.

"Actually," Marty said, "we could really use a camel. If we can heal the king, we'd love it if we could get a camel. Or a donkey, or whatever."

"A wagon," François said. "And jars to carry water."

Wagguten met Marty's gaze with guileless, open eyes. If he was making the Machiavellian calculation François had suggested he would, he didn't show it. "I'm a believer in my own arts, and I must warn you that the king is in a very serious fight against the demon that infests him." He sighed. "I love my king, and wish him health. But I'm also a believer in trying all possible remedies, because you never know what's going to make the difference in this infernal battle. I will take you to see the king."

He took them through a narrow passage in the back, its entryway set at such an angle that Marty hadn't even noticed it. A hallway led over the front gate, and narrow windows let Marty look and see the two spearmen in white sashes standing guard, and his own warriors, standing at ease a hundred feet away. The sounds from the front of the street carried up into the hallway.

"You can see the gate," he observed to the physician.

"If you're asking whether I watched you talk to the guard, the answer is yes. It is wise to stay informed. About everything that happens in Jehed."

Another angled, inobtrusive gate brought them into the throne room of the king. They emerged behind the throne itself, a heavy wooden chair with arching legs, wide arms, and a back nearly seven feet tall, thick with carvings of eyes and mouths.

The king didn't sit on his throne, he lay on a bed in front of it. The bed was a raised wooden platform and it bore a thin pallet. The king—it could only be he—lay under a sheet and trembled. His features were hawklike, his hair long, but if he was a hawk, then he was a hawk who had been shot down. Blood stained his pallet and the sheet, especially near his face. A clay spittoon lay beneath his head, stained dark with old blood and glistening with blood that was fresh. The room's air was close, and smelled of death.

A single woman stood beside him; she was the singer in the white burnoose, and now Marty could see that she had coppery red hair and chiseled, fine features. She held a bowl of water on the corner of the bed and pressed a damp cloth against the king's forehead.

"Tuberculosis," François murmured. "It has to be."

"No it doesn't," Gunther murmured. "Could be pneumonia."

"Lung cancer," Marty said.

"My lady Lunja," the wizard said. "These men would attempt their arts upon the king."

Tears streaked the queen's face. "What of *your* arts, Wagguten?" she asked. "What of our sacrifices, our pleas to the gods?"

"You were brave to let me try my skills," the magician said, bowing deeply. "Be brave again, my lady. This battle our king fights is a great one."

Lunja took her bowl and cloth and withdrew a step. Gunther stepped forward and placed his hands on the king's brow. He bowed his own head in an attitude that looked for all the world like a priestly posture and he frowned in concentration.

Nothing happened.

The room felt smaller by the second, and sweat trickled down Marty's spine. He smiled at Wagguten in a manner that he hoped was solemn and trust-inspiring. Wagguten answered with a frown.

Gunther's muscles clenched and he gasped. The lady Lunja stepped forward half a step with a wordless cry and then caught herself. She reached forward, stopped herself, and finally bit down on the cloth she'd been applying to the king.

And then Gunther's hands began to glow.

Gunther groaned as the light poured from his hands into the king's body. It looked like a light transfusion. Marty had the unsettling sensation that he was watching one man give part of his *soul* to another.

And maybe that was right. The Egyptians treated the ba, or personality, as different from the ka, or spiritual energy, of a person. Maybe Gunther was pouring his ka into the sick king.

The king's trembling erupted into spasms. He shook, his body racked by coughs, and then he leaned over the edge of the bed and heaved what looked like a quart of blood into the spittoon.

Marty vaguely remembered that tuberculosis was very transmissible, and he shifted from one foot to the other, trying not to show his nerves.

The king sat up and turned to face the strangers. A dull fire glowed in his eye and a faint smile worked at his lips, visible through the layers of crusted blood. "I am sorry," he said. "I am a poor host."

"You have been ill, Your Majesty," Wagguten said. "Lie down and rest more."

"I am feeling improved," the king said.

"We are not finished with our arts." François stepped forward and reached into his woven basket. Was he going to pull out the extra ankh? Marty didn't want to stop him and cause a scene, so he held his peace. François produced a lump of bread from his basket and unwrapped it.

It was moldy. It was the bread into which he'd planted only the green mold.

Penicillin. François had been working at developing some kind of home-brew penicillin. It hadn't healed his infected scratch, but now he was going to give it to this sick king.

Madness.

Was it worse madness than trusting Gunther to heal by the laying on of hands?

Marty looked at Gunther and saw that the German was shuddering. He slipped himself under his comrade's shoulder to support him, and François sliced the bread neatly in half, offering it to Wagguten. "Feed this to the king. Cut it into twenty pieces and give it to him over ten days. It should finish his healing."

"Barley rot?" The queen's voice dripped with doubt.

"Yes, my lady," François said. "But very special barley rot."

Wagguten took the bread and led them out.

⇒ CHAPTER ⇐
TWENTY-ONE

The market of Jehed buzzed with human voices: hagglers, hawkers, protests of poverty, promises of delight. To François, this was what he loved most about the Middle East, what was missing in much of Western society: lively banter and haggling.

He stopped at a wagon. It was piled high with what looked like dried and crumbling soil, but emitted the faint smell of ammonia.

He looked up at the sour-faced, big-eared merchant in a ragged gray burnoose and asked, "Is this bat guano?"

The merchant looked at François from head to toe and frowned. "It's fertilizer. You don't need it unless you're farming."

"Yes, fertilizer. But from bats, or from some other animal?"

A scowl sprouted on the merchant's face. "I won't tell you where the cave is."

"I don't want to know where the cave is." François held up a gold link from his watch's wristband; it had taken him hours to pry the band apart, link by link, using his pocket knife. He softened his voice, trying to project warmth and friendliness. "Friend, I just want the guano. Tell me how much."

The man's demeanor softened at the sight of the gold. He pointed at the link. "I will have to weigh that to see what it is worth."

The merchant pulled out a two-armed lever scale and set it on the table in front of him. François dropped the small link on one of the trays and the tray immediately lowered. The merchant dropped a clay bead on the other tray, then another, and another until the scale showed even. He looked up at François and said, "For this amount, I will give you one hundred fifty pounds of the fertilizer."

It was François's turn to frown. He hated the idea of getting anything and not being sure it would work. "Actually, before I buy, can I get a small amount to test? I want to make sure it will work."

"Work? What do you mean, it's bat dung! What are you going to do with it?" The merchant stared. "Will you fertilize a gourd and come back in six months?"

"It's hard to explain. All I would need is about *this* much." François cupped his hands together.

The man rolled his eyes and handed him back the gold links. "Go ahead and take what you need for this *test*. But come back to me when you are ready to purchase, understand?"

François nodded as he scooped several handfuls of the guano into a tightly woven basket. "Thank you for being reasonable."

The merchant sniffed and scanned the marketplace for another possible customer.

Walking on, François tucked the basket in his pack and slung it on his shoulder with some of the other samples he'd already cadged from traders. The scent of cinnamon and cumin were floating in the air as he walked alongside spice and food shops.

Spotting a merchant's wagon filled with pottery, François hurried past the people yelling for his attention and the occasional child running underfoot. As he approached the pottery stall, the woman and man standing next to the wagon motioned for his attention. They were darker-skinned than most of the Jehedi, and they were plump. François took the latter as a sign of success.

The woman held up a brown earthenware jug. "Good man, a wine holder for your home?"

Her partner held up a large earthenware bowl with a matching top. "We have the best clay wares that you will ever find. The king himself purchases our goods. You cannot make a bad choice from among our vessels, good man."

François smiled. They had an impressive variety of ceramics. "Do you make all of these yourself?"

"Of course," the woman answered.

"And do you do custom work?"

The man nodded proudly.

François noticed a basket filled with chunks of red clay. Probably what they shaped their wares from. François pointed. "Can I show you what I want with the unbaked clay?"

The man motioned for the Frenchman to come behind the table. "Please, show me what you think you want."

François grabbed a fist-sized chunk of the clay and began to work it. He was surprised how well it molded and kept its shape. It had been a long time since he'd made a finger pot, but the motions came back to him easily.

After flattening the piece of clay in his hand, he molded it into a hollow sphere with a thick opening on the top. As he deftly rotated the ball in his hand, he pinched a simple screwlike groove into the neck of the opening.

Once done, he placed it on the table, grabbed a smaller chunk of clay, and made a matching screw-top for the base. They were crude and the grooves wouldn't actually fit, but they would illustrate his intent.

Both merchants watched his every move with increasingly strong expressions of astonishment. "Sir, you have a talent for this," the man said. "But what is it that you've made?"

François picked up both pieces and focused the merchant's attention on the screwlike grooves in both pieces. "Do you see these lines on the neck and the lid? I have done it poorly, but you will do it well, so that the two pieces will attach together by their grooves. When hardened, the lid will rotate onto the neck." He demonstrated what he was talking about without letting the two soft pieces of clay touch. "And when the lid has been turned all the way, it will stay there even if you knock the vessel over or turn it upside down."

The woman put her hands to her mouth.

"I think that would work just as you described," the man said. He turned to the woman. "Lalla, you have smaller hands than I. Do you think you can do this thing?"

She nodded. "The difficult part will be to make sure the grooves match and are the right size. A good seal can be ensured with beeswax."

"Exactly," François agreed. "Now, I want the lid to be heavier than the bottom—that means the clay walls for the bottom would be thin."

"Won't that make it easier to break?" The man asked.

"It will. I also want a little hole in the middle of the lid. The hole should be about the thickness of . . . this." François snatched a hollow reed that was about half the thickness of a pencil from the wagon.

The man stroked his chin with thick fingers. "Sir, we can do this. How big do you want the vessels, and how many do you want?"

"Ten," François said. "The size of my fist."

The merchant looked at his partner, then nodded and turned back to François. "We will make these for you, and we will charge you the same as we would charge for our ordinary wares."

They quickly sorted out a deal; two gold links for the jars. "How long do you think it would take to make these?" François asked.

"I'll start right away," the woman said. "I'll have at least the first set of completed vases cooled and ready for you to use by tomorrow at sunset."

"That's perfect." François clasped forearms with the merchants, sealing the deal.

He headed for the nearest exit from the market and made a beeline for their borrowed mud-brick home. He had experiments to run.

Wagguten had arranged for the crew and their warriors to have access to a large mud-brick building a few steps from Jehed's market square. It must have been something like a stable, once, but it held sleeping pallets now, along with a couple of rude benches and a table.

A dozen of the king's spearmen in white sashes stood not far off, watching the shelter at all times.

Marty, Gunther, and Kareem had been relaxing in the shelter as François set up a makeshift workbench. Lowanna had been there earlier, but after a minute or two of her glowering in François's direction, she'd left. François felt guilt over her attitude toward him. He'd obviously done something to earn her animosity, but wasn't exactly sure what.

Kareem blew on the fire he'd just made and François set an earthenware mug full of liquid on the glowing embers. After a few minutes, the liquid began to steam and he poured bat guano into the makeshift mixing bowl.

Surjan walked into the shelter, and as François stirred the

contents of the mug with a green twig, the head of security sniffed and his lip curled up in a sign of revulsion. "Whatever that is, it smells foul."

François chuckled. "Way to go, Super Nose. You have detected bat feces mingled with urine."

"You're not making dinner . . . right?" Marty asked.

"Mouthwatering, eh?" François chuckled. "You know, it would be a very good deed to introduce the humans of the fourth millennium to French cooking."

"Yeah, but . . . that's not what you're doing, right?" Marty pressed.

François peered into the mug and stirred. "Potassium nitrate is soluble in water, so I'm trying to extract it from the guano." He set an earthenware tray with a turned-up rim on the embers.

"And you're doing this because . . . ?" Marty looked perplexed.

François unfolded a piece of cloth and set it on his lap. "You'll see."

Surjan pointed at the mounds of black and yellow powder on the bench. "Charcoal, sulfur, bat guano. Where's the party?"

François looked up at Surjan and grinned. Of course, the ex-soldier knew what he was making. He laid a thin cloth over the mug and grabbed the handle through a slab of rawhide to protect his hand from the heat. He slowly tilted the mug onto the hot tray.

The cloth helped filter out the solids and a clear liquid slowly dribbled from the mug. The guano broth sizzled as it poured across the tray. François watched and, after a few minutes, the water evaporated, leaving behind white crystalline residue.

François emptied the mug of the solids, filled it half full with water, added dung, and began to repeat the procedure.

Marty asked Gunther, "How's the king doing with that moldy bread?"

"He's hating it, even with honeyed tea. But he's taking it."

"Candidly," Marty said, "I worry we might poison him."

Gunther raised his eyebrows in a facial shrug. "The mold is pretty pungent."

"But is he getting better?" François asked.

"He is," Gunther said, "but . . ."

"You saw the light," Marty said. "Gunther healed him."

"Ah," François said. "Gunther's faith healing worked. But my science is misguided."

"I think your science, in this case," Marty said, "is more of a child's cartoon version of science."

"And yet the king recovers." François shrugged.

"Slowly." Marty lay on a pallet and sighed. "I hope so. We need to get going, but the prairie's getting more arid the farther we go. I'd really like to take that camel with us."

Surjan growled. "The king's men watch our every move. If he dies, we're going to be in for a rough go of it."

François nodded. "Fortunately, we have Gunther's healing power to back up my science."

That ended the debate. Marty and the rest of the crew lay on the reed mats splayed across the shelter's floor and rested while François spent the next hour producing mugfuls of his bat-dung soup, filtering it, and creating more of the white crystals.

When he'd finally exhausted his supply of dung and crushed the white crystals with a mortar and pestle, François poured from the mortar a pile of what looked almost like flour. He hoped that it hadn't been a giant waste of his time.

He hoped the same for his experiment with antibiotics, though he himself was beginning to doubt.

He looked over at Marty, who was awake and staring up at the ceiling. "Want to see if my design works?"

"Did you invent a smallpox cure this time?" Marty asked.

"More of a weapon," François said. "Hopefully."

Marty sat up and gazed at François's handiwork. "Did you make a gun?"

"Give me a second." Using a flattened stick, François measured out two parts of the powdered sulfur, three parts of the pulverized charcoal, and fifteen parts of what he hoped was potassium nitrate. He mixed the white, yellow, and black powders together until he had a large mound of dark powder.

After a full minute of mixing it as well as he could on the flat surface of the earthenware tray, he scooped up a small amount of the black powder with the stick and set it away from the rest of the powders on the tray. Taking another small stick, he put its tip into the still-glowing embers of the fire until it began smoking and caught on fire. He looked up at Marty and grinned. "You ready?"

Marty stared at the workbench and nodded.

François carefully took the flaming stick and brought it to the fingernail-sized mound of powder. The moment the flame touched the powder, it flashed brightly, sending up a plume of smoke.

Marty leaned closer and whispered, "Did you just reinvent gunpowder?"

François nodded.

Marty laughed. "I don't know if this is going to cause some paradox, because I don't think the Chinese invented gunpowder for another couple thousand years. I'm assuming you have specific plans for that?"

"Not troubled by the paradoxes caused by the early invention of penicillin?" Surjan grunted.

"Not as much," Marty said, "no."

François imagined a box full of the fist-sized earthenware vessels the pottery merchants were making for him. "With the Sethians and who knows what else is out there . . . I say we risk the paradox."

⇒ CHAPTER ⇐
TWENTY-TWO

François watched as Kareem stirred the large, reeking pot of guano soup, over a fire outside their mud-brick shelter. The crew's expanded team, including its ten Ahuskay warriors, occupied the loaned building and a large patch of the land around it, with two fires built on the ground in addition to François's, and a number of small lean-tos.

After the previous day's successful test of the gunpowder, François had started the manufacturing process in earnest. Instead of distilling the potassium nitrate from mugfuls of bat guano, he'd upgraded to large five-gallon earthenware containers with the help of the couple who'd made him his grenades.

So far, he'd made a two-pound pouch full of the black powder, and now that Kareem and Gunther had volunteered to help with the extraction of the potassium nitrate, the process should hopefully be done before they had to leave.

It was late at night, after the evening meal, and the campfires were being banked for the night. François spotted Lowanna.

"I'll be back, okay?" he said.

Kareem nodded, his eyes tearing from the noxious vapors.

François walked toward the next campfire as two women emptied the remains from a large cooking pot into a smaller pot. Lowanna sat on a bench watching, and he sat down next to her.

Her back stiffened.

François sighed. "I've been thinking."

She said nothing.

"You don't like me. I get it. And I don't think that's on you. I think it's my doing."

"It's always about you, is it?" she muttered.

He bit his tongue. "It shouldn't be," he agreed. "In this case, it is. I didn't respect you. And I used my money to control you."

"How strange that I don't enjoy that."

"No, it's not strange." François took a deep breath. "Look, I have money. Had money, anyway, before this whole thing happened to me. I always had it, and when I put my mind to it, I could always make more. And the easiest way to get what I wanted, my whole life, was to use the money. So I did."

Lowanna flared her nostrils. She looked away, watching lights getting snuffed out for the evening in a building across the street.

"I'm not going to say that you would have done the same," François said. "Maybe you wouldn't. Maybe you would have been wiser than me. Maybe I have been an especially bad rich man. I will point out that I have at least used my wealth to try to advance the cause of knowledge."

"Looking for aliens and Bigfoot," Lowanna said.

"That would have been a much better retort before you and I both traveled back in time," François said. "Don't you think?"

"Fair point . . . *my dear*."

"Ah, yes." François nodded. "I'm sorry. I have tried to indicate that I thought you were a beautiful woman, but this was unwise of me. Perhaps I should have stuck to complimenting your anthropological insights."

"Perhaps you should have made your own tea," Lowanna growled.

"Yes. Yes, I'm sorry for all of that. I insulted you, and I'm sorry. What else do I need to apologize for?"

Lowanna sat still as a statue.

Nodding, he stood and walked away.

Someone in the distance yelled, "Fire!"

François saw the yellow and orange glow of flames near the marketplace. He rushed toward the commotion as residents of Jehed poured out of their mud-brick homes to see what was going on.

He paused for a second at the well, located at the center of the town square. Was water too precious a commodity to be used against a fire?

He followed the crowd to the market. The smell of burning grass and wood filled the air. Men and women grabbed buckets of sand and rushed toward the conflagration.

François had seen the piles of sand strategically located throughout the marketplace, but hadn't given it much thought before. Seeing an empty bucket, he scooped up a load of sand.

As he raced past several merchant stands, the glow ahead took the form of flames licking at a wide wooden structure. It was a single-story warehouse.

Following the example of others, he tossed the sand at the fire. It barely had any effect. He raced back for more sand.

For twenty minutes, François and others battled the flames.

In the surging crowd he spotted Marty and Surjan, their faces streaked with sweat and soot.

Even some of the king's guards were present, throwing large bucketsful of sand, and temporarily preventing the flames from spreading.

But the contents of the storeroom—timber and cloth—were now on fire, and the flames were getting close to an adjacent warehouse.

But was sand really his best firefighting tool?

François tossed the bucket and ran to the crew's camp. He grabbed both earthenware grenades from his supply pouch and turned to race back. He hadn't yet inserted the flint-based ignition systems he'd worked on, but it wouldn't matter in this case. There was fire enough to do the job.

But he needed to clear the crowd.

He ran back across the market to the burning warehouse. Warmth flooded through his body and pressure built up within him. For a second, François felt as if he was about to explode. His chest vibrated like the engine of a muscle car and he yelled, "Everyone back! Move away from the fire!"

This should work.

The grenade would explode, and shock waves would put out the flames.

Might put out the flames. As his bread-mold antibiotic might heal the king.

Or might not.

The people of Jehed scrambled backward, away from the fire. François held a grenade in his right hand, wound his arm back, and hurled the little ceramic weapon through the open door of the structure.

This would work.

Almost instantly there was a loud *whoomph* followed by a shock wave that knocked François prone. Debris flew over his head and rained down on him.

The building collapsed. Dust and soot rose in a billowing cloud, and the flames were instantly gone.

People rushed forward with more sand to snuff out the glowing embers. Two townspeople lifted François up by his arms, talking to him. His ears rang, and it took him a moment before he understood what they were asking. "What form of magic was that, stranger? I've never seen the like."

François felt a tingling sensation running up and down all his limbs. Like electricity, but . . . it felt good. So good, in fact, that he could have probably run a marathon at that moment. He felt euphoria in the midst of chaos.

Was this what Lowanna and the others had described?

A woman in the distance screamed. "They're gone!"

A second woman took up the cry. "The king's boys, they've been taken!"

François spotted Marty rushing in the direction of the king's two-story home. "Thank you. Thank you," he mumbled. Pulling himself from the grasp of his well-wishers, he raced after Marty.

He caught Marty in the king's open doorway just as one of the king's maids burst from the building. She threw herself on Marty, thumping him with her fists.

"It's because of you!" she yelled. "Your people brought this upon us!"

François put on a show of calm that he did not feel and tried to make his voice soft. "Please . . . can you tell me what happened?"

The woman stopped hitting Marty but didn't unclench her fists. "The king's three boys. Nine years old, seven, and five. The youngest two have been taken. The eldest was left with a cut across his cheek and a message." Her eyes blinked rapidly and she swayed on her feet.

François grabbed her shoulders and steadied her. "What message?"

The woman's expression melted into one of utter sorrow. "'Send the strangers to the ruins and we'll return your whelps unharmed. Don't do this and they'll be eaten.'"

Marty paced back and forth along the outskirts of the town, waiting for Surjan's return. The kidnapping of the king's children had been a surprise, but the more disturbing thing was that his crew had been mentioned by the kidnappers.

Send the strangers to the ruins...

The only thing Marty had been able to learn from the king's women about the ruins was that they were northwest of the town and that they were haunted.

He'd been to his share of allegedly haunted places in his archaeology career, of course. But that was before he'd encountered the Sethians and the Hathiru. If ancient Earth held those monsters, what other surprises might it contain?

Nobody had gotten any sleep that night, and it had taken all of François's sweet talking to prevent the crew from being tied up and thrown into the ruins. By the time the first light of dawn appeared on the horizon, the Ahuskay warriors had been isolated into a makeshift prison while Marty and the rest of his crew were escorted from the town.

The Jehedi warriors leaned on their spears with scowls on their faces, watching Marty closely.

It had been Surjan's suggestion that he go alone and scout the ruins to see what they faced. He'd argued that it would be easier for him to both track and avoid being detected if he was alone.

"There he is, praise God!" Kareem pointed.

Marty focused in the indicated direction and waited for a full minute before he saw the first sign of Surjan's form jogging in their direction.

As the large man slowed and finally came to a stop, he took a moment to catch his breath. "About three miles northwest, there's a set of dodgy ruins in a green valley. Looks like human settlements, but they're old. Really old. Those nippers could be hidden in any of those buildings."

"Did you see anyone?" Marty asked.

Surjan's face took on a sour expression. "I thought I saw some people moving within the ruins, but they... moved wrong."

"What do you mean?"

He sighed. "This might sound barmy, and I know we're in the

wrong part of the world, but what I saw looked like incarnations of the Hindu god Narasimha. One of Vishnu's avatars."

Marty furrowed his brow. "Narasimha is the one with a head of a lion. You saw cat-headed people?"

"They had the heads of cats. They moved like cats."

"On all fours?" Marty asked.

"On their hind legs. But they prowled. And they smelled like cats. But their bodies were the bodies of men." Surjan shrugged. "It was a great distance, and the winds were unreliable, so I couldn't get any closer without alerting them."

Gunther nudged Marty. "Are you thinking what I'm thinking? That sounds like Bast."

Marty nodded. "Why not? We already have Sethians, the cow-headed Hathiru, why not a bunch of Bast clones running around? I suppose something had to have inspired Egyptian mythology. Call them Bastites."

François grinned. "Call them Bastards, perhaps?"

Marty turned back to Surjan, in no mood for jokes. "You didn't see any kids?"

The Sikh shook his head. "I didn't, but I smelled them."

"You're sure?" Marty asked.

"The . . . Bastites . . . smelled catlike," Surjan said. "But when they traveled, they had humans with them. I can now appreciate what a bloodhound must experience, because to me I can smell the difference as clearly as if I was being asked to tell the visual difference between an orange and an apple."

Marty scanned the crew. "We're persona non grata in the village until we get those kids back, and it seems that they were taken because of us." He turned to François. "It looks like your grenades are working. Do we have any more?"

François extracted one fist-sized ball from a pouch hanging off his belt. "Just this one. And my supplies for making more are all back in Jehed."

"Surjan," Marty said, "you saw the terrain and the Bastites. Do you have any suggestions?"

The big man turned to face northwest and remained silent for a few seconds. "About two miles from here, the land dips into a valley and it's pretty treacherous terrain. We're going to have to be careful. I have no idea how many of those monsters we're facing, but I guess my nose should be able to sniff its way to where the kids are being held."

"Is there any cover on the approach?"

Surjan nodded. "Thick forest down in the valley."

Marty didn't like it. The enemy had picked the terrain, and it was one that they presumably knew well. A little cover at least meant he might get the advantage of surprise. On the other hand, the Bastites had apparently invited Marty to come.

He looked at the rest of the crew. "Any thoughts or concerns before we head out?"

François frowned. "All I have is the one grenade with an ignition system I haven't even tested yet. So, if we're engaging in melee of some kind..." He held up his sharpened ankh. "I'm not exactly a kung fu master or trained with weapons."

Marty patted the Frenchman on the shoulder. "Surjan is taking point with his nose. I'll be near the front as well. Kareem, I assume you're somewhere right behind or next to me. Gunther, are you comfortable with your weapon?"

Gunther made a so-so motion with his hand and Lowanna cleared her throat. "I'm very comfortable with both the ankh and my throwing stick, thank you very much."

"And you?" Marty asked the Jehedi warriors. "Will you fight with us?"

"We come only to make certain that you do not flee," the foremost grunted.

Surjan pointed at François. "Just watch our six and yell if you see anything."

François nodded.

"And if you're about to toss your grenade," Marty added, "yell so we aren't caught by surprise." He took a deep breath. "Let's go see if Bast turns out to be as much fun as Seth was."

Marty crept forward on the balls of his feet, amazed at the difference in climate between the arid village and this humid, mist-covered subtropical valley. Hanging in the air were the scents of grass, mold, and something rotten.

About half a mile ahead, Marty spotted multistory stone buildings squatting in the mists. The edges of the buildings were worn smooth, and several walls lay tumbled into the grass. Marty wanted to map them, measure them, and look for inscriptions.

Grandpa Chang's voice rang softly in his head, on the occasion of a broken action figure.

The root of suffering is your attachment.

No archaeologists had ever uncovered ruins of any great age in this area. Then again, in five thousand years, this entire area was going to be covered by the vast dunes of the Sahara.

Taking a deep breath, Marty set aside his archaeologist's curiosity and focused on what lay ahead. The ancient-looking buildings were to the north. Several crevasses bordered the southern edge of the city, and skirting along the western edge of the valley was a thick forest, something he'd never seen in this part of the world. A leftover microclimate from the last ice age?

There was one visible path into the ruined city and that was the north-south path between two of the crevasses.

As Marty crept beside him, Surjan pointed toward the buildings. "I smell the kids somewhere over there."

"You sure?"

"Has to be them. Smells just like the king's women. They eat a lot of cumin."

"And our cat-headed friends?"

"They're there as well."

Marty pointed in the direction of the trees. "Assuming the western crevasse stops ahead of the forest, I was thinking maybe we could skirt along the edge and go into the forest. We should be able to get closer without being seen, and from there we can scout out the possibilities with a bit more accuracy. The more information we can get, the better. What do you think?"

Surjan nodded. The group slowly progressed through the rocky terrain and entered the forest.

Lowanna murmured, "I've never seen so many sycamore fig trees in my life."

"Amazing, isn't it?" François plucked a yellow fruit from a nearby tree and bit into it. "Delicious. And these kinds of trees were mentioned in both the Old and New Testaments. I don't think these exist in North Africa anymore, at least not outside of someone's private garden." He plucked another of the ripe fruits and handed it to Lowanna.

She stared at the offered fruit for a moment, took it and bit into it. Her eyes widened and a smile bloomed on her face. "It's sweet like honey."

"Guys, let's eat later." Marty motioned in the general direction of the stone buildings and Surjan led them forward.

The temperature inside the forest was at least ten degrees cooler than the surrounding prairie. Surjan sniffed, motioned to the east, and said, "The kids are close."

"The cats?" Marty whispered.

"Closer. But I think we're downwind."

Marty nodded as the big man moved forward, leading them toward the buildings. The structures were built of carved sandstone blocks, worn into saddles and red drapery-like ruffles by wind and time.

There were no windows in the buildings, yet there were doorways with what looked like wooden doors. How old were the buildings, and who had built them?

Kareem hissed. "Cat people on the other side of the crevasse."

Marty glanced toward the entrance of the valley and saw a group of nearly a dozen figures approaching. He crouched and hissed, "To the forest. Get out of sight!"

The group hugged the shadows and raced toward cover.

Keeping a low profile, Marty motioned for everyone to push ahead. He brought up the rear. The thickness of the undergrowth forced the crew to walk along the lip of a crevasse, where the footing was at a steep angle and was strewn with loose rock.

One of Lowanna's legs shot out from under her in the gravel and François grabbed her arm. They regained their balance and raced ahead, disappearing into the shadows of the forest.

Marty followed Gunther, who was struggling with the rocky terrain. Suddenly, the ground under the German archaeologist shifted. Marty lunged for Gunther and yanked him back to solid ground, but in the process the ground under his own feet shifted and he slid toward the yawning crevasse.

He grabbed an exposed root, which snapped taut and stopped his slide.

"Marty!" Gunther knelt slowly and extended his hand.

But then the root broke, and Marty plummeted into darkness.

CHAPTER TWENTY-THREE

Marty lay in darkness.

He had fallen into a deep crack in the earth. By some miracle, he'd managed to slow his fall sufficiently to land on his feet without breaking anything. His fingers, feet, and knees were scraped to hell, and he prayed that the rest of the crew had gotten away without calling attention to themselves.

But after landing, his memory was mostly a blank. He recalled the smell of rotting eggs. The scent reminded him of a vacation he'd taken to see a childhood friend in South Florida. They'd visited a garbage dump nicknamed Mount Trashmore. It was literally the highest elevation in the southern part of the state. The methane emissions were controlled by burning the gas off through several pipes that reached deep into the grassy mountain. It was entertainment on a low budget for two seventeen-year-olds. Almost forty years later, he'd experienced a similar strong scent of rot and must have passed out.

The floor was smooth. Clay or plaster, or maybe dirt pounded flat by centuries of traffic. He couldn't still be in the crack he'd fallen into. Someone had found him and brought him here, wherever here was.

Taking in deep breaths and letting them out slowly, Marty worked on calming his rapidly beating heart. Who had plucked him from the crevasse?

He was alive, at least. He had to believe that escape was possible.

Horrible images came to mind as he imagined the reasons why the catlike creatures would have wanted him alive.

Food was a distinct possibility. Nothing is better than fresh.

Torture. They had summoned the crew to the ruins. If they really wanted to get all the so-called strangers, and if he was the only one they'd caught, then they might work on trying to extract information from him.

Bait was a third possibility. For some reason, they wanted the crew. One way to get them all might be to hold Marty as a prisoner to lure the others in.

Unless, of course, his friends were also prisoners, held in different cells. In which case, the cat-men might try to play them off one another.

His eyes were useless in the darkness. So Marty closed his eyes and focused on his other senses.

When he was a kid, Grandpa Chang had taught him meditation. It was supposed to help clear his mind, make him more open to clear thinking, and be more receptive to what his body—and his senses— were telling him.

Taking another deep breath, Marty found the air damp. It smelled of the grass, the humidity, and decay. And the air was still.

He was inside. Probably in one of the buildings.

He felt tiny vibrations coming from the floor.

Footsteps.

And the vibrations were getting stronger.

He felt for his ankh; it had been taken from him. Without a doubt, these weren't friendlies.

A door swung open and blinding light poured into the room.

Marty squinted, trying to make out details of the two figures at the doorway, but the door slammed shut and the bright light snapped off. A dim blue light began emanating from a fist-sized rock one of the figures was carrying.

The rock was placed on the ground. As time passed, it glowed steadily brighter.

The interior of the room slowly came out of the darkness. Marty was already crouched in a defensive position, arms raised to deflect attack. The shadows melted away from the two new arrivals.

They sat cross-legged not more than six feet from him.

The stone didn't put out enough light for him to really get a sense of colors, but these monsters had catlike eyes that seemed to glow in their dim surroundings. One had tabby orange fur and the other was tawny yellow. They were as tall as tall men, powerfully built, and dressed in kilts, capes, and sandals.

Marty sighed. For once, he'd like to encounter a new sentient species that was shorter than he was, and not threatening.

Orange Cat leaned forward and sniffed several times, its eyes squinted and its mouth held partially open, revealing long canines. It looked at Tawny Cat and shrugged.

Tawny Cat spoke in a very high-pitched voice. "You smell of the *one*, but you aren't of the *one*."

Marty blinked, trying to process what he'd heard.

Tawny Cat tilted its head. "Do you hear me, of the *one* who is not of the *one*? Do you understand what I am saying to you?"

Marty nodded. "Yes," he lied.

Orange Cat donned a glove and drew a metal object from within its robe, and held up Marty's ankh.

"This was in your possession. Such a thing is not for those who are of the *one*, it is for the others. You held such a thing?"

Marty nodded again.

"Yet it does not burn you," Tawny Cat purred and both of the creatures' eyes widened.

The cat-man had to wear a glove to handle the ankh. Might that explain why the ankh was so lethal to the Sethians? Something about the metal in the ankh was deadly poison to them, or maybe it caused a violent allergic reaction.

The cat-men kept sniffing at him. Did the crew smell different from the humans of this time? He resolved to ask Surjan.

"You are not of the *one*," Orange Cat said, "but you are also not like the rest."

Marty maintained a blank expression. He needed time and he needed more information. "I thought I was the *one*."

Both cat-headed creatures shook their heads, and the one who did all the talking for the pair wrinkled its nose.

As he did so, Marty noticed that each of the creatures had a small ring attached to its septum. Just like the Sethians did.

"What are you doing here?" Orange Cat purred. "You are but one. We are looking for more than just one."

A sense of relief washed over Marty. The rest of the crew must have managed to make it to the forest without catching these things' attention.

Marty's skin began tingling as adrenaline rushed through his system. The door opened, bathing the room once again in blindingly bright light.

The light had a yellow cast to it. Did that mean it was daylight? If so, perhaps the cat-people had fished Marty from the crevasse and stashed him in one of the ruins. If so, the seal on the door was impressive—when shut, it blocked out all light.

Marty squinted against the brightness and saw the outline of a large creature standing in the doorway.

It ducked its head and walked in.

It was a Sethian. And it was nearly seven feet tall.

Its yellow-eyed countenance focused on Marty and he felt malice boiling off the creature like vapor from a Halloween smoke machine. The Sethian spoke with a deep gravelly voice, "Are you Merit Nuk Han?"

Marty stared.

"The *one* asks for Merit Nuk Han," Orange Cat said. "You know this creature, he is of your kind."

So was the *one* the Sethian? Is that what the furball was talking about?

The Sethian snarled, and let out a loud guttural vocalization that was a mix of a growl and a bark. "Do you know where Merit Nuk Han is?"

Marty shook his head. "I don't understand."

The cat-headed creature turned to the Sethian, then promptly turned back to Marty. "The *great one* is clear about this, and the *one* speaks for him. You must die if you don't help kill Merit Nuk Han and those who come with it."

The great one? What in the world could that be? The Sethian's boss?

Marty blinked as he rattled the words the cat creature had said around in his head, desperately trying to make sense of it.

He felt he was in some scene from the Book of the Dead, confronted by gods or demons with the heads of beasts. He couldn't pass on until he produced the password the monsters wanted to hear.

Merit Nuk Han...

The Book of the Dead, or the Pyramid Texts, or the Book of Breathings. These gate guardian or judgment scenes were common in ancient Egyptian writing.

Writing.

Written ancient Egyptian, much like modern Semitic languages, didn't represent vowels very well.

Merit Nuk Han would be written as Mrt Nk Hn.

The Sethian again made a growling noise deep in its chest. "This is your final chance. You will find Merit Nuk Han and kill it and its people, or you will die."

"So, you will let me go if I promise to kill Merit Nuk Han and its people?" Marty was fishing for information.

The Sethian snarled, spittle dripping from its bared canines. "No. You will lead me to him. Understood?"

Marty's mind raced as he visualized the words the Sethian was saying. When encountering unknown words in written Egyptian, his mind strung them together into a single stream of consonants and then tried to find the skeletons of known words within.

Out of force of habit, his mind did the same thing now. *M-r* made an "overseer," and *t-n* could mean "this," but "overseer" was masculine and *t-n* was the feminine form, so that didn't work.

Maybe the words weren't Egyptian, after all.

Then a chill passed up his spine.

Mrtnkhn.

Martin Cohen.

How in the world could this monster know his name?

The Sethian drew a glittering dagger from its belt.

Marty's skin tingled and his hands shook. He stood, backed away, and fell into a defensive stance.

Light flashed into the room as the door banged open. The cat-headed creatures hissed. A huge turbaned warrior raced into the room and slammed into the back of the Sethian.

Chaos erupted.

Marty launched a front kick at the chest of Orange Cat, sending it flying backward, its head smashing against the stone wall with a sickening crunch.

The ankh fell from its grasp and Marty scooped it up.

A bellowing roar erupted from the Sethian as he turned, flinging Surjan to the side.

Marty lunged at the giant creature, who sidestepped him, but crashed into Tawny Cat, knocking it backward through the entrance.

With a blurred motion, the Sethian slashed at Marty with its dagger; the blade buzzed through the air and just barely missed his face.

Surjan sank his ankh deep into the creature's back and then yanked it free. A dark ooze flowed from the wound, splattering the room with its foul reek.

With his ankh in his hand, Marty feinted a slashing attack with it, which sent the Sethian one step back, and with a continuing fluid motion, Marty fell into a sweep of the behemoth's weight-bearing leg and sent it crashing onto its back.

Before the Sethian could react, Marty slashed across the creature's exposed belly, and then plunged the ankh into its inner thigh and slashed outward.

The creature howled and began scrambling to its feet. Blood poured from its wounds. The Sethian's glowing yellow eyes stared at Marty and it growled. Marty backed out of reach.

Those wounds and the amount of blood loss would have felled a water buffalo, yet the creature climbed up into a crouch.

Marty braced himself for the attack and suddenly a metal spike blasted out of the creature's mouth as Surjan yelled, "Surjan Marty *fateh*!" It was a call for their victory in Surjan's native tongue, and the spike was the tip of his ankh.

The Sethian's body convulsed and then collapsed, pulling the ankh from Surjan's grip.

From the corner of Marty's eye, he noticed a shimmering ball of light just as it touched his leg and blinked out of existence. He glanced in the direction it had drifted from and noticed Tawny Cat. Its skin had already started decomposing, just like the other half-human creatures he'd encountered.

Marty felt relief as he looked at Surjan's blood-spattered face. "Welcome to the party."

He stepped around the growing pool of bleach-smelling ichor flowing from the giant Sethian and noticed that Surjan's left arm was hanging motionless by his side. "Your arm?"

Surjan winced. "Popped out of joint."

Gunther and Lowanna poked their heads into the chamber. "Anyone need healing?" the German asked.

Marty pointed at Surjan's arm. "Gunther, did they teach you how to pop dislocated arms back into place in the Army?"

Gunther nodded and walked over to Surjan as Lowanna announced, "We've got the kids. François has them hiding in the forest and is probably making them both fat on figs. Kareem is tracking down some of the remaining cat creatures." She gave Marty an evil grin. "He's pretty dangerous with a sharp stabby object in his hand."

Marty pointed at the decomposing remnants of the Sethian. "Somewhere in that mess is a pretty nice-looking dagger. He might want to play with that."

A blob of light bubbled up from the remnants of the Sethian and drifted toward him.

The blobs came from enemies that *Marty* had killed. Were they souls? Some life essence that only the crew could see? Was Marty a vampire of sorts?

At least, as François had pointed out, he fought to defend himself, and for the purpose of provoking this light-response.

As the ball of light drifted into him, a shock raced up his leg and warmth spread across his chest, making him gasp.

Surjan also gasped, but the world around Marty began to spin as noises and colors filled his senses.

And just as suddenly, it all stopped.

His heart raced as a wave of energy washed over him. Any sense of exhaustion vanished in the blink of an eye.

Marty heard footsteps outside the room.

He looked over at Surjan, whose arm was moving like normal again, and their eyes met. Something had happened to him as well, Marty could tell. "Do you also feel like you've just broken through to a new level of being?"

"I should say so. I guess that would be level number three for me. If we're counting."

"Yup, same for me." Marty chuckled and recalled how as a kid he'd played an arcade game and felt a sense of euphoria after hitting a new level. The real-life version was much better.

If this was, in fact, real life.

Surjan laughed. "I feel reborn."

Marty kicked the dagger away from the goo that remained of the Sethian. He retrieved another Sethian medallion. "Let's take a very quick inventory of what's here, take whatever we think we can use, and get those kids back to the king."

"So far the only things we found are a stash of dried beans, just like in the outpost, and a pouch of gold nuggets, each about the size of a grape."

"Good, now we have something to barter with. I find it interesting that the Sethians would have gold . . . I guess they buy and sell things, too."

"Kareem is coming," Surjan announced.

"How do you know?" Marty asked.

The head of security shrugged. "I can smell him. Believe it or not, I think my sniffer has gotten even more sensitive."

Kareem appeared in the doorway, scanned the room, and nodded. "We've all been busy. There are no more of those cat things in this valley, praise God, but I think some may have escaped while we were ambushing the others."

"Ambushing?" Marty felt a growing sense of camaraderie between the crew members. "Let's take those kids home. On the way back, I'd love to hear what happened while I was unconscious."

⊰ CHAPTER ⊱
TWENTY-FOUR

After the crew delivered the kids, there was rejoicing amongst the people of Jehed, and the warriors from Ahuskay were freed. Marty found himself stopped repeatedly on the street by people who handed him sweets and gave invitations for him and the crew to eat a meal under their roof.

Effusive expressions of gratitude were pretty common in modern Middle Eastern cultures, and given that these people were theoretically the ancient ancestors of the modern people Marty had spent years with, it was interesting to see and feel the similarities in behavior.

Marty, Gunther, and François approached the king's home and this time the spear-wielding guards in white sashes smiled.

As the three walked into the building, Gunther leaned over to whisper, "This is what fame feels like."

"Blessed ones, you are back!" Lunja, the king's wife, greeted them with a warm smile. She motioned for them to follow her back into the main residence and then upstairs. "You need to see Iken."

"Iken?" Marty asked.

"The king," Gunther whispered.

François took deep breaths. "She doesn't seem traumatized by grief. Maybe the penicillin worked."

"What you made isn't penicillin," Marty told him.

The queen wasn't waiting, and they hastened to follow.

Climbing up the mud-brick steps, Marty followed Lunja's multicolored robe into a room they hadn't seen before.

His eyes widened.

King Iken was not only sitting up, he was sitting on a chair beside a writing table. The man was breathing without apparent discomfort. His bloody spittoon was nowhere in evidence.

The graying man turned and smiled. "Blessings on you and your people. I owe you much." The king pointed at Gunther. "I do not know if it was your touch that healed me"—he pointed at François—"or your foul bread . . . but I thank you. I am feeling much better."

François pulled from his pack two more pieces of the mold-covered bread and laid it on the king's desk. "I advise you to continue eating this for at least three more days. The demons need to be killed, otherwise they can come back."

The Frenchman was trembling.

The king grabbed one of the pieces of bread and bit a large chunk from it.

His face twisted into a grimace that showed what he truly thought of the taste, but he spoke through a half-full mouth and said, "Enjoy the taste, demons. More of this is coming."

Marty groaned inside and moved to cut off this medical malpractice. "We killed all of the creatures we found in the ruins, but there likely are more out there somewhere."

"Ametsu?" the king asked.

Marty nodded. "Ametsu and also creatures of the Ametsu. Giant men with the heads of cats."

The king grinned and showed Marty a sheet of vellum, a scraped and preserved animal skin. It bore markings that resembled the characters he'd seen at one of the oases. Unintelligible symbols, a rudimentary map, and an area circled that had an infinity symbol on it.

"I am writing to my brother kings. When the Ametsu, or their creatures, desecrate one of our ancient places and dare to attack us, it is an offense to all of today's kings and to the kings of the past. Others will send warriors, and we will reclaim what is ours."

Marty desperately wanted to wear his archaeologist hat for a moment and ask about the ruins, but for the crew's sake, his questions didn't matter. In fact, questions about something that might actually be common knowledge could only raise suspicion. Being responsible for the crew's welfare, he buried the questions the professor of Egyptology wanted to ask and assumed the role of team leader. He bowed his head with respect and removed from his pack one of the yellow figs from the hidden forest. "You certainly already know that the ruins lie in a fruitful valley."

The king's eyes grew wide and he set aside the half-eaten bread. "Beautiful." He bit down on the fruit and his eyes closed for a moment as he made a low sound of deep satisfaction. "What a gift!" He opened his eyes and met Marty's gaze. "My people promised yours a boon if you could help me recover from the demons in my chest. I will honor that promise. I will need a couple of days to gather what is needed." The king took a large bite of the moldy bread, grimaced, and motioned to his wife. "Lunja, have Ridha and Lalla prepare large jugs for the water. They will need at least a day or two for the pots to bake and cool."

"Thank you, Your Majesty." Marty stood and again bowed his head to the king and his wife. "We'll take our leave."

François pointed at the bread. "I'll be back tomorrow with more of that."

His hand was shaking.

The king bit off another hunk of the bread and turned back to writing on the animal skin.

The three members of the crew navigated their way out of the king's house and Marty glanced at Gunther. "Could you have imagined in a million years we'd be in a prehistoric village dealing with pre-pharaonic North African leaders? Or possibly encountering creatures that almost certainly inspired Egyptian mythology and no modern biologist knows existed?"

Gunther shrugged. "I'm telling you. *The Twilight Zone* . . . we're sitting in someone's imagined story and playing the part of the crazy professor who's worried that he's lost his mind."

Marty chuckled and shook his head. "And, François, what's going on with you? You look like you're suffering from St. Vitus's dance."

François giggled. "I feel . . . invigorated. I'm a healer!"

"Or a poisoner," Marty muttered.

"Probably not," Gunther said. "If the mold was poison, the king would be ill."

"And instead, the king is recovering," François said.

"Okay," Marty said. "I like your enthusiasm. But maybe . . . maybe let's focus on the gunpowder."

François nodded. "If we only have two days, I really need to get stuff ready with the black powder and grenades."

"A really excellent use of your scientific mind," Gunther suggested, "would be finding a way home."

"At this point," François said, "either Marty's vision gets us home or nothing does."

Marty's gaze narrowed as they navigated the town and he thought about what lay to the east. Almost everyone in the town had warned him about the travel and not to go. There was danger. At least François was thinking again. Of all the people on the crew, he was the one preparing for war.

Marty walked with François and Surjan through the scrub grass of the outskirts of Jehed. François talked excitedly about what he'd been working on.

"I've got almost fifty pounds of black powder mixed, and with Kareem's help we have another three hundred pounds of charcoal, sulfur, and guano."

Surjan raised one eyebrow at the Frenchman. "And how are you making sure that all that black powder doesn't blow us all up by accident?"

François waved his arms. "Some of the villagers have brought back some green wood from that hidden valley, so I had one of the woodworkers make storage boxes. There's no way a stray spark is going to set those things off." He stopped at the edge of a downslope and with a satisfied nod handed a grenade each to Marty and Surjan. "We're far enough away that we shouldn't have any weird questions about the explosions."

"If anyone asks," Marty suggested, "we blame lightning bolts." He hefted the one-pound object. "As you know, MacGyver, having explosives in this day and age might cause some crossing of the streams or a breakdown in the space-time continuum if anyone figures out how you did this, so let's keep the details hush-hush, okay? It's the Chinese who are supposed to invent this stuff."

"Fine by me, as long as you agree to leave the hard science

terminology to me..." François muttered. "Space-time continuum...
as if!"

Marty chuckled as he examined the grenade. It was shaped like a
baseball and had a buttonlike cap on one end. The majority of the
weight was in the top of the grenade. "This is not balanced."

"On purpose. The screw-top lid has most of the weight because I
want the grenade to land on the sparker that I installed at the top."

Studying the lid, Marty found a spring with... "Is that flint you're
using as a sparking agent?"

"It's a simple thing. Two pieces of flint held in place with a spring.
Upon impact, the spring scrapes the two together, sending off sparks
into the grenade and setting the powder off."

"Is that a reliable trigger mechanism?" Surjan asked.

François smiled. "That's why we're out here. I think it should
be, but I want to make sure you both know how to throw it, because
it's... well, let's just say you can't throw it like a baseball. The lid is
going to tumble and it'll be hit or miss if the trigger takes an impact
with the target or not. Think of the lid side of the grenade as the tip
of a spear. Throw it that way and the top of the grenade should lead
all the way to the target." He glanced back and forth between Marty
and Surjan. "You guys ready?"

"Wait a minute." Surjan hefted the grenade in his hand with a
concerned expression. "What's the lethal radius of this?"

François bobbed his head to the left and right. "Probably only
about ten feet or so. These have nothing in them but black powder.
The others I'm assembling will have pieces of shrapnel. Mostly rocks,
since chunks of metal are hard to come by. Just make sure you throw
it at least twenty feet."

Marty adjusted his grip. "Okay, guys. I'll count down from three.

"Three...

"Two...

"One...

"Throw!"

Marty heaved his grenade as far as he could. It sailed a good forty
feet before gravity pulled it down and it smacked into the ground
with an explosive *whoomph*.

Followed immediately by two sandy thuds.

"Damn it!" François growled. "That's not what I was hoping for."

Marty shrugged. "Hey, one out of three isn't bad."

"It isn't bad, it's abysmal." François raced down the slope, grabbed the failed grenades, and came back muttering as he unscrewed them, letting a brownish-black powder spill everywhere. "I have to go back and check the formulation. It looks like some of the grinding was not fine enough and the sparks didn't catch."

Marty fist-bumped the banker and nodded. "François, I'd say your experiment is well on its way to being a success. At least for one of the grenades, the trigger and powder seemed to work. Also, there's no chance the grenade is going to accidentally poison someone."

"We need something more reliable," François grumbled. "But, yes, it's okay for a first attempt. I'll get the kinks worked out."

Surjan nodded. "How many of those can you make?"

"The pottery is the limiting factor. I have enough black powder for fifty grenades, and raw ingredients for another three hundred. Assuming I get the bugs worked out quickly, by the time we leave, I'll have a few boxes of grenades."

"How are you paying for the supplies?" Marty asked. "Lowanna has a pouch of gold nuggets from the ruins. Are you two . . . on speaking terms?"

François laughed as the group started walking in the direction of the village. "I don't think she's plotting to stab me in my sleep anymore. Either way, I'm fine. I actually traded a few of the gold links from my watch. It's not like I need to keep time these days."

"Fair enough." Marty looked over at Surjan. "You have plans for those grenades?"

"I'm thinking about getting a bandoleer made." The tall man grinned. "It never hurts to be prepared."

"My thoughts exactly," François chimed in.

They entered the outskirts of the village. Guards saluted as they passed.

Tomorrow night was a going-away feast hosted by the king, and the next day they'd be gone.

Marty clasped forearms with Badis. He looked past the warrior into the corral that housed the group's supplies and his eyes widened. There stood five fully loaded wagons, with oxen and a handful of camels. The wagons were heavy with wrapped supplies, but the thing that was shocking was the huge quantity of giant earthenware containers, which he presumed had water in them. "Where did all of this come from?"

Badis turned to Udad. "Did they leave names?"

The younger warrior shook his head. "They just brought it and said it was for our travels."

"Who is *they*?" Marty asked.

"Some of the king's men. People. The Jehedi."

Marty furrowed his brow. It was probably ten times the amount they actually needed for their journey. Maybe more.

Munatas was feeding a camel a bundle of long green grasses, when it suddenly bellowed.

I have a thorn in my lip!

"What's wrong with you?" Munatas shrieked.

"Check his mouth. He's got a thorn in his lip." Marty froze. How the hell did he know that?

Had he understood what the camel had said?

Marty leaned forward to rest on his knees and took deep breaths.

Munatas turned to Marty and smiled, waving something in his hand. "You were right!" The Ahuskay villager offered the animal more of the grass and the camel resumed munching.

Marty felt vaguely ill.

"Are you well?" Badis asked.

The men looked concerned and Marty patted both of them on their shoulders. "I'm fine." He motioned to the now-filled corral. "Are we ready to go tomorrow morning?"

Badis nodded.

"Good." He clasped the man's forearm once again and said, "There's a feast tonight. Make sure you get your share."

"Seer," Badis said, hesitation in his voice.

"Yes?"

"A host such as this is becoming..." Badis gestured at the wagons. "Such a host should march under a banner."

Marty turned and walked back to the village center where the celebration feast was being prepared.

He liked these people. They were good and honest folk, and he'd have loved to stay longer, but he had a vision.

Eleven days until the end of their journey.

✤ ✤ ✤

Marty stood beside the cooking pit. He smiled as King Iken walked through the town's center. It was the first time Marty had seen the man outside his home.

The king made a beeline for Marty and greeted him with a kiss on both cheeks. "I will be sorry to see you and yours go. You've been a greater blessing to me than I could have ever hoped for."

Marty patted the man's chest. "Are the demons quiet?"

"All gone. Gunther left me two days' supply of that foul bread, which I've promised to eat—just to make sure the demons are truly gone." He motioned to the large spitted camel that one man was rotating over the coals while another basted it with a mop soaked in some reddish, heavily spiced liquid. "The rest of the food is not quite ready yet, but please join me for the King's Cut."

The smell coming from the camel was an intoxicating mix of roasting meat with North African spices like cinnamon, allspice, garlic and more.

"The King's Cut?"

The king motioned for Marty to follow as the man walked up to the crackling fire-roasted camel, retrieved a knife and a two-pronged fork from his belt, and sliced a chunk of the meat from the rotating animal.

He handed Marty the steaming slice of meat, its juices glistening. "Go ahead, take the first taste. It's said that the first bite is always the sweetest."

Marty plucked the meat from the prongs and the king sliced off another chunk for himself.

They took a bite at the same time and Marty closed his eyes.

He'd previously eaten camel, but this was like nothing he'd ever had before. The basting had created a smoky crust on the meat that exploded with flavors that were quintessentially North African. And either this king had access to salt or there was something else enhancing the flavor of the meat, because this was better than anything he'd ever had before.

"What do you think?"

Marty smiled. "It's a good thing I'm going. Because if I stayed here for too long, I'd get fat."

The king laughed and motioned to one of his guards. The man raced off and the king draped his arm over Marty's shoulder. "I told you before how grateful I am that you've come. I want you to know that you and yours are welcome back any time you desire. I have arranged for your supplies, as promised—"

"Speaking of supplies." Marty wasn't sure how to approach the topic delicately. "I saw all those wagons filled with food and water. I don't want to seem ungrateful, but it's too much for my group to manage all those wagons. It's—"

The king laughed and gave Marty's shoulder a squeeze. "I can explain, my friend." He pointed at an approaching crowd. "Here, maybe this will help."

The crowd was huge, at least fifty . . . no, closer to one hundred men. A tall, muscular man wearing a guard's sash and carrying a spear approached the king. He briefly knelt to one knee and then stood. He squinted, making his eyes look tiny in his long face, and his nostrils seemed permanently flared.

The king motioned to the man. "Usaden is one of my most trusted guards. We have many in Jehed, and in the country for many miles around, who have pledged to serve those who have saved their king and his children. I had Usaden pick from the best. No men with wives."

Marty stammered, hoping he misunderstood what had just been said. "Are you saying these people are—"

"They are yours to command. They wish to join your host. Their destiny now lies in your hands. I expect the name of Marty to be famous across the desert sands for many years to come. I hope this can help you on your journey."

Badis stood to one side, leaning on a spear. No, not a spear—it was a long pole with a crossbar on top.

A pole from which to hang a banner.

Badis handed Marty's pack to him and nodded.

The gathered men all faced him, dipped down to one knee, and stood. Their earnest faces made Marty realize how over his head he now was. It was something to lead a group of six. A bit more a group of sixteen. But this . . . this was the beginning of an army.

It was indeed becoming a host.

He wasn't ready for this.

But he had no choice.

He pasted on a smile and raised his voice so it could be heard across the group. "Welcome and thank you for uniting with our group. You join us at an important moment." He signaled Badis to come forward.

The Ahuskay warrior grinned and advanced, holding the banner pole proudly. Marty dug into his pack and found what Badis wanted him to take out.

"We have a long trip ahead of us," Marty said, "and we are leaving at dawn. We travel under this banner, the sign of the Broken Ametsu." He affixed his banner to the pole and Badis raised it.

"The Broken Ametsu!" Badis bellowed. "The living banner of the Host of Marty the Seer!"

"The Broken Ametsu!" the new members of the host shouted. "Marty the Seer!"

Living banner? What had he done? Marty cleared his throat. "Make sure you are well rested and we'll gather at the corral just before the sun rises."

The king yelled, "And make sure to join in the feast at sunset! There will be much to celebrate and I wish you all the best on your journeys." He made a dismissive motion and the group dispersed, drifting to their various corners of the town.

The king turned to Marty and grinned. "You will do well."

The king and Marty clasped forearms.

A vein in Marty's temple began throbbing as he thought about what to do with this army of people.

As Marty worried, he remembered one of Grandpa Chang's sayings.

The biggest mistake you can make is to constantly worry about making a mistake. Things have a way of working themselves out.

Marty nodded.

Regardless of everything else going on . . . he knew one thing.

He needed to take one step at a time.

Eleven days to go.

⫷ CHAPTER ⫸
TWENTY-FIVE

"Okay," Surjan said. "Everything you know about spear-fighting is great, if you find yourself fighting an enemy one on one. If you're isolated and in hand-to-hand combat, you can forget most of what I'm about to say to you."

He faced two dozen men, lined up in two rows. Each held a long stick, which Surjan had carefully collected and kept along the road for this very purpose, and an oval shield made of leather.

In the distance, the host's banner watched, flapping in the breeze.

Two dozen men, and one woman. Tafsut.

Surjan's female friend, from Ahuskay village. She had joined the spear fighting training he had organized, and for the three days during which Surjan had been observing their sparring, she had willingly thrown herself into the fights. Like any of the men, she fought with great personal courage. She was beautiful, with her dusky-clay complexion and her shimmering black hair. They leaped, they threw their spears when they had openings, they slashed as well as they thrust. It was a fighting style that exposed their bodies to counterattack but also generated strong, violent hits.

It was also totally unsuited for fighting in a unit. It was the fighting style of barbarians, and Surjan aimed to teach them all an additional way to approach battle.

He wasn't entirely sure where they were going with this army, but it seemed they were heading into combat. And specifically, against the violent, thick-skinned Sethians. When that battle came, Surjan wanted them to fight like a unit, not like a mob of uncoordinated heroes.

"We are going to learn how to fight together!" Surjan bellowed in his parade ground voice. "The first, the single most important thing you need to know has nothing to do with the spear. We must learn to stay together as a single body. Shoulder to shoulder."

"If we stand shoulder to shoulder," Badis said, "are we not easier for enemy archers to shoot?"

"We will prepare for archers later," Surjan said. "But the answer is no. Shoulder to shoulder you will protect each other from arrows and other missile weapons. But let us consider an enemy with a spear or sword. Badis, raise your spear into a guard position. Back hand near your waist, blade at eye level. You two, to his left and right, do the same. Now observe." He made as if attempting to break through their guards. "To either side, you have a brother, Badis. Behind you are brothers. All you have to worry about is the two feet in front of you."

"Yes," Badis said. "But if we move, we will have to move together."

"That is correct!" Surjan bellowed. "So here is the first rule of fighting together: hold the line."

"Even in retreat?" Munatas asked.

Tafsut spat. "We do not retreat."

"Hold the line," Surjan said.

"What if we have to turn?" the other woman in the spear-fighting group asked.

"We will learn to turn together," Surjan said. "And when we turn, we will hold the line."

"What if a fighter falls?" a short spearman pressed.

"Hold the line," Surjan said.

"Do we go back to get our wounded?" the same man wondered.

"We go forward together," Surjan said, "and we go back together. The second rule of fighting together is this: follow your leader." He tried to think of a word for sergeant, and couldn't, so he made one up. "Each platoon will have a Speaker for the Spears. A Spearspeaker. He will tell you when to turn left, when to turn right, when to step forward, and when to step back. And you will do as he says."

"We will hold the line!" Usaden barked.

The other warriors all looked at him and nodded.

"We will walk with bent knees," Surjan said. "Torso straight up and down. For now, we'll hold our spears in guard position if we're in the front line, and in shoulder position if we're on the second line. Watch your brothers to left and right out of the corners of your eyes. You want neither to get ahead, nor to be left behind. We will learn by doing, and we will drill until we know without thinking how to take steps that are the same length, so that our line holds."

"Hold the line!" Usaden grunted.

"Hold the line!" others answered.

"Are you the Spearspeaker?" Tafsut called to Surjan.

"For now, at least. I will call out your steps, one at a time. First, forward. Step! Step! Step!"

The line was ragged at first, and tended to become more ragged as it moved. But Surjan kept barking, moving the line forward and then backward until they did so without breaking formation. Then he taught them to pivot one hundred eighty degrees, swinging their spears with the hand placements that ensured the shortest possible range of motion for the weapons, and then marched them back and forth again, until the sun went down.

Eating roast antelope beside a fire an hour later, he found himself sitting next to Tafsut.

"I think I won't be Spearspeaker," he told her. "I'll command the Spearspeaker. Or maybe there should be two Spearspeakers, who both answer to me."

She nodded. "Are you asking my advice?"

"Your thoughts, at least."

"Badis should be Spearspeaker," she said. "Or Usaden. The other warriors all respect them."

"The *other* warriors?"

"That is not why *I* joined the spear-fighters."

Lowanna held up her sling to demonstrate to the crowd of assembled warriors. "Some of you are shepherds or hunters and already have experience with this weapon," she told them. "We'll be shooting stones at the target I have painted in goat's blood on that large rock over there. If you can hit the target three times in a row using your own form, and that's different from what I'm about to show you, then you can ignore what I'm about to teach. Otherwise, this is how you use the sling."

She had made the slings with Kareem's help, and Kareem himself stood with the group, brow furrowed as he focused on learning how to use the weapon. Lowanna had been unable to bring herself to eat meat since arriving in the ancient world and discovering she could hear the speech of animals, but she had made her peace with using and crafting things from leather. She had chosen the sling because it was portable, and deadly, and because projectiles were abundant.

She had grown up using the sling as a child in the Northern Territory. First, it had been a toy. Later, she had taken small game with it and driven off predators.

She held her sling up. "The entire length should be about as long as your two arms together. The small patch of hide in the middle is where you put the stone. A good stone is the size of your thumb or maybe a little larger. Notice that one length ends in a loop and the other ends in a knot. Place the loop around your index finger and hold the knot loosely between your thumb and forefinger. Just pinch it, lightly."

The group followed along. Several of them were already lethal with the sling, but no one showed any impatience. Lowanna herself had learned to use the sling to protect sheep on her uncle's ranch in the outback, using stones to chase away dingoes, and then to kill rabbits. She'd taught grad students on three continents to shoot with the sling. She'd never had to use it to attack a human being, but she knew she could cause damage.

She taught her band to swing the pouch in a figure eight and release, and also to hold the loaded pouch at arm's length and then fire in a single overhand throw. They practiced pacing out the distance they'd need from one another so they could stand together, and then she took them to the target she'd marked on a boulder by splashing blood on it.

"The main thing to do with the knife is stab." Marty demonstrated, thrusting. "If you slash, like this, you can only wound parts of your enemy that are near the surface. You can blind him, or maybe you'll get lucky and hit a vein."

He had thought that he would work with their warriors on

moving quietly. He'd expected Surjan to be helpful with that, and that he might be able to enlist Kareem, as well. They had quickly learned that their warriors walked differently from the people from the future. Rather than rolling heel to toe by habit, they stepped with the blade and ball of their feet first, and then rolled the heel down. Was that because they didn't have lifetime habits of wearing heavy Western shoes? In any case, it made for a naturally quiet walk.

So Marty had moved on to teaching them to fight hand to hand. He'd worked through some punches, kicks, and throws, and now he was instructing them to be effective fighting with knives, and fighting against knives.

His warriors were all comfortable using knives as tools, but few had fought with them. By preference, they fought with spears.

"But if you thrust, you can hit him in an organ." Udad grinned. It was a shocking expression on the face of a young man still several years shy of twenty, but Marty reminded himself that ideas about adulthood were very different in the ancient world. Udad was no child.

And if Marty was going to allow him to be part of the host, he couldn't very well fault the boy for understanding Marty's point about how to use a weapon.

He couldn't fault the *man*.

Marty nodded. For the next point, his grandfather had explained how wrong movies usually were, but that was obviously not relevant now. "You hold the knife up in front of you," he said, demonstrating. "Point up. The knife itself keeps your enemy away and protects you, and is here in a position to strike at the belly and the chest. That's where you want to attack." He gestured at his own center of mass. "This space is full of organs that make great targets."

"And you parry the knife with your knife?" Udad asked, hesitantly.

Older men clucked their tongues and shook their heads.

"Good question." Marty grabbed Tafsut by the elbow and brought her forward to demonstrate. Surjan watched her intently; was that jealousy? "No. That would be you trying to catch a tiny piece of metal with your own tiny piece of metal, and it will almost certainly go wrong. When someone attacks you with a knife, you have two options. You can move out of the way. Or you can block the attack."

"Block the attack?" Tafsut stared at him.

Marty chuckled as he realized this was the first time in his life he'd ever taught anyone any piece of martial arts. "Like this. You attack me."

They both had short sticks snapped to the right length to represent fighting knives. Marty held both hands at his centerline, his right tightly gripping the stick, ready to block any incoming attack. Tafsut held her practice knife low and forward, as Marty had described. She circled to her right, encroaching on Marty's left and forcing him to join her in the same slow circling motion. "Good," he said.

After a quick feint—not a maneuver he had demonstrated—she lunged in to stab him in the belly. He shifted slightly to the right, and slapped the inside of Tafsut's wrist with his stick, sending her attack flailing outward.

He gently poked Tafsut in the belly with his own stick and grinned.

"I see," she said.

"By keeping your weapon, even if it's only your fist, at your centerline, you can make yourself ready for an attack for any direction." Marty said. He quickly walked them through examples of an inside, outside, high, and low block. His men nodded their recognition and then their approval. Several cheered.

Surjan stepped forward. "Everyone, practice. With your partner, take turns. One of you attack and the other block and counter. Then switch."

The Sikh stepped between Marty and Tafsut, who promptly put up her practice knife and circled. Marty found himself bumped aside and partnerless.

Marty withdrew a few paces and watched them. There was a spark in the woman's eyes, a kind of combative laughter as Surjan returned her smile. Marty felt a sudden sense of unease. Not because of any jealously—on the contrary, it was because he knew that Surjan and the rest of the main crew were to return home to the future. Her heart might certainly be broken if Surjan vanished from this world, but would he have misgivings about leaving her behind? Marty had never interfered in the relationships any colleagues had had with locals on any archaeological dig in his career, and wasn't this the same thing? Was he worried about discipline? But fundamentally, he and his companions were organizing a premodern war band, a host, not a company of the U.S. Army.

It wasn't his business to interfere.

Marty sighed and left the warriors drilling with Surjan.

Marty and the rest of the crew stood on a low rise to watch. He leaned on a practice spear as if it were a staff. Below them, gentle hills spread in all directions. To the west and south, the hills were anchored and carpeted by tall dry grass, while to the east and north, they churned into coppery red sand, giving way on the eastern horizon to long dunes.

A knife ridge of rock, fifteen feet high, had been marked with two circular targets, each three feet across. The company's warriors stood in a spear-bearing division nearer the rock, and on their far side, slingers. Usaden stood as Spearspeaker to one side, and the First of Sling was a sling fighter named Idder who had joined them in Jehed. He wasn't from the town, apparently, but a shepherd who lived in a village nearby. With the slingers was a platoon of archers, warriors who had their own bows as well as slings.

Badis began belting out orders in a voice he had learned from Surjan. His warriors advanced toward the ridge and then moved away from it. They turned one hundred eighty degrees. They pivoted ninety degrees one direction and then ninety degrees the other. They thrust in unison, they planted their spears to take a charge. They raised their shields and drew them back into an overlapping carapace, like a turtle withdrawing into its shell—leaving more than a few spears poking out between the shields, so the turtle was also prickly. The shields had been fitted with long straps tying them to the warriors' bodies, to make it easier to fight with shield and spear; the straps had been Gunther's idea, but Kareem had made them and Surjan had taught the fighters how to use them.

Marty felt a sense of pride growing within him as he watched the warriors drill. In a few weeks' time, they'd transformed from a pack of individual fighters into a cohesive force, and that was impressive.

He also felt disquiet. What was he doing at the head of an army?

And when he took this army into battle, and its soldiers began to be wounded and even die, how would he feel? What would he do then?

These were not game pieces, wooden meeples or cardboard chits to be tossed back into the box. These were people who would bleed and die, based on the fortunes of war and on decisions Marty made.

He looked at Surjan and saw pride and satisfaction on his face. Pride, satisfaction, and appreciation—Surjan was keeping a special eye on Tafsut.

At a barked command from Idder, the slingers and archers went into action. He ordered them to march left, and right, to change direction, to take cover. They didn't move shoulder to shoulder like the spearmen did, but in a loose swarm. Then Idder called out targets—left, then right—and his slingers hit the targets indicated. The archers mimed shooting, but didn't loose the arrows, which weren't always easy to replace. He marched them backward fifty feet and the slingers hit the targets again. He marched them back a second time without hurting their accuracy, and it was only when he'd marched them back a third time, and they were some two hundred feet away from the targets, that they started to miss.

Even at that distance, they'd still inflict real damage on a massed crowd of soldiers.

If they fought human soldiers. If they fought Sethians, it wasn't clear that they'd be able to do any damage at all.

"Look," Kareem said, interrupting Marty's train of thought. "Look to the east."

"I can smell them." Surjan growled.

Marty looked. At first, he saw nothing, but after a minute had passed, he saw a rising cloud of dust on the road. Someone was coming.

⤜ CHAPTER ⤛ TWENTY-SIX

"There are Ametsu," Kareem said. "Sethians. Three. Or maybe four."

Marty squinted. The sun was high behind his head, beginning to sink into the west. "I swear I see camels. And the riders don't look like Sethians."

"No, those people are fleeing," Kareem said. "Behind them. The things they are fleeing from."

Marty had learned to trust Kareem's eyesight—its sharpness, let alone the fact that he was able to flat-out see in the dark. "Time to test our host."

Surjan and Lowanna raced forward to join their spear and sling companies. Gunther gave Marty a soft smile and a shrug. "It isn't in me to shed blood."

"You're a healer," Marty said. "Can you heal our side?"

Gunther nodded and moved to join Surjan's fighters.

François raced back. He wasn't running away, he was rushing to the supply wagons. Digging out more of his explosives?

Marty and Kareem reached Surjan just as the instructions ended. The spear-fighters divided into two platoons and lay down in the tall grass on either side of the trail. They wore undyed fabrics and hides and their own skin was tanned deep shades of brown and orange; huddled down behind their shields, they didn't exactly disappear, but they became . . . inobtrusive.

Lowanna and her sharpshooters, which consisted of people with both slings and bows, scampered around behind the ridge of rock they had just been using for target practice.

Badis lay down at the front of his men on the far side of the trail while Usaden positioned himself with the warriors on the near side. Surjan told Marty and Kareem, "Usaden's platoon attacks first, on his command. After they turn to fight us, Badis rises and attacks." Then he went and lay down at the front of his own men, on the near side of the trail.

"I sort of want to use my knife skills," Kareem said, "but it's smarter to kill the Sethians with spears."

The young man had a spear. Marty had his stick.

"Yes, it is," Marty agreed. "Your ankh might be better still."

"But I sort of want to use my knife."

Marty sighed and lay down.

The fleeing camels reached them. The beasts were bloodied and panicked, foam streaking from their lips and matting their hides. The riders clinging to their backs were women and children, the women either quite young or aged, and the children all below, Marty guessed, ten years old. Several of the women were wounded. Children shrieked, and their wailing dopplered up in pitch as they drew near, and then dropped off again as they passed.

Behind them came four Sethians, with two doglike things.

Two *sha*, to use the Egyptian name. Two Seth-beasts, as the earlier generations of Egyptologists would have called them. Things with bodies like lions or enormous wolves, but with forked tails. And their heads were nearly exactly the same as the heads of the Sethians—the same tall, square ears and long snout on a generally doglike head.

Usaden hollered and sprang from the tall grass. His men rose with him, and so did Surjan, Marty, and Kareem. True to the training he'd given, Surjan pressed to the side of Usaden's platoon and joined them in disciplined spear-fighting. Usaden bellowed an advance and up-shields.

The four Sethians stumbled to a halt and pivoted to face Usaden's platoon. The sha did not. One turned and sprang at Badis's men. The other raced after the fleeing women and children.

Cursing, Marty chased the running sha.

He yelled as he ran, freeing the sling from his pocket and fitting a stone into it. He was surprised that he had the coordination to do it, but he was able to get the stone cranking around his head, once and awkwardly, and then he let the stone fly, striking the sha in the flank.

It wasn't much of a blow. But the sha wheeled around and roared at him.

Usaden's spear-fighters struck the four Sethians at a brisk march, spears pumping forward like pistons. One of the Sethians fell, but the other three pushed back, swinging axes and long swords. The spears that bristled so fiercely in drill mostly bounced off the Sethians' skins—but in two locations, Gunther saw drawn blood.

The monsters' skin was thick, but it wasn't impervious.

Kareem rushed past him, spear-tip raised to eye level, to hurl himself at the nearest Sethian.

On the far side of the trail, Badis's men were struggling against the single sha. It had taken them by surprise, and they were trying to form up a shield wall to defend against it.

Gunther looked for fighters to heal. No one had yet fallen out of the battle, but he kept his eye on a couple of men who looked faint.

Kareem and two of the warriors together knocked one of the Sethians down and stabbed at it where it lay on the ground.

One of Usaden's warriors staggered away from the fight, bleeding from a gash in his forehead. Gunther moved to intercept the man—Munatas, that was his name. Grabbing Munatas by the elbow and murmuring reassuring words, he induced the warrior to kneel and then laid healing hands on his scalp.

The flesh knit together as light poured over it. Gunther no longer felt strange performing these...miracles? Enchantments? But they drained him. Munatas grunted thanks and rose to reenter the fray.

Gunther looked toward Kareem and froze; the Sethian who had been knocked down first, whom Gunther assumed to be out of the fight for the duration, was rolling over onto one elbow and struggling to rise. He had a spear in his hand, and he was behind Kareem.

Kareem didn't notice him.

Another warrior lurched toward Gunther. Gunther's ears roared with the noise of battle and he couldn't make out words, but the man's arm hung at a sickening angle, and he thought he could make out pleas for help. Idder, that was his name.

But the rising Sethian would kill Kareem.

Gunther pushed past the wounded man. "Sit here, I'll be right back." He stooped to pick up a rock and ran.

In his haste, he had hoisted up a rather large stone. How was he strong enough to even carry it? It was nearly the size of his own chest. It might be adrenaline. But he couldn't focus on his own surprising strength; Kareem was in danger. Gunther charged around the end of the spearmen, staggered up to where the Sethian was trying to rise, and smashed the stone down right into the monster's skull.

He fell to his knees. The Sethian's skin shimmered and light collected in a pool on its sternum, just above where its head was now pounded flat into the ground. The light rolled into a ball and rose into Gunther. He felt it like electricity, like the tingling before a thunderstorm. He felt it also like the same energy that flowed out of his body when he was healing, only now it was flowing in.

He stood, and Gunther felt a new level of clarity. His mind had never felt more focused. He took a deep breath and a newfound energy coursed through him. So this was level three.

He snorted. What a ridiculous terminology.

But he couldn't deny the reality of the experience.

Badis's men had driven the sha attacking them against the ridge of rock. Lowanna's sharpshooters had mounted the stone and were firing sling stones directly down into the monster's hide. Lowanna herself was roaring and howling at the monster. When it tried to scramble up the rock, Badis and his men stabbed it and brought it back down.

Usaden and his warriors had two of the Sethians down. They shimmered and were dissolving into sludge, as was the Sethian Gunther had killed. But the last of the four was wounded and flailing. He spun about, thrashing with an ax in one hand and a mace in the other, like a monstrous free-range Cuisinart, and his violence shattered Usaden's line.

The Sethian broke through and ran—headed straight for the man with the shattered arm.

Idder' was sitting, as Gunther had directed him. His back was turned to the charging Sethian, and he was slumped forward... stunned at least, and maybe unconscious. He was oblivious to the monster bearing down on him.

And Gunther had put him into the monster's path.

Gunther sprinted, but he saw he was never going to make it.

He looked for stones on the ground to throw or strike with, and there were none.

The Sethian raised its mace over its head.

"Stop!" Gunther shouted.

And the Sethian froze.

But it didn't stop moving. Its muscles instantly and thoroughly locked as if it had been tased. Without control of its muscles, the Sethian's forward momentum sent the creature tumbling forward onto its face and it skidded nearly ten feet, plowing a deep furrow into the sand before finally coming to rest just past Idder.

Gunther stopped, too. What had happened?

The Sethian snarled at him, and then Surjan and his men crashed onto the Sethian with their spears.

Marty flung himself at the sha.

He was trying to remember any advice his grandfather had ever given him about fighting wild animals, and all he could remember was, *don't do it*. An animal could be diseased. An unknown animal could have unknown diseases, or this one could have ancient illnesses against which Marty had no immunity.

But the beast sprang at him, and he had no choice.

Marty dodged, forgetting for a moment that he had a weapon in his hands. Then he leaped after the monster, cracking it across its low-slung back with the staff.

It was an animal, wasn't it? An unreasoning brute? If he could sting it or frighten it, maybe it would flee.

Unless it was rabid. Or a trained killer.

The sha whirled about and leaped at Marty, faster than he was expecting. It had a lionlike body but its head was canine. Canine, but enormous, with an ass's ears. Its jaw yawned wide open, so wide that Marty was certain it must have become dislocated. The animal's teeth were long and curved and they glistened about its bloodred tongue.

Marty fell back, dropping onto his haunches and wedging the staff underneath the sha's breast. Planting the butt of the staff into the sandy soil, he let the beast's momentum carry it forward and it lurched like an upside-down pendulum. Marty rolled down and into his shoulders, flattening himself. Time slowed. The sha swiped with its front claws, tearing through Marty's shirt but narrowly missing his skin. Then the beast soared over him, the hind legs raking at Marty in a single blow. If it had landed, it surely would have gutted him completely, but the sha missed.

Marty continued his backward roll, a little surprised himself that it turned into a somersault. He snatched up the staff as the animal launched yowling toward a sandy hill, snapping himself into a defensive position.

He felt fluid, acrobatic, alive.

The sha skidded around when it landed, finally reorienting itself to point at Marty. Marty was already running to attack, taking short, calculated swings with the staff that left him still able to parry, and kept the length of the stick between himself and the beast. He struck it in its face twice, and it hissed like an angry cat.

Then it hurled itself at him. Marty tried again to get his staff under the animal, and this time he failed. The monster struck him with its shoulder and sent him bowling across the hillside. Marty's enhanced reflexes brought him to his feet again. He'd lost hold of the staff, but he had his hands up, and he was prepared to instantly take another full-body attack.

Instead, he found Gunther beside him. He stood with a ramrod-straight back and held his hand toward the sha, palm up, fingers splayed.

"Stop!" Gunther yelled.

The sha roared and leaped at Gunther.

Marty dove, but he knew he wouldn't make it in time. He saw Gunther in his mind's eye, torn to shreds by the sha's long talons.

A hail of stones and arrows crashed into the beast.

The projectile onslaught couldn't knock the beast from the air or push it back, but the sha shrieked and lost its focus. It curled, cringing back from the stones that pelted it, and when it hit Gunther, it was massive and moving fast, but it wasn't slashing.

The sha rolled over Gunther and found itself facing spearmen. Badis's and Usaden's warriors had arrived. They ringed it in on three sides, turning slowly as Surjan shouted commands for both platoons, pivoting so that the open side of the enclosure of spears turned toward the open savannah.

"Kill it!" a woman cried. She rode a camel and she was disheveled and bloody; Marty didn't recognize her. "It's a monster!"

"No!" Lowanna pushed through the spearmen, positioning herself alongside Badis. She faced the sha with empty hands at her sides. "No, it's not a monster. It's an animal."

Marty helped Gunther climb shakily to his feet and met Lowanna's gaze. "It's wise and compassionate and noble to show mercy to animals, but sometimes, if an animal is a threat to the community, it has to be put down."

"Let me talk to it," Lowanna insisted.

Marty nodded slowly. "Okay. But it can't leave if it's going to come back and attack humans. Here or anywhere. Does that seem fair to you?"

Lowanna hesitated, but nodded.

"I don't know what happened," Gunther muttered.

"You stood like a dumbass in front of that monster and told it to stop," Marty whispered. "A noble, beautiful, brave dumbass. Still a dumbass."

"Yeah, but it worked last time, with the Sethian," Gunther said.

Lowanna made calming sounds at the sha. They were plaintive noises, the shushing sounds a person might make to calm a puppy or a baby. The sha slunk from side to side, sniffing at the tips of the spears ringing it in, and then gathering itself into a sitting position in the center.

Lowanna continued making soothing sounds and gestures.

The sha finally opened its mouth, threw back its head, and roared.

Lowanna shook her head. "It eats the flesh of men, and will have no other meat."

"Kill it," Marty said.

The sha sprang forward. The spear-fighters bellowed and surged to the attack. They fell on the animal like a storm, and in a few savage seconds, it was dead.

Lowanna stood to the side and shed silent tears. Marty reached to touch her with a comforting hand, and she pulled away.

François trotted into Marty's view holding a wax-sealed pot, one of the next batch of explosives he was working on. The Frenchman grunted disappointment that he had missed the fight.

The sha soon dissolved and sank into the sand, leaving a wet spot like a nuclear shadow.

≈ CHAPTER ≈
TWENTY-SEVEN

Marty spoke gently to the refugees, asking where their village and kin were, and what had happened. The refugees for their part were adamant—they wanted to stay with Marty and become part of the host.

It took an hour for everyone to calm down, and for Gunther to bandage the injured. Whatever healing ability he had, it was only good for one or two uses before he had to rest. Lowanna helped him; Marty didn't watch closely, but he thought she was doing more than merely applying bandages and packing poultices into wounds. Some of Gunther's healing touch seemed to have rubbed off on her.

What was it Gunther had tried to do? Command the sha to stop in its tracks?

Marty and François examined the puddles left behind by the four Sethians and the two sha. They found kilts, sandals, weapons, and cloaks. They also found one of the Sethian medallions; Marty picked it up and put it around his neck.

When the wounded had all been counted and tended, Surjan came to report that they had suffered no deaths.

Marty felt a weight come off his shoulders.

He and François met with the leaders of the refugees, two women with elaborate tattoos covering their faces and necks. Marty tried one last time to ask the women if he could take them home, and they refused.

"Very well," he conceded. "You may come with us. Let us go look at your former home and see if anything may be salvaged."

They traveled half an hour, mostly eastward and then a few minutes to the north, following a valley that narrowed into a canyon and then opened into a stone bowl full of smoking ruins.

The women had been stone-faced until they reached this valley. Then several of them broke down into weeping and rushed to this pile of burning timbers or that, looking among the corpses, kissing and wailing over the dead.

At Marty's request, Kareem and Lowanna kept the children out of the valley.

Two wet stains on the ground hinted that Sethians had been killed during the attack. Marty stopped counting the human corpses at fifty. They were beheaded, impaled, or sometimes just so peppered with wounds that they had exsanguinated. They didn't look tortured, per se.

But he rolled over half a dozen bodies, and every single one had a slash across the abdomen over the liver.

"Is it worth opening a body?" Marty asked François.

"No," François said. "They're dead, let them lie. We know who killed them, it was the Seth-headed bastards. It looks like they were probably killed for their livers, but does it really matter? If you find that the corpses were all intact inside, and some just coincidentally had a similar external wound, would it change your course of action?"

"No," Marty conceded. Though it might affect his picture of what he thought he knew about the Ametsu. Was it academic interest? Pointless? Maybe.

He chuckled, a grim, haggard sound.

"Let's bury them," François said. "Or burn them, or whatever their women prefer. It's the decent thing."

"Are you worried they might send more warriors?" Marty asked.

"I sort of *hope* they'll send more." François's mouth was set in a flat line. "Give me thirty seconds with one of those bastards and a bomb, and I'll start to feel a little better."

Marty searched among the survivors until he found his two leaders again. He asked about treatment of the dead and they pointed to cave openings visible at the far end of the canyon, above a circle of standing stones. "We wrap and bury them," they explained.

Lowanna took the lead in organizing the burials. She found

wrapping cloths or created them out of the clothing of the dead. Together with the surviving women, and volunteers from the host, including Gunther, she cleaned the bodies with sand. They then packed them with a coarse yellow salt scratched from the ground at one end of the valley and wrapped them head to toe.

Surjan, Kareem, and the warriors guarded the entrance to the valley and also stood watch along the cliff tops above it.

What these people did was not mummification as the Egyptians knew it. The salt was not natron, and Lowanna didn't remove any of the bodies' organs. But, watching her work, Marty felt awe at the fact that he was witnessing something akin to mummification, close to Egypt, worked by some cousin folk of the Egyptians, before Egypt as a political entity had even begun.

He sat down and breathed deeply for a while.

The women sang dirges while Marty, François, and other volunteers carried the wrapped dead up long ladders. Inside a low-ceilinged cave illuminated by the orange rays of sunset bleeding in through the entrance, Marty saw stacks of the wrapped and withered dead, and piled more dead upon them. He filled several chambers with bodies, and by the time the work was done, the valley was cloaked in cold night.

Then Marty sat with François and drank. They sat among the stones, a circle of twelve megaliths each the height of a man. The valley walls were lower at this end—did the villagers use the stones to measure the passage of time by sighting along them to astral events at the horizon? Marty could ask, he had access to actual informants, but he found he wanted to sit and drink, instead.

They drank a thin, watery wine that the survivors produced for them. They lit no fire, and talked in between the sounds of children screaming, women trying to hush them, and the weeping of the women themselves.

"What will they do?" Marty wondered out loud.

"What humans have always done." François sounded tired. "This is the ordinary state of humankind, Marty, and you know it better than I do. War, death, and destruction. And when things go too far south, you move. This was God's command to Abraham. *Lekh lekha*, get up and get going."

"You and I lived in a golden age," Marty said.

"Better than a golden age. The platinum age. The diamond age. The best age there ever had been, to date, even though our teachers spent all their time trying to scare us witless about nuclear war or deforestation or whatever. But there never was a more peaceful time. It was never easier to get an education, or get good medicine."

"It's always been good for the rich," Marty said, with a little more barb than he had intended.

"You sound a bit like Lowanna."

"Sorry."

"But that's the damn point, Marty. It's always good for the rich. The Godspeaker of Ahuskay is doing all right. King Iken, he was going to die of . . . whatever he had, but still, he had lived like a king. The guy has multiple women and a two-story house. The rich always do fine. The amazing thing about the time that you and I lived in, my dear Marty, was how great it was to be *poor*."

"For the record," Marty said, "I never spent my time trying to scare students witless about nuclear war. Or anything else."

"That's because you actually know your stuff," François said. "Ideology is the refuge of the incompetent."

"Sometimes I kind of like you," Marty said.

"Sometimes I do, too." François took a long drink.

"I guess what I really meant," Marty said after some consideration, "is what are *we* going to do now?"

François grunted. "I tried to be leader. I'm pretty sure you won that contest. I've been trying to figure out my role since."

"Help me. I'm a talk-about-things, consensus kind of leader."

"That's true. Or at least true enough." François scratched his chin, and then his neck, and then scratched himself all over, as if he were ridding himself of some persistent pest. "Agh!" he finally cried. "I don't know. We started with some volunteers who wanted to go kill Sethians. And then we developed into a war band, except a band with caravan drivers and merchants attached. And now women and children. We're the children of Israel, we're *Battlestar Galactica*."

"True epic literature is always rooted in great human migrations," Marty said. "From *The Iliad* to the stories of Jacob to the *Shahnameh*."

"That's your consolation?" François laughed. "That one of these people might write some really fantastic *poetry* some day?"

Marty shrugged. "Maybe that's all there is, in the end."

"No," François said. "Hell, no. You . . . okay, *we* . . . are going to save these people. I can't quite figure out this version of the fourth millennium B.C.E. we've wandered into. Is this an alternate universe, in which there are monsters? Or is this really our past Earth, and there were monsters here all along, and we didn't know it?"

"Or was there always lots of evidence of monsters?" Marty suggested. "The cryptid people were right, after all. Maybe it's the Egyptologists to blame. Maybe all that stuff that we read as mythology was history all along. It's crazy if you think about it . . . so much evidence exists about what we're seeing, drawings, stories, even in some cases oral traditions. We just didn't believe it, because we never found a body."

"Because these monsters melt into goo," François said. "Which, by the way, suggests a body chemistry not of this Earth."

"Aliens?" Marty took a long drink.

"You can't say it isn't possible."

Marty shrugged. "Monsters, anyway. And we turned a blind eye to it, because we preferred automobiles and television and penicillin."

"Don't knock cars and TVs and medicine," François said. "These people would kill to have those things, and rightly so. But it doesn't matter what the answer is, we're here and we have to decide how to react. It's like the existentialists say, life is screwed up, so try to take on a noble cause."

"That's a pretty concise summary of existentialism."

"I skipped those lectures and read other people's notes. So we're going to choose a noble quest. In fact, Marty, I think if you look into your heart honestly, you'll see that we chose the noble quest a long time ago."

"What do you mean?"

"We killed that first Sethian almost by accident," François said. "Maybe . . . certainly, it was my fault. I was too eager, I wasn't careful, and Abdullah died for my sin." His voice dwindled to a thready rasp. "A day doesn't pass that I don't think about that, and wish that I could take it back."

"I know," Marty said. "Me too."

"But then we got to Ahuskay. And they were scared. And you could have said, 'Screw these people, let's go. Our quest is to get to Egypt, or get home, or whatever.' But you didn't. And you didn't

hesitate, either. You jumped right in and said you'd fix everything."
François chuckled. "Hell, I was pretty sure for the first twenty-four
hours that Badis was going to murder me. And fixing everything
meant defeating that Sethian outpost. And beating those guys put us
on the track where we had to defeat the Bastites, and everything else
has basically just followed in a straight line. You committed to this
fight back in Ahuskay, Marty, and you can't back out now just
because you see the stakes. In fact, you know what I think?"

"I'm learning quite a lot about what you think."

"I think maybe the destruction of this village here was a message
to us."

"They stole their livers," Marty said. "What's the message?"

"Yeah, they stole their livers, but think back. At Ahuskay, the
Sethians treated people like farm animals. Just harvest one or two,
now and then. Why would they come to this village and wipe
everyone out?"

"You think it's a warning to me?" Marty asked. "To *us*?"

"I'm saying it's definitely possible. To you, the warlord Dr. Martin
Cohen, who has been rolling up their western network. What did
you say they called you? 'Merit Nuk Han'? The message is, 'Stop now,
uppity human, or we will do terrible things to you.'"

Marty's mouth tasted terrible. He wanted to vomit, but he leaned
forward and spit a long string of acidic saliva into the sand. "You're
right, we're committed. I'm committed. I don't know whether this is
an alternate universe to our own, or if maybe we're learning some
surprise history lessons. But in a fight between human beings and
anything else, I'm on the side of human beings."

"Me too," François said. "We all are. Even Lowanna, though I
think she might feel conflicted sometimes."

"So do we send a message back?" Marty asked.

"Too late," François told him. "You already sent it. You killed the
raiding party. Including their dogs. So the raiders won't come back
and the home base will sit around wondering what happened. That's
a message, and you've also knocked them off balance."

"What do you think the home base looks like?" Marty asked.

"I'm starting to think it might be the pyramids." François snorted.
"Joke's on you and Gunther, you've been studying aliens all these
years and never knew it."

"The guy on TV with the crazy hair was right."

"Actually, I don't think their home base can be that big," François said. "I mean, think about the size of their outposts. Groups of four or five. That's not a colony, that's just a few people to hold the fort. I think if they were really numerous, we'd have seen more of them."

"We've just been following this one trail," Marty said. "There might be another string of outposts down into Nubia, and another one out across Mesopotamia."

François clapped Marty on the shoulder. "So if we're stuck here and can never go home, we have a life's work. Breaking up all the other Sethian networks."

"But the goal isn't really to defeat them all, we just want to get home to our own time—"

"Marty..." François shook his head and gave him a sad smile. "You're ever the optimist. I don't think there's any going back." He held up his hand as Marty opened his mouth to retort. "And if there is, great, but we can't assume there's an easy way back out of this. We've got to assume we're stuck."

"What if peace could be made?" Marty wondered.

"They eat our livers," François pointed out. "Tell me what you think the terms of the peace would be."

"I'm just...I hate fighting." It wasn't entirely true. But he hated the suffering of innocents.

"Good," François said. "But I don't think we're destined to make peace with these bastards."

"Because they eat our livers?"

"Because there are none in our time." François shrugged. "Something wiped them out. Something wiped them out before written history started, or at least reduced them to the level of cryptids. I'm inclined to think the something was Kung Fu Cohen."

They sat in silence a while. The cries and weeping had quieted, and the smoking had mostly subsided.

"The aliens aren't even the weirdest thing," Marty said. "Not for me."

"So you agree they're aliens."

"Working hypothesis."

"How anything can be weirder than the melting monster-headed aliens, I don't know."

Marty sighed. "When I was a kid, I made up a hieroglyphic script. When I was first getting excited about Egypt, I'd been to a museum exhibit, I learned how hieroglyphs worked, and I went right home and made my own."

"Gunther told me."

"Yeah," Marty said. "Well, here's the part Gunther doesn't know. Back there at the dig site, in the tunnel. You remember how Gunther pointed out some odd writing to me in the corner, and that writing told me how to open up the wall?"

François nodded. "Wait . . . you're not saying . . ."

"That writing was in English," Marty said. "Using a hieroglyphic script only I can read, because I made it up."

"No way."

"If Gunther had looked more closely, he would have noticed that the script included pictures of ballpoint pens and a guitar."

François laughed. "And you didn't think to tell anyone?"

"Things happened fast," Marty said. "And I've had a lot on my mind."

"Liar," François said. "We've had multiple conversations to sit down and inventory our discoveries and powers and whatnot. You had plenty of opportunity to tell someone."

"I found it embarrassing," Marty admitted. "I don't know why. Because, I don't know, this thing I made up as a kid showed up at a dig site . . . But . . . I felt . . . I don't know, it seemed to me I should tell someone."

François shook his head. "Maybe Gunther's right and we *are* in the Twilight Zone."

They drank some more.

"I don't think the Sethians took anything other than livers," François said. "So in the morning, we should collect what we can make use of."

"Loot the place?"

"No, it's the opposite of looting. The rightful owners are part of our tribe now. Let's conserve what is ours, for the good of our people."

"Our tribe." Marty shook his head. "Wow."

"We should get this written down when we can," François said. "I mean, in hieroglyphs. If I die, I want you to put an account of this great migration on the wall in my tomb. But maybe make my part sound more noble than it really was."

"You discovered penicillin," Marty said. "Or at least you tried to. So maybe you healed a king. That's pretty noble."

"Don't forget the bombs," François said. "I'm grinding the powders even finer than before. The next batch will work even better, you'll see. This is my true calling. I'll be the Alfred Nobel of the fourth millennium."

"In the morning, we'll gather up what we can use here," Marty said. "And I want to send Lowanna on ahead."

"To scout?" François asked.

"Yes. The animals will help her. They tell her things I'd like to know."

"I know they do," François said. "So there's some competition for what's the weirdest part of this whole experience."

⇜ CHAPTER ⇝
TWENTY-EIGHT

Lowanna leaned forward against the camel's furry hump and fell into the rhythm of the animal as its soft padded feet traveled across the sandy terrain.

The grass of the prairie had now almost completely given out. It still stood in sparse patches here and there, but they now traveled through a true desert.

She had learned how to ride before she'd ever even seen a horse. Being born near the Tanami Desert in the Northern Territory, it wasn't so strange in that part of the world for feral dromedaries to share territory with her people. In fact, her parents had tamed the beasts and had started a dairy. Other kids grew up learning how to ride a bike, she'd grown up riding camels.

The motion of the camel as it walked had always felt to her like the movement of a rocking chair. She scratched the side of the large animal's hump as he trotted eastward. "You let me know if you get tired, okay?"

The big animal let out a gurgling noise that sounded like a human trying to cough up some phlegm. But to Lowanna it clearly communicated to her that the big bull was not tired; also, he wanted to know whether she was thirsty, because he smelled water up ahead.

"If there's water, let's stop so we can both drink."

The camel shifted his direction to the southeast, veering off the east-west path that they'd been traveling. Within ten minutes, she saw the first signs of palm trees.

Camels weren't famous for their ability to detect scents generally, but when it came to sniffing out water, these big guys knew what they were doing.

As the camel trudged down a rocky slope toward the oasis, Lowanna saw a small lake with a dozen palm trees lining its edge. She'd seen such bodies of water in Australia. They were created by cracks in the bedrock and an upwelling of water from the water table below. The result was a natural well.

Lowanna hopped off the camel and approached the shore. A two-foot-long yellow lizard basked in the sun; it hissed a warning and scooted away. She rubbed the side of the camel's neck and said, "Ignore him. He was just scared you were going to step on him."

The lizard settled on a rock twenty feet away and gave one last hiss.

The camel snorted and flared his nostrils, unimpressed by the reptilian machismo. He dipped his lips down to the water and began drinking.

Lowanna scanned their surroundings, paying careful attention to the palms. She walked over to the trees and saw that they had been picked clean of dates. There were date pits strewn along the shore.

She crouched down and picked up one of the pits. Its surface was dry, but the pit hadn't lost all of its moisture to the air yet.

Other than maybe bringing the animals to the lake to water them, there really wasn't a reason for the group to come to this oasis. They had plenty of water still, and if Marty's vision was right, they only had two days left before they arrived at wherever it was they were supposed to go.

Which was what, exactly? A way home? A trap? The Sethians' home base?

Hearing a chirp, Lowanna walked over to the nearest palm tree and found a nest with a sparrow in it, gray-breasted, with brown and black feathers in its wings. "Hello, little one. Have you seen people like me recently?"

The bird hopped up onto the edge of its nest and peered at her. It tilted its head and stared.

"Have you seen any humans around?" she tried again. "Any Two-Legs?"

Yes.

"Did you see any today? Since the sun came up?"

Yes.

"Where?"

The bird just stared.

Lowanna pointed north. "Were they that way?"

No.

"That way?" She pointed south.

No.

"That way?" She pointed east.

Yes.

Interesting. People east of here. "One person?"

Yes.

Lowanna's eyes widened. A single person wandering around the wilderness had to be an unusual thing. She was herself a bit nuts to be doing it, but then again, she was with a big brute of a camel, so she wasn't *really* alone. She looked at the bird, who was still staring at her. "Are you sure it was only one person?"

Yes.

She pointed east again. "And he came from that way?"

No.

"Wait a minute, I thought you said . . . was there more than one person?"

Yes.

Lowanna waved at the stupid bird and gave up trying to talk to it. Sometimes the animals she encountered were simply not very useful to talk to.

She walked over to the camel just as he lifted his head from the lake. Lowanna pulled a fig from her pack. "Come here, big boy, you'll like this."

She held out the yellow fig for him. The camel used his thick leathery lips to grasp the fruit, then chomped down.

Lowanna rubbed his neck. "Did you like it?"

The camel turned his head and wrapped his neck around her shoulders, giving her the equivalent of a camel hug.

"Aww, you're welcome."

Lowanna looked up at the sky; it wasn't quite yet noon. She could scout out the path east for another couple of hours before having to turn back. "Let's go a little farther and see what else we can see."

The camel knelt down and Lowanna hopped onto his back.

✣ ✣ ✣

Lowanna and her one-humped companion trotted eastward. They were covering a lot of ground, and so far, other than the oasis, she hadn't spotted anything of interest.

With the sun just past noon, Lowanna heard the cry of a hawk. At the same moment, the bird itself blurred past her and slammed into a mouse who'd scurried out of his hole at exactly the wrong time.

The camel stepped sideways a bit, skittish over the surprise appearance of the raptor.

She patted the side of his hump. "It's okay. No need to be worried, my friend."

The gray-colored hawk was big, almost two feet long from tail feather to beak. It settled on a twisted log. Lowanna called out to it. "Have you seen other humans nearby?"

The bird of prey squawked. *Many. You will see them.*

Lowanna's eyes widened and she pointed east. "That way?"

Yes. The mouse's tail hung from the hawk's beak like a book ribbon from a Bible.

"How many?"

Many, the bird responded. It swallowed what was left of the mouse, shrieked, and vaulted into the air.

Lowanna patted the side of the camel's hump. "Let's keep going straight, but let me know if you see or smell anything unusual."

They resumed their brisk canter.

Did the hawk know better than the sparrow? Were they both wrong, or too stupid to understand her questions?

Might a bird lie to her? Animals could be stupid . . . could they be venal?

It was time to get back.

She stopped and scanned the road ahead. A faint yellow haze clung to the eastern horizon.

She scanned to the north and south and the horizon didn't have the same look to it. Normally, heat would create a haze in the distance, but it just made things slightly out of focus, like a smear of petroleum jelly on a camera lens. This haze had color.

The camel continued east as Lowanna focused on the horizon. She heard the susurrus of mice and snakes, but they had nothing useful to say to her. As they drew closer to it, the yellow haze became more pronounced.

Taller.

She wished she had Kareem's or Surjan's eyesight.

Having spent the first half of her life in terrain just like this, she knew that the horizon was not much more than three to four miles away across a flat surface.

An eagle perched on one of the top branches of a desiccated and skeletal tree. Lowanna pointed to the east. "Hey, what do you see in that direction?"

The eagle fluttered its wings and stared down at her.

Danger.

A chill raced up Lowanna's spine and she patted the camel's hump. "Let's stop."

The camel immediately came to a halt and Lowanna called out again to the eagle. "Can you tell me more about what's ahead of me?"

Men.

Men?

Lowanna stared to the east, a knot of uncertainty in her belly.

The eagle might be right. That yellow haze could be the dust being kicked up by people on the march. By a *lot* of people on the march.

Who?

She leaned forward and whispered, "Let's go back, quickly!"

The camel turned around and she yelled back at the eagle, "Thank you!"

The eagle flapped its wings and took off with a loud squawk.

It's not the men that are the danger.

⤜ CHAPTER ⤛
TWENTY-NINE

It was past sundown. A vein in Marty's temple throbbed as he paced back and forth outside the host's camp. Lowanna was still out there somewhere and he cursed himself for thinking it was a good idea for her to go scouting on her own.

He should have gone with her.

He turned to Kareem, who sat cross-legged on the sand and stared eastward. "Do you see anything?"

"Not yet," the young man responded.

It was the fifth time Marty had asked.

Somewhere in the darkness a bird cawed. Marty couldn't see the bird, but knew that the voice belonged to a hawk.

I'm hungry!

Marty winced. Did he have a screw loose? Was he actually understanding what the raptor was saying? Ever since he'd had that euphoric sensation in the ruins, hitting level three, he'd begun hearing meaning in animal cries.

Would he start healing by the laying on of hands, too, like Gunther? And seeing in the dark?

I'm hungry! the bird cried again.

It was somewhere ahead, in the darkness.

"Then get yourself some food, you stupid animal!" Marty yelled into the night, suddenly feeling foolish.

Do you have food?

Marty stared into the darkness and shook his head.

Kareem looked up at him and tilted his head to the side. "Are you talking to that bird?"

"Maybe," Marty said.

Kareem handed Marty a strip of dried meat. "Maybe you can feed the bird."

Feeling utterly foolish, Marty took the long strip of meat, ripped it in half, and then held one half up above his head. "Here, take some meat."

He heard a single flap of wings. Flashing talons snatched the meat from his outstretched hand and vanished.

Marty shivered.

"That's impressive, by God, Dr. Cohen." Kareem smiled. "You can talk to the birds like Lowanna talks to her camel."

"Any sign of her?"

Kareem shook his head.

"Hey, bird! Are you still hungry?" Marty yelled.

He felt a little less stupid this time.

The hawk replied, *Do you have more food?*

Marty pointed east. "I'll give you more food if you can find my friend who is in that direction. A human woman, traveling with a camel."

Somewhere not too far away, he heard wings flapping and then nothing.

"What do you expect the bird to do?" Kareem asked.

Marty shrugged and stared into the darkness for a full ten seconds before responding. "I don't know. I'm just frustrated that it's late and—"

He heard an angry squawk. *Where is the food?*

Marty held the strip of meat up. The bird snatched it out of his hand and flapped away. He called out to the hawk. "What did you see?"

Two-Legs says she can see the campfire. Returning soon.

Marty looked over his shoulder at the campfire about a quarter mile behind him.

Kareem hopped up onto his feet and pointed. "I see her, God be praised! She and the camel are racing directly for us."

Marty stared into the darkness and saw nothing.

About three minutes later, Lowanna burst from the darkness on the lathered and exhausted dromedary.

Jumping off the animal, Lowanna almost crashed into Marty. He scooped her up and gave her a bearhug. "What the hell took you—"

"Marty, we've got an army heading this way!"

Marty's blood ran cold. "An army? How many people? How far out?"

I'm tired! the camel bellowed. *I'm hungry.*

Lowanna kissed the camel's neck and began rubbing it. "I promise you'll get some rest." As they began walking back to camp, she turned to Marty and said, "I couldn't tell how many. I encountered a hawk that clued me in and then I saw a large cloud of dust being kicked up by an army on the move."

"More people than we have?"

"A lot more." Lowanna lightly smacked Marty on the upper arm. "And how in the world did you send a hawk to look for me? Can you—"

"I can." Marty shook his head. "And I'm still wrapping my head around that." His stomach cramped. There might be a battle. Could they avoid the army? If not, could they pick the field of battle? Above all, he needed to know more about the oncoming forces. "How far away are they?"

"The army was at least a few hours march east of where I saw them, and my friend raced the whole way back for about half a day to get here. I'd say if we stay right here, and they don't change direction, they'll probably be here in a day, maybe two."

A day or two?

Marty paused midstride as the vision he first encountered replayed in his mind's eye.

The sun rose and fell dozens of times as his view headed eastward, past villages, farmlands, the outskirts of the desert and off in the distance dust was being kicked up by a large amount of people traveling on foot, heading west.

He approached what looked like an army and rose up above it, getting a full view of what turned out to be hundreds of people, all equipped with weapons of ancient war—some spears, bows, an occasional sword and staff. At the center of the moving army was a covered wagon and his mind's eye flew toward it.

Into the tent, past the attendants, and to the throne where a man sat.

He looked up as if he could see Marty. The glow of the man's bronze skin shimmered and he smiled.

"Welcome, Seer. It is time."

Marty shivered. Kareem and Lowanna looked at him with expressions of concern. He continued forward, stumbling toward the campfire, and a thousand thoughts raced through his mind. The vision . . . could it really be playing out as predicted?

It was just before dawn and the camp buzzed with activity. François directed a squad of cooks as they prepared meals. The animals were being fed and people were preparing for a day's march.

Marty stood on a low rise northeast of the camp and stared eastward with Kareem by his side.

The sun cracked the horizon. "What do you see?" Marty asked.

Kareem shaded his eyes with his hand. "I don't see an army, praise be to God." He glanced to his left. "We have a visitor."

A tall spearman walked up the ridge, heading directly for them.

"Usaden," Marty called. "Good morning."

They clasped forearms. "Lowanna said that you wanted to talk with me."

Marty chuckled. He had said no such thing to Lowanna, who was meddling. She wanted him to talk to Usaden, apparently.

But . . . maybe Usaden could be useful.

He pointed east. "We don't yet see them, but we have visitors coming from that direction."

"Visitors?"

"They might be an army," Marty said cautiously. "I was wondering if you might tell me why there might be an army in the field."

The strong man scratched his throat. "King Iken is at peace with his neighbors. I know of no king who is at war. I would be surprised if one of our neighbors marched with an army. There are robber bands, but those are never in numbers greater than a dozen or two."

"And the Ametsu?"

"The Ametsu and their creatures are small in number," Usaden said.

Marty frowned. "So, what would you expect if there was a force of people heading our way? What could their reason be? Is it something you'd expect to turn into a battle?"

Usaden furrowed his brows. "Perhaps a king has heard that a sovereign without lands passed through his domain. Perhaps a king fears that you will take his land, or that you are a robber. Perhaps he wishes to meet with you, or warn you off."

Marty took a step back. "A sovereign without lands?" That might be stretching things a bit.

Usaden nodded solemnly.

Marty decided not to argue. "So would you expect them to attack us?"

"No. Certainly not at first meeting. They will want to know more about us. But, of course, if they foolishly choose combat, we are prepared."

Marty nodded. "Thank you. I like to hear other people's thoughts."

"I see something!" Kareem pointed to the east.

Marty focused to the east and saw nothing but the horizon. "What do you see?"

"I think I see the first hints of dust in the air, by God. Either it's a storm, or it's an army on the move."

"How long before you think they'll get here?"

Kareem shrugged. "Impossible to tell. Are they on foot? Do they have supply wagons? No earlier than tonight, and maybe tomorrow."

A hawk screamed high up in the air and dove straight to the ground, pulling up only at the last second and landing on a waist-high boulder directly in front of Marty.

Two-Legs calls you to return. To prepare.

Kareem handed Marty a piece of dried meat from his pocket.

Marty ripped off a piece of the meat and pocketed the rest as he turned to face the bird. He offered the jerky and the hawk plucked it from his outstretched hand, swallowing it whole. He held out his arm and the bird gingerly climbed up on the new perch. Its talons clutched his arm painfully, even through his sleeve. "Tell her I'm coming."

He raised his arm. The bird stretched out its wings and took off.

"You talk to the birds?" Usaden stared.

"It's worse than that," Marty said. "They talk back."

The sun stood just past its midday height. Marty stood on a tall rock just north of his new encampment; the host had marched only a few hours before he had called a halt. He watched as plumes of dust were kicked up by the approaching army, revealing what at first seemed like hundreds, but eventually gave way to a thousand or more soldiers on the march. It was just like the dream vision he'd been plagued with since coming to this time and place.

And if the rest of the vision were to be fulfilled?

The next part would be the real challenge. Not getting everyone killed and somehow managing to meet with the enthroned man in the main tent. Marty's vision was very specific.

Marty took a deep breath and let it out as he walked back down to the encampment. It was time to greet whatever fate had brought for him.

The front line of the arriving force slowed and then stopped. The rest advanced, consolidating to settle finally into a solid body.

Marty felt calm. He met François one hundred yards ahead of their host, and two hundred yards from the new arrivals.

François spoke without really moving his lips. "And now what?"

"If they wanted to bulldoze us into the ground, they would have done it already."

They waited ten minutes. There was discussion in the other army. Finally, two soldiers separated from the front line and walked toward them.

Marty spoke softly and forced his words out in English. "Okay, sweet-talker. You're up."

Both soldiers wore thick leather vests and kilts under plain white capes, and sandals on their feet.

François showed his empty hands. "We bring greetings and peace from afar."

The Frenchman's voice was warm and hypnotic. The hair on the back of Marty's neck stood up.

One of the soldiers smiled, but the other's lip curled in a snarl and he tightened his grip on his spear. "Who are you to expect that we'd parley with you?"

François motioned in a grandiose manner toward Marty. "King Marty is leader of this host. I am but a repeater of his words."

The smiling warrior continued to grin and nod agreeably. The snarling one turned to Marty and sneered. "A king without even a single armed man with him? Very foolish." He swung the tip of his spear in a chopping motion toward Marty's head.

François gasped. Marty sidestepped the clumsy swing and kicked high. He slammed his foot down on the middle of the weapon, snapping it in half. The fighter staggered back two steps.

The soldier growled and lunged at Marty, a dagger aimed for his chest.

For Marty, it seemed as if his attacker was moving in slow motion. He gripped the man's extended wrist and squeezed, and the dagger dropped from the soldier's hand.

"Senbi!" the other warrior yelled with a surprised tone. "Have you gone crazy?"

Marty advanced on the soldier, who took another two steps back. "You would strike the king?" He grabbed his assailant by the front of his robe and almost lifted him off the ground. "You show poor hospitality."

The man's eyes widened as he stammered an apology. "I'm sorry. I was a fool and I cannot—"

"Shut up," Marty snarled.

Senbi clamped his mouth shut. He dangled in Marty's grip, only his toes touching the ground.

Marty motioned for François to pick up Senbi's weapons as he set the soldier back down on the ground. He smoothed out Senbi's robe, and handed him back the dagger and broken spear. "I wish no harm to you or yours. Do you understand?"

"Senbi understands," the other soldier said. He gave his partner a glare.

Marty extended his hand to the soldier he'd just humiliated.

The man shuddered. He stared at Marty's hand as if it were a scorpion's tail.

"We can be friends," Marty said.

Senbi accepted the offer and they clasped forearms. Then Marty did the same with the other soldier.

Marty turned to the less hostile warrior. "I would meet with your king."

The man nodded. "I'll report back and say that your people are peaceful and will cause us no trouble. That's correct, right? We can be friends?"

Marty and François both nodded.

"We *want* to be friends," François said.

The soldier who had attacked Marty looked distraught. "I'll talk to the captain of the guard."

The other soldier beckoned and they both walked back to their army.

François folded his arms over his chest. "That took a couple of unexpected turns."

Marty nodded. "Well, I suppose the next step is trying to get in to see the king."

"Would you rather I take over the role of poobah?" François asked. "Do all the talking?"

Marty chuckled and shook his head. "I've established myself as the king, now. I think I'd better continue in the role."

⊰ CHAPTER ⊱
THIRTY

Marty waited as the crew assembled on the east side of their encampment. Tafsut argued with Surjan about his going into the "enemy" camp without her. Surjan was wielding a seven-foot-long spear and despite his being the best fighter in the entire group, the tiny woman wasn't having any of it. He calmly took the argument and then told her again that he was doing what he had to do.

As Tafsut stomped back into their camp, Surjan watched with a perplexed expression, shrugged, and walked over to where Marty was waiting. He hitched his thumb in her direction and said, "She's just overly protective."

"I think it's adorable how you two get along." Lowanna laughed. "If she gets any more protective, she might kill you in your sleep just to make sure no one else can."

"You and Marty are adorable, too," Surjan growled.

"What?" Lowanna ground her teeth.

Marty patted Surjan on the back and took inventory of their group. Kareem and Gunther were talking in hushed tones and so far, there was no sign of François. "Has anyone seen—"

"I'm here, I'm here..." François came jogging toward them, his pack slung over his shoulder. "Sorry I'm late, but I was making sure the other cooks didn't screw up the midday meal."

Marty motioned for everyone to walk a bit farther into the no-man's-land between camps so that the crew could talk in private. "This is ... this *may* be ... where the vision takes us."

"A road home?" Lowanna asked.

"A new enemy." Surjan glared.

"A meeting with destiny." Marty shrugged. "The time is now, and here is the army we've been marching toward. We need to meet with whoever is leading this group. Whatever happens, we can't leave these people who've hitched their wagons to ours high and dry." He shifted his gaze to Surjan. "Did you leave instructions with your guys?"

He nodded. "Usaden has overall command. He and Badis each command a platoon of spear-fighters. Idder commands the sharpshooters. They know that if we don't return by nightfall, their priority is the safety of the group."

Marty looked over the group. "We may need to show our talents once we're inside there."

"I will sniff like a madman." Surjan snorted and shook his head.

Kareem rubbed his fingers and grinned.

"I can heal three of them, I think," Gunther said. "And freeze one of them in his tracks. Not sure whether I have a limit on dropping rocks on people's heads."

Lowanna grinned mischievously. "Oh, I think I've got something that'll make them think twice about messing around with us."

Her expression gave Marty pause. "Are you going to give us a hint about what you have planned?"

"A flock of pigeons," Gunther guessed, "to poop on everyone who gets in our way?"

"Gunther!" Lowanna feigned outrage. "I'd never do something like that. Besides, who poops on demand?" She turned to Marty and winked. "I think it's best that I just keep it a secret for now. Most of the fun is being surprised, isn't it?"

Marty shook his head and raked his fingers through his hair. "Just be ready, anything could happen." He turned to François and wagged his finger. "Let's keep your special voice in our back pocket, though. I don't want to persuade this army . . . artificially . . . and then have them get angry with us later."

"So I do nothing, then?"

"You carry the banner."

As Marty led the crew across the quarter-mile gap between the two large groups, he felt a sense of inevitability. The vision he'd had from the beginning laid out a nearly two-month journey, and even with the unexpected delays along the way, somehow it all had managed to work out such that on the exact day they were supposed to encounter an army—the meeting had happened.

It gave him a feeling of confidence; it also bothered him. Marty had no idea what he was getting himself into. These people hadn't attacked, which was great, but they could be waiting for him to go into the spider's den and then set off their own trap. Might this be an army of Sethian vassals?

Might they be potential recruits for Marty's struggle against the Sethians?

But there should be a man seated on a throne, and Marty believed he was supposed to meet him.

This king's army had dug a ditch around their encampment and set wooden spikes into the bottom of it. The excavated dirt had been heaped up to make a bank on the inside of the ditch. Marty wished he'd done the same with his camp, though it wouldn't matter if this encounter went well and peace was the result. And anyway, he didn't have nearly the manpower.

Marty approached a gap in the ditch that had five spear-wielding soldiers on each side. He waved to them and they bowed. "Hail, King Marty."

King Marty. It was ridiculous, but François had stuck him with it and it had obviously been communicated to the guards. "Hail, good men. I seek an audience with your king."

The soldiers looked at one another and among them all, not a clue was available.

The soldier who'd attacked him had mentioned someone. "Is there a captain of the guard?"

The soldiers nodded and one of them pointed to the southwest. "The captain has a tent in the southwest corner, not too far from the king's quarters. But he's often walking the interior perimeter of the camp, inspecting his men. He could be anywhere in there."

Marty nodded. "We will find him."

The guard who'd spoken snapped his fingers, pointed at two warriors on each side of the entrance, and announced, "You will be provided an escort—for your protection, King Marty."

Four spear-wielding warriors left the entrance and began shadowing the crew's every movement.

Marty smiled at the soldiers. These men were following certainly not for his protection, but in order to keep an eye on the crew's activities.

He walked into the king's camp, with François at his side, carrying the banner of the Broken Ametsu. The rest of the crew followed, and behind them came four nervous-looking soldiers.

Within the perimeter, the tents were set up in blocks with evenly spaced alleys between them. He saw small ditches that looked like latrines under construction, and cooking fires.

"How does anyone find anything in this place?" Surjan whispered.

François motioned to one of the passing soldiers. "My good man, how can we find the captain of the guard?"

The soldier turned and pointed south. "I saw him on patrol not five minutes ago. Follow this path and you should encounter him." The soldier then rushed in the opposite direction.

They walked through the grid toward the south. They found nothing but the outer barrier and some tents.

A soldier approached along the outer perimeter and Surjan turned to him. "Where is the captain?" the Sikh barked.

The soldier stared at the group and pointed in the direction he'd come from.

Marty and the crew traveled the path between the tents and found themselves in a clearing devoid of tents, a square plaza of packed dirt. Fighters sparred with long sticks as well as blunted swords.

A tall man approached. He wore a thick leather vest, a leather kilt, and sandals; sheathed at his waist was a long-handled bronze mace. He looked up at the banner.

"Strangers, which of you is King Marty?"

François pointed in Marty's direction.

The man slammed his fist against his own chest. "I'm the captain of the king's guards. A warrior named Senbi told me you want an audience with the king. No audience will be granted. We have met in peace, we will part in peace. It is enough."

"I am King Marty. I am also known as Marty the Seer." Marty drew his ankh and displayed it. The soldier took a step back, his eyes growing wider. "This has given me visions and led me to this place at this time. The gods have told me that I am to meet with your king."

He had taken some theatrical license, but Marty didn't feel he was actually lying.

"Nonsense!" A second man approached, shaking his head. His only weapon was a dagger on his belt, but he had a thin gold fillet encircling his forehead. His cape was long and his tunic had a blue fringe. "Stories are easy to come by, mere air. I am Prince Mesu-Ptah, Keeper of the Seal, Sole Companion to His Majesty. Who are you, King Marty, that we should respect your blood? What are your deeds? Who are these gods who cloud your mind? You will not see the king."

"My good captain, my good prince ... there must be something that can earn an audience with the king." François's voice flowed like warm honey through the clearing and Marty found himself focused on the Frenchman's every word. "We believe that an audience with King Marty is what your king would want."

"Prince ..." Lowanna murmured. "Is this guy the heir?"

"No," Marty whispered back. "There are lots of princes. He's just a courtier."

The captain turned to the prince and said, "Did you see the silver sigil he bears? It must mean something."

Marty was mildly annoyed that François had gone ahead and used his voice hypnosis trick.

But maybe François couldn't really help it. Marty couldn't choose not to hear animals speaking.

The prince's expression softened a bit. "The king is ill and needs his rest."

"We can help with healing," Gunther volunteered. "We have skills in that area."

The captain shook his head. "Thank you, but we have the best healers. You cannot help."

Lowanna stepped closer to the prince, put her hands on her hips, and gave the man a smoldering glare. She wore her long-sleeved Tool shirt, travel-stained and torn, and it gave the confrontation an unearthly appearance. "Our magicians are the greatest in the land, Sole Companion of the King. As our gods are the greatest. Turn away King Marty the Seer at your peril, Prince."

The prince smirked. "I do not fear your gods, Cushite barbarian. Nor your magic tricks."

Lowanna swept her open palm across the dirt plaza, pointing at all the soldiers who'd paused their sparring to watch their prince and captain interact with the foreigners. "Choose your champion." She pointed at the center of the clearing. "We fight with our bare hands alone."

The captain snorted. "Any of my men would kill you."

"Not only will I defeat your champion," Lowanna said, "but I will cause him to leave the ring without even touching him."

Marty imagined boars charging the fighting ground.

"Madness," the captain said.

Lowanna took two steps toward the captain and stared him in the eyes. "I take it you are the champion?"

Marty's heart thudded in his chest.

The captain walked over to the sparring circle. The other soldiers fell back and Lowanna also stepped into the circle.

Surjan and the others on the crew shot one another sidelong glances. They looked at Marty and all he could do was shrug.

Lowanna had said and done some strange things on this journey, but she had always made good. Marty watched the encounter with as much apprehension and curiosity as anyone else.

It is warm and dark. Must we leave this nest?

We must do as we are told.

But I have been so comfortably asleep.

Marty looked around. Was he hearing camels talk? Groundhogs?

Lowanna pointed at the captain's mace and made a flicking motion. "Remember, Captain, no weapons."

The head of the king's guard smiled and handed his mace to another soldier, along with a dagger from his belt. He showed his empty hands, spat, and grinned.

Lowanna showed her empty hands as well and took a step closer to the captain.

Did she know judo? But surely, she would have mentioned that to Marty before now.

"You said that I'll leave this circle without you even having to touch me." The captain took a step closer to Lowanna and shook his head. "I'm not leaving this circle before you."

The dark-skinned woman gave the captain a warm smile and purred, "I love a boastful man." She held her arms out as if she were looking to embrace him, palms up. "Come, give me a hug."

From each of Lowanna's sleeves a snake slithered into her outstretched hands. They reared up to show their hooded heads.

The man is frightened.

Do not bite him.

The captain let out a high-pitched yell and scrambled backward. The cobras hissed. The captain danced one way and then the other, and the snakes pivoted to watch him move.

What if he attacks?

He will not. He flees.

"Outside the circle, Captain!" Lowanna called.

He snarled but nodded, and she set the snakes gently on the ground. Marty guffawed at the sight of the captain standing outside the sparring circle while Lowanna's reptilian friends slithered away.

Lowanna stepped closer to the captain and with a dulcet tone said, "We command the birds of the air and all the beasts of earth. We see all things and we sway the hearts of men. We can heal your king."

The soldiers gathered in the open space all turned to the prince and the captain. Marty read surprise in their faces, but also uncertainty and hope.

The captain turned to look at the prince, arching his eyebrows.

Prince Mesu-Ptah shook his head at Lowanna and smiled. "Sorcery! But impressive sorcery. Perhaps you will indeed be able to heal the king."

Marty and the crew stood in front of a tent that was easily five times the size of any of the others. The tent was guarded by four soldiers who were bigger than Surjan, standing beside a broad table. With them stood a short, thin man, clean-shaven and dressed in a light tunic threaded with gold. The short man held the pole of a banner; he must be a herald.

On the banner were painted two hieroglyphs, the same glyph repeated twice. The hieroglyph was the rectangle-and-three-dots sign for *ta*, meaning, the land. "The two lands" was an old way to refer to Egypt, which meant this had to be an Egyptian force.

But Marty didn't know an Egyptian king who had used The Two Lands as a throne name.

The herald pointed at the table and motioned to the turbaned warrior. "No weapons inside the tent." His voice was booming and sonorous.

The prince and captain bowed.

Surjan placed his spear on the table. The herald then opened the tent flap; the tent within was lit, but was darker than the space outside, so Marty saw it as shadow.

The herald announced, "King Marty of the..." He looked to Marty and whispered, "What is the name of your kingdom?"

Marty leaned over and whispered, "Connecticut."

"King Marty of the Kingdom of Connecticut draws near the throne. King Marty is..." He looked at Marty, prompting more information.

Marty shrugged.

"The Seer," François said, "master of many obscure lores."

The herald repeated the words and looked at Marty again.

Marty shrugged.

"Victor of the battle of Two Shas," François said, "Scourge of Bast, slayer of the Ametsu. Author of a very well-received monograph on uses of the subjunctive in Afroasiatic languages."

The herald said the words, stumbling in the second half, then looked at Marty.

Marty looked at François.

"Famed healer," François said, "freer of the oppressed, giver of food to the hungry, bringer of water. He commands the beasts and they obey. He knows the tongues of the dead. Favored of Thoth, he invents the written word. Wide is his kingdom, bold is his action, and gentle is his heart."

"That should be enough, right?" Marty asked the herald.

The herald nodded and repeated François's words.

Marty stepped forward to enter the tent, but the herald stopped him.

"King Marty, I give you the golden Horus, whose crown crushes enemies, whose tongue unites the land, whose word strengthens the weak of heart."

Marty smiled politely.

"Who strikes foes dead with a mere glance, whose breath blows down kingdoms, the arrow of Sekhmet, the Only True King."

Marty nodded.

François pushed the banner into the herald's hands. The herald frowned, but took it.

"How excited are the gods by his presence in their temples! How fearful are the Nine Bows of his presence on their borders! How emboldened are the children of the land at the sound of his name!"

Marty forced himself to keep smiling. He felt he was listening to the introduction of a commencement speaker.

"The King of the Two Lands, he of the sedge and of the bee, Narmer."

Marty's heart stopped.

Narmer?

The time was right, but . . . Narmer?

He and the other members of the crew stumbled forward into the tent.

He saw now a throne, the same throne he had seen repeatedly in his vision. But the throne was empty. Beside the throne was a palanquin, and in the palanquin, tended by two priests, lay Narmer of Egypt.

Sick.

Dying.

⫷ CHAPTER ⫸
THIRTY-ONE

Narmer.

Actually Narmer.

The man whom Marty knew as the unifying first king of Egypt lay on an austere palanquin. He was propped up on two leather bolsters and covered with a thin sheet. He trembled as if the weight of Marty's gaze weakened him. Marty was used to imagining Narmer with the tall curving *hedjet*-crown of the Narmer Palette, but here his head was bare. The king had big ears, big lips, wide nostrils, and goggle eyes. His skin was the dark, cracked leather caused by a life on the road.

Narmer didn't look old. But he looked broken.

Narmer's was the face he had been dreaming for weeks.

A stench of rot filled the room. Marty gagged.

The tent, like the palanquin, was simple and sturdy. Its only other furnishings were two tables, which bore knives, bones, inscribed stones, and feathers. Magical objects? Medical paraphernalia?

Between the tables and the king stood two old men. One wore a long robe and the other a panther skin and a leather skullcap. They stared at Marty as if he were a threat.

Two mace-wielding soldiers stood inside the entrance.

"I kind of want him to stand up and swing a mace," François murmured. "You know, smash Lower Egypt. Unite the kingdom."

"Take a selfie?" Lowanna snorted.

François nodded vigorously. "Yes. I took a selfie with William Shatner at a bar in Vancouver. *Of course* I would take a selfie with King Narmer. If only I had a phone."

Slowly, the king opened his eyes, and then he smiled in one corner of his mouth. "You behold a marvel." His voice was a gravelly croak. "The last king of the Black Land, the beaten former defender of civilized man. The great flaming hope of yesterday, and the cold ashes of this morning. Look and remember, that you may tell your children."

"See?" François muttered. "He's up for selfies."

"Your Majesty." Marty made the arm gesture of reverence familiar to him from ten thousand hieroglyph panels, raising both arms, and he bowed low. Gunther joined him, and then the others followed.

As if provoked by the respect, Narmer fell into a spasm of coughing.

"You are not from here," Narmer said.

Marty looked down at his own checked oxford shirt, stitched in several spots and obviously out of place. His slacks were even more egregiously wrong—the king's soldiers all wore kilts, as had the Sethians. Marty smiled. "I'm from far away. We all are."

"Perhaps you are also not . . . from *now*." Narmer arched an eyebrow in Marty's direction.

Marty froze. He was very conscious of the men with maces at the tent of the door, and all the men with spears outside, and the two priests who stood to the side of the king, rubbing their hands and frowning. What did the king know? And was he trying to elicit an admission from Marty?

But he was, after all, the man from Marty's vision. And the vision had led him to Narmer, and in the time it indicated. This could not be coincidence.

Still, best to show his cards carefully. Just because Marty was being led to Narmer, did not mean that Narmer expected Marty. Or that he would be friendly.

"The world is eternal," Marty said. "It endures and it repeats." He hoped that was vague enough, and perhaps profound-sounding enough, to satisfy the king.

"No," Narmer said. "Some things endure, and some things repeat. But some things go backward in time, against the sailing of the sun-bark, and appear in the world thousands of years before their own creation. Some *things* do, and so do some *men*."

"He knows," François said.

"I know many things," Narmer said. "But I do not know *you*. Though I have seen your faces, and have been waiting for you."

He coughed again, violently. One of the men in robes raised some gauze to the king's lips and he coughed blood into it. The priest discreetly dropped the bloodied fabric into a pot.

"We're scholars," Marty said.

Surjan snorted.

"Scholars, and friends of scholars," Marty continued.

"And a host," Narmer said. "A war band such as a small nation might be proud to field."

"Yes," Marty agreed. "We were born approximately five thousand years in your future. Not all of the host. But those of us who stand here."

Narmer scanned the group. He shook, and his lungs rasped as his chest rose and fell. "Is any of you a child of the Black Land?"

Marty rested his hand gently on Kareem's shoulder and brought the young man forward. "This is Kareem. He was born in the Black Land, near the marshes at the mouth of the Nile."

Narmer took Kareem's hand and squeezed it. "At last."

"Your Majesty," Kareem said.

"And the rest of you are from the Nine Bows." Narmer sighed. "It is humiliating that I must fail humanity. It is more humiliating that those who come to supply the deficit must always be of the Nine Bows."

"Nine bows?" Surjan murmured.

"He means foreigners," Gunther said. "Non-Egyptians."

"I am from so far away," Lowanna said, "that I am not of the Nine Bows."

"Nubia?" Narmer asked. "Punt?"

"I'm from across the ocean," Lowanna said. "Many months of dangerous journey from here. You have not heard of my home, Your Majesty, but even in my distant land, the name of the Black Land is well known. As is the name of King Narmer."

"You flatter me," Narmer murmured. "I am a failure. The Lower Black Land battles me, the Children of Seth eat my people. My domain is diminished to a grain of wheat, and now even that grain is to be eaten. Soon I and my kingdom shall be cast into the latrine."

Was this, after all, an alternate universe? One in which Narmer never unified Egypt, but died a failure?

Or did this Narmer have a future ahead of him still?

"You entered the tunnel," Narmer said.

Marty's heart stopped.

"Yes," François said. "What do you know about that tunnel?"

"You entered the tunnel," Narmer said, "and then you found yourselves here. You found yourselves *now*. And you are looking for the tunnel again."

They all stared.

"How did you know?" Surjan asked.

Narmer chuckled. "I have seen some of the others. They always look like you. They are always from the Nine Bows. Lands with strange names. Harsh and uncouth to the ear. And they always come looking for the tunnel. I think the tunnel makes them search for it. The tunnel seduces them. Which means that what becomes of them is my fault."

Marty shivered. "Did you build the tunnel?"

"I must warn you that it's futile," Narmer said. "I have seen many champions such as yourselves over the years. I have seen them enter the tunnel. They die and turn to dust. All of them."

François whistled.

Marty felt betrayed. By his dream. By himself, too—or whoever had put the hieroglyphs of his personal invention into the tunnel.

"I was a believer in my father's visions as a young man," Narmer said. "But I have seen too much death. I have *caused* too much death. It is time to let go of the visions, accept that my death, too, is inevitable, and that there will be no great kingdom."

"Visions?" Marty asked. "Visions of the future of the Two Lands?"

"And more," Narmer said. "Visions of each band of heroes before it came. Visions that the end had come, and that there would be no more heroes. And then, unexpectedly, visions of you. One final band. One last chance."

"But there will be a great kingdom," Gunther said. "Or, at least, there *can* be. We've all seen its ruins. We've seen the ruins of the kingdom that lasted three thousand years. And you will be the one who unites that kingdom."

"If you don't surrender," Surjan added.

Narmer wheezed in and out and shook his head faintly.

"Who built the tunnel?" François asked. "Was it your father, then?"

"My father did not build the tunnel," Narmer said. "But he inherited the tunnel and its lore from the men who knew the Builders." He seemed to be sinking into the bolsters before Marty's very eyes. "The Builders were not men such as you and I."

"What do you mean?" Gunther frowned. "Were they more heroic than us?"

"You mean the Sethians," Marty said. "The Children of Seth built the tunnel and summoned us here?" He felt betrayed again.

"No," Narmer said. "The Builders were a greater people. They came down from heaven in mighty vessels. They were tall as giraffes and they had breath like storm winds."

"Breath . . . like a crocodile?" Marty asked, thinking of the text on the tablet.

"If you prefer." Narmer tipped his head slightly.

"How do you know this?" Gunther asked.

"I have seen their works," Narmer said. "Their buildings, their canals, their plazas . . . their tunnels. My father told me of hearing their stormy breath. The Children of Seth were some of their servants and their creation, who rebelled and were left behind as a punishment. The Children of Bast and the Children of Hathor were also their servants, and there are others. If my father is to be believed, then there are many others, all over this world. But they are all fallen, degenerate races, much weaker and stupider than their masters. The Builders had mighty tools and powerful vessels such as mankind has never known, and the Builders came down from heaven to save mankind."

"I can't tell if I'm listening to some creation folktale," Lowanna grumbled, "or watching *Ancient Aliens* on late-night cable TV."

"Your father inherited the tunnel." Marty tried to stay focused, against the thousand images and ideas swirling in his head.

"My father's father was a foreman for the Builders. And when their work on the tunnel was complete, they consigned it into his hands. He was to operate the tunnel, to cause it to function, and he was to pass that burden on to his sons."

"Its function is . . . what, exactly?" François said.

"It calls heroes," Narmer said. "And then it kills them."

Marty felt he was standing up to his waist in ashes. "Is that what the Builders told your grandfather?"

Narmer's breathing was slower. His skin, brown and cracked, still managed to appear translucent, revealing thick webs of blue veins beneath. "The Builders said they had come to this planet to prepare its people. They said that a great trial was coming this way. They said that humanity as a whole could never be ready for that battle, but if the Builders had their way, they would prepare champions to fight for humanity. They told my grandfather that the Black Land stood upon something they called the 'Way.' That heroes who were tested here and went forward would be tested at other 'Stations' along the Way, in order to become greater and nobler, until they were brought to stand in the appropriate place and time in order to fight for all mankind."

"And we're the last." François whistled. "The last, after the last. The postscript, the afterthought."

"Are there other tunnels, then?" Surjan grimaced.

Narmer shrugged.

"How do you operate the tunnel?" Marty asked.

"There are procedures," Narmer said. "It is a machine, though a very complex one. It does not matter now. I have come to the end of my days. I have no child to learn the methods of operation from me, and we have lost the Black Land. Perhaps the Children of Seth will work the tunnels. Perhaps they will create their own champions, mighty in all their evil, and those champions will stand against the greater evil when the time comes."

"What is wrong with the king?" Gunther asked the nearer of the two priests, the one in the robe.

The man shrugged. He was tall, with a blocky head. "He fails, and his failure is beyond our arts to cure."

The priest wearing the panther skin worried his fingers. He was short and rotund with jowls that moved as he spoke. "We fled the Black Land looking for a famous healing spring. It seems that we fled too late. Even now, we are wasting time, when every second might mean life or death for the king!"

"Why would the Builders devise such an engine?" Marty asked. "You say it calls men and then it kills them?"

"I said that it calls heroes," Narmer murmured. "And they reach the tunnel at the end of a long journey, and enter into it to solve its mysteries, and the tunnel kills them. They turn to ash. I have seen it with my own eyes, many times. My father believed the tale he passed on to me. But as far as I have ever seen, it is a lie. Perhaps it was always a lie."

"What if the Builders are mankind's enemy?" François asked. "What if the function of the tunnel is to call for mankind's great potential defenders and murder them so they can't do any good?"

"I don't know." Marty bit his lower lip. "What we're saying is that it doesn't make that much sense that some advanced people built a machine to attract and, uh, train heroes for some kind of final battle, but that makes a bunch much *more* sense than aliens building a machine to summon potential heroes and murder them. That's a bit far-fetched."

"I can't believe I'm even hearing you say the word 'far-fetched,'" François said, "after everything you've already witnessed and done. Do I need to remind you of all the crazy things you have already personally experienced, or shall I just draw a picture of a ballpoint pen?"

"Pen?" Gunther muttered.

Marty closed his eyes and rubbed his temples.

"It seems indirect," Surjan said. "If these Builders could identify you as a threat before you were born, François, why not just kill you in the cradle?"

Marty's heart was flat. Did it matter what the motivations of the Builders were, if the end result was that Marty and his companions got reduced to ash, regardless? The difference between a lie and a broken machine was, practically speaking, nothing.

"If the story the Builders told is true," Lowanna said. "Does that mean that we're humanity's last hope?"

Marty rubbed his eyes. He was tired and he didn't want the responsibility. "Because there will be no more champions?"

"Because there will be no more champions," Lowanna said. "Some kind of monster enemy is coming for the entire species, and friendly aliens set up a training gauntlet for heroes, but we're the last to get through before the engine falls out of use."

"In fact, we made it through *after* the engine had fallen out of use," François said. "If you think about it."

"This is a very strange story," Surjan said.

"I failed," Narmer said. "I lost my war with the Lower Black Land. I had no children to whom to pass the lore of the tunnel, and I never summoned heroes who could survive the journey."

"Except us," François said. "So far."

"Don't go," Narmer said. "Don't choose the tunnel. It is death."

Marty bit his lip. Did he really have a choice? Hadn't the tunnel chosen him? And if he wasn't going to enter the tunnel, what on earth would he do instead?

Simply choose to live here and now, in the fourth millennium B.C.E.?

Under Sethian rule?

"My only consolation at my early death," Narmer said slowly, "is that I will not be there to see you reduced by the tunnel to ash."

He coughed again, so violently that his priests had to catch him from falling off the palanquin.

⫸ CHAPTER ⫷
THIRTY-TWO

This time the priest brought the pot over to the palanquin and held it below Narmer's face. The king spat blood directly into the pot, which reeked of death and corruption.

Then the priests levered Narmer back onto the palanquin. His breath had become a constant rattle.

"This is why I must keep my men from seeing me," Narmer rumbled. His words came slower by the minute. "A king can only reign as long as he inspires confidence. No one seeing me now would believe I could defeat the Nine Bows, or the kings of the Lower Black Land, or the Children of Seth. No one would think I could hold on to life until the setting of the sun. And they would be right."

"What is the illness that plagues the king?" Gunther asked the two priests. Lowanna leaned at his shoulder, listening. "How does it kill?"

"We have no name for it." The blockheaded priest shook his head. "It turns his insides all to blood. He is rotting alive."

"We are wasting time!" The rotund priest stamped his feet. He looked at the guards as if to give them an order, but only scowled.

"Show them my feet." Narmer grinned the ghoulish grin of a little boy excited about something disgusting. "If you can stand it."

"I'm a healer," Gunther said.

One of the priests peeled back the sheet from Narmer's feet. The king's feet and legs were black and necrotic. Herbs were packed in bundles around the flesh, but the stink that rose off Narmer's uncovered body nevertheless nearly knocked Marty unconscious.

The rot ran up Narmer's legs in black and yellow streaks. His shanks were hairless and withered, and the skin hung loose on his bones, as if the flesh was all gone.

"This is the true majesty of mankind," Narmer moaned. "Death. Our common lot, our royal cloak, our universal end."

"What do you think?" Marty murmured to Gunther, drawing him and Lowanna to one side.

"I'm not a medical doctor," Gunther said. "I'm only trained as a military medic. This isn't something I can run an IV for or stitch up. My only options are, you know, I can do things." He wiggled his fingers. "And what I can do, I'm not really sure that I can do anything about *that*. And besides, I don't even know what that is on his legs. Leprosy? Isn't leprosy a bacterium or something? So I don't know, as long as we're taking long shots, maybe we try François's uh, penicillin? But does leprosy make you cough like that? Can he have leprosy and also tuberculosis? Is it gangrene?"

"We had a camel that had a section of foul-smelling blackened skin like that." Lowanna wrinkled her nose. "It was gangrene, and we had to put him down."

Gunther shook his head. "If it's gangrene, I think he's a dead man. Look how far up his legs it's gone. We're not going to amputate his torso."

"Yes, but the things you can do," Marty said. "Your gifts."

"We can try," Lowanna said. "This is *the* Narmer, isn't it? We have to try. It's like if we could save Churchill's life in 1939, or if we could stop Martin Luther King from getting shot. Without this guy, there's no Egypt as we know it."

"You think the bread mold, too?" Marty asked.

Gunther shrugged. "We try that, too. Why not? It's like that wizard Wagguten told us, try everything, you never know what's going to work." He buried his face in his hands. "I can't believe I'm taking professional advice from a wizard."

"Not professional advice." Marty grinned. "Magical advice. And magic is really more of a hobby for you."

"I feel so much better."

"I'll help," Lowanna said. "I can heal, too."

"I know you can," Gunther said. "And if some dormouse or passing squirrel tells you what plagues the king, and how to remedy it, please don't hesitate to pass the information on to me. Sincerely. Anything that may help."

Gunther laid his hands on the king's legs, one hand on each shin. Lowanna put both her hands over his sternum, as if she were going to give him CPR.

Marty and the others stepped back.

"They say no incantations," the blockheaded priest muttered.

His colleague shrugged.

Light trickled down Gunther's and Lowanna's arms like running condensation down a window, pooling in the king's sheet and seeping through into his body. Marty stepped back, found he was fidgeting, and crossed his hands in front of his body to hold them still.

The light from the procedure—Marty couldn't quite bring himself to think of it as a *spell*—cast black shadows across the faces of the two priests. Their mouths were open in astonishment, their eyes black pits.

And they were fidgeting, too.

Marty couldn't hear a sound but the rasp of the king's breath. Gunther's body began to spasm, as if he were having a seizure, or gripping an electrical cable with his bare hands. His head snapped back and forth and Marty stepped forward to catch his friend. Gunther yelled wordlessly, let go of the king, and staggered backward into Marty's arms.

Lowanna collapsed.

Marty smelled ozone wafting off his friend. Gunther was awake but woozy, so Marty loosened his collar and patted him on the shoulder.

Surjan tried to minister similarly to Lowanna, but she brushed him off with a growl and climbed to her feet.

Marty stood and looked to the king. His face was peaceful, but when Marty lifted the sheet to look underneath, the king's rotted feet looked no different.

And the stench of death remained on him.

"Is the king dead?" the fat priest asked, a look of horror on his face.

"Surely not!" The blockheaded priest bent to listen to the king's breathing. "Not yet, he lives."

"We must take him now," the fat priest said. "We have wasted too much time with this delusional talk of tunnels and the Nine Bows and sailing the bark of the sun backward. The king is dying, and we may yet bring him to the healing spring!"

Lowanna took Narmer by the hand. "Your Majesty?"

Narmer made a thick rattling sound as he exhaled.

"He is dying!" the fat priest shouted. "Get these foreigners out of here!"

The two warriors stepped into the room. Marty grabbed the mace hanging on one warrior's belt and pinned it in place. "Wait," he said.

"Wait!" François removed from his shoulder bag a grass-wrapped parcel. The bread inside was invisible under a complete covering of green mold fuzz. "This is a medicine."

"Leave it!" the fat one shouted. "We must go!"

"You must cut this into ten pieces," François said. "He should eat one piece per day."

"He can eat nothing," the priest said. "Look at him. He expended the last energy of his life talking to you, and now he can do nothing but die. We must carry him as fast as we can to the healing spring."

"The healing spring," Marty said.

The warriors at the door relaxed, and Marty stepped away from them.

"We may have brought it with us," François said. They locked eyes briefly, and Marty raised his eyebrows. "Where is this spring?"

"To the west," the fat priest said. "There is a spring to the north of the trail. The sick and the frail are brought there to be healed."

"Are they dipped into the spring?" Marty asked. "Or do they spend the night sleeping in a cave?"

"They sleep in the cave," the blockhead said. "Do you know this place?"

"We know the place," François said. "We brought its magic with us."

"You have captured the spirit of the spring?" The fat priest frowned.

François set the mold down on the corner of Narmer's bed and drew the flat box from his shoulder bag. "Yes," he said. "It is in here, in the great symbol of life."

"Wait," Marty said.

"The ankh," François said. "Symbol of life, and oaths. We met the spirit in the cave above the sacred spring. And we have bound the spring's spirit of life by oaths into this talisman. You know this symbol, the golden ankh." He opened the box with all the conspiratorial drama of a carnival barker, his eyes wide and gleaming. "We must touch this to the king's skin, and he will be healed."

"I do not know that symbol," the fat priest said.

"We might be a little early for that," Marty mumbled. "In five hundred years or so, they'd recognize it for sure."

François was undeterred. "Remember this symbol, for it is the great loop of life."

"It will heal the king?" the blockheaded priest asked.

"It has healed us," François said. "It has made us younger, and cured our illnesses. It regrew my hair!"

He sounded more like a snake-oil salesman the longer he talked. If he was trying to use his hypnotic voice powers, he was failing. Maybe they were like Gunther's healings, they only worked so many times a day. Marty gritted his teeth and tried to smile.

The fat priest reached for the ankh and Marty pulled it back. The priest scowled.

"Only the king may touch this." François hesitated. Marty could see by the squint of his eyes that he was trying to work out how to explain that the priests shouldn't touch the ankh without contradicting the claim that it had healed Marty. "It may harm as well as heal. Best not to provoke the spirit needlessly."

"Is there a ritual?" the blockheaded priest asked.

"The king must grasp the ankh," François said. "Touch it with his bare skin."

The fat priest took Narmer's hand in his own and opened Narmer's fingers. Next to the corpulence of his priest, Narmer looked frail and brittle, just a bundle of sticks. Marty held his breath as François gently worked the staff of the ankh into Narmer's palm and then the priest wrapped the king's fingers shut.

"What now?" the fat priest asked.

"We should definitely say a prayer," François said. "An incantation. Do you know something appropriate, Marty?"

Marty drew himself to his full height, feeling deeply conflicted and guilty.

"Four score and seven years ago," he said, forcing his thoughts to run along their natural English path. He spoke slowly and thoughtfully, doing his best imitation not of Abraham Lincoln, but of the animatronic Abraham Lincoln he'd seen at a state fair when he was nine. That ashen-skinned simulacrum had led him to memorize the entire Gettysburg Address and deliver it to his class for extra credit in history, and he'd never forgotten it. "Our fathers brought forth upon this continent, a new nation, conceived in Liberty, and dedicated to the proposition that all men are created equal."

The gold metal of the ankh appeared to melt in Narmer's hand, leaving behind a familiar silver sheen. Marty watched as the particles of gold flowed onto the king's skin as if they had a mind of their own. The golden hue the ankh had transferred to the king seeped into the man's skin and vanished.

The priests' eyes were fixed on the king's hand. They saw what had happened, as well.

"Keep going," François muttered. He slid the box away so that the ankh gently tumbled onto Narmer's chest.

"Now we are engaged in a great civil war," Marty said, "testing whether that nation, or any nation so conceived and so dedicated, can long endure." The glowing had stopped, along with Marty's sense that the gold from the ankh was leeching into the king. He licked his lips and continued. "We are met on a great battle-field of that war." The priests looked up at Marty anxiously. "We have come to dedicate a portion of that field, as a final resting place for those who here gave their lives that that nation might live." Narmer grunted and lay still. "It is altogether fitting and proper that we should do this."

Except it didn't feel fitting and proper, it felt like a scam.

"The king is dead!" The fat priest dropped Narmer's hand and pulled at his own hair. The ankh lay ignored, its gold sheen gone, leaving only a cold, dull silver object on the king's chest. "The king is dead. You have killed him!"

Grandpa Chang's voice projected in his head.

One moment can change a day, one day can change a life, and one life can change the world.

Marty's hand began to shake. Did they just change the path of history? Was Ancient Egypt doomed by something he'd just done, or maybe not done?

"What?" François fumbled and dropped the box. It clattered dully on the packed earth floor. "No, wait a minute, that isn't right."

"You said the spirit could harm him as well as heal him," the blockheaded priest said.

"I explained that poorly," François said. "What I meant—"

"It has harmed him!" the fat priest shrieked. "It has killed him!"

"We could have taken the king to the healing spring." The blockheaded priest shook his head in sorrow. "You took the king's last moments and ate them up with your petition."

Marty felt his breath coming short, and it was getting difficult to see. He hadn't felt this much anxiety since . . . since . . .

"Seize them!" the fat priest shrieked.

The warriors had snaked their maces into their hands while Marty's back was turned. One now grabbed Lowanna by her hair and held the mace over her, while the other did the same with Kareem.

"Cowards," Surjan growled. "Put down the boy and the woman and I will kill you both with my fists alone."

"Nobody needs to kill anyone." Marty's head was spinning. He had failed. Narmer was dead. He had come so far, he had arrived on time, and then Narmer had died.

He died only after telling Marty that the quest was pointless, because the tunnel would only kill him.

But that couldn't be right, could it? Marty had seen his own hieroglyphs inside the tunnel. Didn't that just have to mean that he was going to arrive, and to leave himself a message? And why would he do that if he knew that summoning himself only ended in death? And Narmer was meant to reunite both halves of Egypt. Regardless of what they'd done here, it must still happen . . . shouldn't it?

He felt both paradox and parallel universe theory yawning like twin pits at his feet, and he was already short of breath and dizzy.

Lowanna slammed a vicious uppercut into the nose of the man holding her and sent him reeling back a step.

Kareem slashed at the soldier with his ankh and pulled away from his grip.

Both warriors raised their maces.

"We'll leave," Marty said. "We're sorry. We'll leave now."

"Go!" the fat priest wailed. "Go, before I summon the warriors of the king and have you dragged to your deaths behind wild camels! Go, and may the gods spit upon you as you have spit upon our people!"

They exited the tent into darkness. Surjan took his spear from the table outside and François reclaimed Marty's banner. Then they walked across the Egyptians' camp in stunned silence.

⇒ CHAPTER ⇐
THIRTY-THREE

Marty and the crew left Narmer's camp briskly. Surjan took point, spear held with practiced grace in a position that looked casual, but would allow him to bring the weapon to bear quickly. Marty brought up the rear. He'd have said he wanted to defend their exit if asked, but also he was in shock.

François carried the banner, which seemed to droop before Marty's eyes.

Narmer. *The* Narmer.

Dead.

Was it Marty's fault?

He had difficulty breathing, and twice had to stop and lean forward, resting his elbows on his knees while he fought back the urge to vomit.

A mournful wail rose behind them, filling the air like the slow-motion explosion at the end of an action film. Marty picked up the pace to catch up to the remainder of his crew, worried that the weeping might be following by the thudding of sandals in pursuit.

But no one chased them.

For all the shouting and recriminations of the fat priest, he wasn't sending soldiers. Marty joined the others in saluting the guards at the picket, and then they crossed over the spiked ditch and bank.

Three hundred yards of no-man's-land felt like a hundred miles, but they finally reached their own camp as the sun fell beneath the horizon. Munatas and two of Idder's archers waved them through.

"We should break camp now," Surjan said. "We need to leave, before Narmer gets a successor, and the new man decides to cement the loyalty of his troops by making an example of us."

"Surjan is right," François said.

"We didn't kill the king." Gunther staggered as if carrying a heavy burden.

"What will you do to prove your innocence?" Surjan asked. "Roll the surveillance footage? Call in the forensic crime scene team? Or just pit your word against the word of the king's own priests and bodyguards, who were present at his grim murder by the strange foreigners?"

Gunther reached out to pat Surjan on the shoulder. "I'll ask my champion to fight for me, in a trial by combat."

Surjan clapped his hand to Gunther's, trapping it in place. "Your champion won't help you then, if you don't listen to him now. We need to get out of here."

"Where to, by God?" Kareem asked. "We have nothing in this world."

"We can make our fortune," François said. "In a million ways, at least."

"Selling penicillin," Lowanna harrumphed.

François shrugged. "Healing people. We could be legends."

"We should dissolve the host," Gunther said. "Send them all home. Maybe even take them home ourselves. They didn't come for this. They certainly didn't come to be part of a pharmaceutical company."

"The healer doesn't like a little competition, eh?" François grunted. "We could strike gold in San Francisco. Or oil in the Persian Gulf."

They hadn't come for this.

"I need to think," Marty said.

"Are you okay?" Gunther asked.

"I . . ." Marty sucked at his teeth. "I feel like I just killed Santa Claus. Or Winston Churchill in 1939. I don't know what I did, or what went wrong, but I think I might be the man who wrecked the history of the world."

"That's awfully grandiose for one man," François said quietly. "And it's wrong. I don't think they could have got to the healing spring anyway, and besides, it looks like it wouldn't have saved the old boy. At worst, you're an ordinary man who had the extraordinary experience of meeting Santa Claus. Or Winston Churchill, in 1939. And then you had some ordinary bad luck and maybe made an ordinarily bad decision, together with your friends."

"Yes, but what do I do now?" Marty asked.

"What you can't really avoid doing," François said. "You continue living, and making more decisions, and hoping that some of them turn out okay."

"That's good advice for a kid who just got dumped by his first girlfriend," Marty said. "I'm not sure that it's any use for the man who just killed the King of Egypt."

"If you really want to lay blame," François said, "the penicillin was my failure, and so was the ankh. All you did was recite the Gettysburg Address. And frankly, I put you up to that, too."

Marty grunted, but he wasn't sure whether he was conceding, disagreeing, or just making a sound to indicate he was still standing there. He found he had no more to say. He turned and left the camp.

He walked slowly, feet heavy as lead. The sharpshooter on watch at the edge of camp nodded to him, and so did the spearman standing beneath the bone-thin tree two hundred feet out into the night.

He trudged on, watching the fires of both camps recede and become twinkling orange gems. When he stopped, he was on the crest of a low dune, facing north and west and feeling the glow of starlight on his face like a bath of dew. In the distance, he heard the rumble of thunder, and beside him, he heard a soft exhalation. Only then did he realize that Lowanna was with him.

He turned to look at her, unsure what to say or ask.

She grunted.

It was permission enough to keep silent. Marty nodded.

What were his options? He could turn and go west, all the way to Ahuskay. He could take everyone home—well, almost everyone. Some members of his travelling folk band came from villages that had been destroyed. But they could continue to the homes of the others, and find lives as members of new tribes.

Leaving the Ametsu, presumably, still a threat.

And leaving Marty and his companions where, exactly?

Whatever the purpose of Marty's vision, it hadn't, after all, led them to a way to return to their own time. They were stuck.

He could take the people elsewhere. Maybe back to one of the unoccupied oases they'd encountered. They could start a new village. Marty imagined himself plowing and herding, and had a hard time seeing the image. He could teach, though. Or just think.

But either of those plans fundamentally assumed that the Sethians were done with Marty and would leave him alone. That they wouldn't pursue him for the wounds he had already inflicted on them, and for the people he had rescued. Since they appeared to know him by name, it didn't seem likely that they'd just let him go now. And if Marty took his people back to a village and left them undefended, then they were worse off for ever having met him.

They could keep on going, and just explore. Marty's knowledge—modern man's knowledge—about the fourth millennium B.C.E. was mostly a lot of blanks on the maps. How fascinating would it be to go peer into some of those blanks! To learn long-forgotten languages. To maybe leave written records. Even written records for his future self to find.

As he had, apparently, already done.

Or would do.

But would Badis want such a life? Would Tafsut?

Would Kareem?

And if he walked away, the Sethians could return along their western route and again subjugate and terrorize the villages Marty had freed.

He sighed.

He could become Narmer.

All that was known to the modern world about Narmer was that he had unified Upper and Lower Egypt. Narmer himself had referred to his struggles to do so, and the resistance of the inhabitants of the Delta. Marty could take on Narmer's name—which was, after all, just a pair of hieroglyphs, a catfish and a chisel. In Narmer's name, as Narmer, he could fight Narmer's wars. He could unite the Egypts.

He could drive out the Sethians.

But could he? He'd had some success so far, but never against large numbers. The most Sethians he'd ever fought was four, together with two of their sha war-beasts. That had been enough of a touch and go battle that he didn't relish the thought of fighting, say, ten of them.

And what if he reached this hypothesized Sethian headquarters, and there were thousands of them?

He would have died trying to rectify his mistake. That wasn't nothing. It would be a death with integrity.

But even if he defeated the Sethians in all their strongholds, however many there were, that still left the tasks of unifying and governing Egypt. Tasks for which Marty was in no way qualified.

He could also walk away. Become a woodworker again. Make dining room sets for the discriminating buyers of the fourth millennium B.C.E.

Marty turned and looked back at the camps. They remained where they had been, but fires were dowsed now.

In mourning, probably.

He heard birds cry overhead. *An army comes. An army comes at dawn.*

He frowned and looked at Lowanna. She was staring up at the sky.

"Time to make some decisions," she said.

Watch the flock of Two-Legs, Lowanna heard the bird overhead calling.

The Two-Legs will slay each other.

"Who is to watch the Two-Legs?" Marty asked.

"I believe they're talking to each other," Lowanna said.

"Why do they watch the Two-Legs?" Marty looked stricken.

"They're carrion birds."

Marty nodded. He trembled. "Maybe the birds are talking about Narmer's army and our host?"

Lowanna threw back her head and called to the birds. "What Two-Legs? Does an army come? Does a flock come?"

A flock of Two-Legs comes from the east.

It comes with the rising of the sun.

"Men?" Lowanna cried. "Children of Seth? Do they have the heads of jackals?"

Two-Legs! Many, many Two-Legs!

Jackals with Two-Legs! Great jackals who stand like men!

They will all feed us their dead!

Lowanna turned to Marty. "A new army is coming. I think Sethians."

Marty nodded. "I heard."

They raced back to camp. Marty shouted the passwords before the sentry even called the challenge, and summoned companions as they sped to the campfires. "Surjan! François! Gunther! Kareem!"

Lowanna faltered, letting Marty run on ahead.

The other camp—Narmer's men—was dissolving.

She saw men in small groups, shouldering their gear, crawling over the ditch and bank and simply walking into the desert. The guards at the entrance were gone. The fires were doused, but in the light of the moon and stars and through the gap in the bank she saw men raiding their own army's supply depots to take food and water. They squabbled over loaves of bread and strips of dried meat, and all the while the army bled men into the night.

She hurried to join her friends.

"Tomorrow, there will be more thinking to be done," Marty said. He stood on a stone to speak to the crew, but also to Badis and Tafsut and Udad and Idder and Munatas and some thirty other warriors. Everyone within the sound of his voice was listening to him, and others were flocking to hear. "Tomorrow, we will have to decide what it means that we have formed together as a host. Is this a people? What future shall we fight for?

"But when today's sun rises, we do not have time to ask these questions. Today's sun brings with it an army of enemies. The Ametsu, the Children of Seth, are not simply some other people with whom we have misunderstanding. They are not cousins, who steal our sheep and want to marry our daughters. They are monsters who herd us like cattle and eat our flesh.

"And we must stop them. Behind us, between us and our people, there is no one. There is no other defender. If we do not stop the Ametsu, no one else will do it. They will rage across two thousand miles of path and destroy every human settlement they find. So we must stand. We have trained for this, and we are ready. We have mighty warriors and mighty weapons. And we have a great host of allies— François and I will go consult with the men of Narmer and agree on a plan of action. We have an hour or two before dawn to prepare."

"I will go speak with the men of Narmer," François said.

"I will go with you," Surjan added.

Lowanna pointed. "The men of Narmer are gone."

The man scrambling over the defense had disappeared. Through the gap in the bank, all lay still and dark.

"No," Marty murmured. "They were so many."

"They were Narmer's men," Gunther said. "Without Narmer to lead them, they went home."

"I will round up those who remain. They're better off with us as a reserve force or auxiliaries than running away into the desert." Marty marched into Narmer's camp at a rapid pace. François followed.

Lightning flashed on the northern horizon. Lowanna felt a prickle of electricity run up along her spine, and her breath filled her lungs with nervous energy.

The sky in the east was turning from dark indigo to a deep royal blue. The smudge of a marching army furred the horizon, under the dust cloud thrown up by its own feet. How numerous were they?

Surjan gave Usaden and Badis orders and went to join Marty. The Ahuskay and Jehedi warriors barked at the host, driving them to their pallets to recover spear and shield or sling and rejoin their files. Gunther approached Lowanna, shaking his head.

"This is my fault," he said.

"Everyone feels like it's their fault," she told him. "Marty sure does. I feel like it's my fault, too. But it isn't. François . . . I don't always agree with the way he thinks, but he has the right of this. Shed no tears, not right now. None of us killed Narmer, we all tried to save him. And there's nothing we can do about it now, anyway, except stand and fight."

"Or in my case," Gunther said with a sudden boyish grin, "stand and heal."

"Who do you think you're fooling? I saw you smash that Sethian's head in with a rock."

"So push our feelings back to tomorrow, then?" Gunther asked.

Lowanna nodded. "At least until then."

"Sounds healthy."

François and the others returned with a crowd of men. They were armed with spear and shield, and there were officers among them, so they even moved in something like formation. There were few of them, though, maybe only fifty—the large mass of the army had disappeared, along with the officers, the herald, and the prince.

The priests had gone, too. Had they taken Narmer's body with them?

The eastern sky showed a stripe of burnt orange between a blue-gray plain and a blue-gray sky. As Lowanna looked, the approaching army seemed to spill out of the orange band like smoke pouring from a fire.

Marty returned to Lowanna and shook his head. "I'm not sure I can get used to hearing animals talk."

"Well, we know who the cool kids are," she said.

"I feel so excluded," Gunther complained.

Marty laughed. "Can you find a bird," he asked Lowanna, "and ask it to count for us? I want to know something more specific than 'there are lots of them, and not very many of us.'"

"I don't know how high birds can count," she said. "But I'll ask."

⤛ CHAPTER ⤜
THIRTY-FOUR

With a sour taste in her mouth, Lowanna stared at the horizon and worried. She and Kareem had ridden two hours east from their encampment and nothing about what they were seeing looked good.

When she and Kareem had left, the host had been marching north a few miles to avoid direct contact with the incoming army. And now that they were staring at the incoming mass of people, she could see that they too had shifted their approach. Instead of heading due west, the newcomers were now heading slightly northwest.

The oncoming army was changing course to intercept the host.

Lowanna's camel fidgeted. Kareem's camel snorted and nipped at its companion.

Kareem shielded his eyes from the midmorning sun as he stared east. "I see the troops, praise be to God. I can also see the enemy under the dust. They're going north and west. It is a much bigger army than our host. Oh my!" He pointed all along the eastern horizon. "I see a long line of blue," he said. "That must be the Nile."

Lowanna pressed her lips together and watched for a moment longer. "See anything else?"

"They're moving fast," Kareem said. "We have half a day before they reach us."

Marty felt envy as he watched the eagle jump from the palm tree and flap into the sky.

The host stood massed on a low rise, the only hill within sight. Marty had marched here in hopes that the approaching group would continue straight and pass the host by. But it seemed to his eye that the arriving army was turning to intercept his host.

And Lowanna's message, sent by eagle, had confirmed the perception.

"They're heading straight for us?" Surjan asked. The Sikh was wearing a leather bandoleer he had fashioned, and it held several of François's smaller grenades.

"That's what Lowanna says. It looks like there's no avoiding this fight." There would also be no getting around behind the approaching army to attack it from the rear.

"Good." Surjan sniffed loudly, his nostrils flaring. "Let's bring it to these pillocks. Do we fight here, on the hill?"

Marty looked around at the gently sloping sand, a few strands of savannah grass still stubbornly poking out of it as it sloped down toward the east. "I wish there was a canyon or a butte to defend, but there's only this little mound. Better a little hill for defense than no hill at all."

"And better still a ditch and bank." Surjan pointed back at the fortifications Narmer's people had left behind.

"That's a lot of area," Marty said. "I don't think we can defend the whole thing."

"We can't," Surjan agreed. "But there are only two ways into that area that don't cross a spiked ditch and climb a steep bank. If these people insist on a confrontation with us, then we need to get into that fort right now, finish the ditch and bank, and hold it."

"Do we have time to get back there and finish the fortification?" Marty's spine felt tight.

"Probably," Surjan said. "Our odds improve if we move right now. And they improve even more if we can slow them down. If we can get settled in before they arrive, maybe we can look tough enough that they won't even fight."

Marty nodded. "Where's François? I've got some ideas for his black powder."

François had cleared one of the supply wagons of everything but the raw ingredients for explosives. He had imagined he would mix just a little more gunpowder as the wagon rolled down to the ditch-and-bank enclosure, but had given up on the idea the first time the wagon bumped over a stone and sent his work flying.

Still, there was less delicate work that could be accomplished.

The host was on the march, heading back into Narmer's fortification. Marty and Surjan were at the front of the host. Gunther and Lowanna raced ahead on camelback, with a small group of volunteers who were going to seal the fortifications shut by digging the entrances out.

Kareem held an empty jar. François pointed at the sealed wooden boxes and said, "That container is completely dry, right?"

Kareem nodded. "Bone dry. The lid was left off of it."

"Good. Go ahead and empty one of the boxes of black powder into the container and then"—François pointed at one of the lumpy bags—"open that bag, it's full of gravel. Scatter a few handfuls of the gravel into the container and then repeat again with the black powder. Try to be even and level. I know it's hard when we're being jostled like this. I want four layers of gravel and black powder."

Kareem cracked open the first wooden case and carefully poured the contents into the large wide-mouthed container. He looked into the container and said, "Four layers won't fill this."

"Right." François pointed at the nearby palm tree. "After the four layers, you go ahead and gather some of the dried fibers from the palm tree and put it loosely into the container. That'll be our wick."

Kareem quickly sprinkled rocks on top of the black powder. "This is going to be a real fight, isn't it? A big battle."

"I'm afraid so, Kareem."

"They outnumber us," Kareem said. "By a lot."

François grinned. "That is why we must cheat."

The Egyptian smiled and nodded. "Good. Fight to win."

"Fight to win." François took another empty jar and set about following his own instructions to Kareem.

If he was going to die here, he was going to take a lot of his attackers with him.

Marty paced the east-facing bank with Surjan at his side. François and Kareem had finished their work only twenty minutes before the arrival of the other army's first troops. They had unhitched the oxen, driven them away, abandoned the wagon where it was, and scrambled through the ditch and over the bank to join the host.

The ditch and bank were no great obstacle to a single person, if they were undefended. With defenders armed with spears and missile weapons, Marty hoped they would stop an army.

Or maybe even make it decide to go away.

Lowanna, Gunther, and the diggers had finished the great square. It was over a hundred yards to a side, so there was no way the host could defend the whole thing, if they were completely surrounded and attacked from all sides at once.

The host all waited inside the eastern bank. They were crouched down so as to be invisible to the approaching army, other than Munatas, who stood, holding the Broken Ametsu banner.

Behind the bank were lit several large fires.

Marty wished he had a palisade wall along the top of the bank. He wished he had more warriors. He wished he had secret forces in reserve. But the battle was here, and he had none of those things.

The enemy came on in a loose and growing mob of men with spears, bows, javelins, and swords. Marty looked but made out no chariots, and no Ametsu.

Marty turned to Surjan. "What can you see?"

"There are Sethians among them. They are farther back, and they drive on the horde of men. And the men outnumber us, three to one or more."

Marty pondered what he was about to order.

"The army's almost in range of the bowmen," Surjan said.

"The mines?" Marty asked.

Surjan smiled. "Bob's your uncle. Ready to detonate, on command."

Marty gritted his teeth. If his sharpshooters shot too early, and the enemy retreated, he lost his best surprise attack.

Marty signaled to Munatas. The Ahuskay warrior climbed the bank with a grin on his face and a straight back. When he reached the top, he waved the banner.

Marty cupped his hands around his mouth, but then François was at his shoulder. "This part is for me," the Frenchman said.

"No fair," Surjan murmured. "You also get the land mines."

François shrugged. "You'll get your turn." He stepped to the top of the bank and called to the enemy army. "Go home! This land belongs to King Marty the Seer!" His voice rang out as if through a megaphone.

The forward section of the advancing army stopped. Men bumped into one another, jockeyed for position, stepped on each other's toes, and punched each other.

"Marty Cohen is the slayer of the Ametsu!" François continued. "He is the great rescuer of mankind from its enemy! Flee now and live! Attack us and die!"

For a moment, Marty thought it was going to work. The enemy army milled about, hesitated, and looked as if it might dissolve.

Then drumbeats started.

They boomed out from the back of the army somewhere. With each shuddering *tom*, the enemy warriors stood a little straighter and looked a little more determined. They shuffled into formation, the ragged mob forming up in ranks.

"Nuts," Marty said.

Trumpets blew, and the enemy advanced.

"Trumpets," Surjan said. "We could use trumpets."

"They're almost to the ditch," Marty said.

François raised and dropped an arm, signaling to Kareem.

Surjan shouted orders out to his two platoons of spear-fighters, as well as to Lowanna and Idder in command of the sharpshooters. The archers waited, but the slingers began hurling stones over the bank, dropping them onto the front ranks of the enemy.

Marty didn't see where the fuse ran, but he saw the explosions.

Whoomph . . . whoomph . . . whoomph.

Three buried explosives went off in quick succession, throwing enemy warriors into the air. Hadn't there been four, though? Maybe there had been a misfire. The sudden craters separated the foremost ranks from the main body of their army. When the warriors in front crouched to shelter from the explosions, and turned to see the pits, they exposed their backs.

Marty's skirmishers armed with slings rushed to the top of the bank and fired down into the separate front ranks. The archers, meanwhile, loosed their arrows at the larger, unseen mass of the enemy force, so that those who rushed forward were caught under a feathered hail.

The enemy shrieked.

The explosions had to seem like magic to the enemy, and Marty did his best to reinforce that impression. He stood at the top of the bank and waved his arms like a wizard. If the enemy had been within earshot, he'd have shouted the Gettysburg Address.

The enemy front line dissolved.

Kareem scrambled up to the top of the bank and pointed. "They are sending fighters around the south side."

The enemy knew they outnumbered Marty's host, and were trying to encircle him.

"Archers?" Marty asked.

"Not yet." Surjan nodded to Kareem and signaled with an arm.

François, Kareem, and a handful of skirmishers with slings rushed to the southern bank.

"Arrows," Surjan warned.

Marty crouched. Three of his warriors holding large hide shields rushed up to provide a wall of protection for him, Surjan, and Munatas. Arrows stuck in the thick hide or bounced off. Marty alternated watching the enemy host through the gaps between the shields, and the outflanking advance party. The outflanking party consisted of maybe thirty warriors with mixed weapons and shields, and they were running flat out, stretching into a line.

The enemy knew that Marty's army was small.

At Idder's command, the skirmishers let loose a volley of stones at the outflankers. They shouted to one another, then collapsed their line into a more compact formation, shields up.

The sling stones rattled off the enemy shields.

And then François and Kareem threw grenades.

Whoomph.

Whoomph.

Whoomph.

Not all of the grenades exploded. Two hit the ground and simply cracked open. Still, the outflankers scattered, leaving a dozen corpses and two pits in their wake.

Off to the east, Marty saw dark clouds gather.

He saw a flash in the sky and heard the rolling echo of thunder.

Kareem frowned as he peered eastward. "I see more dust on the horizon."

"Are you sure that's not rain?"

"I'm sure." Kareem looked up at the sky. "They won't get here until tonight or tomorrow morning."

Marty sighed.

Lowanna patted Surjan on his arm. "It looks like we're about to get a charge straight down the middle."

Surjan looked up at a golden eagle circling overhead. He pulled a grenade from his bandoleer and showed it to her. "How smart are the birds, really? I mean, if we wanted a grenade dropped from a height in the middle of our enemy, could they do that?"

She looked up at the golden eagle and grinned.

"And it wouldn't accidentally drop it on top of us?" he pressed.

Lowanna looked up at the eagle and held out her leather-wrapped arm. "Come here, beautiful boy."

She took the grenade from Surjan and explained what she needed.

The enemy had regrouped, and moved forward again in columns, swarming over the craters. Marty shouted gibberish and waved his arms, but it didn't seem to deter them.

The eagle lifted one of its feet. As soon as Lowanna offered the grenade, its clawed foot wrapped completely around the earthenware explosive and took off.

Surjan and Lowanna watched as the eagle flew higher.

The ground shook. Enemies raced forward.

Suddenly, the bird tucked its wings and plummeted to the earth.

Before Lowanna could even register what was happening, the eagle had pulled up and there were a *whoomph*, a dust cloud, and an eruption of astonished cries in the middle of the enemy ranks.

Arrows flew across the sky, resulting in more screams of pain.

"Ready spears!"

The voice sounded like Surjan, but it was Usaden, imitating the Sikh. Badis then bellowed out the same thing.

The enemy swarmed down into the ditch. They slowed to avoid the spikes. Some weren't nimble enough and impaled themselves. Others fell to the slings and arrows of Lowanna's skirmishers. Some made it through the ditch and began to climb, shouting harsh, guttural chants of war.

"Hold the line!" Surjan shouted to his two commanders as the spearmen moved to the top of the bank to defend it.

"Hold the line!" they shouted back.

"Hold the line!" the men roared.

And then there was a clash of the front lines as the two armies met.

The two spear-fighter platoons fought side by side. Surjan prowled behind them, stepping forward to fill the gap when a warrior staggered, or reaching with his long spear to slice one enemy after another.

Not always going for a kill, but more often attacking unarmored spots to incapacitate.

A slice through the back of the knee, a stab between the shoulder and the neck, a smash across the bridge of the nose.

Blood was everywhere.

Whoomph.

Another grenade exploded somewhere in the crowd of clashing bodies. Lowanna wasn't sure who was throwing them now.

More screams.

And just as quickly as the advance had started, the enemy's front line retreated. The ditch was full of corpses.

But there were corpses on this side of the bank, too.

Surjan bellowed, "Fire arrows!"

"Fire arrows!" Idder repeated.

As Lowanna saw the enemy retreating, flaming arrows flew overhead. She knelt at the top of the bank to watch. The earth shook with a tremendous explosion that tossed bodies of the retreating enemy in all directions.

An enemy arrow whizzed by Lowanna's ear and thudded into the earth beside her.

Surjan staggered from the melee, blood trickling down the side of his face from a deep and ugly gash. Lowanna rushed to him and pressed a glowing hand against the wound.

"Did François just have one last surprise?" she asked.

Surjan pressed at the healed flesh where his wound had been. "I guess so. I'll take it."

The spear-fighters cheered, shouting taunts at their retreating enemies.

"Do you think that might be it?" Lowanna asked.

Surjan nodded. "I suspect so. At least for today."

⇐ CHAPTER ⇒
THIRTY-FIVE

The sun had set. Guards watched for the enemy from the top of the bank. Around the fires clustered near the eastern side of the enclosure, men recounted their brave deeds to one another, cursed their moments of evil luck, and remembered their comrades who had fallen.

Marty watched as Gunther tried to heal yet another person, and even though his face was turning red with the effort, he was spent. At least for the moment. Gunther and the wounded warrior both settled for bandages and a poultice.

Marty draped an arm over his friend's shoulder. "You've figured out how your healing powers work?"

Gunther nodded. "At first, I could only really do it once in a day. And that was pushing it. But I guess over the last couple weeks, as I . . . gained new levels, I guess . . . I seemed to be able to do more at any given time. Nowadays I can heal up to three times before I hit a wall and need some rest. Using that . . . talent . . . really drains my batteries."

"Guess we better hope the enemy stays away until morning." Marty handed Gunther a flagon of wine.

"Or just runs," Gunther said. "We administered a beating today."

Marty nodded slowly. "They won't know for sure that we're running out of explosives. On the other hand, they might guess. And I'm pretty sure they know how few of us there are. And they have reinforcements arriving in the night."

"If we get surrounded, we'll be in trouble."

"Surjan and Kareem and Lowanna are out there now, trying to make certain that doesn't happen. Or at least, keep us apprised."

Gunther took a long pull at the flagon and sighed. "That's actually pretty good."

"Personally, I was never a big wine person, but...I could be swayed."

The German took another drink and handed it back to Marty. "If I have any more of that I'll definitely be swaying." He looked over at Marty, reached forward and patted his knee. "You look haggard. What was the final tally?"

"We had six people who died. Many more wounded, but by some miracle, between you and Lowanna, I think almost everyone is combat-ready. They should sleep in shifts."

"We were lucky," Gunther suggested.

Marty nodded. He was a bit numb to the deaths and that really bothered him. Six people had died under his leadership. But he wasn't sure he'd have done anything differently. All things considered, today's fight had been a victory for the Kingdom of Connecticut.

"I'm going to get some rest and see if afterward I can heal a few more people." Gunther stood and patted Marty on the shoulder. "You get some rest, too. We need an overwatch that's awake."

Marty watched Gunther stagger off to a sleeping mat and collapse.

Then he climbed the earthen bank and scanned the perimeter of their camp. There were plenty of people awake and perched on the bank, keeping watch.

The ache creeping up the base of his spine was a sure sign Marty needed rest.

Tomorrow would bring another battle.

He prayed wordlessly to whoever might listen.

Kareem looked up into the darkness and smiled. The clouds were blocking the stars and moon tonight, leaving the world cloaked in darkness.

His night vision was a blessing from the Almighty. Dr. Cohen and the others talked about levels and abilities, but what power could cause a man to rise in level other than the power of the Merciful?

Despite the lack of light, the world for him shimmered with an almost satin-like texture. The ground and everything around him were varying shades of some kind of fuzzy reddish tone.

Except for those things that walked in the night. Those stood out like torches.

Off in the distance, Kareem saw a palm tree jutting up from the scrub, but hidden in the palm fronds was an orange hue that took on the shape of a rat. Several of them.

When he was just a boy, he'd snuck into a Cairo theater and watched a rerun of an Arnold Schwarzenegger movie called *Predator*. The way the alien in the movie saw the world was how Kareem, too, now saw it.

Kareem was the Predator.

He had climbed through the ditch, where warriors of Ahuskay and Jehed worked together to drag out the bodies of the enemy dead, and continued walking toward the enemy's camp.

The enemy camp had no fires burning.

Suddenly the hairs on the back of his neck stood on end. Something... there was something wrong in the night, something that his senses had detected, even if his mind had not noticed. He crouched, scanning the empty terrain for whatever lurked there.

If only he had Surjan's sense of smell, he would be a truly lethal predator.

He held his sharpened ankh in one hand and the Sethian dagger in the other, prepared to strike with either. The knife was a more comfortable weapon in his grip, but the ankh had proven itself against these vile monsters, the demons of the ancient tomb paintings come to life.

Kareem heard the sound of sand crunching, once, and he held his breath. Was it the sound of a footfall? Would the sound repeat?

Crunch.

Swiveling his gaze toward the sound, he saw something that put a smile to his face. It was one of those cat-demons, emerging from behind a boulder.

Kareem watched as the cat stared into the darkness and slunk eastward toward Kareem's encampment. It believed it was being stealthy, no doubt. It believed it was unseen.

To Kareem, it burned reddish-white like a bonfire.

Kareem picked up several pebbles. He watched as the creature slowly scanned left to right, peering into the night and sniffing.

He tossed the pebble to the left of the cat-person and it immediately spun to face that way. The creature's tail swished back and forth.

Kareem advanced slowly. The wind blew at his face, bringing the cat-demon's scent to him, and hiding Kareem's own odor. He tossed a pebble straight past where the cat creature was already staring.

It crouched low. Kareem brought up both of his weapons as he crept forward.

The tail swished and the creature hissed just as Kareem sank both of his weapons into its back. The dagger barely penetrated the skin, but the ankh sank in without resistance.

The demon yowled and lurched forward. Kareem kept his grip on his weapons and moved with the monster.

He slashed between the vertebra with the ankh, severing the spine, and the half-beast fell face forward, its body convulsing and its voice silenced.

It took only seconds for the foul rotting odor to seep from the wounds and a blindingly bright ball of light to leak up from the cat-creature's body.

Kareem reached for it. The moment his fingers touched the light it became an electric shock racing up his arm, across his chest, and to the rest of his extremities.

A warmth bloomed within Kareem's chest and he felt goose bumps rising all over him. There were more shades to the darkness, subtler red from every source of heat. Almost as if he could see the different temperatures flowing through the wind.

Praise be to the Merciful and Compassionate, who had shown mercy to Kareem.

He was now level three.

Kareem smiled as he turned back and continued toward the enemy's camp. He was within one hundred yards, which once would have felt very risky to him. With his ability to see heat, he knew that he was seeing the enemy and they weren't seeing him, and that made him feel invulnerable. He watched the ordinary movements of the camp, men eating and sharpening weapons and bickering and playing games and mostly sleeping.

Then he saw the Sethian.

The creature's body temperature was slightly different from humans', and it was noticeably larger.

It astonished him to see a Sethian mingling peaceably with the humans. Prior to today, he wouldn't have believed that possible; now, scanning the enemy army, he saw several of the Ametsu.

But something else about this particular Sethian caught his eye.

This creature was at the edge of the enemy camp. It was bent over and in obvious distress, shuddering and scratching the earth.

Kareem slowly approached, making sure to be conscious of the wind's direction. As he got closer, he heard a wheezing sound coming from the monster.

Kareem stared.

He'd never seen a Sethian in pain. They seemed to be either fully alive and trying to kill you or suddenly dead and decomposing.

This one was neither.

As it bent over and struggled for breath, the Sethian kept touching its nose.

Kept touching the ring on its nose.

Which was cracked.

Broken during the day's combat?

Kareem had assumed it was ornamental. And it probably was.

But maybe it wasn't.

He turned and headed back to his camp.

Dr. Cohen needed to know about this.

⇌ CHAPTER ⇌
THIRTY-SIX

"Livers," François said. He'd woken Marty from a disjointed dream.

Marty had dreamed of Narmer's face, slipping away into darkness.

François spun a ring in his fingers and said again, "Livers."

Kareem stood beside him, an anxious look on his face.

Marty realized that he hadn't actually spoken out loud. "What? What about livers?"

"There's something wrong with the Sethians," François said. "What did Narmer tell us? That they came from another world?"

"That's not exactly what he said," Marty mumbled. "But that's what we think he meant."

"So their bodies aren't used to the environment here somehow," François said. "Maybe it has something to do with the iron. The human liver is the most iron-rich part of the body, so maybe they eat human livers to enrich their own blood."

"Why not cattle livers?" Marty asked.

"Maybe they eat those, too." François shrugged. "And Hathiru livers and who knows what else. But why exempt humans? And maybe eating human livers is also a convenient way to terrify a population that might otherwise resist. And maybe they want humans generally to stick around, for whatever reason. To farm. To keep down the lion population. Who knows?"

"Maybe they find human liver delicious," Marty suggested.

"Also a possibility. So what's the function of this ring?"

Marty realized where he'd seen the ring before. "They all wear nose rings. The Hathiru, the Bastites, the Sethians."

"They all wear nose rings," François agreed. "As fashion, it seems to show astonishing uniformity. So I think it isn't fashion."

"My brain is throbbing," Marty said.

"You're sleep-deprived and adrenaline-shocked," François said. "It's kind of impressive that you still have a brain at all."

"But say this part slowly," Marty said, "so I make sure I follow."

"Maybe the nose ring helps them process the iron in the liver," François said. "Think about the crops we've found at their outposts. Beans, near Ahuskay village. And figs near Jehed. Both iron-rich, right? Or maybe the ring helps them breathe, binding the oxygen to the iron they consumed. Maybe there's something wrong with our atmosphere, for their bodies." He chuckled. "Maybe their native atmosphere is iron-rich, so they need help breathing here, and they have to eat iron. Can you have atmospheric iron, is that a real possibility?" He shrugged.

"Or maybe the ring controls them," Marty suggested. "Maybe the big one uses the rings to send commands, or electric shocks, or guiding stimuli. Or maybe it heals them."

"Maybe." François jerked a thumb at their Egyptian companion. "Except that Kareem saw one of them without his ring tonight, and he said the monster seemed to be struggling. Choking to death."

Kareem nodded vigorously.

Marty hesitated. "Coincidence?"

"The scientific method does not jump to a conclusion of coincidence, Dr. Cohen," François said. "The scientific method comes up with a theory to explain the known facts and then tries to devise a test."

A sheet of black clouds hid the sunrise. Marty had slept only briefly and fitfully, wrapped in a blanket and lying on the bank of earth. As he looked eastward from the top of the bank, trying to gauge both the hour and the enemy's numbers, a flash deep inside the cloud and the rolling boom of thunder washed over the battlefield.

The enemy advanced again.

Surjan bellowed, and under his command, his Spearspeakers Usaden and Badis organized their battle lines along the bank, left and right. Lowanna and Idder placed the sharpshooters in mobile squads spaced evenly apart along the flat ground behind the bank.

They'd tallied at least one hundred twenty enemies killed yesterday. During the night, Surjan, Lowanna, and Kareem had killed three Bastites as well. Scouts? Assassins? Whatever the intended role of the cat-people, they were the only forces the enemy had sent out during the night. No further attempts had been made to outflank the host.

And Kareem had reported seeing a Sethian that struggled to breathe.

But none of that knowledge lightened Marty's heart. Looking down at the enemy this morning, their forces were, if anything, greater than the day before. Now he saw multiple Sethians among them, and here and there a Bastite.

"Kareem," he said, "I can't see anything else approaching on the horizon. Do you?"

"Nothing."

"Good." Marty handed a grenade to the only bird he had that was capable of carrying one and gave it instructions.

He watched as the tawny eagle flew over the battlefield and he winced as the animal dropped the grenade and careened awkwardly away.

It had almost been hit by an arrow.

Whoomph.

But the bird had been startled off its aim, and the grenade hadn't hit any enemies.

"Dr. Cohen, there is one thing... have you seen the giant Sethian?"

Marty frowned. "They're all giant."

"I mean the really big one." Kareem wrinkled his nose as he focused on the scene below. "About twice the size of a man."

"Twice the volume?" Marty asked. "Twice the mass. Twice the height?"

Kareem shrugged.

Marty grimaced. "Is the giant Sethian over ten feet tall?"

His mind immediately raced back to the ruins.

The great one is clear about this, and the one speaks for him. You must die if you don't help kill Merit Nuk Han and those who come with it.

The so-called Great One sent another Sethian to find Marty. Could a mega-sized Sethian be the Great One that had been mentioned? And if it had some way to find Marty, that might explain why the advancing army had swerved to the north to intercept the crew.

Narmer had had visions of Marty and his people. Was there a giant Sethian that had had similar dreams?

Marty felt sick to his stomach.

"Yes, over ten feet," Kareem said. "And he's fast, by God. He's either knocking things out of his way or people are just fleeing."

"We need to let the others know—" A bolt of lightning slammed into the other side of the bank. Marty and Kareem both staggered and fell.

With his ears ringing, Marty motioned to Kareem. "Let's get down before we get electrocuted."

They both slid down the dirt.

One of Idder's skirmishers approached Surjan. Surjan couldn't recall his name in the moment, but he remembered the man as one of King Iken's men, from Jehed. "You asked for someone who is an expert with a sling?"

"Yes." Surjan pulled a grenade out of a large box. "I need this to be flung over the top of the enemy. Almost straight up, so that it falls on him from a great height." He mimicked the trajectory he had in mind with his hands. He thought that gave the grenade the best chance of landing heavy-side down, and igniting. "Can you do that?"

The man nodded. "I think so."

Surjan put his hand on the man's shoulder and gave it a light squeeze. "Are you sure? Because if it accidentally goes in the wrong direction, you could really make a pig's ear of it."

"A pig's ear?"

"You might kill our friends."

The warrior nodded again. "I've hunted with my sling for more than twenty years."

Surjan handed the man a grenade and ducked under a makeshift shield as a barrage of arrows landed in the vicinity. "Okay, show me what you can do."

The man placed the grenade into the well-worn pouch of his sling and with a practiced rotating motion spun the sling around his head and suddenly let go of one end, sending the grenade flying.

The grenade went up like a rocket.

The grenade came down.

The *whoomph* sound of the explosion put a smile on Surjan's face. The screaming from the approaching army was just a cherry on top of a sundae.

Surjan heard a load roar.

It sounded like a Sethian.

But much, much louder than he'd ever heard.

François inspected the jar filled with powder, gravel, and tinder. It was ready, and he motioned for two soldiers. They awkwardly carted the bomb toward the front line where Surjan would find a use for it.

The Frenchman had barely slept a wink. Taking a deep breath, he let it out slowly and held his hand out to Kareem, who was assembling the last of the grenades.

The young Egyptian rubbed beeswax into the threads, screwed the cap on tightly, and handed the finished product to François. François checked the seal, placed the bomb into a box with several others, and passed the box back to Kareem.

Kareem rushed away.

That was the last of the explosives. François sighed. His penicillin had been a bust, but his bombs had worked. The screams on both sides were awful, but he didn't try to shut them out. He owned the screams. Some of the dead had died and were dying because of his bombs, and he would deny no man his final cry.

But they were necessary deaths. They were deaths to end the scourge of the Sethians.

He wished there was more that he could do, but for now he bowed his head and prayed.

Lowanna stared up into the sky and felt a heaviness in the air. It was more than just the unusual humidity. There was a pressure building up in her chest and as she breathed it almost felt like static. The air around her felt as if it was filled with electricity and that was a dangerous thing.

She'd never been struck by lightning, but her Aunt Sally had. Twice. Sally Lancaster had had her drinks paid for for twenty years on the back of her account of getting hit by lightning on repeat occasions. The detail that Lowanna could never forget was her aunt's insistence on the prickly feeling of static electricity just before getting hit.

Crouching down on the top of the bank between two files of spearmen, she saw the enemy flooding over the ditch. Behind them, Sethians roared and drums pounded. The front ranks of the enemy fell shrieking on the spikes and died, and the seconds were simply crushed by those coming behind them, but then the ditch slowly filled with corpses. The later waves marched over the bodies of their fallen comrades, and then clashed with Surjan's spear-fighters.

As people waged battle all around her, she touched her knees and hands to the ground and felt the sensation abate.

A roar erupted from somewhere just ahead.

She saw the monster-headed creature rising from the mass of the enemy. It rose head and shoulders above the tallest men and with one swipe of his hand three people went flying. They landed in twisted, unnatural positions, necks and spines broken.

One corpse lay at Lowanna's feet.

She looked down and gasped as she recognized Udad, the young man from Ahuskay who had been healed of lameness as a boy.

The creature turned and locked eyes with Lowanna.

Kareem stabbed a Sethian in the back with his ankh. The spike sank all the way to the crossbars and it must have pierced the heart, because the Sethian dropped like a stringless marionette. No shuddering, nothing.

To be certain, Kareem pulled the weapon out and stabbed it into the base of the demon's skull.

The glowing life essence bubbled up from within the monster and Kareem absorbed it with a smile.

Kareem was out beyond the embattled bank and the corpse-filled ditch. He slipped between enemy ranks, trying to attack heralds, drummers, officers—anyone whose death would impair the enemy.

It was especially satisfying to kill one of the Seth-headed devils that had murdered his uncle.

He heard a tremendous roar and he raced toward it. He slipped past two enemy squads, moving laterally, averting his face, and finally putting on a red helmet stolen from a dead man to go unseen. Up ahead he spotted the back of a Sethian that was literally twice his height. There was no way for him to reach a critical organ.

This was the big one he had reported to Dr. Cohen. It was immense, and it was growling at a corps of drummers and trumpet players.

But as the demon's attention turned to something else, Kareem ran in and sliced across the back of the giant Sethian's knee. He felt the blade part the creature's skin and scratch roughly against a tendon, not quite severing it.

Suddenly, Kareem was launched through the air. The blow stole his breath and he crashed into two enemy soldiers.

The lines of both armies had broken.

Where there had been a rank of disciplined spearmen holding back the enemy horde, there was now a chaotic swirl of sweating, cursing warriors, spraying blood.

Marty waded through that swirl, looking for key targets. He found Kareem's giant Sethian, a dozen yards away.

If anything, Kareem had understated its massiveness. The thing looked unearthly, like two bulls had been bound into a single, muscular body, and now lurched together across the landscape. Its jackal head with the square ears was bigger than Marty's chest.

If the others were Sethians, then this monster was Seth himself.

It had charged up the bank, trampling its own men. Behind it came a burly armored warrior gripping a tall carved staff in both hands. From the tip of the staff flapped a green banner bearing the Sethians' infinity symbol. Now the monster was surrounded by Marty's warriors, and fighting them all hand to hand . . .

And winning.

Seth bellowed loudly and spun around, showing a wound across the back of its left knee.

Someone had managed to wound it.

Marty threw a spear directly at the beast, and with preternatural speed it caught the weapon in midair.

Then it leaped forward, knocking down two of Marty's warriors and two of its own men as it chased Marty.

Marty ran.

Somewhere Surjan yelled something barely intelligible, "... water jug..."

Marty slammed a fist into an enemy soldier's face as he ran past him.

Seth's ponderous footsteps were getting closer behind him. They were faster than Marty's steps, and his stride was much longer.

Whoomph.

Marty looked over his shoulder at the sound of the explosion, hoping to see Seth on the ground. No such luck.

The creature bellowed and spun on its heels, looking for whoever had thrown the grenade.

Had the explosion missed?

Had the grenade hit, and simply done no damage?

They had no plan for Seth. They had planned to hold their ground on the fortifications until the enemy decided it wasn't worth their time, or broke on the ditch and bank and the spearwall.

But they hadn't counted on this monster. Their defenses would not stand up to that thing.

How could Marty possibly kill it?

⇜ CHAPTER ⇝
THIRTY-SEVEN

"Move them off the bank!" Marty shouted. "Isolate Seth! Isolate the big one!" Alone, maybe, Marty could find a way to take the giant Sethian down.

Surjan spat blood into the dirt. "This is not some judo match, Marty. It's not about motion at this point. We grind on them and they grind on us, until one of us collapses into the sand."

But Usaden bellowed a command, and his platoon marched sideways. Idder's sharpshooters harassed Seth with a storm of hurled stones, which only caused it to roar and paw at the ground with its massive sandals.

But the few moments gained allowed Usaden's platoon to swing around, turning to face Seth without turning their backs to the human enemies.

Most of Surjan's spearmen now stood in a square atop the bank.

A couple of squads, and the sharpshooters, raced about in the general chaos.

Seth charged at Surjan's lines again. It ran head-down, as if it intended to head-butt the front rank of the host. Perhaps because the way it ran limited its vision, or perhaps simply because of its indifference, it ground half a dozen of its own men to the ground. Their screams sounded both agonized and ecstatic.

"Hold the line!" Badis shouted.

The square of spearmen bent, sagged to one side, but held.

The host hunkered together behind their shields, spears thrusting forward. Seth crashed against them. Spears poked its chest and shoulders. Some snapped, some stuck. Several spearmen fell to their knees, planting the butts of their spears against the earth itself as the enormous beast-headed man threw its weight upon their shields. The line bowed.

"Skirmishers!" Surjan rushed forward with his long spear. Marty followed. Surjan stabbed at Seth's face, and at the very last second, the giant ducked and twisted its head to one side. The sharpened tip of Surjan's spear jabbed into Seth's ear.

Those should have been soft tissues. The spear should have penetrated the monster's brain, leaving it dead on the field. Instead, Surjan's spear shivered into splinters and he was knocked to the ground.

The second rank of the formation stabbed repeatedly at Seth's head and shoulders, striking him but doing no apparent damage. Tafsut had fallen out of formation, and she now appeared at Surjan's side, stabbing the beast. Marty slipped forward and threw kicks against the beast's wounded leg, trying to knock it down.

"Skirmishers!" he yelled, repeating Surjan's cry.

"For Marty!" he heard Usaden bellow.

"For Narmer!" Marty bellowed back. And again, "For Narmer! For Narmer!"

"For Narmer!" the men in the square shouted, and they pushed.

As they pushed, sharpshooters arrived. Stones rained off the monster's forehead, rattling down and bouncing off the taut leather of the shields. A stone struck Seth in the eye and another in the pink of its snout. Arrows mostly struck its hide and fell harmless to the earth, but several pierced its shoulder and stuck. It roared, seeming more irritated than wounded. Then it shook its head and leaped back, away from the shield wall.

Marty had no great skill with the spear, but he picked one off the ground, anyway, to use as a staff.

Then he saw the face of the man whose spear he'd taken—it was Munatas, the young Ahuskay warrior who'd explained trader tallies to him on the road.

There were numerous spears lying on the ground.

Among numerous bodies.

A few of them were Sethians, but the larger number by far were humans. Their bodies were trampled, mangled, torn apart, and even chewed on. But mostly they were impaled on spears.

Marty felt ill.

"You flee too fast, abomination!" he shouted. Then he struck Seth with his staff, two-handed, behind the knee.

Seth stumbled forward, catching itself on one knee and the knuckles of both hands. Marty struck it again, repeatedly, across the back of the head and on the spine. For a moment, Seth was silent, and Marty thought the giant might have finally tired, bowing to defeat.

But then Seth laughed.

Marty swung his staff and Seth whirled, viper-quick, and grabbed the staff in one hand.

Lightning crashed. It felt close, at the edge of the battlefield, and screaming came hard on the lightning's heels. Rain slammed into Marty like a broad, flat hammer, soaking him instantly and sluicing through the sand and springing from the taut leather of his men's shields like a New York City spring rain off the black umbrellas of its bankers.

He'd lost his sense of the larger battlefield.

He was pretty sure he was losing.

Seth ripped the staff from Marty's hands with a single violent tug. Then it struck Marty across the face.

Marty sailed across the battlefield and crashed to the earth at the feet of his own men. He tried to stand and found he couldn't. The world spun and vomit surged up from his belly, splashing on his own arms and legs as he tried to drag himself to his feet.

Seth sprang forward, and Marty saw death coming.

Sandals swept over Marty. He saw the soles, and mud, and kilts. And spears were being planted into the ground to either side of him, and he heard a crash and a heavy groaning sound as Seth slammed again into the line that had moved forward to enclose Marty.

Then Surjan was there, dragging Marty to his feet.

"For Narmer!" Surjan bellowed, and he pulled Marty away.

Seth's warriors had regrouped and came charging forward. Marty's men were off the bank and on flat ground now, and the enemy swarmed on all sides. Idder shouted directions to a platoon of skirmishers within the square formation and they unleashed a continuous volley at the Sethians' auxiliaries. Men screamed and fell. Was that good? Marty wasn't certain who was doing the dying.

And did it matter, really? The human levy massed under the Sethians wasn't really Marty's enemy. He wanted to rescue them, not kill them.

Only, they resisted rescue.

Surjan left him and returned to the fray, shouting at the top of his lungs. Lowanna was there, staring into the storm and mouthing something. Talking to animals Marty couldn't see? François held a large ring that looked familiar to Marty, but he wasn't sure why.

His vision was blurry. Was it the rain?

Or had he been hit on the head?

Marty realized he was lying down. He stood, looking for Kareem, and found the young man holding a spear and shield and standing in the battle line. The man beside Kareem went down, a Sethian spear through the center of his chest, and Marty felt sick.

Livers, François had said.

Kareem had seen a Sethian without a nose ring and struggling to breathe.

Was it possible?

Thunder crashed into Marty's ears and behind it came the cacophony of battle. He heard the whir and snap of slings, the shattering of spears, and men chanting, "Narmer! Narmer! Narmer!"

How many of the men in the battle line had actually been followers of the dead king, and how many were simply chanting what Marty chanted? How could they possibly have seen in the would-be unifier of Egypt what Marty saw, from the perspective of five thousand years later?

Maybe the Sethians had a vulnerability. An Achilles' heel of sort.

An Achilles' nose ring, as it were.

He wished he had more to go on.

Marty heard screaming.

He looked for Kareem and didn't see him. Had the young man fallen? Was he trampled?

And did he also hear trumpets? Or was that a ringing inside his own head?

"Hold the line!" Surjan bellowed. "Fighting withdrawal! Step! Step!"

Seth crashed against Surjan's square. Ironically, what stopped the spear-warriors from being pushed up and over the bank into the ditch might have been the pressure of the Sethians' own troops on the other side. The square bowed in, trembled, but held.

Human fighters with spears on the other side of the wall shrieked hideous threats and hurled themselves on the shields and spears of Marty's host. Others raced toward the right wing and beyond, attempting to outflank the spear-fighters and being frustrated by their square formation.

Idder shouted commands and the skirmishers let loose on the outflanking soldiers, who melted like an April snow.

Arrows fell on the square, too, but the inner line of Surjan's men kept their shields raised. Most of the arrows struck in the thick hide and stayed.

Seth roared and charged forward, spears poking it fruitlessly in the head and chest. At the same time, the enemy warriors on the bank gave way, and Surjan's square moved—

But not all together, and the square opened at one end.

A platoon of enemy soldiers charged at the ragged opening. Where had they come from? Marty snatched another spear from the ground, but this one was already cracked in half. He ripped the two halves entirely apart and held them like fighting batons.

Leaving François, he charged toward the advancing flankers.

But Tafsut got there first. She ran at the head of a squad of warriors. Marty didn't know all the host by name, but he knew their faces, and these men were strangers. They weren't all armed with spears, either—some had maces and clubs, and at least one had a long bronze khopesh.

These were some of Narmer's men who had stayed behind.

"Narmer!" Tafsut shouted. She carried a shield and spear and she made good use of them. There was no line to hold, but she flung herself into the enemy, slashing, tripping, and stabbing, and when her spear was left impaled through a dead warrior, she stooped and grabbed a short sword.

Behind the charging enemy came two Sethians.

Marty rushed to Tafsut's aid. The Ahuskay warrior ducked under the swing of a Sethian ax and slashed the inside of the monster's thigh. As Marty had seen far too many times, the blade didn't cut the alien's skin. Tafsut deflected a second swing by moving to intercept it early and batting it aside, and then stabbed the Sethian harmlessly in the side.

The wave of Narmer's men broke on the two Sethians and ebbed back. The second Sethian seized a spearman bodily and hurled him into the ranks of his own comrades. Then he lunged to grab for Tafsut.

Marty arrived. He bent backward as if dancing the limbo to duck beneath the tossed spearman, then leaped over the swing of an oversized ax. Then he swung both his batons in a violent scissorlike motion, cracking them together on the second Sethian's outstretched wrist.

The Sethian roared and turned to punch Marty. One on one, these ordinary Sethian warriors were simply not quick enough to hit Marty. Marty had become faster in his three months of traveling, training, and fighting his way across ancient North Africa. He ducked, then parried a second punch by slamming it aside with both batons held close together.

Then he heard Tafsut yell—a short, violent sound that ended in a choking noise.

His foe was lunging for him and Marty had no time to look at the other Sethian. Instead, he leaped forward and planted one foot on his opponent's shoulder. As the Sethian dove to try to seize Marty, Marty propelled himself upward and backward using the Sethian's own energy. He arced his back, imagining himself a leaping dolphin, hurling his body back toward Tafsut.

The Ahuskay warrior was bleeding from a bad gash in her leg, which dangled limply. Her Sethian foe had one hand around her neck and had her hoisted off the ground. It shook the woman and roared into her face.

Tafsut's cheeks were purple and her eyes were rolling in her head.

Marty swung first one baton and, rolling over in midair, then the second. Both blows struck the Sethian in his nose ring. The first cracked the ring in half, and the second batted it out of sight, sending it flying in two fragments across the fray.

The lunging Sethian roared in frustration, missing Marty.

The Sethian who had Tafsut by the throat shrieked, an animal sound of terror, and slammed the woman against the ground.

Marty stepped over Tafsut protectively and slammed both his batons into the ringless Sethian's belly. The Sethian gasped, coughed, and began to choke.

Kareem and François were right. There was something about the rings.

He shot a glance over his shoulder and saw that the square of spearmen had closed up again. Had Tafsut saved them from a rout?

But the square bowed on all sides.

Marty leaped to attack the second Sethian, aiming a barrage of pummeling blows at its muzzle. The Sethian swiped once with a hand, and then a second time, and then it put both hands over its face and started to stagger backward.

"Back, monster!" Marty shouted. "I know your secret!" He shouted just in case the Sethians could understand him, and also for the benefit of his host. Narmer's men swarmed forward, dragging down the ringless Sethian. The other Sethian fled.

But at the same moment, Surjan's formation collapsed.

"Hold the line!" Surjan shouted, as the square crumpled.

A few men formed up here and there in clumps, fighting back-to-back or in small rings. Others fell, ground under the feet of the Sethians, Seth itself, and their human levies. Still others simply evaporated, fleeing or falling or disappearing from Marty's view.

Trumpets blew. Seth roared and lurched forward at its berserker pace, snapping up warriors and rending them with its jaws. Marty and the knot of warriors he was with formed up in a confused tangle, trying to stay over Tafsut to protect her as the host broke.

Kareem wiggled through the curtains of fighting men around them and tugged at Marty's sleeve. "Tafsut," he said. "Is she...?"

Marty took advantage of a momentary respite in the fighting around him to kneel and check.

Tafsut was dead.

⤳ CHAPTER ⤳
THIRTY-EIGHT

The host crumpled in separate ragged lines. Marty or Surjan might have intended some sort of fallback maneuver, but that intention didn't last beyond a few brief seconds, and then the fallback became a stampede.

Lowanna stood her ground, hurling sling bolts at the enemy. Lowanna's stones didn't seem to faze Seth, the biggest of the monsters—who had turned his attention away from her to focus on the battle—and rarely seemed to bother the ordinary Sethians, either. Still, she couldn't bring herself to concentrate on just shooting humans.

A few of her sharpshooters, including Idder, rallied around her. Idder's left arm hung bloody at his side, which slowed down his slinging considerably; he had to pick up the stone and put it into the pouch, start the pouch spinning and fire, all with just one hand. He fired at maybe a third of his ordinary rate.

But he kept slinging.

It was hard to feel that the humans on the other side were really the enemy. They were slave conscripts, or duped conspirators, maybe, but did they really want to crush and rule other men?

Also, she didn't feel that victory could come from killing them, no matter how many human warriors might die. She saw herself on a living chessboard, and the enemy king was the hulking, lightning-fast Seth, and until Seth died, the battle wasn't over.

Or could Seth be captured? Could Seth surrender?

And who was the king on Lowanna's side? Whose loss would ensure their defeat?

She thought of Marty Cohen falling in battle and felt sick to her stomach.

Three enemy swordsmen rushed toward her, and for a moment she thought she would have to retreat. But two spearmen crashed into the enemy from the side, downing one man instantly and trampling him underfoot, and then setting themselves as a defensive hedge in front of Lowanna.

But they couldn't hold for long. A wave of enemies was running their way, and with them Sethians, and behind them Seth.

Marty and Kareem stood with a knot of warriors, totally surrounded by the enemy now. There were bodies heaped under their feet.

Was this how they were going to die? Five millennia before their own births, in a forgotten battle in the desert? On the day of Lowanna's birth, were her bones lying desiccated beneath the dunes somewhere west of the Nile?

Abdullah's were.

Her skin crackled with excitement, and with the distant flashing lightning of the oncoming storm. Her chest felt that it would burst. The tempest had started as a damp wind at their backs, but now the dampness was all around her and the sky overhead was a scudding lid of dark gray and lightning struck here and there in the broad valley. It came fast, with only brief interludes between the electric stab and the rumble of the following thunder. She was a sitting duck, an easy target for the lightning, standing on the open ground, but she didn't run for cover.

Could she hear voices in the lightning, too?

But no, those were trumpets.

A volley of missiles launched overhead. They weren't the stones of Lowanna's slingers, but a swarm of javelins. The projectiles slammed into the charging enemy, dropping every fifth man with an injury, some of them mortal. The charge slowed.

Lowanna's slingers jeered, and three more men rallied around her and resumed slinging stones at the foe. But who had thrown the javelins? The missiles were too short to be the spears of Surjan's warriors.

The two spear-fighters defending Lowanna broke ranks to run forward and down two enemy warriors, battering them with their heavy shields and then running them through.

Lowanna risked a look over her shoulder. A host was advancing, in a rapid but disciplined march. She blinked to see clearly as lightning flashed behind the army, but she could make out the banner, and it showed two horizontal rectangles with dots alongside them.

The Two Lands, Marty had said.

Narmer's flag.

And where was the banner of the host?

Lowanna pivoted to face the enemy again and began to advance. She had long run out of sling stones in her pouch, but the ground was stony, and she had perfected the quick, fluid movement of stooping to grab a rock, snapping it into the sling's pouch, and winging it at a chosen foe.

Marty was in motion, and she tried to give him cover. He left Kareem and their warriors where they were and moved like a fish, ducking, diving, and spinning his way through the enemy. Like a fish moving upstream, or like a talented forward on the football pitch. Lowanna dropped a hulking man with an axe who loomed up to threaten Marty, sinking a stone into his forehead. When a swordsman rushed him, she struck the enemy under his arm, knocking him sideways; Marty's attack looked like a gentle touch, but he planted a knife-hand into the warrior's throat and the man dropped.

A Sethian swinging a mace charged Marty. Lowanna hit it three times with stones, but the Sethian didn't slow down. Marty dodged a mace attack, and then he had his sharpened ankh in his hand. The Sethian parried Marty's first attack, and then when Marty pivoted to stab at the Sethian's side, the Sethian caught his hand and held him.

Lowanna nailed the monster with a stone in the eye.

The Sethian dropped Marty with a howl and Marty stabbed it.

The ankh sank into the Sethian's hide like Surjan's spears never did. The Sethian's howl ended in a gurgle and it collapsed, dead.

The tide of the battle surged back toward Lowanna and she found herself skipping backward. She kept her eye on Marty and saw him rushing toward Seth. He was doggedly moving toward Seth. He was going to kill the enemy king.

And he was going to do it with his ankh.

"Help Marty!" Lowanna shouted at Idder and her other men. They dropped a storm of sling stones into the fray around the Egyptologist, knocking down warriors here and there who were trying to stab him in the back or tackle him, and then he was out of range.

Marty charged Seth, and Seth hit him with its mace.

Marty went flying across the battle, sailing like a baseball, body limp as a rag doll.

Kareem and his warriors began to drag themselves through the murderous fight in Marty's direction. For the moment, he lay away from enemy soldiers, and he had an arm raised to the sky. Was he shouting? But Lowanna couldn't hear what he was saying.

Her body shook. She felt like a vibrating guitar string, like the skin of a booming drum. The wind seemed to blow *through* her.

Seth turned and stomped in Marty's direction. It moved like a freight train, rushing past its men and sometimes even trampling its own wounded warriors. It roared, an ear-splitting sound that started in the bass register and then echoed against the distant cliffs with the shrill shrieking pitch of angry gulls. Lowanna slung stones at the monster, but it was moving too fast.

Birds circled over Marty's body. Carrion birds? Was he dead? But his arm was still raised.

Lowanna felt a shiver race up her spine.

But it wasn't from the roar.

The lightning struck closer to her. She felt a strange connection to the crackling power overhead. She heard its static-filled singing, she felt a reverberating sensation in her chest that matched the cadence of the noise she was hearing. Lowanna focused on the clouds above and she could almost taste the energy buzzing all around her. Her heart began racing as she felt the gathering power.

She felt as if she was suffocating on pure energy.

It made her feel scared . . . no, not scared . . . uncertain. Flexing her fingers, the energy coursed through her and she felt like she was communing with the clouds above. She imagined a tendril of power reaching toward her and through.

It was seeking a target.

She pointed at the monster Seth.

Seth raised its mace to strike Marty.

The entire world flashed white as a tremendous bolt of lightning erupted from the cloud and slammed into Seth. Thunder exploded in the same instant, deafening Lowanna.

Her own men staggered away in confusion, surprise, and awe, and the oncoming ranks of enemy soldiers tumbled to the ground, stunned.

The monster convulsed, jerking from side to side like a marionette whose puppeteer was having a seizure. It dropped its mace and sank to its knees. Its own men drew back, leaving it standing in a circle of scorched grass on a sand dune that was now crusted with an upper mantle of glittering glass.

Fatigue washed over Lowanna. She nearly fell.

There was a moment of silence across the battlefield.

Except for birds, singing over Lowanna's head.

The nose ring, they sang.

Shoot the nose ring.

Her head snapped around to look at Marty. His arm was still raised. Had he passed her a message by shouting it to the birds?

She looked back to Seth. The big monster was shaking its head and lumbering slowly to its feet. The lightning strike that had melted sand into glass hadn't killed it. Like every Sethian Lowanna had seen, it did indeed have a ring through its nose.

"Hit the monster's nose ring!" she shouted to her slingers. "Every Sethian you face, destroy its nose ring first!"

She trusted Marty.

And she fired a stone at Seth's nose.

So did Idder, and so did the three other men who stood beside her. A volley of sling stones crashed into Seth's face. It shook, like an annoyed cow swishing its tail when stung by a deer fly, and then it raised its hands to cover its face.

But it was too late. Lowanna thought she could hear a bright cracking sound, or a tinkle, as of shattering glass, but that was probably in her imagination. She didn't know whose stone it was, either, but one of the projectiles hit Seth directly in its nose ring, snapping it in two.

The fragments fell to the ground.

Seth bellowed. The sound was less fearsome than its roar of only moments earlier. This was a strangled sound, with notes of bleating in it.

The trumpets blew again, and soldiers surged past Lowanna with a roar, moving forward. They didn't march with the careful precision of Surjan's trained fighters, but they were more numerous, and they were fresh.

They swarmed over the western bank and into the battle-plagued enclosure.

Narmer strode among them. The sight of him took Lowanna's breath away—he wasn't lying ill, broken, and nearly dead any longer. He looked the vision of health, a warrior in his prime. His limbs were long and muscular, with no obvious sign of the rot that had afflicted him, and his lungs were hale. He shouted out a battle song in time with his men, and he carried a shield and mace like any warrior.

This was her side's king.

They had thought him dead, but he lived, and was back in the battle. Had the penicillin done the trick? No, he'd "died" before he'd been able to consume any, and it was doubtful François's mold had ever been anything more than wishful thinking, in any case. And she and Gunther had failed in their attempt to heal the king.

Had it been the ankh, after all?

Seth staggered forward through the line of its own men. It was gasping for air, a loud, industrial rasp that Lowanna could hear now, but its assault on Narmer's front lines threw the men back, and Seth's lines gelled and held.

The enemy king was not dead. Lowanna's heart sank.

But Marty had earned a reprieve, at least. With the Sethians' lines moving forward to meet Narmer's men, Kareem and the knot of warriors with him darted forward to grab Marty. They dragged him aside; Gunther was with them, and he knelt to minister to Marty. A white glow spilled around the ankles and spear butts of the warriors, and Lowanna took a deep, steadying breath.

Where were Surjan and François?

She found that she was kneeling over a corpse.

Not just any corpse—the warrior Usaden. He lay dead, clutching Marty's banner, eyes open as if he was astonished.

She shook herself, like a dog emerging from water. There was a battle to be fought. She and her band of slingers, which had grown to ten, were now unmolested, at least for the moment, and with plenty of targets. The Sethians' troops seemed to be out of arrows, and Lowanna should take advantage of that fact.

"High ground," she said to Idder. "We'll get better shots from high ground."

She seized the banner and stood.

Idder pointed to the nearest bank, and she staggered up with sharpshooters in her wake. From there, she could see the battle lines more clearly; they had ground to a halt and the forces stood toe to toe again, slugging it out. But Narmer's forces had lost their impetus and they didn't have the crisp, disciplined lines of the host's spearmen. They now began to slide back, one foot at a time. In terms of human troops, the armies had reached an equilibrium. But a dozen Sethians or more remained among the enemy forces.

And there was Seth itself.

The biggest of the Sethians moved more slowly, now, and its breath sounded like the chains of a ship, thundering through its hull as it struggled to raise anchor. But it still moved, and it still swung its mace. Narmer's men shattered their spears on its hide and lost their swords beneath the relentless march of its feet and lost their lives as its mace brained and mangled and pulverized them, leaving a slick of blood and a chaotic constellation of severed body parts on the sand.

Had Marty been wrong? Or had he been right, but his insight was insufficient to turn the tide of this battle?

But she had nothing else.

She shoved the banner's butt into the sandy soil of the bank. Beside the pole, she saw shards of pottery and earth stained black— a grenade that had shattered without exploding? In the gathering storm, the flag whipped and streamed magnificently.

"Shoot at their nose rings," she told her men again. "Every Ametsu you can reach, I want you to shatter its nose ring above all else. If enemies approach, bring them down, but otherwise, we are up here to break jewelry."

"For Narmer!" Idder shouted.

"For Narmer!" Lowanna cried, and began to fire stones at the enemy. "And Marty!" she added, under her breath.

⇒ CHAPTER ⇐
THIRTY-NINE

Marty heard the monster's rasping breath. It sounded as if it were right over him, the beast looming and raising its hand for the death blow. It also sounded as if it were coming from Marty's own chest.

He felt squashed and shattered. Surely, he had broken ribs. He opened an eye to the blinding spears of the daylight sun and found there was no monster looming over him, only Gunther. He tried to sit up.

"Not yet," Gunther said. "I'm working on you."

"You'll have to work later, Doc." Marty rolled over onto one elbow and almost screamed in pain. From this vantage point, though, he could see Seth. It stood swinging its mace, mowing down Narmer's and Surjan's warriors with casual muscularity.

Narmer's warriors—they had returned! And that couldn't be Narmer in the lead, could it? Something had restored the dying king.

Probably not the Gettysburg Address.

The battle had passed Marty by. He stood with his friends and a small squad of spear fighters, to the side of the battle and behind the enemy. A rear guard glowered at him from Seth's flank, but didn't make any move to advance.

And Seth was moving more slowly, wasn't it? And it lurched from side to side as it moved.

Had Lowanna got the message? He couldn't tell from this angle, but some god of storm had heard his plea, and dropped a lightning bolt. Good luck. You couldn't count on it, but when it happened to you, you had to press your advantage, and maybe, just maybe, Marty's side had had a stroke of good luck. *Two* strokes of good luck, even.

And maybe just in the nick of time.

Gunther was trying to lay his hands on Marty, and Marty pushed him away.

"There's a time for everything," he grunted as he climbed to his feet. "The time for healing comes later. If it comes at all. Use it for someone who needs it. Like Tafsut did."

"Tafsut is dead, Marty," Gunther said.

"That's my point." Somewhere in his brain, Marty knew he wasn't making a coherent argument, but he would hate himself for taking Gunther's healing at this moment.

Then François was there, pressing an orange pot into his hands and giving another to Gunther and Kareem.

"Has anyone seen Surjan?" Marty asked. "Or Lowanna?"

François cackled. "Surjan is working with me. Narmer's arrival has given us the time to roll one last cracker out onto the field. God willing, as Kareem likes to say."

"Praise God," Kareem said. "You are learning to talk like a civilized person."

"Lowanna, I'm not sure," François continued. "She was on a hill, at one point. About when that lightning fell."

"Remind me not to fight in a storm next time," Marty said.

Gunther looked down at the pot in his hand. "I don't know," he murmured.

"What is this cracker?" Marty asked the Frenchman.

"Big bomb," François said. "All the remaining gunpowder. But that makes it heavy and awkward, you know? Hopefully we don't need it, though. See if you can get the huge guy with the grenades I've given you. Pretty sure if he goes down, the rest of them run away. And if you can't get close to him, maybe knock out some Sethians."

"If only we had a cannon," Marty said.

François chuckled. "I wish."

Marty nodded and François shuffled away. Marty lost sight of him in the sheets of rain. Had he somehow slipped past the fighting lines and back to Narmer's side? Or were he and Surjan working in some other corner?

"I don't know how good my aim with this thing will be," Gunther said.

"Feeling qualms about throwing a grenade?" Marty asked.

"Sort of," Gunther said.

"I feel no qualms," Kareem said. "Let's blow these demons up."

"I'll throw yours," Marty said to Gunther. "Just hold it for now."

Were they demons? Marty jogged toward Seth and his rear guard, grenade in his right hand. Functionally, they were. They oppressed and murdered mankind. They seemed to be from another world, with strange technologies that might as well be magic.

And they were damned hard to kill.

The rear guard was a squad of men with swords and shields. They glared at Marty and his companions and then one of them shouted a command. Seth turned and looked over its shoulder briefly, and Marty saw that it had lost its nose ring.

Had Lowanna heard his desperate shout to the birds, then? Or had someone else seen what he and Kareem had seen, Sethians with ringless noses struggling to breathe? Or had the crew simply gotten lucky?

Then Seth turned back to face the fighters in front of it. Marty saw Narmer, on his feet, mace in hand. The king waded slowly forward through the enemy line, his face fearless. But he was making his way directly to Seth.

"You throw first," Marty said to Kareem. "Let's get these swordsmen out of the way."

Kareem nodded. He waited several seconds. The swordsmen picked up their pace, raised their blades over their heads, and hollered.

Then Kareem threw the grenade at them.

It exploded as it hit. The four men closest to the center of the blast fell shrieking and clutching grievous wounds.

"For Narmer!" Marty shouted.

"For Narmer!"

The spear warriors with him surged forward. Kareem charged with them, and Marty recognized only now that Badis was among their number. Was Usaden commanding the remaining spear fighters of the host, then? Or Surjan himself? Marty's men fell on the enemy, downing two more of them immediately and driving the others into a blind and panicked flight.

"Here we come, monster!" Marty roared. "Hold the line!"

"Hold the line!" Badis shouted. The warriors formed up in a defensive rank in front of Marty.

"Monster!" he bellowed. "Come get this!"

Seth wheeled about. It was tottering and unsteady, and at the sight of Marty and the grenade in his hand, it hissed.

Marty hurled the grenade.

Seth's reflexes were not entirely gone. The pot arced neatly through the air, and the hulking monster swiped with one enormous paw. Marty thought Seth would bat the bomb aside. Even, for a split second, he feared that Seth would swat the grenade back in Marty's direction, and that Marty would die in the explosion at the end of history's first, and worst, tennis match.

But Seth caught the grenade.

Boom! Smoke enveloped Seth. Stinging sulfurous smoke and microfragments of pottery struck Marty in the face, making his eyes water. A ragged cheer went up from Marty's men and from Narmer's front line. Marty, his companions, and their warriors jogged toward the enemy.

The sky opened and rain crashed to the ground. In moments, the falling sheets of water obliterated the smoke, as if pushing it into the soil itself.

And Seth was revealed, alive. It was down on one knee and one hand, shaking its head slowly. It sucked in loud, rattling breaths. Blood ran down from its ear.

The grenade hadn't killed it. It had been holding the bomb in its hands as it exploded, and it hadn't died. Another grenade likely wouldn't kill it, either. Unless Marty could get Seth to eat the explosive, or maybe hold it against its face.

Marty's heart fell.

"Give me the grenade," he said, and Gunther did.

Marty took a deep breath. There was nothing for it but hand-to-hand combat. And Marty would try to press the grenade against Seth in some vulnerable spot as it went off. Marty would die, but maybe he could kill Seth in the process.

Or could Marty maneuver Seth into falling on top of the grenade as it detonated?

No way.

"Look!" Kareem shouted.

Marty looked where the young Egyptian pointed; into the seething mass of humanity where the two armies stood toe to toe and pushed and bled each other. At first, he saw nothing new or interesting. But he knew Kareem had better eyesight than he did, vision that had served Marty in good stead before, so he kept looking.

He saw François and Surjan.

They were carrying a pot with a fuse. Like the grenade Marty held in his hand, except that it was significantly bigger. This pot was big enough that an adult human could curl up inside in a fetal position.

The last bomb. The big one.

But they stood behind the line of Narmer's men, stuck. They moved left, and the enemy moved left. The enemy tracked them to the right, too, and each time they moved, the enemy pressed the soldiers in front of François and Surjan, keeping the line impenetrable, and the bomb trapped on the other side.

"Shield wall!" Marty yelled.

Surjan's head snapped up. The acute senses that allowed him to smell water from two miles away let him hear Marty, too.

"Shield wall!" Surjan bellowed, and Marty barely heard him across the two lines of fighting men.

Seth was on its feet and rumbling toward Marty. Behind it came its standard banner, holding the carved staff and flag high. Marty hefted the last grenade.

Surjan's men formed into a shield wall. Narmer's soldiers to their left and right were confused. Surjan yelled at them, and then Narmer yelled, too.

Narmer's men formed into a shield wall, too. It was ragged and gap-riddled, but it was approximately right. The Sethians' human soldiers pounded on the heavy leather shields of the wall with swords and spears, and yelled taunts and jeers at their enemy.

Seth picked up speed.

Marty threw the grenade. It flew barely over Seth's head. It struck the ground right behind the heels of a squad of the Sethian's swordsmen, top-down, and exploded.

The blast knocked Seth off its feet again and sent it rolling sideways. Marty himself staggered back, wiping grit, sweat, and smoke from his face. The explosion also cleared the line in front of Surjan and François. They lurched to their feet, picked up the pot, and rushed forward.

"Light it!" Marty shouted to his companions.

He had to keep Seth near the bomb. Near enough that, when it exploded, Seth would be killed. Which might mean that Marty would also be killed.

Which would be worth the sacrifice.

Narmer's men pushed the Sethians' troops, inching them back one step at a time and peeling them away left and right past Seth.

Surjan and François set the bomb down beside Seth. François struck fire to the superweapon's fuse, and then he and Surjan retreated.

Marty circled to the right. He felt like a fighter in a sparring match. You circled to look for weaknesses in your opponent's stance and guard. You circled to make him move, to keep him off balance, and maybe to get around the outside of his defenses.

Here, he was circling to try to get Seth to watch him.

And turn its back on the bomb.

Seth shook itself and rose to its feet. "Human!" it bellowed. "Finally, your kind vomits up a champion who can stand against us, however briefly. Your triumphs have been admirable, in their fashion."

"Why won't you leave mankind alone?" Marty shouted. He had reached the point he wanted, so he stopped circling and prepared to battle. The smoking fuse grew shorter. "What gives you the right to prey on my people?"

Surjan and François retreated.

"Why won't you leave cattle alone?" Seth huffed and struggled to breathe. "What gives you the right to herd and eat them?"

Marty shook his head. Not giving an answer, but counting down the seconds as they elapsed.

"Because you are superior!" Seth roared. It looked at the standard-bearer in its shadow and laughed. "This is not only the way of mankind, little man. It is the way of all life."

The soldiers of both sides had settled into an uneasy stasis, the lines two paces apart, all eyes watching Seth and Marty.

"Hilariously, you believe that you are my superior." Seth stepped back, stooped, and picked up the large pot with its smoking fuse. It hoisted the bomb casually over its own head, despite the rattling, ragged sound of its breath. "I have watched you throw these for two days. Do you think I do not understand how they work? Thank you for this. Let's see if your King Narmer can catch it, shall we?"

Marty's heart sank.

Then he saw a streak out of the corner of his eye. It was a javelin, and it was only the first. A storm of short javelins launched over the top of Narmer's battle line.

They were on fire.

The javelins slammed into Seth and into the jar all at once. One moment, Marty was looking at the orange clay vessel gripped in the monster's enormous hands, and the next, a deafening thunderclap and an orange ball of light threw Marty to the ground.

Marty screamed. Pain lanced his ribs. He tasted blood in his mouth and felt a tightening around his chest.

Before he could see, before he could hear again, he dragged himself to his feet and charged into the cloud of dust. Rain sloshed down around his ears and chest, his feet slipped in mud, and he kept upright as he drew his ankh from his belt.

He found Seth. The monster had lost both hands and both ears, and one eye was sealed shut with blood. Seth's herald was crushed beneath his master, only one leg protruding. Seth's breath came thick and throaty, and bloody foam bubbled from its lips. But as Marty approached, it roared, showing massive teeth, and rocked forward, trying to rise.

Marty leaped. He hurled himself on the enormous Sethian's body, straddling the giant like a child astride his downed father when wrestling on a living room floor. And then he jammed the sharpened stem of his ankh down into Seth's one good eye.

Seth screamed.

Marty lunged forward. He grabbed the arms of the ankh like a construction worker grips the handles of a jackhammer, putting the weight of his belly onto the loop and driving the silver emblem of life down into Seth's head as a messenger of death.

Seth swung his arms. Screaming, he knocked Marty aside.

The giant rolled over, rose to all fours.

Then collapsed onto its face.

Narmer's men cheered. "Narmer!" they shouted. "Narmer!"

Marty saw Gunther looming over him, his hands glowing as he pressed them against Marty's chest.

Marty gasped as he felt bones snapping into place. He immediately vomited blood.

Sethians turned and fled. Some men fled with them, and others threw down their weapons to surrender. Some took up chanting the victorious king's name. Marty rose and staggered away from Gunther's ministrations. He tried to get at his ankh, but couldn't; it was pinned beneath the monster's head. However, within moments, Seth's body began to shimmer.

Marty was exhausted. He sat down beside the corpse as it glowed, dissolving into mud that the rain beat into the sands and dissolved. The light that pooled on Seth's body and then entered Marty made him feel younger and lighter and refreshed, but not refreshed enough.

He was level four now, whatever that really meant. But no amount of leveling would allow him to forget the corpses piled all across the battlefield.

Munatas.

Tafsut.

Others.

When he was certain that Seth was really gone, he lay back on the sand and let the rain pummel him.

⇐ CHAPTER ⇒
FORTY

"Marty," François said. Had a million years passed, or twenty seconds? "Marty, the king."

The king. Narmer.

With François's help, Marty stood.

Around him, he heard warriors shouting victory cries. Some wept.

The rain was washing away the last of the puddle of goo that had been Seth. Its crushed standard-bearer lay dead in a pile of jewelry and clothing, gripping the standard.

Marty picked up the carved staff and was finally able to see the detail; its head was shaped like a stylized animal's head. The bottom end of the staff was forked.

Involuntarily, he whistled. He ripped away the infinity-symbol banner and cast it aside. In the corner of his vision, he saw warriors seize the flag and tear it into shreds, hollering as each man claimed his trophy.

He stayed focused on the staff. This was the *was* scepter, a symbol of royalty used by millennia of pharaohs. Like many ancient Egyptian practices and symbols, its origin was shrouded in the mists of time.

The hooting and yelling calmed, the crowd of men parted, and Narmer approached. His step was vigorous and steady; he looked calm, while Marty felt broken.

He carried Marty's banner in his hand, and he planted it now in the mud beside Marty.

"A proud flag for a mighty king," Narmer said.

Marty looked up at Narmer and shook his head. "How can you have healed so completely in such little time?"

Narmer winced as he crouched to look Marty eye to eye. "I am not yet fully healed. Often a leader must show strength, even when he isn't strong." He clapped his hand on Marty's shoulder and grinned. "Though I can say that I am much better than when you last saw me, despite my foolish priests and soothsayers. Whatever it is that your people did"—he nodded grimly—"it worked a miracle. Because I could see myself from above my bed the moment I stopped breathing. I still felt the power of the ankh coursing through me. And then something happened that pulled my *ka* back into its body and I began to breathe again. And now here I am."

Marty handed the *was* staff to Narmer. "Your Majesty, this is for you. I know this as a scepter of power, a proper emblem for a king."

Narmer hefted the staff. He smiled and nodded. "Thank you." He pointed at the other items and motioned to Marty. "The rest is yours. I am content."

Marty looked at what remained. The oversized kilt and sandals likely had no real value. On the other hand, he saw earrings, rings, bracers, pendants, and other jewelry. Some had been Seth's, and some was worn by the herald.

He turned to François. "We don't need this, but . . . the men."

"I'll handle it," François said.

Narmer looked at Marty and asked, "Are you content?"

"I have lost much today, Your Majesty."

Narmer nodded. "Brave companions have laid down their lives. But you have saved me, Your Majesty, for what that is worth."

Which meant that Marty and the crew had kept history on track. Was history inevitably on track? Or had Marty been born into the Earth timeline in which he had saved Narmer, allowing him to unify Egypt?

He knew there were no definitive answers. What had Lowanna said? Something about chasing their own tails down theoretical alternate universes, but at the end of the day, having to make their choices and live with it.

"It's worth a lot," Marty said. "Perhaps I'm not content, but . . . accepting. However, there is one thing we will need to talk about. I know you don't like the idea, but my crew and I still want to visit the tunnel."

✣ ✣ ✣

They buried their fallen comrades in the rain, in separate graves. Gunther spoke words over the graves of Udad, Munatas, and Tafsut, and then sang "Poor Wayfaring Stranger." Marty didn't know the words, so he hummed along.

Narmer pronounced a blessing.

Then the people of Ahuskay and Jehed sang their own songs.

When the singing was done, Surjan and Marty stood alone. Marty looked over all the graves—over a hundred—and felt stunned.

He had failed them all.

And Carlos and Pedro, and their families?

Surjan wept over Tafsut's grave for hours.

The rain stopped the next morning, and Marty's visions stopped with it. It took three days for everyone to recover some semblance of health. For the entire three days, Marty had pleaded with Narmer to take them to the tunnel and show them its operation.

Marty and Narmer walked within sight of the Nile, the other members of the crew trailing not far behind them.

Marty turned to Narmer and said, "The people who came with me. Some will return to their homes across the deserts. Others would like to stay with you. Not all of them are warriors. There are merchants and other good people in the group."

They had all fought beside him. They were all family.

Narmer nodded and waved in the direction of the Nile. "The gods will provide. They are all welcome at my table. You are also welcome. You know I believe the tunnel is a death sentence."

Marty took a deep breath. "The tablet said this would be a battle, and it certainly was. The tablet also said there would be a contest for all of our people."

Narmer frowned. "What tablet?"

Marty laughed as he spotted stone markers ahead. "One second." He jogged toward the complex circle of stones and marveled at what good condition they were in. "In my day, this place is called Nabta Playa. It's in ruins...when I'm from." Marty ran his hand over the stones. "The weathering is only barely noticeable."

Narmer nodded. "This is very old. We know it to show the summer solstice, and the rising of Sirius, and other important days."

Marty waved Gunther over. The rest of the crew came with him.

"Hey," Marty asked, "isn't this where you found the tablet?"

Gunther stared wide-eyed at the stones. "Wow."

"So you read in a tablet that you would fight for all our people," Narmer said.

"I think it's the whole human race," Marty said. "I don't know what the Builders wanted or who they were, but I think we're supposed to be the champions of mankind. And I think we're the very last, so we have to take our stand on behalf of humanity."

"Even if it means being reduced to dust?" Narmer asked. "Even if there's no real chance."

"Yes," Marty said.

"Yes," the others agreed.

Narmer motioned to the west. "Come, we're not far from the tunnel."

Marty was close to tearing up when Narmer led them through the chamber to the tunnel. There was no hydraulic ramp, but a wide descending ramp, and then a massive wall, all obscured in the twenty-first century. Lowanna's face was streaked with tears; they all stared.

Narmer motioned for the crew to follow and said, "I cannot tell you how much I do not want you to participate in this act. I know what you've said, and I know what has been passed down to me from my father and my father's father."

They entered the tunnel, which glowed dimly with light from some unseen source.

"The contest you speak of is like the test my father repeatedly taught me about. The heroes that are brought forth must endure tests to weigh the worthiness of us all. The Builders organized this contest to weigh our worthiness, and from all that I have seen happen in this tunnel . . . we are not worthy of anything but death. I implore you. Do not do this."

Marty looked over his shoulder and smiled. "Last chance."

"I'm in," Lowanna said.

"We all are," Surjan added.

"Amen," François finished.

Kareem and Gunther just nodded.

"Thank you, Your Majesty," Marty said. "We're committed."

Narmer nodded and led them to the blank wall at the end of the tunnel. The wall was clearly made of six slightly different colored panels, as it would be five thousand years later.

Narmer reached up and touched the top left corner of the first colored panel of the wall.

Marty glanced down at the tunnel wall and noticed a blank unengraved spot.

No instructions to himself.

Did he risk paradox by adding those instructions now? Did he risk paradox if he failed to add them? Was paradox even a relevant risk?

"Your Majesty," he said. "Will you tell me the operation before you do it?"

Narmer obliged.

Removing his ankh from his belt, Marty crouched beside the unmarked spot. He took a deep breath and remembered Grandpa Simcha guiding his first motions with a wood chisel over a block of cherry. Steadily, calmly, Marty himself engraved the instructions that he'd end up following over five thousand years later. The guitars, the ballpoint pens, and the other images emerged easily, the stone peeling away like sculpting butter.

Narmer then touched all the panels in the prescribed order.

The six stone slabs blinked out of existence with a sound like the crack of a whip, followed immediately by a strong gust of dust-laden wind. Beyond lay a round, domed chamber.

Marty clasped forearms with Narmer. "Thank you for everything. All life, prosperity, and health to you, Your Majesty."

Narmer smiled and patted Marty on the shoulder. "Life, prosperity, and health to *you*. And in these battles you believe you will face, I wish you . . . victory."

Marty turned to the crew and grinned. "I suppose I'll see you guys on the other side."

Lowanna put her hand into his and he clasped it tight.

Narmer watched as the six walked into the dimly lit chamber. The moment they lined up next to one another, there came a brilliant flash of light, the chamber made a loud snapping sound, and the room sealed itself shut.

The king stared, then cocked his head to one side.

The adventurers, mankind's would-be champions, had not been reduced to ash, as he'd expected.

He rubbed his hand across the smooth wall. What had happened?

Gingerly, Narmer touched the top left corner of the first panel and continued on through the sixth and final panel.

Nothing happened.

He tried once more and again nothing. For the first time, the chamber was sealed, even to him.

"Your Majesty."

Narmer turned to see his lector priest, bowing his head. "What is it?"

"The path to Lower Egypt. The armies stand ready. They await your word."

Narmer turned back to the wall and stared. If he could no longer open it, then he was no longer responsible for this thing that he had been burdened with.

A feeling of relief washed over him. "I am ready. Let us go forth. We shall rid the Two Lands of any remaining Children of Seth, and we shall make Egypt one."

Marty walked into the round chamber holding Lowanna's hand. He noticed six darkened spots on the ground he had missed before. He took his place on the leftmost mark as the others walked in; Lowanna stood on the mark beside his.

He sensed a static buildup in the air as the hairs on the back of his neck stood on end.

The others followed his lead and one by one took their corresponding spots next to him.

He was about to say something when Kareem took his place on the final scorch mark and the world flashed white.

The hive mind sensed the interrupt the moment the test triggered it and launched a thread to service the interrupt.

"High-priority thread 4CR9J5 servicing a test trigger out of the Orion arm of the Milky Way galaxy. Planet Earth, local relative year is 3104 B.C.E.

"Interrupt Service Routine has received six test subjects for the next

entry in the test queue. Forwarding the hash of the received data from the processing chamber. Awaiting command packet."

The hive mind launched a separate thread to verify the hash of the data packet representing the test subjects and retrieve the next test entry.

"Verification routine complete. Status is success.

"Next test entry retrieved from the queue. Brane selected is sigma+654PWJZBE. Relative time is 252 B.C.E."

The hive mind constructed a command packet with the necessary parameters and transmitted it to the awaiting thread.

"Command packet received. Processing . . . location: Indian subcontinent. Launching test subjects."

A ripple in space-time confirmed the launch and the hive mind sent an alert to the Administrator. *"Earth test subjects have completed phase one. On to phase two."*

Marty heard the *thud-thud* of six individual heartbeats as the chamber faded.

The beats continued even as the white all around him shimmered. Marty felt disoriented as he sensed himself moving. At the same time, he felt as if he didn't have a body at all. He was a mind floating in the whiteness surrounding him and this time he knew something major was happening.

But what?

From the featureless surroundings something began taking shape.

A swirling vortex of color appeared in front of his mind's eye. Again, just like last time. He was looking through a portal into another place.

Could it be another time as well? Maybe home?

But this time, instead of clearly seeing an image of where he was going and what he and the crew needed to do, the image was completely blurred.

Only occasionally did he see himself swooping down to eye level to catch a glimpse of land speeding by.

It was all a giant unfocused blur.

And just as his view through the portal seemed to pause on a single blurred image, he heard a deep voice echo loudly in his head.

"Welcome, Seer. It is time."

The portal and the world of white exploded as Marty's ears popped. He fell forward onto all fours as an intense bout of dizziness struck him. He clenched fistfuls of wet sand and held on as the world spun around him.

He smelled smoke and looked up, his eyes opening to a vast river just ten feet away.

Thousands of floating flower petals drifted by.

Surjan gasped. He staggered to his feet and walked to the shoreline. He breathed in deeply and panned his gaze all around them. "I can't believe it!"

"What?" Marty asked.

Surjan pointed upriver. In the distance, a crowd gathered around a fire near the shore. They wore white tunics. And then Marty shifted his gaze downriver and saw the same image repeated. Another gathering of people. Another fire.

Marty climbed up to his feet and felt a wave of nausea. He knew where they were, or least he had a very strong suspicion.

"I believe we're in India." Surjan said it with a note of certainty. "And this looks like the Ganges River."

"Yeah, but *when*?" Gunther asked.

The team looked to Marty.

He was the so-called seer.

He was supposed to have a vision of where to go.

Marty's heart thudded loudly. He'd had a vision, but how was he going to help if most of that vision was completely blurred?

François patted Marty on the shoulder. "Well, Dr. Cohen. It looks like we're on a new adventure. Where to now?"

Marty looked at all of their expectant gazes and shook his head. "To be honest, I have no idea."

◄ AUTHORS' NOTE ►

Well, that's the end of *Time Trials*, and we sincerely hope you enjoyed it.

This was the first, but certainly not the last writing collaboration between Mike and Dave. We wanted to have a section in this book where we can introduce ourselves, give you a little insight into who we are, what our thought processes were with regards to this book, and maybe even where we're going with what will be a series of books.

We are authors with a rather lengthy list of books to our names, but we are by no means similar in how we came to be authors, nor in the type of things we normally write. I guess the easiest way to introduce ourselves is by just diving in, and let's start with the Rothman portion of the Rothman/Butler duo.

I started this author thing accidentally, and by that, I mean years ago I had two young boys who enjoyed their bedtime stories. And my attempts to create off-the-cuff stories were pretty elaborate and to remain consistent I began to write things down. That was the beginning of a slippery slide into authordom for me.

As to my background, I've worked most of my life in various engineering disciplines, with my formal education being in the hard sciences. And I've spent most of my career in Silicon Valley companies as a designer and inventor of cool things. And during that long career, I've traveled the world and seen many things that help bring color to my work. My writing has naturally evolved to focus on stories heavily laden with science, action, and adventure.

I'll hand the virtual microphone over to Dave so he can introduce himself:

I have wanted to write novels since I was seven years old and first read Tolkien. Compromises with the real world have led me to spend a lot of time practicing law, consulting, training, and editing. That experience has included lots of travel (I lived in Italy for two years and in England for almost five) and immersion in a broad spectrum of languages, cultures, history, and music (personally, I play guitar). I write about things that I think are important, which generally lie closer to the human heart and unconscious mind than to the hard sciences.

The two of us have known each other for years in author circles and have been friendly, but generally didn't write the same kind of stuff. While Mike's focus is often around thriller elements and science in our world, Dave's writing tends to have a distinctive historical flavoring to it that lends itself to different worlds, and certainly different times in history.

Mike had recently found some success in taking an unusual approach to a genre called LitRPG, and when talking with Dave, the idea of putting their talents together in a similar fashion struck a note that seemed both unlikely and possibly new and exciting.

Could we convince a reader of thrillers to enjoy a book that had elements of "magic" in it? Could we "sciencify" (a technical term) a novel that had fantasy elements in it and keep a fantasy audience entertained? And all the while, base the story out of our own ancient historics . . . ? It was either madness or genius, and we suppose time will tell if it's either of those or lands somewhere in the middle.

Now that we're done and we can look back at all the work that went into this, the writing process was somewhat hilarious.

You can imagine the "discussions" between the science guy moaning about the fantasy guy's fantasy elements and the fantasy guy being exasperated with the science guy's insistence that every single thing needed to have a non-hand-wavy basis behind it.

In the end, we're both pleased with how things have settled and it clears a pathway for us moving forward.

Did we say moving forward? We did . . .

As the story clearly indicated through the last scene, we set up what will be the beginning of the next book in the series.

We can't say too much about where we're going. Suffice it to say that we have a very clear objective (ending book) in mind, but the path to that book may take us through different places and times.

You may be exposed to historical events that you're barely aware of, and maybe some you're intimately familiar with.

The path will be a rocky one for our intrepid team of adventurers.

But we hope you'll appreciate the payoff once we get you to the end.

Thanks for reading *Time Trials*, and there's lots more where that came from.

—Mike and Dave

We should note that if you're interested in getting updates about our latest work, we have links below so you can join our mailing lists.

M.A. Rothman: mailinglist.michaelarothman.com/new-reader

D.J. Butler: davidjohnbutler.com/mailinglist/

⇥ ADDENDUM ⇤

The addendum is the place where we as authors get to roll up our sleeves and talk about the technical pieces of the story you've just read. When you have an author with a strong science background cowriting with an author who has a strong background in ancient history, you can imagine you might get a story with a bit of both.

And that would be true with *Time Trials*.

Even though this tale fits squarely in the realm of fantasy, or at least it is most certainly fantasy adjacent, we started it in a very mundane, non-fantasy way. After all, we believe that readers who would enjoy this tale would be anyone who enjoys an action-packed story of the unknown. So that's how we started it.

Even though this story is not at all related to an old series that some readers may be familiar with, *The Twilight Zone*, that show was a good example of a series that told tales that inevitably skirted across genres and you never knew what was about to happen. The only guarantee you had would be that you'd be entertained and to expect the unexpected.

That's what we're striving for in this series.

We are mixing elements of traditional fantasy, alternate history, and even science fiction or technothriller, with the goal of providing the reader maximal entertainment.

In this tale, we've aimed to maintain some level of historic and technical accuracy for many of the story elements.

This addendum will contain a few items that we didn't have time within the story to elaborate on, and even though they may seem like a bunch of mumbo jumbo, they may not be. Some things that you've read fit squarely into science fact or historical truth, and we picked a few topics to at least give you a little insight into some of the things that are real, or are based on real science or history.

Ultimately, the goal of any good story is to entertain, but we tend to believe that the best stories leave you with a question that you ask yourself:

Could that have *really* happened?

The answer to that question we leave to the reader's imagination.

We both hope you enjoyed the story, and there's much more to come.

Brane Cosmology:

Brane? What in the world is a brane? Is this some weird misspelling and you meant to talk about zombie food?

Well, this is where the science part gets weird. Just as a review, the word brane was mentioned a few times by the mysterious Administrator.

> *The Administrator felt the ripple in the fabric of space itself, well before the hive reached out to alert him.*
> *"We have a primary test triggering malfunction."*
> *The Administrator frowned. "Give me its local description."*
> *For the Administrator, the time it took for the hive to process the request and return an answer seemed like an eternity. But for those living within the **brane**, a thin membrane-like universe in which the test had been triggered, the processing time would have seemed like an instant.*

Also it was mentioned at the very end of the book:

> *"Next test entry retrieved from the queue. **Brane** select is sigma+654PWJZBE. Relative time is 252 B.C.E."*

These passages may have seemed pretty obscure, because let's face it—unless you're a super nerd like one of us, brane cosmology isn't part of the normal person's lexicon. Given that, let's talk about what a brane actually is and how it applies to this story.

I'll define brane twice. First I'll speak in "science" terms, all of which you'll be able to look up if you like, then I'll explain it in layman's terms and it'll be much clearer why I referenced this in the story.

The central idea behind brane cosmology is that the visible, three-dimensional universe is restricted to a brane inside a higher-dimensional space, called the "bulk" (also known as "hyperspace").

If the additional dimensions are compact, then the observed universe contains the extra dimension, and then no reference to the bulk is appropriate. In the bulk model, at least some of the extra dimensions are extensive (possibly infinite), and other branes may be moving through this bulk.

Interactions with the bulk, and possibly with other branes, can influence our brane and thus introduce effects not seen in more standard cosmological models.

This can also explain why we see the "dark" influences at the galactic level for expansion being faster than expected for the known mass in the universe—in other words, it can be the influence of another universe in one of the n-dimensions that's causing the faster than expected expansion of our universe.

Okay, most of you are probably saying, "Those were all English words, but I don't know what in the world you're talking about."

Let me further explain:

Imagine our entire universe has three dimensions. Front to back. Side to side. Up and down. Those are all easy concepts to grasp. In the science nerd community, we often refer to the fourth dimension being time, and that's where the term space-time comes from, which you may have heard of before.

Okay, now let's zoom out from our universe and imagine it's all sort of a flat pancake. A membrane of sorts (thus the term "brane" cosmology). The idea being described here is very complex, but at its most coarse level, imagine there are many other pancakes that exist. An infinite number, potentially. Each of those is a universe unto itself floating around in a bigger soup the scientists call the bulk—but for this explanation, let's suffice it to say that these branes are big flat objects floating in a soup next to each other.

Now the weird thing is, these branes, our universe being one of them, may be no more than a hairbreadth apart from one another. And yet, we cannot see or touch them from within our universe.

Admittedly this is freaky science, and without going too deep, it's totally speculative at this moment, but it's real science. Theoretical physicists and others are actually doing research on this topic and studying the various possibilities associated with the concepts that unfold from it. From such studies come breakthroughs. You never know what may come.

And without complicating the explanation too much, let's just say that each universe, or brane, has their own relative concept of time. Some of you may have heard of the multiverse. It's a concept where almost anything that could have happened has happened in another copy of our universe. That's complementary to the concept of brane cosmology. In fact, if you had a machine that could transmit you from one brane to another, you could pick a brane that was in the past, the future, the same time, and had any number of permutations built into it.

It's hard to imagine this is all science, but it is.

It wouldn't be the first time today's science fiction becomes tomorrow's science fact.

You want an example?

I'm so glad you asked, because here's a nerdy example that I enjoy tossing out: everyone hopefully remembers that in *Star Trek IV*, Scotty was talking about needing transparent aluminum for building some water tanks to hold two humpback whales. No? Well, that was mentioned back then, and it sounded cool, but there was no such thing.

Fast forward to today and we have aluminum oxynitride, which is a ceramic composed of aluminum, oxygen, and nitrogen. Oh, and it's clear.

There's plenty more examples of that sort of thing, but that's the fun one that may be in some reader's pop culture arsenal that I hope would be appreciated.

Aliens? And what's up with their bodies dissolving?

Throughout the story you saw various creatures from the Egyptian pantheon appear. Whether it was the jackal-headed Sethians, the cow-headed Hathiru, or the cat-headed Bastites, they all seemed to have one key thing in common: when killed, their bodies dissolved.

Before we get too deep into the body dissolving, let's talk about where these things came from.

It was Narmer who said, *"The Builders were a greater people. They came down from heaven in mighty vessels. They were tall as giraffes and they had breath like storm winds… The Children of Seth were some of their servants and their creation… The Children of Bast and the Children of Hathor were also their servants, and there are others."*

Of course, the implication is that there were people who came from elsewhere and created these creatures, and it would be reasonable to assert that these so-called Builders that created these creatures were extraterrestrials of one kind or another.

Let's talk about the science of such a thing. Do aliens even exist?

Honestly, nobody knows for certain, but if you ask most scientists, they'll say that they almost certainly do.

Why?

It's actually a game of numbers. When you don't know something, you try to predict the outcome of any question by using the data you have at your disposal. Sometimes you can derive a definitive answer based on the information you have, or more often than not, you can make an educated guess about what the answer might be. We obviously don't know if there are aliens, but could there be? What are the chances?

As it turns out, there was an astrophysicist named Frank Drake who went through this mental exercise. He's now famously known for the Drake Equation, which was used to at least start the dialog of approximating how many communicative civilizations exist in our galaxy.

How does it work? It's actually very simple, and the results are fascinating. However, for purposes of brevity, I'll skip the details of the equation and simply give you the answer—those of you who want more information can of course simply look up Drake's Equation and enjoy.

Using such an equation, the accepted estimate from low to high is hugely varied, but it's almost certainly greater than one, meaning there's probably someone out there. And with some of the accepted estimates plugged into the equation, there are those who believe there might be millions of communicative civilizations just in our galaxy.

Considering that there's an estimated two hundred billion galaxies in the universe, I'll leave it as an exercise to the reader as to whether you believe life exists.

So, the idea that aliens exist isn't that out of the mainstream nowadays.

And if we presume aliens exist, and could have even visited, that's not just a modern phenomenon. It's a phenomenon that could have happened eons ago or even in our recent history.

Imagine if the Builders were just such a species of alien. And they took inspiration from the land and the creatures they saw, and created new creatures.

Creatures that ended up in the pantheon of many civilizations, including the ancient Egyptians.

The natural retort might be, "We'd have hard evidence if they really existed."

Well, we have lots of pictorial evidence of some rather strange creatures. There are also many written records to corroborate what the pictures show. That's still hard to believe, right? Where's the bodies?

What if those creatures were built with a different physiology? Maybe their internals were driven by a different set of chemicals than we're used to seeing in everyday animals. What if the internals of such creatures, when exposed to air, would dissolve into a gas or a liquid and vanish, leaving nothing for the archaeologists that might look for them thousands of years later?

There are many examples of strange creatures on Earth that resemble nothing most people are familiar with. One simply needs to look at thermophiles or extremophiles to see just how varied life can be, even on this planet.

Some life-forms on this planet will die if exposed to oxygen. Others survive only at temperatures above 180 degrees Fahrenheit. Some require strong acidic environments to survive, while others require environmental pressures of higher than 7,500 pounds per square inch.

With our Egyptian creatures, imagine their chemical makeup is exotic. Not an unheard-of thing. I'd wager that many of you have example of just such an exotic chemical. Mothballs are a classic example.

Yes, the lowly mothball is a perfect example of a chemical that is normally solid, but when exposed to air, over time it turns directly into a gas.

I leave you with these thoughts: Imagine that the things we *know* are mythology might actually be based on real things that no longer exist. And that the only evidence we have of such things are images and stories. What if they did exist? Again, an exercise for the reader to contemplate.

Wait, how do they know they're in ancient times? What's this about the Zodiac?

So we think of the stars as basically being fixed into place, from the point of view of us Earth-bound observers. In fact, that's where the word "planet" actually comes from—in Greek, the planets are the "wanderers," which means that the stars basically all move in a fixed relationship to each other, and the planets are the wanderers that don't stay in one place.

All this, of course, as observed from Earth.

Fun fact: the original seven planets were Mercury, Venus, Mars, Jupiter, Saturn, the Sun, and the Moon. Earth wasn't a planet, it was the world we lived on. And we couldn't see Neptune and Pluto at all. And the Sun and the Moon "wandered" along the same path through the sky as Mars and Jupiter and the others, which made them planets, too.

We call that path the Ecliptic, and there are twelve famous constellations on the Ecliptic, called the Zodiac. (Fun fact: there's a thirteenth constellation on the Ecliptic, called Ophiuchus. He's a giant carrying a snake, and we cut him right out of the Zodiac, the poor shmuck.) So the seven visible planets chug along this Ecliptic at different speeds, sometimes lining up and sometimes lapping one another.

For our purposes right now, the interesting planet (heh, heh) is the Sun. It takes about a month to cross the thirty degrees assigned to each Zodiac sign. Now, in reality, some signs are tiny, like Cancer, and some are enormous, like Virgo, but for this purpose, we divide the 360 degrees of the Ecliptic into twelve Zodiac signs, and say that each sign covers thirty degrees.

You all know this because at parties on TV shows (though not so often in real life parties, in my experience), people ask each other, when they're getting acquainted, "What's your sign?" And what they mean is, "When you were born, where in the Ecliptic was the Sun?"

And D.J. Butler tells those people that he's a Taurus, and they know that he was born between April 21 and May 20, because that's the month in which the Sun is in Taurus. And on the spring equinox, which is to say, March 21, the day in the spring when the day and night are equal length, the Sun is right on the edge of Pisces and Aquarius.

But if you could rewind a map of the sky over the centuries, checking in only on the spring equinox, you would see the sun slowly backing its way across Pisces. About 2,200 years ago, at the time of the equinox, the sun was on the border of Aries and Pisces.

And about 2,200 years before that, the sun was on the border of Taurus and Aries.

This movement, this slow backing of the sun across the Zodiac, is called the "precession of the equinoxes." We've known about it *at least* since the time of the second-century B.C.E. astronomer Hipparchus, but there is some evidence that humans have been aware of it much longer than that.

So when Lowanna Lancaster believes that she's close to the spring equinox, and the sun is not in Pisces but in Taurus . . . she realizes that she's not in (chronological) Kansas, anymore.

Is Narmer real?

Probably Narmer was a real person, who lived around 3100 B.C.E. Probably he was a king of Upper Egypt (the south, the desert) who unified Egypt, the "Two Lands," by conquering Lower Egypt (the north, the Nile delta, the marshes). Probably he was called Narmer in some sources and Menes in others.

What we can say for certain is that there is a stone object called the Narmer Palette. You can easily find images online, so go check it out. The Narmer Palette shows a man wearing the white *hedjet*-crown of Upper Egypt, personally subduing enemies with a mace. That crowned man seems to be identified as *n'r mr*, probably meaning something like "fierce catfish" or "stinging catfish." We pronounce that identification

"Narmer," and we treat it as a personal name. In the palette, he's a giant, bigger than his enemies, and the victory belongs to him.

So even if we ultimately conclude that Narmer is a legend, Narmer is associated right at the beginning of the Egyptian written record with an idea that would last right through Egypt's history and even, in some forms, down into the modern age. That idea is the ideology of kingship: it's the king who counts, the king is the nation, it's the king who wins the victories. In Egyptian art, that meant that the king was always a conquering giant and his enemies were always tiny. That's what the Narmer Palette shows, for instance. For another famous example, look up the Kadesh inscriptions online. Ramses II seems to have fought the Hittite enemy more or less to a draw in real life, but in the pictorial accounts, Ramses is a giant who *personally* shot or trampled the Hittite army.

This ideology, by the way, lies ultimately at the root of the game of chess. The game is over when the king is dead, and not before, because the game is a personal battle between two kings.

So we incorporated Narmer into this story, because it's a fun conceit to have our heroes enabling the beginning of Egyptian civilization as we know it. And we also built a lot of the storyline around the ideology of kingship, including Marty's discomfort at the idea that people see him as a king, the personal guarantor of victory, and his genuine relief when he realizes that his side has a king, and it isn't Marty.

To learn more about LitRPG, talk to authors, including us, and just have an awesome time, please join the LitRPG Group and Gamelit Society on Facebook.